END OF STORY

Also by A. J. Finn

The Woman in the Window

END
OF
STORY

A Novel

A. J. FINN

WM

WILLIAM MORROW

An Imprint of HarperCollins*Publishers*

END OF STORY. Copyright © 2024 by A. J. Finn, Inc. All rights reserved. Printed in the United States of America. No part of this book may be used or reproduced in any manner whatsoever without written permission except in the case of brief quotations embodied in critical articles and reviews. For information, address HarperCollins Publishers, 195 Broadway, New York, NY 10007.

HarperCollins books may be purchased for educational, business, or sales promotional use. For information, please email the Special Markets Department at SPsales@harpercollins.com.

FIRST EDITION

Designed by Bonni Leon-Berman

Library of Congress Cataloging-in-Publication Data has been applied for.

ISBN 978-0-06-267845-4 (hardcover)
ISBN 978-0-06-335695-5 (international edition)

23 24 25 26 27 LBC 5 4 3 2 1

for

Jennifer Joel

and

Felicity Blunt

Aye, and even in gen-teel families,
in high families, in great families . . .
you have no idea . . . what games goes on!

Bleak House

Tuesday, June 23

IN A MOMENT THEY'LL FIND HER.

Find her where she floats, fingers splayed wide in the marbling water, hair spread like a Japanese fan. Fish glide beneath it, push through it; skate along the line of her body.

The filter hums. The pond simmers, shimmers. She trembles on the surface.

Fog prowled the ground earlier this morning—San Francisco swirl, velvet-thick and chill—but now the last of it burns off, and the courtyard basks in light: paving stones, sundial, a chorus line of daffodils. And the pond, that perfect circle sunk near the wall of the house, with its glowing fish, its lily pads like stars.

In a moment a scream will crack the air.

Until then, all is silent and all is still, except for the shiver of the water, and the slow traffic of the koi, and the ripple of her corpse.

Across the courtyard, the French window opens, sun sliding off glass. A breath. Then that scream.

They've found her.

Six days earlier:

Wednesday, June 17

1.

"YOU LIKE MYSTERIES?"

Nicky cuts her eyes to the rearview mirror. The cabbie is squinting at her through lenses round and thick as shot glasses.

"Looks like you're reading a mystery there," he rasps. The car coasts over a pothole, shudders beneath them.

She brandishes the paperback. "Agatha Christie. *Murder in Mesopotamia.*" The man fancies a chat, and Nicky aims to please. Cabbing must be a lonely gig.

"You smoke?"

"No, sir."

"Good." Poking a cigarette between his teeth. "Too pretty to die young."

He sparks it with a bashed Zippo, and Nicky taps the window switch. White air spills in, cool and damp, swamping the backseat; she presses the switch again to a half inch up top and tilts her head toward the glass, sees herself twinned there: lashes spiky with mascara, gloss glinting on her lips. She isn't too pretty—she knows this, doesn't much care.

The cab jolts. Her bag jumps to the floor. "I think you clipped the curb there."

"Yeah, well." Glaring at the windshield. "Surprised they were landing planes. Miracle you touched down."

For Nicky, who is not a flyer born, it's always a miracle when she touches down. She peers past him into a stagnant tide of evening fog, lustrous as pearl in the headlights.

"June gloom. Bet you don't get weather like this back east."

"Nope." *Back east*—it sounds impossibly distant, mythical.

He grunts, satisfied, then bats the turn signal as they hug a corner and surge uphill. Nicky gropes at her seat belt.

"Mysteries, I was saying." Smoke chugging from his mouth, roiling in the cold air. "Lots of mysteries in San Francisco. You heard of the Zodiac?"

"They never caught him."

"They never—yeah." He scowls in the rearview. Nicky shuts up; it's his city, his story. "He's our Jack the Ripper. Then we got the *Romance of the Skies*. She was a jetliner disappeared back in the fifties. Flying to Hawaii, and she just—" A suck of his cigarette. "Gone." A puff of smoke.

"What happened to . . . her?"

"Who knows? Same with the ghost blimp. Wartime, coupla army boys float up in a Goodyear, and when she crashes in Daly City, no one's on board. It's a mystery, like I—that over there!" He flaps a hand to the right. "Oldest house in Pacific Heights."

Nicky spots an albino Victorian with wide-eye windows, rearing back from the street as though startled. "Built fifty years *before* the quake," brags the cabbie. "That was a middle-aged house, and she *survived*."

"She looks surprised," Nicky observes. "Like she can't believe she's still around."

He grunts again. "I can't believe she is, either."

They tunnel ahead. On either side, white street signs flash in the fog, phantom fingers pointing forward: *This way, keep going.*

"Said you're from New York?"

"Yes."

"Well, *this* is the most expensive neighborhood in the country."

The houses loom roadside, spectral in the haze: nineteenth-century ladies, slim and prim, dressed in pastels; a Spanish-style sprawl swarming with ivy; a mock Tudor, timbers and plaster atop herringbone brickwork; two Queen Annes, wood trim lacy as a doily.

"Some of 'em are tech people," the cabbie informs her. "Google. Uber. Uber, I'll tell you something—" He glowers, but doesn't tell her something. "Still a lot of old money here. We've-been-rich-forever types."

Vapor haunts the streets ahead. They ride swells of pavement, waves of it, now cresting, now dropping. Nicky catches her breath.

"We got mystery writers in San Francisco, too. Dashiell Hammett— he lived back there. Post Street."

Another sign thrusts through the mist, urging them onward. *Keep going. This way.*

"Oh, here's one for you." Chewing the cigarette. "Mystery writer used to live in—was it Pac Heights? Somewhere swell. Well, fellow's wife and son up and vanish one night."

Nicky shivers.

"Thin air. Like that plane. Must be twenty-five . . . no—twenty years ago. New Year's Eve, nineteen ninety-nine." The words float in a cloud of smoke, bob there like buoys.

"What happened to them?"

"Nobody knows! Some folks suspected the brother—the writer's brother, I mean—or his wife, or maybe both of 'em. Some folks swore it was their kid. The brother's kid, I mean. There were employees, too, a guy and a gal. But most people . . ." Curving around a corner. "*Most* people believe it was the writer himself. And here we are," he announces, as the cab brakes against the curb with a yelp and Nicky pitches forward, her book skidding from her lap.

She watches the cabbie unpack himself from the front seat, circle to the trunk; the tip of his Marlboro glows in the mist, bright as a will-o'-the-wisp.

Nicky tucks the paperback into her bag. Inhales deeply, coughs—the cabin of the car smells like a fire pit—then pushes the door open and steps into the fog. The street is a ghost town, the hulks of houses mere shades, façades like skulls, staring each other down across the pavement. She shivers again.

"You came ready in that sweater," says the cabbie as the door closes behind her with a clack.

Nicky inspects herself. Her single most expensive piece of clothing: cashmere, a simple charcoal V-neck, newly dry-cleaned. Somewhere over Nebraska she'd knocked a beer down the front. Her jeans, she sees, are still dusted with coarse mutt hair, even though she spent an entire time zone trying to tweeze them clean.

When she glances up again, the cabbie is gawking at the steep pitch of the driveway. He turns to her.

"This is that house," he says. "The mystery house. Did you know?"

"Guilty." She feels it, too.

"Shoot. You let me blab."

"I didn't want to interrupt," she explains gently—she hadn't meant to deceive. But she's read all about the wife and son who up and vanished; by now she knows as much as anyone. Or almost anyone.

The cabbie huffs his cigarette, casts it to the street, a little comet-tail of sparks trailing it. "How 'bout that. Just visiting?" A glance at her luggage, a compact roller and a small vintage steamer trunk, leather clasps and nailheads, spotty with travel labels.

"On a deadline." She dips a hand into her bag, digs out three twenties and a five.

He fondles the bills. "Don't see cash much anymore."

"I'm ol'-fashioned."

"And you ain't frightened? You don't think he killed 'em?"

Sotto voce, like he's asking if she doesn't suppose she's had too much to drink. "I hope he didn't," says Nicky brightly.

"Well. Enjoy that mystery of yours." Moving past her in a waft of nicotine; Nicky wonders if he means the murder in Mesopotamia or the disappearance in San Francisco. As he ducks into the front seat, the car wheezes, and the cabbie with it. "Enjoy the city, too," he calls. "Fifty square miles surrounded by reality." The door bangs shut.

Nicky remains gazing at her luggage, her back to the vehicle. The engine clears its throat; the tailpipe spouts exhaust against her leg; she listens as the car rolls away.

When she turns around, the fog has closed in upon itself, iced over, smooth and still as a mirror, as though the cab and its driver had never been there at all.

2.

SHE STANDS IN THE MIST, arms folded across her chest, hands curled around her shoulders: hugging herself, as is her custom when excited or anxious, or both. Behind her she feels the house holding its breath. She holds her own.

Nicky isn't much for theatrics, not usually—among her friends, she is acknowledged as both sweetest and sanest—but she's waited five years to introduce herself. Her mind rewinds: past five summers, an electric-blue blur; past five winters, Manhattan under snow; five years exactly, this same month, when she wrote that first letter.

Dear Mr. Trapp: You don't know me . . .

Nicky had fan-mailed mystery novelists as a teenager, pleading for insight and autographs; later, during her graduate studies, more thoughtful letters, more probing questions. She still keeps up with the few willing to ditch their screens and tip letters into the postbox. Nicky, a sentimentalist, values pen and paper. Ink sinks into stationery, indelible as a scar; email is breath on glass, an instant dissolve.

Then, in the dregs of July—a pale blue envelope, her name slashed across it, scored deep in the paper: *Mr. or Ms. Nicky Hunter.*

She inspected the flap, the San Francisco address. Smiled, softly.

For three weeks she workshopped a response before at last batting back. (*Dear Mr. Trapp: I am in fact a woman.*) Another month, another blue envelope. And so on into autumn, into winter, into the New Year, into four more—perhaps a paragraph or two from her, a few sentences from him—until their latest correspondence, typewritten in that same cracked ink, the letters heaving and jostling like passengers at sea. `We look forward to welcoming you to our home.`

She rubs her arms. Turns, slowly. The fog ripples, parts like curtains, unveiling the house, risen above her in a great frozen wave.

Château revival in soft cream, built by Bliss and Faville in 1905, the year before the earthquake; since then home to just four families, present occupants included. "One of Pacific Heights' most elegant and tasteful mansions, commanding a spectacular view of the Golden

Gate Bridge," panted *Architectural Digest* in a piece headlined MYSTERY HOUSE. "Grand in its proportions, gracious in its décor, and jealously guarded by the lord of the manor." The article was breathless to the point of asthma.

Still: More than thirteen thousand square feet, spread across four stories (aboveground). Seven bedrooms. Eight bathrooms. A walnut-paneled library housing some six thousand books; a parterre court-yard with sunken koi pond. White-oak flooring throughout. Dormer windows peering from the steep slate roof. Vaulted foyer. A fireworks display of exotic finishes.

Nicky eyes the front door, damming within all that elegance, all that grandeur. And somewhere inside, the author who most intrigues her. She feels little-girl giddy.

Thirteen steps glide up in a smooth sweep of marble. Nicky scans them, squares her shoulders. Her body is light yet wiry, pared and planed; five years ago, when she took up boxing, Nicky Hunter—a happy person, a softie, a hugger—discovered a talent for battery.

She hoists her trunk, hikes the roller bag under her other arm, and mounts the steep front steps.

At the landing, she sets the luggage down. A black-bronze knocker bulges from the door: a question mark, extravagantly curled and swollen at the top, like a hooded snake. Nicky traces the curve with one hand, then aims a finger at the doorbell.

The chime cries, dies.

Dear Mr. Trapp: You don't know me, but I found what might be an error in your novel . . .

The quick snick of a lock. Nicky retreats a step.

The door opens.

There before her, backlit in amber, stands the most beautiful woman she has ever seen.

3.

As she pours Darjeeling, Nicky studies her.

She appears lit from within, a lantern lady. Fortysomething, lavish lashes and Cupid's-bow lips. Her hair tumbles loose over one shoulder. Modest powder-blue dress—modest woman, for all her glories: shy smile, one leg laced demurely across the other. Her voice ("Milk or sugar?") is quiet, as though dusty from disuse.

Diana glances up, and Nicky's eyes abruptly tour the parlor: its butterfly-print wallpaper, its pillar lamps flanking the sofas, the miniature chandelier. Through a pair of French windows, she can glimpse the courtyard, dim in the dying light. Against one wall, a narrow bookshelf; beneath her feet, a Persian rug, artfully distressed. *We've been rich forever.*

Or rich long enough, anyway.

"Your trip was . . . ?" The question burns off. Diana's accent is like fog, English and soft at the edges.

"Bumpy."

"All the way from New York?"

"All the way from the airport. We couldn't see four feet ahead. I felt like I was being whisked someplace mysterious. Like in 'The Adventure of the Engineer's Thumb.'"

Diana blinks politely.

"Sherlock Holmes," adds Nicky.

"Ah."

"There's this engineer—no, thanks; just milk—an engineer who travels from the train station to this mystery house twelve miles away. The carriage windows are blacked out, and the journey seems to take forever. Then his clients at the house try to kill him. Death by hydraulic press. *Then* Holmes figures out that the house was near the train station the whole time. The carriage ride was a feint: the engineer had been driven six miles away and six miles back."

Diana purses her lips. "I confess"—she does sound confessional—"I'm not a mystery fanatic the way you are. Both of you." Now a frown. "I don't mean *fanatic* in a bad way."

"I don't take it in a bad way. What do you like to read?"

Diana names a Nobel winner and two French novelists.

"We have nothing in common," says Nicky.

"Well, I taught French for years. Latin also. But I've read some of your work—the Edgar Allan Poe essay, I remember, and Ngaio Marsh. You've a very human touch. I suppose we tend to think of crime writers as would-be killers, don't we? Murderers manqués? But this made me want to know them. Made me want to read their books, too." She sips. "And you supervise mystery writing?"

"I offer a crime seminar in the spring semester. Otherwise, the kids can write whatever they want. Literary fiction, usually. I remind them that plenty of great American novels are crime stories. *Lolita. Mockingbird. Native Son. Gatsby*—that's a detective novel. The detective isn't wearing a badge, or a fedora, but he's still trying to solve a mystery."

Diana sips her tea, and Nicky stares at her lap, pinches a dog hair from one knee. Vows to talk less. "Oh—I come bearing gifts," she says, talking more, unzipping her bag. "Didn't manage to wrap this very well . . ." Despite working for forty minutes, tongue poking from between her teeth like she was a child trying to draw inside the lines.

It is very obviously a magnifying glass, but Diana has the grace to ask whatever could it be before peeling off the wrapping. "Oh, how lovely—what a beautiful handle. Copper? How old is it?"

"Early nineteen twenties."

"He'll be enchanted."

"Least I could do, truly." Nicky watches steam play atop her tea. "I'm very grateful to you," she hears herself saying, and she lifts her eyes to Diana. "This is a—really extraordinary privilege."

A smile, the shyest tilt of the lips. "Have you worked on a project like this before?" Diana asks. "A—private biography? Just for loved ones?" Gesturing to herself, tentatively, as though unsure that she is in fact loved. "Is there a proper term?"

"Never. And not that I know of."

"How very like Sebastian to toss in a last-minute twist. I suggested—I hope you won't mind—I did suggest he might write it himself, but . . ." A shrug. "He worries he won't have time to do it properly. Besides, he's only got his perspective. He wants a record with . . ." Again the sentence fizzles like a match.

"Multiple narrators," Nicky suggests.

"Precisely."

"How is he?"

The saucer rings when Diana sets it on the table. "Evidently renal failure doesn't kill you until—it kills you. You don't drop dead, exactly, but it's pretty much business as usual right up to the end. With more naps. So a few months. Approximately."

Nicky nods.

"Although I've learned never to underestimate him," says Diana, stroking one shin with both hands. "Besides, he's so looking forward to meeting you."

"Oh, not as much as I am."

"You two can argue about that. He loves a sparring partner."

The gong of a clock somewhere outside the room. Diana eyes her watch. "Have you eaten?"

"I could do things to a sandwich," Nicky admits. "Or a fried egg."

"How about both? I'll fix you a croque madame." In the accent of a native. Diana smooths her dress as she stands. "Pretentious ham-and-cheese sand—"

And then a wave crashes into the parlor.

Fills it, floods it—Nicky expects the furniture to float up on a tide of sound; waits for the windows to burst, gushing noise; for the chandelier to swing, raining crystals.

"Bring me the child!"

4.

HER HEART STALLS.

The echo drips from the ceiling, ebbs from the floor—dark and full and thundergodly.

"Doesn't sound like a dying man, does he?" Diana asks, and Nicky catches the sunset of a blush in her cheeks: a woman fond of her husband. "Careful in this house," she adds. "Sound travels. No secrets."

Nicky rises, slings her bag over one shoulder, wipes her hands against her thighs (what *is* the point of palm sweat?), and trails her hostess into the vast vault of the foyer, where Diana's pumps—modest, naturally—tap against the floor. A grand staircase, fanned at the base, sweeps up to the second story and forks there. She follows Diana in silence to the landing.

A painting hangs on the wall between two high windows. Oil, but so clear and fine that the effect appears photographic. Nicky pauses before the subjects.

A couple on a bench: the man slim as a sword, sheathed in a suit the color of bone, ascot boiling over at his throat, one eyebrow archly arched; the woman, grinning, in cranberry slacks and navy polo open at the neck. Standing beside the man is a plump girl, thirteen or so, wearing a white sundress, her arm laced through his. A small blond boy perches on the woman's lap, his shirt and shorts identical to hers. He too smiles, exposing what Nicky's uncle used to call summer teeth ("summer here, summer there"). In his hands he holds a white paper butterfly.

Fellow's wife and son up and vanish one night, the cabbie had said. *New Year's Eve, nineteen ninety-nine.* When Hope and Cole Trapp, wife and son of the acclaimed detective novelist, disappeared from two separate locations in San Francisco . . . never to be seen again.

Words that, to Nicky, rumble like stage thunder. Except the Trapp mystery proved authentically sensational—one magazine hyped the disappearance as "the most baffling literary vanishing act since Agatha Christie's eleven days on the lam in 1926"—and now, two decades on, still haunts the Internet, haunts the brains of taxi drivers, even haunts Nicky Hunter.

Diana turns right, past a flight of stairs, and then left again, leading Nicky down a corridor, footfalls quiet on red carpet. Sconces line one wall; dusk spills through a row of tall windows. The house is a horse-shoe, Nicky sees, its wings squaring off across the courtyard, where a knee-high hedge maze coils in upon itself. She spies the pond in a far corner, at the juncture of two walls, orange fish like embers beneath the surface.

His fish. *His* maze. His *home!* "The champion deceiver," critics hailed him in bygone days; the creator of Simon St. John, gentleman English sleuth (and his trusty French bulldog, Watson); her correspondent these past five years. And now she's walking his halls.

Nicky can feel her veins glowing, like neon tubing.

They arrive at an oak door, slightly ajar. Fixed upon it is a fist-sized ivory skull, loop of metal clutched in its jaws, crossbones jousting behind it. *The man likes a knocker*, thinks Nicky, peering into the eye sockets as Diana raps three times. Waits.

"*En-tah.*" The door all but rattles.

They en-tah.

Into what she can only describe as a *chamber:* deep and broad and tall, hardwood underfoot, the ceiling coffered in walnut. A range of windows faces Nicky, panes scrubbed clear, the Golden Gate springing across the dark bay beyond; but the room—cavernous, ravenous—sucks up the evening light, eats it alive.

Floor-to-ceiling shelves line the walls, groaning with those six thousand books, all packed tight as teeth. There, near the floor, a batch of leather omnibuses, JOHN DICKSON CARR etched in gilt letters; above her, baby-blue paperbacks in stacks (*Gaslight Crime, Victorian Women Sleuths, Locked-Room Mysteries*), bindings chipped and creased; by her hand, an Ellen Raskin novel in glossy laminate and what appears to be a first edition of *The Moonstone,* three volumes in violet cloth. Tier upon tier of spines, cracked and foxed and tattooed with tiny foil letters that flicker like gold dust in a mine.

Spectacular, thinks Nicky. *Absolutely spectacular.*

A ladder slants against one wall, feet shod in casters; at its top, it hooks over a bronze rail curving along the uppermost shelf. She tracks the rail to the deepest, most distant end of the room.

Housed within the far wall is a fireplace, flames waving, as though inviting her to kneel beside the hearth. She would ignite, she thinks; she is dry tinder.

And before the fireplace sits a desk—old, wooden.

And on the desk, a typewriter—old, metal.

And behind the typewriter, a man—old, but older than he looks, Nicky knows. Slowly he stands, unfolding like a switchblade every inch of his impossibly long body. He inclines his head.

"Hello, Mr. or Ms. Hunter," he says. "I'm Sebastian Trapp."

5.

"I'M SORRY TO HAVE KEPT YOU WAITING. Rotten way to begin a story. You don't want too much lounging around." He calls to Nicky in a crushed-velvet baritone, rich and deep and scuffed; it rolls effortlessly down the length of the room.

To her surprise, she's trembling.

Suddenly his voice drops an octave: "'I have seen those symptoms before,'" he continues, actorly. "'We may take it that the maiden is perplexed . . .'" And now she clocks it: Holmes, "A Case of Identity," as the detective observes his new client pacing in Baker Street. A smile tugs at the corners of her lips.

"'But here she comes in person to resolve our doubts,'" he prompts her.

At her back, Diana murmurs, "After you."

Nicky advances cautiously, while behind his desk Sebastian continues: "'There is always a look of fear upon her face,'" he says. "'She would do better to trust me. She would find that I was her best friend.'" He tilts his head. "'But until she speaks, I can say nothing.'"

Now Nicky sees the spindly chair before the desk; now she perceives the instruments arranged across the blotting pad beside the typewriter: a small noose in wrought iron; a bronze candlestick sans candle; a viper-green poison bottle, unstoppered, empty; a dagger, slender and silver; a Webley-Fosbery automatic—Simon St. John's weapon of choice.

The desk is dark oak, the desktop itself a glass shadow box, a few inches deep and swarming with insects, a dazzle of butterflies, red and cloudless blue and tropical pink, each pinned to a corkboard, wings flung wide in surrender.

Three more steps and Nicky stands across from him. Resists the urge to hug herself. *He's just a man,* she remembers. A man who, as one critic remarked, wrote "the best Golden Age detective stories since the Golden Age." A man whose books have astounded her for years.

He's so *tall*.

Patrician, too, with a saber-sharp nose and square cleft chin, blades of bone beneath the cheeks, a sweep of steely hair. He wears a three-piece suit, shadow-gray, a crimson tie knotted at his throat. "You sense that he shares a wardrobe with his series hero, down to the pocket-watch," someone wrote—and there it is, a fine chain slung from the pocket to a button below his chest.

"'Why should you come to consult me?'"

Nicky says nothing.

"You're much chattier in your letters."

Nicky says nothing.

His eyes narrow. *"¿Habla inglés?"*

"She's perfectly chatty," says Diana, appearing at Nicky's side. "She's excited to meet you, is all." Presenting him with the magnifying glass. "And she's brought a lovely gift."

"Beware of Greeks bearing gifts," he says. "You're not Greek, are you?"

Nicky shakes her head.

"You're right, my wife, she simply won't shut up."

"If you'd stop quoting Agatha Christie—"

"Conan Doyle," reply Sebastian and Nicky in unison.

Diana throws her hands up. "I'll be back in a few minutes. It's an early night for you, young man."

They regard each other as she walks away. Flames gossip in the fireplace, low and soft.

"What about *Murder on the Orient Express?*" Nicky asks at last.

"It's alive!" He sits, gestures to her chair. "Please. What about *Murder on the Orient Express?*"

She cradles her bag in her lap. "You said there shouldn't be too much lounging around in a story. But that story's basically just a series of interviews."

"Not at the beginning. At the beginning it's hustle and bustle and all-aboard. You want to yank up the curtain quickly. Set things in motion." He flicks a fountain pen atop his blotting pad; Nicky watches it roll across the leather. "So let's pick up the pace, shall we?" He pulls out a desk drawer, pulls out an envelope, pulls out the single sheet of paper within.

And begins to recite her first letter.

Dear Mr. Trapp,

You don't know me, but I found what might be an error in your novel <u>Little Boy Blue</u>. It feels like sacrilege even to suggest this!

He glances at Nicky, grave.

On page 222 of my edition, St. John says that "The Adventure of the Blanched Soldier" and "The Adventure of the Lion's Mane" are the only Sherlock Holmes stories narrated by Holmes instead of Dr. Watson. Unless I'm mistaken, "The Adventure of the Musgrave Ritual" is also—technically—narrated by Holmes.

Yours,
Nicky Hunter

"Now, look at your letter. No—first observe the envelope." He pushes it across the desk.

Nicky observes: the creased paper, the publisher's address in her clear script. The faded waves of the postmark. The butterfly stamp, still vivid.

"I appreciated the *Limenitis archippus*," Sebastian adds. "Thoughtful touch. As is this—" Wagging the magnifying glass. Through the lens he inspects the stamp.

"That's a monarch, I believe?" she says. Simon St. John's insect of choice.

"Common mistake. It's a viceroy. A mimic. It evolved to *look* like the monarch, which is poisonous. Although lepidopterists discovered a while back that in fact *both* species are poisonous."

Nicky wiggles her mouth from side to side. It's a habit of hers since childhood; *You'll dislocate your jaw,* her parents used to warn her. "Why mimic another poisonous species?"

"Perhaps it doesn't realize it's poisonous," replies Sebastian merrily. "Perhaps the viceroy isn't so *innocent* after all. Where was I? Yes: I consulted a graphologist on my fifth book. That's a handwriting expert."

Nicky knows what it is.

He taps the stationery. "Your letters have been blown by an easterly wind. They lean to the left. A rebellious personality."

Nicky waits.

"Here, on the envelope: 'Sebastian' and 'Francisco.'" The pen moves between them. "You dot your i's to the left of the stem. That suggests you procrastinate."

She smiles politely.

"And . . ." But something flickers in his expression, like flame behind a screen. He sits back. "Where did I go wrong?"

"Very beginning. I'm left-handed."

Clapping a palm to his forehead. "Of course. Of course."

"So the slant of my letters actually means—"

"—you play by the rules."

"And the dots on my i's—"

"Methodical. Oh, the left-handed assailant. I never saw it coming. What would Simon say?"

"Don't you control what Simon says?"

"We aren't on speaking terms anymore. Are you warm? This is a gas fire, but it still throws off some heat."

"I'm fine," says Nicky, her brow damp.

"Good. It's always burning. I do like a fire." Sebastian's eyes dart to the envelope. He grins, taps the postmark. "Has it really been five years?"

Practically the longest relationship of her life. "I brought your most recent letter with me," she says, tugging a blue envelope from her bag. "May I?"

"I wish you would."

> Dear Miss Hunter:
>   Death has come for better men. Death has come for worse. Now Death has come for me.
>   Five weeks ago, I learned

"We know what I learned," he says.

Nicky skips to the next paragraph.

```
...I am a storyteller. Very old trade, to which I
have brought but seventeen novels that will, I hope,
endure for their full term of copyright.
```

They both smile. His dims first.

```
However, I lived a life before Simon St. John.
Alongside him, too, and after. There are passages
from that life, that story, that I would like to
share, in hopes they might entertain (I am of course
an entertainer), or even--dare I say it?--illuminate.
```

She pauses. "I seem to recall there was more," says Sebastian.
There is more, but Nicky feels uneasy with compliments, at least
when she is the complimented.

```
Your published work is searching and humane--
rare qualities in a critic. You know Simon well, and
of course I am a part of him just as he is a part of
me. In you, Miss Hunter, I see the audience for the
final story I will ever tell. I see someone who can
tell it in kind to anybody who cares to know.
    I'll be dead in three months. Come tell my story.
```

"And in the postscript you recommended that I bring—"
"A gown and a party mask, yes. What does my penmanship tell
you?"
"It tells me that you used a typewriter."
"Not for the signature, I'm sure."
"The signature is just two letters."
He chuckles. "That's the idea."
Nicky folds the paper. Somewhere outside the library, the house
groans like an old man rising.
"That elevator," sighs Sebastian, "will be the death of me. It'll have
to hurry, of course." He traces two bony fingers along the chain of his

pocketwatch, dipping across his front, tightrope-walking to his vest button. "We aren't discussing a proper *biography*—nothing so dull as that. More like a . . ."

"A memory book?"

The fingers pause midstride. "Upon my word, Watson, you are coming along wonderfully. A *memory* book." A quick jerk on the chain and the watch rolls from his pocket. "This was my father's," he says. "One of his few gifts to me. This watch and my military bearing." Reaching across the desk.

Carefully, Nicky lifts the watch from his hand. The metal is cool; the engraving reads TIME IS THE BEST KILLER.

She slips her thumbnail into the groove of the lid, wonders if she should open it. Glances at him. He wears a faint satisfied smile, and his eyes glitter like razors. Nicky nearly shudders.

She presses the watch back into his palm. When her fingertip brushes his skin, she catches her breath.

"Have you met my daughter yet?" he asks. "No? What that child needs is a darn good spanking. Well, speak to Maddy; speak to my idiot nephew. He hates to be left out. Speak to Simone, my—his mother. She *refuses* to be left out. Diana, of course. A few guests at our party next week, perhaps; people feel generous when you're dying. When you're dead, too—*nil nisi bonum,* you know—but I'd like to hear it in advance."

Nicky nods. "I wondered if I ought to speak to your former assistant? Isaac—"

"Isaac Murray." Sebastian looks sly. "Haven't seen the boy in twenty years. But I liked him. More importantly, he liked me. So obviously Isaac must be quoted at length. I'll ask Diana to phone him."

"And how long have I got until . . ."

"My premature death. Three months." Sebastian places a hand atop the Webley, caresses its anteater snout.

"No, I—I wanted to ask how long you'd like me to stay."

"Not *longer* than three months, certainly. Who knows you're here in San Francisco, by the way?"

"Oh—friends. All of them. Not *all* of them, but—"

"But enough of them." He smiles.

"Has he behaved himself?" Nicky twists in her seat to see Diana in the doorway, a phantom in the half-light.

"Mostly," she replies.

"Mostly," agrees Sebastian. "Was that you gambling with your life in the Otis?"

"That was Freddy, bringing Nicky's bags up to the attic. Fred is Sebastian's nephew," Diana adds.

"Yours, too, darling."

"Well. During the school year, he coaches high school baseball and football."

"Soccer."

"Known everywhere else as football, involving as it does both a ball and feet, unlike some sports. Fred's got summers off and he's been good enough to help his uncle with dialysis and medication and errands. He's very devoted."

"He is an ass."

"Stop that. It's an early night for you—lots of chat tomorrow. I'll wait here."

Nicky rises with Sebastian, prepares to say goodbye.

But he's already beside her, shoulder to shoulder, she facing the fire, he the door. "Thank you for coming all this way," he says. "If you can find the good in half the authors you've written about, I hope you can find the good in me." A grin. "And I hope you won't have to dig too deep."

He smells very faintly of salt water and soap. She breathes deep; he bows his head to hers, as though to kiss her cheek. Her heart pounds.

And then, in a voice so quiet she almost doubts whether he spoke at all, Sebastian Trapp whispers:

"You and I might even solve an old mystery or two while we're at it."

6.

Not until she's felt him leave the room does a little shudder ripple through her.

You and I might even solve an old mystery or two.

For a mad moment, Nicky imagines herself a girl detective in the pages of a book, a creature of pulped paper and black ink. A *character*.

She eyes the typewriter, keys glinting in the firelight, casing flexed like muscles, as though ready to pounce; it's a Remington, she knows, and it's spat out every page Sebastian Trapp ever published.

The man himself.

Even with three months left, he's able to conduct electricity: just sitting before her, he seemed to radiate energy, like a dying star. His eyes as she examined his pocketwatch; his voice as it melted in her ear. She's in awe. She's afraid.

She's curious.

Slowly she circles the desk, the flames whispering about her. "Oh," she gasps when her phone shivers in her back pocket.

"Murdered yet?" he asks in that bruised voice Nicky still likes.

She smiles, resists the urge to park herself in Sebastian's chair. "I should be so lucky as to get murdered in this house."

"Why are you muttering?"

"Why are you *calling,* Irwin?"

Irwin is his middle name. Throughout the two years they dated, Nicky took to teasing him with it; when he broke up with her, her first words were "Is it because I call you Irwin?" (No: It was because she was "too nice for me." So nice that they've remained friends. So nice that not once in six months has Nicky pointed out that he calls or texts almost daily.)

"Why am I calling? I refer you to my previous question re: murder."

"I'm in his library right now."

"Weapons everywhere, I bet."

She surveys the desk: Noose, dagger, poison bottle. Gun. She wonders if she might touch it.

"Seriously, babe." He catches himself. Old habits. "Seriously, though: don't you think dude's a killer?"

"Would I be here if I thought dude's a killer? He wrote books I love, he's lived an *interesting* life—I'm lucky to be invited. How's Potato?"

"I've told him you're never coming home."

"I will cut you."

"Christ. You're supposed to be nice."

"Some would say too nice." She pauses. "So how's my dog?"

"Wanna talk to him?"

The world beyond the window suddenly dims; the flames ebb in the fireplace, the desktop shadow box fills with darkness—the library is fading. Night falls fast here.

"I don't want to confuse him. But thanks for puppysitting."

"Feels like old times. I assume I was your third choice."

Fourth. "First. You'll find a little thank-you beneath the pillow. Gotta go." A packet of Oreos. No sense being too nice.

A snap in the fireplace, like a cracked whip, and Nicky hurries to her bag, hurries past the ranks of books, past the ladder, past the windows, into the low light of the hall. To her right a narrow back staircase winds into gloom, as though up to no good, so Nicky walks back the way she came, along the corridor. She'll wait for Diana in the parlor.

At the landing she slows. A man stands before the portrait, glaring at the family.

Six feet of built-to-last, muscles bulging within his sleeves. Linen shirt tucked into jeans. Ink-dark hair, so black it's nearly blue; stubble gritty on his cheeks and chin.

"Even after all these years," he says, studying the painting, "I keep waiting for their eyeballs to follow me around." His voice is deep. His accent is Californian.

Nicky waits. Nicky is good at waiting.

He glances at her with brown eyes, pupils full, lashes thick. "Freddy."

"Nicky." His grip is firm, but so is hers. She grins—it's exciting to meet another Trapp, after all—and he grins back.

"Freddy," he says again, as though for the first time. "Sebastian's my uncle. I'm the houseboy. Nah, kidding: three times a week I fire up the ol'—the ol' dialysis machine, is all. And tonight I lugged your luggage upstairs. Your hero, right?"

"Thank you."

"Not much to lug. You lost?" Thrusting one finger past her, toward the library hallway. "That's Sebastian territory. And thataway"— jabbing a thumb over his shoulder—"you've got Hope's office and the *solarium*, I kid you not. Overgrown now." His eyes snap away from hers, and suddenly he smiles: a megawatt beam, that of a first-time waiter or a child actor. "All good?" he calls.

Nicky turns to see the lady of the house descending the staircase. A key dangles from her fingers. "Freddy, I'm sorry for reeling you back here. That wasn't much of a job."

"Anytime." He shifts the smile to Nicky. "Want me to show you to your room?"

"Lead the way."

"I'll lead the way," says Diana, before her hand springs to her mouth. "Your sandwich. Your croque madame. How stupid of me. I don't know why I'm so scattered lately."

Nicky does not point out that her husband is months from the after-life. "That's okay," she says, her stomach complaining. "I'd like to head out anyway. I haven't been to San Francisco in years."

"I can stick around another couple minutes," Freddy offers. "If you need a lift. Part of the service."

"I definitely will."

Diana continues to frown. "Thank you, Fred. And again—well." She turns, begins mounting the stairs. Nicky follows.

The steps curl up to a long hall wallpapered in Tiffany blue. "The bedrooms," Diana explains, still climbing. "Most of them stuffed with *curiosities*, he calls them. Suits of armor, and spinning wheels, and a worrying number of taxidermied animals, and . . ."

Approaching the fourth floor, the staircase fading underfoot, Nicky dimly sees her bags at the top of the stairs, in front of a door. Diana slows; her knuckles bulge as she grips the key.

"Sebastian thought you might like some space to yourself. So—here's the attic." A pause. "And here's this." Pressing the key into Nicky's hand.

Nicky lifts it—weighty, snaggletoothed—and, with a scrick of metal, slides it into the lock.

Twists.

The door opens.

And the room exhales a fug of dust, almost coughs it. Diana coughs, too. "I thought we'd aired it out properly," she mutters, hoisting Nicky's trunk and stepping inside.

Nicky stands by her roller, peers into the attic, rinsed in gray light. A vast sprawl of floor, loaded at one side with disused furniture—a damask divan, a spiderwebbed floor mirror, a harp the size of a whale jawbone—and arranged at the other with a double bed, a dresser, a rolltop desk; flush against the wall, a long row of children's books, broken spines in candy colors. She recognizes the same Agatha Christie paperbacks she read as a girl.

Dormer windows dominate the attic, six on either side, and between them galaxies of dust re-form themselves in the dusk.

Diana crosses to the bed, lays the suitcase upon it, switches on the floor lamp. The depths of the room swallow the light whole. "It's a bit Miss Havisham. I don't suppose you play the harp?"

"I'm a little rusty." Nicky remains in the doorway. This is the bedroom of a lost child.

Diana walks to the desk; the lampshade flushes traffic-light green. "The bathroom is over there." An open door in a far corner—penny tile and a claw-foot tub. "This used to be staff quarters, back when there were staff."

"I see." Nicky wonders if she ought to be here after all.

"The house key." Diana sets this on the desk beside a sheet of paper. "I've written down my mobile number, and Madeleine's, and also Freddy's, in case you'd like him to drive you anywhere. Sebastian doesn't believe in phones. The Wi-Fi password is 'Watson7.' Uppercase W, numeral seven. Come in, come in!"

Nicky steps into the attic, slowly walks ahead, passing through soft-edged beams of light, one after another, three, four, five. The area by the bed glows like a campfire as she draws near, the roller bumping behind her. "Our housekeeper will be in tomorrow afternoon," her hostess says. "If you'd like her to spruce it up. Adelina is a saint and a terror."

"Thank you."

Diana returns to the doorway. "Consider it your room and your house. And—"

Nicky waits.

Diana smiles, leaves. Her footsteps die in the depths of the staircase.

Nicky turns. Beside the mirror stands a plaster bust, a shapely head crowned with laurels, and next to that a clutch of croquet mallets leaning against a martini table. A chandelier overflowing in a cardboard box, strands of crystal dripping to the floor; a rocking horse, decapitated; four or five old maps in flaking gilt frames; and there, low to the floor, a pair of eyes glinting.

Nicky recoils. The eyes stare.

She spies another set beside them. And another. And another. Eleven eyes altogether, in the faces of six French bulldogs, heads lifted, ears pricked. A firing line of undead canines.

Nicky nearly laughs. She crouches in front of the nearest, black and jowly, and reads the tag on its collar: WATSON VI. Its neighbor, a beefy brindle: WATSON V. Then a small fawn, and so on, until Nicky finds herself eye to eye with a pied cyclops: WATSON.

She crosses to the desk, pockets the house key. Pulls the drawer open—safety scissors, a plastic magnifying glass, Magic Markers. She imagines the hands that held them, watches her own hands tremble.

At a dormer window, she gazes down. A lonely streetlamp. Clouds swarm the rising moon.

Her toe knocks against a Magic 8 Ball, filmy with dust. She grasps it, thinks, shakes, watches the blue pyramid float into view on a raft of bubbles: CANNOT PREDICT NOW.

A glimmer overhead. Above the bed, beyond the lamplight, the ceiling is spackled with pale white stars—glow-in-the-dark, faint against the paint. Nicky squints, and the little cosmos resolves itself:

COLE

She sits on the edge of the bed—surprisingly firm, clean linen sheets—and as the light seeps from the attic, as the windows darken and the furniture disappears, she sighs.

Cole Trapp's bedroom. Imagine that.

7.

FREDDY'S SCRAWNY NISSAN is equipped with a six-CD player. "Pretty much the reason I bought this beauty," he explains.

"What's on rotation?" Nicky hopes he won't say anything douchey.

"Mostly Maroon 5. Also an Uncle Sebastian audiobook. *Jack Fell Down*." Introducing Simon St. John's nemesis, a Moriarty figure known only as Jack. "Figured it'd give us something to talk about. Me and him. Before he punches out."

"And does it?"

"Nope. Where to, by the way?"

They cruise out of Pacific Heights; when Freddy spins the wheel, bands of muscle shift in his forearm. Nicky studies his face. *My idiot nephew*, Sebastian had said. She'd like to make conversation—she's here for the Trapps, even the idiots of the species—but between the cabbie and the missus and the mister, finds herself fresh out of chat. Instead she looks at Freddy, compares him to the boy he was in photos twenty years ago, when the news cast him as the teen-dream cousin in the Trapp family mystery. Still handsome, baseball-jockishly, but affable, too, with a reckless smile and that slightly ditzy voice; the pictures hadn't captured that.

Freddy brakes at a light and grunts, wincing in the red dashboard glow. "Tore my labrum last year," he explains. "Every so often my shoulder complains. No reason at all."

"Like a bratty kid. Maybe there?" A small corner diner on loan from 1955.

Freddy points, rucking up his sleeve, and Nicky spots a tiny line of text inked into the skin above his elbow. He shrugs the car to one side, brakes.

"Would you like to join me?" she asks politely.

He chews his lip. "Yeah, but—I got tournament plans." He names a video game. Nicky, who outgrew games right after beating that one, fumbles with her seat belt. "You got my number, though? In case you need a ride. A car ride." When she glances at him, he's blushing. Could be the dash light.

The belt slithers across her chest. "Diana wrote it down for me. Thanks for the car ride." Climbing out, laptop case slung over one shoulder.

"Welcome to San Francisco. Don't talk to strangers," he adds, and the Nissan coasts away, Maroon 5 whining in its wake.

The diner: jukebox, laminated menus, pictures of the entrées. Nicky parks in a booth and checks her warped reflection in a metal napkin dispenser. Unfolds her laptop.

Closes her laptop. Reclines—

"Getcha anything?"

Sits up. "Corona, please. With a lime." Sits back once more.

A mystery or two . . .

Cole and Hope Trapp disappeared on New Year's Eve 1999—or, technically, the following day, when they were reported missing, as both had been seen after midnight, albeit in separate locations: Cole in his cousin Frederick's bunk bed, a quarter past twelve, when Freddy himself fell asleep; Hope outside a liquor store in the Presidio, where Sebastian's brother and sister-in-law dropped her off at 1:30 A.M. so that she could reload on a particularly exotic mezcal for the Trapps' fabled New Year party ("Glittering!" "Swank!" "Glamorous!" chorused the papers). She would summon a cab, she told them, and return to Pacific Heights with nightcaps for the stragglers.

Ten minutes later, Dominic and Simone peeked into their son's bedroom. Freddy they saw curled up in the lower bunk; they assumed Cole was up top, but later admitted that they hadn't looked too closely. ("Mysterious!" "Shocking!" "Unthinkable!")

Madeleine Trapp, the daughter, returned to Pacific Heights from her off-campus apartment in Berkeley a few minutes before nine A.M. on New Year's Day (her roommate's boyfriend confirmed he had bumped into her outside the bathroom just after three), around the time Sebastian called his brother's house to ask after Hope, who hadn't made it back home before he went to bed; he'd concluded she was battened down with her in-laws.

She wasn't, Dominic informed him. And—as Freddy, awoken by the phone, had reported that very moment—neither was Cole.

The investigation commenced within hours. Surveillance footage was scrutinized—airport, train station, taxi ranks, highways. Neighbors were questioned; classmates were quizzed; the (glittering, swank, glamorous) party guests eagerly submitted to interviews. But—

"Corona with lime."

Nicky smiles and swigs, beer rushing through the lime wedge.

The waitress fans herself with a menu. "Anything to eat?"

"A burger, please. Bloody."

"We're vegan, doll. 'S why we're called Give Peas a Chance."

Goddammit, San Francisco. Nicky swallows a sigh, orders carrots and a bowl of hummus. Shuts her eyes again.

At last, the lead investigators—a creaky veteran soon to retire and his partner, a keen-eyed, green-haired young woman only two years on the force—back-burnered the case. Hope and Cole had been missing for six months.

Did they choose to flee? Was it a double kidnapping? No mere coincidence, surely? Online—this was the midmorning if not the dawn of the Internet—conspiracy theorists spun spiderwebs, click-starved magazines posted lurid captions beneath photos of Hope and Cole: CULT! WITNESS PROTECTION! ALIEN ABDUCTION!

In February, the police publicly cleared Sebastian of suspicion, thanking him for his cooperation. That same day, he traveled to England, where years earlier he and Hope had bought a country house in her native Dorset, and there he remained as Madeleine returned to school and Dominic and Simone and Freddy returned to their lives.

Without a carcass to circle, the media eventually flapped away.

When, at the end of that year, Sebastian Trapp reappeared in San Francisco, he vanished again, as completely as the vicar's ward in *London Bridges,* as the pilfered urn in *Ashes, Ashes.* As his own wife and child.

He wouldn't write a new book for ten years. He wouldn't remarry for another fifteen, although his choice of bride did not go unnoticed.

Because—lest anyone forget—there were the aides. Husband and wife had each employed an assistant, his to help with research, hers to manage her committee schedules. Sebastian's was a graduate student called Isaac.

Hope's was a young Englishwoman called Diana.

8.

NICKY REMAINS AT THE CAFÉ for nearly two hours. A half dozen friends have texted today, each cracking the same are-you-dead-by-now joke; she submits proof of life, assures them she's hiring a security detail, or at least a body double. Outside the window, fog again blurs the air again, cars swim through it—nothing like the lava flows of taillights in New York. She counts nine Teslas before paying the check, summons a ride.

Again she scales the steps; again she strokes that question-mark knocker with one slender finger. But this time Nicky slides the house key into the lock, twists, and pushes the door open. The cavernous foyer is lit low and warm; far away, the staircase glides up into darkness, the portrait at the top just a box of shadows. The windows on either side are black.

In the silence, she feels like a teenager returned late from a night out.

"And what have *you* been up to?"

Nicky starts, glances to her right.

It's a room she hadn't noticed earlier. Through the doorway, she sees the back of a woman bowed over a card table. Nicky counts five other tables as she approaches, each strewn with jigsaw pieces: in the corner there's a cloud of clownfish, creamsicle orange-and-white; nearby, Sargent's *Madame X*, two bare arms and a narrow waist and no head.

She steps over the threshold—into the nineteenth century, across the ocean. An extravagant mural covers the four walls: London by gaslight, cobbled streets glistening, alleys soft with fog, horse and carriage, both glossy and black . . . and stumbling over the stones, walking through the mist, darting around the hansom: urchins and drunks and green-grocers and rats and cats and a pair of gentlemen clutching silver-topped sticks. The façade of a tavern spans one wall; its windows, frosted and sooty, paupers raising pints behind the glass, appear to be blackout blinds drawn over the front of the house.

Nicky studies the woman from behind. Her hair is careless and blond, her shoulders round. Hazy smoke drifts over her head. In one hand she cradles a wineglass, shallow tide of red within. Nicky longs to see her face.

The woman plucks a cigarette from the ashtray. "Someone very dangerous is standing right behind you."

Nicky turns, zeroes in on him instantly, just beside the open door: a figure in the distance, beyond the arch of a viaduct, posed in the sallow light of a lone streetlamp; top hat on his head, cape billowing from his shoulders, mist swirling at his feet. Jack the Ripper. She tries not to shy from him.

"Come over here and let's take a look at you."

As she moves forward, Nicky assesses the woman's work: a tabby, reared on its hind legs, clawing at a caged canary. "This is a trick puzzle," she explains, carefully unpicking piece after piece until the cat is disarticulated, just a scattering of whiskers and fur. "It can fit together any number of ways. But there's only one true solution."

Now she turns, and at last Nicky beholds her plain, pleasant face. She's on loan from the prow of a Viking ship, yet she appears very slightly amused, as though she's got a secret and it's dirty.

Nicky tries not to gawk: this person, in her sloppy sweater, with her sloppy hair, scarcely resembles the college athlete pictured in the press twenty years ago.

Beneath the table an animal stirs, snorts—a squat French bulldog, face a crumpled black mask, two bat ears poking from its head.

"That's Watson." The dog regards Nicky with bulbous eyes, sighs as though disappointed. "And I'm Madeleine." Her handshake is a single brisk pump, the way Nicky was taught.

"I'm Nicky."

"Oh, I know." Madeleine sweeps one arm around the walls. "My father loves the late Victorian. Gaslights and penny dreadfuls. He would've set his novels back then, except Conan Doyle beat him to it. I'm a whore, by the way."

Nicky frowns.

"See?" Pointing to a prostitute in an alley, her skirts muddy at the hems, her bosom overripe. Her face is Madeleine's.

"Dad asked did I want to be the lady in the carriage, and I was like, 'Hell, no—I want some action. And gimme a rack, while you're at it.'" A sip of wine. "Sorry about your room." Lifting her cigarette. "It's where my brother used to sleep." She drags deeply, arrows smoke to one side, mashes the butt into the ashtray—"Filthy habit"—and rinses with wine. She stands, rising six feet tall, her body soft and full, and turns to another table—a kitten dangling from a branch above the words OH SHIT. Underfoot, Watson ambles slowly after her, like a homely familiar.

"So not a week ago, Dad announces he wants to"—shrug—"*reminisce* in print. Okay, sure—eighty million books, of course he's got stories. Places he's been, people he's met." She thrusts a hand into her sweater pocket, pulls out a dented pack of cigarettes and a lighter, fires up. Drifts over to the decapitated *Madame X.* "He knows everyone. Well—he *knew* everyone. Until twenty years ago."

Nicky hears the hitch in her voice, feels the urge to console.

Madeleine gazes down at the headless vision and with two fingers reconstitutes a shoulder. "But I don't think," she says at last, "he should spend what time he's got left dredging up the past. He *never* talks about *them,* you know. You're not unaware of . . . all that."

"I'm not."

"So if that's what you're after . . ." Madeleine steps back to her wineglass, finds it drained.

"I'm not after anything," says Nicky to this unexpected version of Madeleine Trapp.

"You better not be a Trapper Keeper."

Nicky nearly grimaces. True-crime rubberneckers and paranoiacs and self-appointed Sherlocks, usually preoccupied by the drama within their own ranks, who continue to obsess over Hope and Cole's disappearance. They tout alleged sightings; they reenact—in print, anyway—the double murder; they debate elaborate methods of corpse disposal (acid bath, as in *Baa Baa Black Sheep;* butchered, cooked, and served to a family dog, per *Everywhere That Mary Went*); they gossip about Diana, whom none of them appear to have actually met. Nicky has knocked on the doors of those chat rooms over the years, waded through the sewers of social media—it's an intriguing story, after all—but only to observe.

"I'll take that as a no." The cigarette hisses in the dregs. "Nothing against *you,* by the way. I'm sure you're a damn delight. Dad says so." A smile—her smile is perfect: just enough teeth, just enough mischief. "I'm also sure you'll be exquisitely sensitive."

"Sensitive is my middle name."

"Very few people use their middle names." Madeleine crouches, and the bulldog shuffles into her arms. "Well—oof—I've seen you. That's enough progress for tonight, I think."

They quit the vermin and the vice and emerge into the serenity of the foyer. "Over there's my hidey-hole"—Madeleine nods at a door in the far wall—"by the grandfather clock. My sweet little suite. Watson is my roommate."

Their footsteps are silent on the marble. "How long have you lived here?" asks Nicky.

"As a grown-up? Moved back in three terms into law school, never moved out. Never finished my degree, either. Never did lots of things, in fact."

"What do you do?"

Madeleine adjusts Watson in her arms. "Christ, she's getting heavy. Dad feeds her pâté. You got a dog? Don't feed it pâté. Let's see: I wrote a terrible book. I won't ask if you've read it. You'd be embarrassed if you hadn't. I'd be embarrassed if you had. Stunt publishing. Dad's editor asked if I had a decent mystery novel in me." The dog snorts. "Correct, Watson. I did not."

The terrible book starred a female private eye tracking an arsonist in fifties San Francisco—"Not so much hard-boiled as scrambled," sniffed one critic. Nicky wonders if she ought to change the subject, if she ought to reassure Madeleine, if she ought to suggest lunch or maybe one of those GoCar city tours (not *now*, though, not at night, after they've both been drinking) or—

"I helped Dad with a few Simons back in high school," Madeleine continues. "Research, I mean. I was bad at that, too. I'm good at taking care of him, though. You've been warned about the Otis?" They've reached her door.

Nicky looks to her right at a latticework elevator grate. Before she can reply, Madeleine drops Watson to one hip, opens her other arm like a wing. Nicky steps into the hug—Madeleine Trapp's hug! She can feel the dog snuffling against her side.

"Night." Cigarettes and a surprisingly flowery shampoo.

"Night," Nicky answers.

A squeeze. "I really wish you weren't here."

Nicky decides to squeeze back all the same—it's only polite—but Madeleine releases her, smiles. Disappears into her suite.

What that child needs is a darn good spanking, Sebastian had said of his daughter. Nicky can't imagine anybody less spankable.

She stands alone in the foyer, black shadows steeped in the corners, white steps unfurled before her. Around her all is quiet. The walls say nothing to one another; the floors don't settle. Not even the whisper of pipes. Not even the creep of a clock. A house without a voice. Nicky stamps on the marble floor beneath her. One pitiful thump—no report, no flock of echoes.

Doesn't sound travel in this house? Or is that only human voices?

Her gaze travels up the staircase, to that portrait suspended in the darkness, the phantom family.

A moment later, she arrives at the landing. On the wall before her, Madeleine flanks her father in her white dress, staring at the foyer. Her posture is excellent, her plump face sober and somber. The woman downstairs had slumped at her table, appraised Nicky through a scrim of smoke.

Why, she wonders, would a man who never talks about his first wife and child hang their picture here?

9

MADELEINE PARKS HERSELF AT HER DESK, a dainty escritoire that chafes her thighs, and rouses her laptop. Observes that she has left two lamps lit all day. San Franciscan of the year.

She'd *hugged* her.

Why did she *hug* her?

Pity, probably. Pity and cheap wine. The girl seemed nervous; quiet, too, and Madeleine distrusts quiet people. Why in royal hell had her father recruited such a homunculus? Why had he recruited anyone at all? Is the homunculus to have the run of the house? Does she expect a tour guide? Will she want to visit Madeleine's room?

She swivels. "And here," some museum docent announces, "we see a bedroom from the late twentieth century, preserved intact." The battered sofa and twin armchairs, vainly awaiting a party of five; the bed in its nook, vainly awaiting a party of two; drapes tumbled in thick crimson tresses over three tall windows facing the street; the bureau and mirror and en suite—all as they were twenty years ago. "Observe the Cyndi Lauper concert poster," the guide continues, "and the enlarged reproduction of a nineteenth-century German postcard. We might conclude that the occupant enjoyed retro popular music, possibly ironically, and was also, at some point in their life, pretentious." And along the far wall, the same broad scaffolding of shelves, crowded with tennis trophies and paperback novels and CD cases and framed photographs (assorted Watsons in assorted poses) and a lava lamp (extinct) and an aquarium (droughted) and a maidenhair fern.

In her arms, Watson complains. "I agree," says Madeleine. "No visitors." She turns back to her laptop.

The file, stashed in an obscure folder, is named pap smear photos, which seems likely to discourage interest. Madeleine clicks.

SIMON SAYS

A screenplay by Madeleine Trapp

Based on the novel by Sebastian Trapp

She scrolls through twenty-five pages, two murders, and many, many cameos from Simon's dog. It's bad in all the ways she feared, certainly, but also in ways that she appears to have invented. She's glad her father knows nothing about it.

Three of the St. John mysteries have already been adapted for film, each handsomely mounted, each well received, and each long ago—a point emphasized by the movie producer who this past February reached out. Madeleine's is a stubby CV—four years of college, three terms of law school, assorted volunteer posts, all these details last revised online in 2008—but the producer wasn't looking for an unemployed half lawyer: he wanted to revive the Simon St. John franchise, reboot it from the top, and could Madeleine put him in touch with the author?

She could, but she hasn't, and she won't. Not yet. If Simon is to be restored to life onscreen, what better resurrectionist than—here's a twist—Madeleine Trapp? She imagines her father leafing proudly through one hundred pages of crisp banter and mild violence; she hears him praising her fresh ideas, so fresh that as of yet she hasn't actually had them. "You've made Simon your own, my puffin," he'll chuckle. "Tell this producer that if he changes a word I shall haunt his toilet."

Madeleine fidgets in her chair. This represents her first compelling professional opportunity in more than a decade. And time is short.

10:13 P.M. Her fingers dance over the keyboard. She'll write until midnight. Two hours in 1920s London, chasing a killer armed with a poison-tipped umbrella.

At 10:16, she steams into the kitchen, finds her cousin at the stove. "Thought you'd punched out for the evening," she says.

"Forgot my phone." Freddy pokes an egg frothing in the skillet. "Got hungry."

He's always hungry. "Where's the wee Boswell?" asks Madeleine, leaning into the fridge.

"The what?"

"Dad's fan club. You want some inferior pinot noir?"

"No. You want some superior sandwich?"

"Sure."

She pours, sips, settles at the island, surveys the kitchen: Scandinavian-spare, slate floor, window seat, courtyard view. In the corner, an outside door, and beside it the entrance to the dim back stairs. All renovated four years ago, her father's wedding present to Diana. Diana, who scarcely ever cooks.

Her mother had never set foot in this room.

"You'd never guess your dad's a goner," Freddy is saying. "Remember volunteer week at the nursing home? In high school? And that one lady who just wandered around predicting deaths? 'Henry's going tomorrow,' she'd say. 'He's getting fainter. I can almost see through him.'"

"Life of the party."

"But her hit rate was, like, unnerving. I started to wonder if this granny was actually *killing* the people she said were gonna die."

"Did you talk to her?"

"Hell, yeah. She was hilarious."

"Sorry—I meant did you talk to the creature upstairs. Nicky." With mild distaste.

"She bummed a ride. Nice. Not too chatty." He sets before her a toasted sandwich.

"What delectation is this?"

"It *was* grilled cheese and ham," Freddy answers as he airlifts the egg from the skillet. "It *was* a croque monsieur. But dress it in a saucy little yolk hat, and your croque monsieur becomes"—tipping the egg onto the sandwich—"a croque madame."

Madeleine blinks.

"Diana mentioned it earlier. I asked the Internet."

If Diana had mentioned arsenic, Freddy would've gargled with it. Shouldn't a crush stale after twenty years? Shouldn't a man move on? "What did she say?"

"Diana?"

"*No.* That Nicky girl. We are talking about that Nicky girl."

"Are we? I dunno—she likes his books? She's sweet. Good vibes. Didn't ask about any *family* drama, if that's what you want to know."

Do you believe he killed them? That's what Madeleine should've asked. Pointed to the very large, very dead elephants in the room and just asked.

"Well, our family drama is more dramatic than most."

"Madeleine." Freddy wags the spatula at her solemnly. "They've been pen pals for three years. If she had some, like, tabloid agenda, I'd think he'd know by now. And if she thought he'd . . . you know—"

"Killed them."

". . . that, then she probably wouldn't've come here, right?"

Madeleine considers this. "Five years," she corrects him, grudgingly.

"There you go." He nods the spatula toward the sink once, twice. "Think I can swish this?"

"From four feet away?"

"That a yes?"

"That's a no, actually."

The spatula clatters into the basin. "Suck on that."

Madeleine takes the plate back to bed, splits the sandwich with the dog. The screenplay can wait. Her father can wait. . . . Although not for very long.

She subsides into the pillows. Twice now he's attempted to speak to her about the future, and twice Madeleine has balked. It isn't the bequests that concern her—she knows he'll provide amply for her, and for Diana, and for Freddy and his mother, too, probably—but life (hers) after death (his): What will it look like? What will it *sound* like? Who will call her Maddy? Her mother called her Mad; her brother called her Magdala, though only sparingly, and only in private—his code name for her, and hers for him, cribbed from some Agatha Christie novel co-starring two cousins christened thus. Madeleine forgets how it began, but she remembers Cole murmuring *Merry Christmas, Magdala* as he pressed a gift into her hands by the tree, before their parents sloped downstairs; she remembers the notes he slipped beneath her door those nights when they'd watched an even barely scary movie:

> *To: Magdala*
> *Can I please sleep with you tonihgt.*
> *Sincerly: Magdala*

He would knock, and she would climb from the sheets and read his request and open the door and say, "Get in here, Magdala," and in the morning he would whisper, "Thanks, Magdala," and the name was retired until next time.

Magdala, Mad, Maddy. Soon just Madeleine.

On the desk across the room, the laptop screen falls asleep. So should she, she decides, reaching for her bedside lamp.

After a moment in the dark, she hears herself ask, "What do you think my name is, Watson?"

The dog snorts.

"I assumed as much," sighs Madeleine.

10

A BEAUTIFUL ENGLISHWOMAN; A FADED DAUGHTER. A vast house. A koi pond and a grand staircase. A skein of halls, a grandfather clock. A library. An attic—a *spooky* attic. The house is Styles, where Poirot investigated that first mysterious affair; it's 221B Baker Street, the walls pocked with bullet holes, the windows braced against London pea soup. It is Manderley. It's the Piccadilly flat where Lord Peter Wimsey styled himself a detective.

It's perfect.

Nicky excavates a book from her steamer, tiptoes to bed with it. Sheathed in linen sheets, her skin scrubbed clean and her hair still damp, she examines the cover: *The Crooked Man: The New Simon St. John Mystery*. Not so new anymore, of course, and neither is her copy. She turns to page 4, where the collected works of Sebastian Trapp teeter in a column.

THE SIMON ST. JOHN MYSTERIES
Simon Says (1983)
Everywhere That Mary Went (1984)
The Man with Seven Wives (1985)
Little Boy Blue (1987)
Jack Be Nimble (1988)
There Was an Old Woman (1989)
Jack Be Quick (1990)
The Itsy Bitsy Spider (1991)
Roses Are Red (1992)
Jack Fell Down (1993)
Baa Baa Black Sheep (1994)
Ashes, Ashes (1995)
London Bridges (1996)
And When She Was Good (1997)
Seven for a Secret (1998)
If You Have No Daughters (1999)
The Crooked Man (2010)

NONFICTION
The Nerve and the Knowledge:
A Writer's Thoughts on Detective Fiction (2000)

It's been more than a decade now since *The Crooked Man*—itself ten years in the making. Nicky folds back the cover.

And hears a fusillade of sharp pops, hard rain pelting glass.

She sits up, turns to the dormer window. The sky is clear.

Another moment of quiet. Nicky sinks back into her pillow.

Those pops again, bubble wrap bursting: a-rat-a-rat-a-tat. And then a soft chime.

Sound *does* travel in this house.

Now her eyes are wide. The Remington, surely, two floors below.

. . . More letters? To whom? Or just paperwork—being-of-sound-mind-and-body-I-do-hereby-bequeath stuff? Still: fun to imagine he's at work again, plunging into the alleys of Spitalfields, sifting through the Bermondsey sands. One last night in Soho.

She bats an arm at the lamp, switches it off.

When in 2010 his publisher released a new Simon St. John novel, the first since the previous century, booksellers rejoiced: Sebastian Trapp, invisible lo these many years! Sebastian Trapp, whose infamy had long endured! But would readers remember Simon, a jovial aristocrat in twenties England tortured by his time in the French trenches? Would they remember, perhaps even more fondly, his canine companion, Watson, among literature's less astute fauna? ("Watson has never snouted out a single clue, never chased down a single suspect," St. John explains to a client in one of his adventures. "He is simply my friend, and I could ask for none better.") His opera-singer sister Laureline, killed off to much public dismay in *Seven for a Secret* but frequently glimpsed in flashback; his friends and foes at Scotland Yard, particularly ambitious Inspector Trott; Mr. Myers, the gorgeous Essex pharmacist (and "the best man in England"), as well as St. John's paramour in countless online fan-fiction stories, who ably dispenses our hero's medicine and expertly identifies assorted poisons—would readers embrace them anew?

And dared they reacquaint themselves with St. John's archenemy, his Moriarty, the ingenious serial killer known only as—

A-rat. A-rat-a-tat-trapp. Ting.

—Jack! A lean figure in a ghoulish mask—shock-white skin, tiny sunken eyes and enormous nose, two demon horns, a grin like a gash. "The very likeness of Spring-Heeled Jack," as Inspector Trott says, "that Victorian bogeyman always jumpin' 'cross rooftops and rappin' on kiddies' windows."

Nicky draws her feet from the foot of the bed.

Yes: readers would remember; readers would dare. *The Crooked Man* stormed bestseller lists worldwide. Reviewers praised it, some extravagantly. Sebastian Trapp, at long, long last, was back.

He never wrote another word.

A-tat a-rat a-Trapp!

. . . Until now, it seems. Oddly soothing, these staccato blasts, the bright cry of the bell; Nicky wonders if the fire is burning, flames licking at the logs, the spines of his books rutilant in the light.

She rolls on to one side. The strings of the harp are silver silk; the headless horse glimmers; the glass eyes of the mummified dogs gleam.

She burrows into the sheets, into her head.

In the years since his second retirement, Sebastian Trapp has emerged, here and there, to dine at the Baron Club, or to attend library benefits, or to scud across the bay on his yacht. Stories about him have demoted Hope and Cole to supporting roles in a long-ago drama; his legacy seems ever more to be that of a very popular novelist. A very popular novelist who suffered a devastating misfortune, perhaps. Or a very popular novelist who committed the perfect crime.

Nicky urges herself to remain calm. Their interviews will be informal, amiable. Not even interviews, really; conversations.

Conversations are always dangerous if you have something to hide. Who said that?

Her phone wakes up on the pillow—

Call Nicky

—and then it rings. Aunt Julia is not tech-savvy.

"I told the phone to call you," she explains when Nicky picks up. "Are you still alive?"

"Not the first time I've heard that joke tonight."

"It isn't a joke. I'm not up past midnight because I'm joking."

"I'm sorry," says Nicky, meaning it, sitting up. "I am alive, and I'm excited. It's exciting!"

"Living with a murderer is not exciting. Stop picking at your nails."

"I'm not." She is. "All good in Savannah, Aunt J?"

"Oh, I *hate* this idea."

"You don't *hate* it," says Nicky, who tries not to hate anything. "You're uncomfortable with it. *I'm* sort of uncomfortable with it. In an interesting way, though. Spending time with—"

"Someone who killed—"

"That's not what I was—I'm here to tell his story, remember."

"So you say."

"And maybe I'll learn something nobody else knows." She can't help but hope she will. "I'm not frightened, though."

"Not frightened *enough*, certainly."

Nicky hears the gurgle of a straw, pictures Julia on her porch swing, sipping a julep and swatting at mosquitos. A widow's life for her.

"You're too *nice*, Nicky. You always think too *well* of people. People take advantage, you know." Silence. "Have you seen him?"

"I saw the whole family, except for his brother's wife."

"What are they like?"

Nicky thinks of Madeleine with her cigarettes and wine, of Freddy chattering at the wheel. Diana, too, polite but removed. "A bit . . . a little sad, maybe. Like they're not where they should be. Misplaced. I sort of want to hug them."

"You sort of want to hug feral cats, young lady. And what about"— deep breath—"Sebastian Trapp?"

"Sebastian Trapp," says Nicky, "is a force."

"You expected that."

"He's like a fire. You want to pull up beside him and warm your hands."

"Why didn't you say so? Nothing safer than a fire."

"Well, he invited me, so I'm going to make the most of it. Here— wanna know what today's word was? Is?" Julia had given Nicky a supremely unnecessary word-of-the-day calendar last Christmas, half as chunky now as it was then. Nicky packed it this morning, just to please her aunt.

She excavates it from the steamer trunk, peels off yesterday's sheet, looks at today's.

"Well?"

After a moment, Nicky says, "Foreboding."

Gurgle. "A little on the nose. Remember you're supposed to use it in a sentence before the day's out."

"I feel no sense of foreboding in this house."

After Nicky hangs up, she considers that this isn't strictly true. He *is* like fire, and being here—in the Mystery House, a staircase away from him—is like passing your hand through flame. The thrill of contact with a dangerous substance.

She's amazed he chose her, this author whose books she loves; amazed he chose anybody at all. She hugs herself—in excitement, in anxiety.

You ain't frightened? the cabbie had asked.

Not frightened enough, Julia whispers in her ear.

Nicky shuffles on her knees to the foot of the bed, unlatches the steamer trunk propped against it. She excavates a slim paper packet, sits back, slides a stack of nine postcards into her lap. On the front of the first card is an indigo-blue butterfly, wings like petals burst apart.

On the back, in lumpy script:

> *Dear Nicky:*
>   *I'm Cole, I guess wer'e Pen Pals! I like reading, milk chocloate, animals esp Dogs + the "Beach Boys." Tell me abuot your life, what is up?? What kind of music do you like? What sort of cloths do you wear? I look forward to keeping in touche!*
>   *Your Freind, Cole*

The date is *April 1999.*

Nicky inspects the next postcard, *May 1999,* a golden retriever swimming and smiling.

Dear Nicky:

I went to the postcard shop at the warf but they didn't have a French bull dog. Our French bull dog is called Watson 4, he a good boy. My freind Issac gave me a new t shirt but it's to big for me, it says: BLONDIE. Do you want it? If you want to read a good book maybe read Dad's books, they are cool

Your freind, Cole

A teacher had enrolled her in a "correspondence program for young teens interested in ecology and wildlife preservation," as she recalls— "Let's find you some friends," he explained, meaning well—but after her assigned pen pal failed to write back, she found herself in touch with Cole Trapp. Each month a new postcard arrived: the butterfly, the dog, the red panda, the sloth, one by one—the seahorse, the fruit bat—until the final greeting in December 1999.

Pen pals weren't often reported missing on national news. Alongside their mothers, no less.

Again Nicky settles into the pillows, studies the pictures in the moonlight. The honeybee, the box jellyfish . . .

She won't tell her host—he certainly doesn't need to hear about a few messages his son sent twenty years ago to a fellow animal enthusiast. That's not why she's here. Even if she has wondered ever since.

Her breathing deepens. Her lips part. The final postcard slides from her fingers. The scorpion.

She gazes at the ceiling, the constellation of four letters. Glowing— ghostly; but glowing in the dark.

And as her eyelids flutter and fold, Cole's name seems to shine a shade brighter.

Thursday, June 18

11

"'WEAVING SPIDERS, COME NOT HERE.'" Sebastian spoons each word like it's relish, a shimmering beer in one hand. "Club motto. Yet here you've come."

Nicky smiles, struggles to right herself in a leather club chair so buttery that she's slid almost to the floor. Across the table, her host sits up straight in a balding velvet wingback. She grips the armrests, smiles harder.

She slept deeply the night before—fairy tale–princess sleep, poisoned-apple sleep—and awoke to an attic whitewashed with sun; as she padded to the bathroom, shafts of light kindled Nicky's hair, set her skin aglow. She felt reborn.

A text and photo awaited her: Irwin and Potato beneath the sheets, dog's snout burrowed into human's armpit, one paw at his lips. Kinky.

Irwin hadn't slept in her bed since February. Does she envy her dog? Is she so lovelorn?

. . . Not really, no. Hope you've had your shots, she replied before dressing. Walked out. Walked back in. Found her aunt's calendar in the sheets. The word of the day: *absquatulate*, "to decamp or suddenly leave a social gathering." Below: *Use this fun word in a sentence today!*

"Fat chance," answered Nicky.

Then the ride to the Baron Club in Sebastian's green Jaguar, the streets unspooling before them, the speakers exhaling classical music ("I don't actually *like* it, but I feel I'm *expected* to"). Outside a hulking block of red brick in Lower Nob Hill, a valet swapped places with Sebastian ("Good morning, Mr. Trapp"), a doorman admitted them ("Been a while, Mr. Trapp"), a concierge sat them at a low-rise table huddled in a corner ("Your usual, Mr. Trapp?"), a waiter supplied a pilsner glass of beer ("And for the lady, Mr. Trapp?").

"Pineapple juice, please," says Nicky. The waiter doesn't glance at her, just flicks a table lamp to life, its black shade speckled with light.

The club lounge is airy for an old masonry building. Waiters glide past, all male, like the membership, ice cubes chiming in glasses.

Pictures on the walls, mostly horses and white men, but the odd owl, too—even a few stuffed specimens, staring at her with headlight eyes.

"Weaving spiders—we're not meant to talk shop between these walls." Sebastian admires his pilsner.

Today's suit—with waistcoat—is brown houndstooth, forest-green tie. Sebastian Trapp, unless adventuring on tour—Nicky recalls photos of him in safari gear, triumphant atop an elephant, swaddled in a parka on the Siberian tundra—was always famously formal in his attire. She squirms in her jeans and blouse; she feels a flock of glares settled upon her like birds on a wire.

"I'm underdressed," she murmurs.

"You're dressed as a woman. This club is no-girls-allowed." Sebastian stands and addresses the room: "That's enough, gentlemen, show's over. Just a human woman. It's fine," he assures his guest. "What, they'll expel me? I'll be dead before the motion passes!"

The waiter returns with apple juice. Nicky doesn't complain. "To you," she says to Sebastian as he sits.

"To dying," he says.

And they drink. *Look at me,* she thinks, *toasting with Sebastian Trapp.*

"God, it tastes better before noon," he sighs. "Are you comfortable in that museum upstairs?"

"Very. You have a beautiful home."

He sips again, sucks foam through his teeth. "I s'pose I do. I don't see much of it anymore. The dining room, when I'm feeling civilized. My library."

"I heard your typewriter last night."

"Did you? There's a spare room right below yours. It must conduct sound."

"Can I ask what you're working on?"

"I'm working—straight to the chase with you, isn't it?—working on my affairs. Who inherits what. How much to bequeath the dog. So that's the library. Where else do I roam? My bedroom, where I sleep and dream and get my blood cleaned thrice weekly. Such a satisfying word. *Thrrrice.*" He crinkles his face in pleasure. "Say it with me."

"Thrice."

"That was shit. Savor it."

"*Thrrrice,*" she trills, and feels her face crinkling, too. *Look at me, joking with Sebastian Trapp.*

"Ha!" he thunders. A ripple through the room as a half dozen diners half rise from their seats, scowling at Sebastian. "Now, Diana has her own bedroom. As did my first wife. Same room, in fact. I've mentioned my first wife?"

Nicky jolts. He's mentioned her—glancingly, in three or four letters. "You have."

"Well, when we moved in, we each claimed our own territory. Just before my son was born. I've mentioned my son?"

"You have." Glancingly, in two or three letters. Nicky pounces. "Would you like to start with them?" She sets a notepad on her lap, swipes her phone to life, and places it on the table, in the halo of the lamp. Reminds herself to focus—this is an opportunity to do some good work. Taps record.

"Are we on the air? Oh, where to begin—'my mind is like a crowded box-room with packets of all sorts stowed away therein, so many that I may well have but a vague perception of what was there.'" He eyes her.

"That'd be Sherlock, 'Lion's Mane.' You were saying—"

"Do you know your saints?"

Nicky shakes her head. "Not my genre."

"My father did. Military man. Survived Omaha Beach. Bullet here"—he touches his hip—"bullet here." His stomach. "So he had hopes for his line. Now, Saint Sebastian is the patron of soldiers and athletes. Painters love Sebastian. Obscenely handsome heretic, arrows plunged into his flesh like he's a pincushion. Usually looking distressed." The twenty-first-century Sebastian waves undistressedly at a passerby. "The scene: an army base in West Berlin. Enter a new Sebastian, hefty child. Only infant laid out on a stretcher." He sips his beer, swallows, upper lip creamy with foam. "Eventually I acquired a brother, named for the patron saint of astronomers, so I won that round. Two parents. Then one parent. Then no parents. Then no brother." He has leapt five decades in as many sentences. "I was . . . ten, twenty, and sixty, in that order. Nice round numbers. First my mother died of lupus; it was quick. Then my father died of a gun in his mouth, which was quicker. Remind me: are your parents alive?"

Nicky blinks, startled. "No." He waits. "My mother died when I was in college," she says, "and my dad had a heart attack five years ago."

"It happens. Dominic found the body at the kitchen table." Crossing his endless legs, one foot wagging in its loafer. "The Sergeant—that's how we addressed our father; he was a sergeant major by then, but *Sergeant Major* is a mouthful—the Sergeant had been drinking coffee. Waste of caffeine." His foot goes still; slowly he zippers his fingers along the crease in his trouser leg. "I was singing in the shower, shaking off a bad dream, when Dominic tugged on the curtain."

She finds she's holding her breath. The man can tell a story.

"He died at seven fifty-eight in the morning." Nicky, unsure how to react, writes this on the pad, strikes it out. "You see, the bullet had passed straight through his skull and slammed into the clock above the oven. Just like in a mystery novel—a smashed wristwatch confirming time of death. Even today, when Detective Whoever points to a stopped clock, I remind myself that it could happen. Not that I ever stooped so low, of course. A stopped clock; honestly." He sips.

"By then I'd been living in San Francisco for a little while. I was back in Berlin only to pack my brother off to Berkeley. We postponed. But not very long." He raises his eyebrows. "And then there were two."

Nicky observes a moment's silence. "That must have been hard," she says, with feeling.

"Life is hard. After all, it kills you." He strokes his tie. "It came for Dominic on a dark road. Left him there, too. Midnight hit-and-run on the Pacific Coast Highway. Talk about stooping low. A cruel twist—he'd kept me alive after Hope and Cole disappeared."

Nicky twitches, static-shocked. *He never talks about them.*

"Dominic cooked—he owned several restaurants—and the idiot Frederick tended to Watson the Fourth. He and Cole had grown up together. Freddy, I mean. Same age, almost. Same school, sometimes." He cups the beer in both hands, fingers caressing the glass. "He was Cole's only friend."

All the papers ran the same photo: dark-eyed, dark-haired Freddy standing beside his small, pale cousin, both wielding tennis racquets. To Nicky they looked like different species.

"And Simone talked," concludes Sebastian.

"Talked?"

"Yes. Simone is that ideal conversationalist who doesn't particularly care if you're listening or not. I've written some of my best work with her soliloquizing somewhere nearby. She supplies superb ambient noise. I find it soothing."

"I see." Nicky is curious to speak with Simone.

"The family visited nearly every day, separately or together. Although Dominic stopped swinging by after he died."

"And what were you doing?"

Sebastian frowns. "When?"

"All that time. Until *The Crooked Man*."

"I've just told you. I was at home, bouncing like a squash ball between four walls. What did you think I was doing?"

"I don't know." Suddenly she feels shy. "Nobody knows."

He drains his glass and signals for another. "Young Hunter," he says, "there is one pursuit, and one alone, that engages a man who has lost his wife and son in a single night, and that is resisting the almighty urge to blow his brains out."

12

Nicky stares.

He's primping the handkerchief in his breast pocket, one foot bobbing up and down, steady as a pulse, even as his death wish rattles in the air.

Sebastian Trapp has never commented publicly on Hope and Cole—not even in the days following their disappearance, when the police pleaded for information at press conferences, when radio and TV hosts urged their very willing audiences to come forward with useless tips.

Sebastian promptly offered a million-dollar reward for information leading to the recovery of either wife or child. A week later, he doubled it. Phone lines lit up. Skeptics jeered.

But how he felt—how he mourned (if he mourned)—was a mystery.

"Death had obsessed me for a very long time," he says, sipping a fresh pilsner and easing into his chair, as one accustomed to an audience. "Ever since our mother." Nicky wants to linger in those lost later years, pin him there like a butterfly to a board; yet already he's flitted away. "She worked as a librarian on the base, and there I would go after school to read. My mother set the syllabus. Adventure stories, for a time; Tintin, of course—very fun, very racist—and *Swiss Family Robinson*. Oh, to live in a tree house!" He dashes a hand against his knee, gleeful, and Nicky finds herself grinning. "Or *The Count of Monte Cristo*. Imagine plotting merciless revenge!"

He knits his fingers, touches them to his dimpled chin. "Our mother was—she felt a special *tenderness* toward anyone who might be perceived, or self-perceive, as inferior. The loveless. And the luckless. The hopeless. The helpless." With each word, his voice sinks lower, softer, as though tethered to a weight.

Now he grasps his beer. "Hadn't thought about that in years."

"Hadn't thought about what in years?"

"You're going to have to stop repeating my every word. It could get annoying."

"We were talking about your wife and son."

"My wife and son." He drinks, smacks his lips. "Cole struggled with reading, you know. Got it from me. Oh, yes," as her brows lift. "Back then, of course, parents didn't consult a specialist. They simply hoped their child would work it out."

He's slipped her grip again, retreated into the mists of time. Quietly Nicky sighs; she's interested in his past, certainly, but that turn-of-the-century vanishing act is like a scar—she can't look away from it, even if she wanted to.

"I made reading a game," explains Sebastian. "Each word was a mystery in miniature. Line after line, I slugged away, because I knew there must be a solution. All that chaos was really just a scene to which order might be restored."

"Like a detective story."

"Elementary, my dear Hunter. And my mother, bless her, was a perfect fiend for a detective story. We turned every page of *The Sign of Four* together—very slowly. Then she dropped half a dozen Agatha Christies on my desk. I wrote Dame Agatha a letter when I turned thirteen, asking for her autograph—she was still alive and kicking, remember. And a few weeks later, I held it in my hands: a signed, matte-print, eight-by-ten picture of a seventy-five-year-old lady wearing a plain black dress. I very nearly wept. You'd have thought it was from Jayne Mansfield."

Nicky smiles politely; she recognizes this story from interviews. He's speaking in spirals, circling back to his opening chapters the way Simon revisits witnesses, exposing the next layer of the story, the secret beneath the skin. "Did the Sergeant ever read with you?"

"The Sergeant," says Sebastian, "did very little with me." He cracks open the lid of his pocketwatch, presses it shut without observing the time. *Fidgety as a schoolboy with a secret,* somebody once wrote. "Reading those books, I would plot alternative endings, devise another way out of the maze. Motive was trickier, but then motive is always tricky. Especially when you're a child. After my mother died . . ." He swallows beer. "I became—obsessed with it."

"Obsessed with *her* death?"

"Obsessed with death in general." He squints. "Wondering if it would come for me. *When* it would come for me. Because I would not stop for death, would he kindly stop for me?"

And there it is again! That dark voltage in his eyes, in his voice. The bared tooth. The power, too. He's a dangerous substance.

He sets the glass on the table. "After moving to Boston in 'sixty-eight, the story goes, I became a mechanic. Electrician, too. Mazes beneath the hoods! A mystery in every volt! I liked gears, I liked wires, I liked puzzles. I had half a dozen little gray cells"—he taps his temple with a slender finger—"and I was good with my hands. Those people are magicians. Noble professions." He glares at the room, the stock cast of pale men in dark suits; now he grimaces, waving them away like so much smoke. Nicky expects him to say *bah*.

"I moved to California the following year, apprenticed myself to a watchmaker. That was the summer of the Zodiac. And his cryptograms." Shaking his head. "He sent four to the press—one in early August, the rest later that year and the following spring. The first, you'll remember"—Nicky doesn't remember, wasn't alive, hadn't much thought about the Zodiac until yesterday's taxi ride—"was chopped into thirds and submitted to three different San Francisco newspapers. Each printed their portion, as instructed. And within a day, it was solved."

"Who solved it?"

"Most people would say it was a couple in Salinas. Took them twenty hours."

"Would most people be wrong?"

"Took me just over twelve." He traces a finger along the rim of his glass. "I phoned the paper before work, left the number for the shop. But when the paper called me back, the watchmaker refused to put me on. I'd always punched in late—the irony is not lost on me—and so it was that day, and he was annoyed. I spent the afternoon wrist-deep in clock guts, thinking about the cipher I'd cracked, thinking about the killer. And by evening, when I finally got an editor on the line—St. John was his name; Michael St. John, very Catholic—the Salinas duo had contacted the *Chronicle*." He shrugs. "'Man is the most dangerous animal of all,' the Zodiac wrote. Christ, what a monster."

Sebastian drains his beer; streaks of foam crawl down the inside of the glass. "Couldn't spell, either."

"I'm not a great speller," Nicky admits.

"So now you're the Zodiac."

"Then what happened?"

"'Then what happened? Then what happened?' You sound like my children when I told them a bedtime story." Nicky sips her juice. "Then what happened was Michael St. John explained that the paper's crosswords editor was getting senile—apparently they'd published several puzzles with interesting spelling errors—and he invited me to submit some samples. And ta-da—" He spreads his hands as though presenting himself, like a prize on a game show. "Crossword editor, age twenty. Not bad for a kid who couldn't read, eh? I liked the work. Took not one holiday in four years, not until it came time to pack Dom off to school. We know what happened when I returned to Berlin." He gazes at the dregs of his beer, then slides his eyes to her phone.

Nicky's skin prickles; he's about to say something he hasn't said before.

When he speaks again, he does so slowly. "I called Michael St. John, explained I'd come down with pneumonia. Tacked on an extra three days for the funeral. Didn't tell anyone I'd buried my father."

"Why not?"

Sebastian sighs. "People your age—young people, I mean—you treat your lives like galleries, for public display, open to all. My life is no gallery. It's a vault, a black box, and—I'm sorry I can't put this more elegantly—it's nobody's damn business."

Nicky pauses. "I don't believe my life's a gallery."

"Good. It isn't. And also," he continues, patting his pockets, voice in retreat, "I felt ashamed. That's illogical; I know that, intellectually. But you don't feel with your brain, and I felt ashamed. I wondered if someone might assume I was of a mind to take my own life, too."

From his coat he fishes a pipe. "Genuine cherrywood," he whispers. "Started last month. Good time to pick up bad habits, no? Should I do it?"

Again he grins, that contagious grin—he sounds like a child inviting a friend to dare him. "Smoking indoors is a capital crime in California, isn't it?" says Nicky. "Maybe wait?"

"I suppose." Sebastian hides the pipe in his pocket. "Where was I? Ah, yes: in 'seventy-five, I met my wife—"

"At a New Year's Eve party."

"You *have* studied. We married, we honeymooned, we scrimped, we saved. And for years I built crosswords. Didn't pay much, but more than Hope earned as a social worker. I found it soothing, always knowing the answer." For a moment he's quiet. Then he applies a fingertip to his temple and rotates it in a circle, as though winding a clock. "Nineteen eighty-four. I've been working the puzzle beat for some time. One day—you'll know this, of course—one day I say to myself, 'Sebastian, you unconventionally handsome devil, what about an ex-soldier turned sleuth?' The First World War ends, aristocratic veteran seeks distraction. He's independently wealthy, I decide, because they all are. You don't want a detective on a budget. I don't, anyway. By this time I'd met a few people in San Francisco who were very comfortably off, and I found it inspiring. Oh, you spoil me." Another pilsner has been set in front of Sebastian, crowned with foam. Nicky's glass is juiceless, but the waiter has disapparated.

"Now, that was Dorothy Sayers's blueprint, of course. But I hadn't read Dorothy Sayers, so my hero didn't trip over Peter Wimsey as he strode into my head. I named him St. John, after Mike, and I chose Simon for my father. Rare sentimental moment." He brings his beer to his lips. "Death would obsess him as it obsessed me. Coined a catchphrase, just before the finale: 'I should have wrapped this up in a ribbon a long time ago.' Thought it sounded self-deprecating. So many detectives are such know-it-alls, yet it takes them forever to crack the case." Nicky nods in agreement. She's never read this anywhere.

"A fellow I knew, another writer, steered me to his publisher, and—well, the details are dreary, but at last my late editor took me on. For a pittance. Put me to *work*. She envisioned the story not simply as a book, printed and bound, but as a bestseller. To some people that's a dirty word. Those people do not write bestsellers."

He drinks deep, swallows, exhales—and Nicky wonders if the man doesn't seem a touch nervous.

"The rest is legend. Terrific success. I know not why. Once the royalties began rolling in, we moved into our house—a foreclosure; talk about a pittance—and I waded upstairs, two flights, Hope in my arms. Cole was born a few weeks later, a few months early." He nods. "October sixteenth, nineteen eighty-five."

Nicky writes the date in her notepad, below the Sergeant's time of death.

Sebastian watches her left hand move across the paper. "I was good to St. John. He was good to me. For a long while, he was good *for* me. Until he wasn't." He swirls his glass, the beer rolling within it.

"For ages, I couldn't understand writers who resented their characters. Those characters were their meal tickets! Golden geese! Conan Doyle killed off Holmes, as you're aware. Pitched him over the Reichenbach Falls. He stayed dead for nearly ten years. Christie loathed Poirot—called him a 'little creep.' A bit ungrateful, I thought." He sets down his glass, perches on the edge of his seat. "But one day, I suddenly felt the same way about Simon. Always in disguise, always playing dress-up. Couldn't abide those twee anglicisms of his: his Pimm's and his cricket paddle and his 'Poppycock!' and his morning tea and his afternoon tea . . ."

"I love Simon," says Nicky before she can stop herself. "And I love your books. They're probably my favorite detective novels."

He lifts a brow. "Probably?"

"Probably." But her heart is thumping proudly, her teeth are set; Nicky will defend a beloved book as if it's her young. Even from its author.

Sebastian settles into the wingback, beaming. "So I wrapped Simon up in a ribbon. Trussed him like a goose. Threw that goose into cold storage. And here's the thing . . ." He reaches for his glass. "I didn't miss him."

Nicky hesitates. Worth the risk. "When did you decide to give him up? Was it right after"—she softens her voice—"was it after that night?"

Sebastian regards her neutrally. She braces herself, holds her breath.

His eyes drift to one side. "That's enough for now, methinks. I'm fading fast." One final pull on his beer and he pushes himself to his feet, slaps his thighs, smooths his sleeves. "Our chariot awaits."

But as Nicky retrieves her phone, he still hasn't stepped away. She looks up, finds him looking down. "You know," he says, "for a very long time, I kept almost dying."

His brow is furrowed, his gaze troubled; she wonders if he's surprised himself. And then he's gone.

13.

FOR A MOMENT NICKY REMAINS SEATED, wiggling her jaw, thinking.

Then a shadow drapes her. She looks up.

Up and across. The man is vast, an eclipse in coat and tie, pink linen shirt taut around his belly, like the skin of some unwholesome fruit. Black eyes lurking beneath zigzag brows. Face the color of rare beef. Fluff clinging to his scalp.

"Lionel Lightfoot," he says, offering her a ham hock. "Yes. Ah. I overheard—*quite* the handshake—I couldn't *help* but overhear you just now."

Nicky doubts this. She apologizes anyway.

"Ah. No. Yes. Well. Ah. You must be the person collecting *stories*. Like a Brother *Grimm!*"

"That's me."

He beams, a garden of greens in bloom among his battered teeth. "Very *clever*, our Sebastian. I used to say to my late wife, I used to say, 'In a room of *ten men*, Trapp is cleverer than—'" A cough racks his frame; he shudders, splutters.

"Cleverer than nine of them," supplies Nicky.

Lionel Lightfoot blots his lips with a handkerchief. "Cleverer than the other nine *combined*," he finishes, thrusting a stiff card at her. "I've known the *family* since the *Jurassic*. Come see me in Sea Cliff. I *insist* that you do, I really *demand* it."

She palms the card, gathering her bag and jacket. "If you insist and demand."

"Ah! Yes. Lionel Lightfoot," he reminds her.

"Nicky Hunter."

"How charming. Ah. Yes. Ah. Until then."

He recedes like a blimp unmoored.

Had he not identified himself, she wouldn't have recognized Lionel Lightfoot: scion of an ancient San Francisco family, author of numerous novels about scions of ancient San Francisco families—and the man who, a year after Sebastian's wife and child vanished, published a roman à clef in which a crime writer's wife and child vanish.

Perhaps she won't tell Sebastian he said hello.

"Lightfoot said hello?" Sebastian asks when she emerges from the club. She squints in the white sunlight, finds him slanted against the brickwork. "Not really a name for a person, is it?" he adds, the pipe wobbling between his lips. "Sounds more like a hobbit."

"He seems very—old money."

"So old it died." Sucking on the pipe. "Silly fellow, Lionel. Silly place, the Baron. All that posturing."

"Eyewash," agrees Nicky. It's one of Simon St. John's signature oaths, invoked whenever a suspect offers a dubious alibi.

Sebastian winces. "There's an expression I regret digging up. 'Eyewash'—honestly."

Again her skin prickles. He can mock his own work, if he likes, but he ought to consider how he's also mocking his readers.

"I'm sorry."

He has stepped toward her, between Nicky and the silver sun, so that the long fallen tree of his shadow breaks upon her.

"I don't mean to sound ungrateful. To St. John or to a reader. The greatest joy in any writer's career is the attention of his audience. And mystery readers are the most attentive audience of all. So ignore me when I complain," he says, turning to the street, his shadow sliding off of Nicky. "It's just eyewash."

The Jaguar runs over her answer ("I'll ignore you"). "Anybody teach you how to drive?" asks Sebastian.

She blinks. "No, in fact. You don't need to in New York."

"Then today's the day." Smoke spills from his lips when he coughs. "The young lady will take the wheel," he announces, opening the passenger door. "Nothing easier than driving. Ever play bumper cars as a child?"

Only once, she remembers, at an amusement park, some kid's tenth birthday; neon sheen, blaring pop, cars like bees, swarming her and stinging her until her teeth rattled. *Girls can't drive!* the boys shrieked. *Girls can't drive!*

"I can't drive," she says.

Sebastian tucks himself inside, grins. "And I've drunk three beers, and I'm suddenly quite tired, and I don't like that setup. I'll steer you through it."

By the driver's seat she pauses, her hands trembling; quickly she squeezes herself, and then she steps inside. The door shuts. Sebastian clears his throat. "Foot on the brake." She obeys. "Shift into drive and step on the gas. Gently. Don't run over Theo."

Nicky grips the gearshift, slides it closer, feels the Jaguar relax. She applies one foot to the pedal.

"Step on it."

The car jolts. Her foot darts left, mashes itself into the brake.

"Try again."

This time the car glides forward. Nicky twists the wheel, carefully, and they peel away from the curb. Again she brakes. "Sorry."

"Sorry won't get us home." Reclining.

Nicky exhales. Presses the gas.

Slowly they roll ahead; slowly—though a bit faster—she curves the car into a side street; slowly—yet faster still—Sebastian guides her through a crossword grid of roads.

"So: who is Nicky Hunter?"

A stop sign. She meerkats her head from one side to the other. "Sorry?"

"Stop apologizing. I've talked my jaw off its hinges. What about you? Describe yourself."

"I thought you had me all figured out. By my handwriting."

"Five words."

She tries to signal a turn, swats the windshield wiper instead. "Dammit. *Curious.*"

"We'll count that as one word. Curious. How so?"

The wipers squeak to a halt. "I like to know. I like to understand."

"Ah—you like to detect. What else?"

"Sensitive." Pushing the Jaguar through an intersection. "Or empathetic, maybe. If that doesn't sound immodest."

"It does not. How do you empathize?"

How smoothly he's turned the tables! She tries to back out—"Oh, I . . . silly ways. Unhelpful ways"—but only silence from the passenger seat. Nicky sighs, spots a FOR RENT sign in a dusty storefront, AMY'S LAUNDRY painted across the glass.

"When I see a sign like that," she says, "I think, Man, it must've been so *exciting* for Amy, watching them stencil the window, getting business cards printed, the grand opening . . . Her family must've felt proud." They slide beneath a green light. "And then working, probably very hard, for whatever it was she wanted, and putting up with whatever she put up with, only to wind up like that." The Amy-less store recedes from view.

"Opening a business must be like a marriage," Nicky concludes. "Nobody goes into it assuming they'll fail. But she did. Amy, I mean. So I feel terribly for her. Because she had a dream and it died and that's sad. I know what failure's like; most people do, on some scale. It's humiliating! And unfair! And I think most people—not all people, but most—I think they deserve better."

A respectful silence. After a moment, Sebastian opens his eyes and says, "Amy's Laundry was a drug front."

Nicky frowns. "What?"

"Money laundering. Serious criminal enterprise. There was a methamphetamine lab in the back, right where Amy would've kept her boxes of business cards."

"You're kidding."

"No, and neither was whoever executed two drug dealers in the parking lot behind the store last month, on the very spot where Amy's family would have celebrated her grand opening."

Nicky pauses. "Amy, you bitch."

He laughs. "It was your own doing! There's no trap so deadly as the trap you set for yourself. Also, your driving is improving."

She laughs, too, can't help it.

"Your third word, please. Take a left after the park."

"*Loves reading*. That's two words," she observes, triumphant.

"Two important words, but I can't allow it. Settle for *bibliophilic*. Fourth word?"

"I thought I'm supposed to be learning about you."

He waves four bony fingers.

Nicky spins the wheel. "*Adventurous*. Not as adventurous as *you*, but I'll travel anywhere, eat anything. A couple of friends and I are learning Mandarin."

"How's that going?"

"I don't yet know the word for 'really badly.' I also like to box—"

He faces her. "You do?" he says admiringly.

"I mean, against a punching bag. Don't put me in the ring, please."

"A boxer. How unexpected. And your final word?"

She thinks of her friends, her family, her dog; thinks of Friday-afternoon classes and the New England sea in summer; thinks of lasagna, of musicals, of her steamer trunk. "Happy."

A car in her rearview flashes its lights. Sebastian taps his window switch; air musses his hair. "I realize I haven't spoken much about Hope or Cole," he says, and Nicky, in her surprise, eases up on the gas. The driver behind them revs past, screams.

"What did he say?" she asks.

"I would blush to repeat it. Two blocks and we're home."

They roll forth. "Your wife and your son," Nicky prompts her passenger—but he merely gazes out the window.

At last they slow to a crawl, three houses too soon ("This isn't a tour bus, Hunter"), finally stopping at the foot of the drive. Nicky twists the key in the ignition. The Jaguar breathes its last.

"Was that your first driving lesson?"

"Practically."

"You're a natural."

"Am I?" She feels pleased.

"Not really, no. But we survived."

A prick of disappointment. "Thanks for taking me to your club."

"You'd make quite the psychoanalyst. Or at least a priest. There's a whiff of the confessional about you." Sebastian's eyes are narrowed, as though he's trying to locate the exact words. "A man finds himself saying what he hadn't meant to say. That's a gift. And a weapon."

He gazes up the drive. Nicky studies the back of his scalp, silver waves flowing down to the nape of his neck.

"Are you really happy?" he asks.

"I am," she says, sincerely.

In the sudden quiet, she can hear him breathe, deep and even. "I was thinking, as we spoke"—still addressing his house—"that the past is a strange place. My past, anyway. What about yours?"

She glances over his shoulder, toward the marble steps gliding up to the front door, the question-mark knocker coiled like a snake in the sun. "Maybe. Isn't everybody's?"

"As Simon St. John tells us, the past is a poison. Tolerable only in trace amounts."

"I remember. But the past is gone."

"Oh, no." Now he turns to her, and his smile is so sad she could cry. "The past isn't gone. It's just waiting."

14

AFTER SEBASTIAN RETIRES TO HIS BEDROOM, Nicky crosses the foyer, the laptop in her bag knocking against her hip, the phone in her pocket full of his voice. The courtyard will be her studio today.

In the parlor, a woman's body lies curled on the sofa.

Eyes closed, hair roiled across the cushion. Her dress is gray. Her narrow feet are bare. One hand clutches a photo album.

"Oh," says Nicky.

An eyelid flickers. Diana spies her guest, sighs; then her eye springs wide. The album tumbles to the floor as she sits up. "I didn't see you," she says, throaty. "I—of course I didn't see you. Tea?" Two fingers on the pot. "Still warm. No? Just me, then."

Nicky seats herself on the opposite sofa as Diana pours with one hand and smooths her hair with the other. "How did you like the Baron Club?"

"Lots of owls," Nicky replies. "I met Lionel Lightfoot."

Diana pauses. Even her frowns are lovely; she must sulk very prettily.

"Sebastian had left the room," adds Nicky.

Diana sips, swallows. Lifts the photo album to the table. "That's a saga. Lionel's people—well, they're the sort of people you'd refer to as 'people.' Voices full of money. His novels were—oh, high-society melodramas, really. *The Not-So-Great Gatsby,* Sebastian says."

Watson has appeared at Nicky's ankles. "She'd like you to pick her up," Diana translates. Nicky obliges.

"After *Simon Says,* Lionel and his wife—Cassandra, she was called, terrifying woman—you could say they *inducted* Sebastian and Hope. Into San Francisco. Sebastian joined the Baron. Hope joined committees—the library, the rehab center, *real* work, not just save-our-park. And the Lightfeet were made Cole's godparents. But when he left . . ."

Left. As though Cole had excused himself from the dinner table. Nicky strokes the dog's cue-ball skull, the steep peaks of her ears, and waits.

Again Diana sighs. "Lionel wrote that novel. *Had a Wife—*"

"—*and Couldn't Keep Her,*" Nicky murmurs.

"He needed money, I suppose, at last. Or attention." Reaching for the teapot. "This was long before me, of course."

Nicky scrolls through microfiche in her head until she finds a newspaper photo dated January 2, 2000: *Diana Gibson, assistant to the missing woman, leaves the precinct after giving a statement, accompanied by Lionel Lightfoot, family friend.* His mouth at her ear; her eyes on the ground, a curtain of hair drawn over one cheek. They look like unlikely conspirators.

"But you knew Lionel before then, didn't you?"

The dregs of the tea trickle from the spout. Slowly, Diana sets the pot back on the table.

"I suppose so. I mean, yes. I don't really think much about that part of my life." She gestures to Nicky. "Not until recently, anyway."

"Which part?"

"Quite a lot of it, actually." Staring at the cup in her hands. "Quite a lot of my life. And now I can feel it changing again." She knits her fingers. "But where were—oh, Lionel. He wants to make peace, after all these years. His book was cruel, really, though I don't think *him* cruel."

"Well, he *was,*" says Madeleine.

15

SHE HAS LISTENED TO THEM for a couple of minutes now, hovering just outside the parlor door. Then "Lionel wants to make peace," Diana says, and Madeleine nearly sniggers, because Lionel couldn't make a sandwich—and why should she eavesdrop in her own house, anyway?

". . . I don't think *him* cruel."

"Well, he *was*," says Madeleine, stepping into view: barefoot, shoes hooked on two fingers, jacket over one arm. Her stepmother swivels in her seat; Nicky perches on the sofa, lap overflowing with French bulldog.

"Hello there," says Diana. "Have you met Nicky Hunter?"

Madeleine beams. "You're still here."

The homunculus nods.

As Madeleine crosses the room, she catches Diana's perfume, that minor-key chord of flowers and water; she has never asked for its name. She flops on the couch beside Nicky, hikes one heel to the edge of the table. "Oh, my aching limbs."

"Madeleine works at the library," Diana explains.

"I *volunteer*. In the kids' section. My compensation is the magic of a child's smile." Scratching Watson's rump. "Dr. Seuss today."

"How were the children?" asks her stepmother.

"I do not mind them in a room, I do not want one in my womb. I ducked out during fingerpainting."

"You absquatulated," says Nicky.

Madeleine stares at her.

"Sorry," Nicky adds.

Diana stirs her tea. "Nicky met Lionel Lightfoot at the club this morning."

"I love how Dad is just escorting women into the Baron," says Madeleine, whose father has never escorted her into the Baron. "Next time he'll show up with a cheerleading squad."

Nicky giggles, a sweet little chime, very winning; Madeleine chooses to hate it. "He asked about your father's memoirs—"

"Word travels fast. Don't bother with Lionel. Dad took all that personally, you know."

"Probably the only way to take it," suggests Nicky.

"Of course, when *he* lost a wife under what some"—Madeleine raises her hand—"might describe as 'suspicious circumstances,' no one cranked out a novel about *that*. Did you ask him about *that*?"

"Not really my business," murmurs the homunculus.

"Well, none of it is, yet here we are."

"Cassandra fell down the stairs. At their home in Sea Cliff," says Diana, with the gravity of an army officer notifying the next of kin.

"Heart attack at the top, corpse at the bottom. That's the official story." Madeleine waits for Nicky to request the unofficial story. When she doesn't: "Sandy was very elegant. I imagine her cartwheeling down the stairs like a gymnast. In flowing white robes, for some reason. I'm such a drama queen," she mutters, swiping at her eyes, rolling her head back. "*Any*way. Sandy doted on that mother of mine. Everyone liked my mother. *You* liked her."

Diana nods. It isn't a question anyway.

"Even Isaac liked her—remember? And he hated the *world*. He was a grad student," Madeleine informs Nicky, "so fair enough." A cough rumbles in her ashtray lungs.

"Isaac was helping Sebastian with his books at the time I worked for Hope," says Diana. "Library runs. Stone Age Internet research."

"Isaac Murray," drawls Madeleine, as a low heat warms her skin. "I had such a foaming-at-the-mouth crush on him." To Diana: "Didn't you two . . ."

"No."

"My mistake. He was studying philosophy," Madeleine tells Nicky. "Which, to a college sophomore, made him capital-D deep. Perfect stubble, too." Again she looks at Diana. "Didn't you go out with him—"

"On New Year's Eve, yes. That once. I never saw him again. Although I rang him this morning, asked if he might have a moment to speak to Nicky. Your request, yes?" Nicky nods. "He said that he's ghostwriting the memoirs of a young 'influencer' who's dumber than a box of hair—his words—and would welcome the distraction."

A sudden silence, as though the electricity has been cut. Madeleine stares at the veil of light slipping off the bookshelves.

Beside her, Nicky shifts. "I imagine a lot changed after that night," she says quietly. Just making conversation? Or is she poking around?

"People have asked me—" Madeleine begins. "Well, they haven't asked *me*; they've asked each other *about* me—how could I live in the same house as my dad." She looks hard at Nicky, who, after all, is also living in that same house. "The answer is that wherever he is, there's no place safer."

Diana turns to Madeleine. "I wanted to ask whether you'd fancy tennis tomorrow morning. Nicky, you're welcome also. Just beware that Madeleine played at university."

Nicky lifts her brows. "Lucky for me, I'm seeing your cousins at ten o'clock."

"Cousin, singular," says Madeleine. "And thanks, but tomorrow I'm scheduled to be overweight and out of shape all day, so I must decline."

Diana nods at the photo album. "I was just about to show Nicky some family pictures."

Madeleine stares. "Does Dad know?"

"He chose them himself."

It's a chop to her throat. A dagger in her back. When had she last heard her father even speak their names? Acknowledge a birthday, raise a glass to their memory? When did he last glance at the portrait still keeping vigil at the top of the staircase? Yet just one day after this stranger arrives—

"Would you like to join us?" asks Diana.

Madeleine bottles a scream. Instead: "You know, I really ought to smoke." She heaves herself upright, collects her jacket and shoes, and steams from the room, Watson waddling in her wake.

In the foyer, her throat tightens. She's been rude.

She returns to the doorway, vision swimming. "I know Dad wants this," she says to two women she can't see. "I know you're just helping him."

Again she leaves, trips over the goddamn dog. And goes upstairs to Diana's bedroom.

There, she lingers outside the door. The ivory bedclothes, the ivory curtains; the walls painted violet—violet was her mother's color. This was her mother's room.

Her mother's furniture, too: the bed, the pearl-gray secretary with glass cabinets in a hutch rising up the wall. The cabinets used to house framed photographs and chunks of brain coral and a collection of champagne corks; now they're bare. But for the amber pill bottle on the nightstand, there's nothing to suggest the room is in any way tenanted.

Madeleine never ventures within, though here, from the hallway, she can imagine her mother just out of sight. Now she touches the door, gently, and the rest of the room swings into view: The small chest that once contained a trove of vintage board games. The smoked-glass floor vase that used to gush birch branches collected in Dorset. The walk-in wardrobe where twenty years ago Hope hung her shirts and slacks, her dresses and gowns. Madeleine wanted to keep them there when Diana moved in: "You don't mind, do you? There's just no room anywhere else." There was room everywhere else, of course, but that was for her stepmother to point out.

"I don't mind." Diana placed her own clothes in the smaller closet. Eventually, Sebastian ordered Madeleine to clear out the wardrobe— yet years later it's still vacant, not a scarf on a hook, not a pump on the floor.

Otherwise, the room remains inviolate, a museum display. Why had her stepmother indulged her for so long? Or could this be some mind game? Madeleine frowns; she can picture Diana playing cards, or golf, but not mind games.

Down in her suite, back at her desk, she steps into Soho's Bellona Club, where a severed head has surfaced in a toilet cistern.

SIMON ST. JOHN

Satan's lips, what's this? The eyes — the
pupils! Fully dilated. This unfortunate woman
has sprinkled belladonna in her eyes within
the past four hours.

                    INSPECTOR TROTT
Enough to kill her, St. John?

                    SIMON ST. JOHN
No, Inspector. What killed her, I'm afraid, was
being decapitated.

Madeleine stares at the screen.

                    INSPECTOR TROTT
In the book, this scene was much less stupid.

                    SIMON ST. JOHN
It's because Madeleine Trapp couldn't write a
grocery list, let alone a screenplay.

                    INSPECTOR TROTT
Ha, ha! What a tool.

                    SIMON ST. JOHN
She could lose some weight, too.

                    MADELEINE
i hate you both

She yanks her copy of *Simon Says* from the escritoire, studies the
scene her father wrote. He'd made it look so easy.

Madeleine grits her teeth, growls, and swats the book against her
desk so many times that pages break from the spine and whirl to the
floor like leaves.

16

"ACTUAL PHOTOGRAPHS, if you can credit it," says Diana, "on actual paper."

She settles herself beside Nicky and opens the album, laminated leaves squeaking. "Sebastian has curated a little exhibit for you. These look so glossy, don't they?" Marveling at the first page. "Nineteen ninety-five." A timestamp glows in one corner of the picture.

But Nicky's eyes are on the boy.

He stands on some nameless beach, copper sand licked smooth at his feet, surf crawling behind him. He's a small child, T-shirt drooping from his frame as if from a hanger, and rather homely: nose a snub, hair and eyebrows white, eyes unexceptionally blue. Graveyard teeth, gappy and crooked.

"Nine years old here," says Diana. "October baby."

"You remember Cole's birthday."

Diana bites her lip. "I suppose I do. His mother adored him, and I rather adored his mother. Mama, he called her. Look—his origami." She taps the shard of red in Cole's hand: a paper butterfly, wings two inches across, sharp and bright as a kite. "He could do swans or fish, if you asked, but mostly butterflies. Sebastian dabbled in lepidoptery"— Nicky appreciates that Diana doesn't define the word for her—"and boys want to be like their fathers, don't they?"

Nicky studies the butterfly, the wings edged in green, the two tiny spikes crowning its head. Then she turns the page to Mama herself, in living color, broad shoulders, broad grin; beside her Cole grins, too, a little older now, his teeth wrapped in braces. Mother and son are pinching a sheet of construction paper, the words CHERCHEZ LA FEMME Magic Markered across it in godawful cursive.

"That's a detective-fiction term, I believe."

"'Look for the woman,'" Nicky explains to Diana, teacher of the French language.

"Oui."

"Sorry. In any classic mystery, a lady's the cause of all the mayhem."

"Just possibly a man wrote that. I think Cole heard it somewhere—in one of Sebastian's books, perhaps—and took it to mean that when i doubt, he should find a female to help him. His mama, specifically. It was a little joke between them. *Une petite blague.*" Diana smiles at the photo, idly stroking her calf. "He liked French. Or he liked the sound of it. I didn't spend much time with him. I hope I was kind. Watson sheds so much these days." She whisks her hands across her thighs, rises. "Take your time with that. Oh!"

The woman even snaps her fingers perfectly.

"We're hosting midsummer cocktails next Monday," she says. "The night of the summer solstice. Annual tradition. His Highness likes to mingle once a year. I don't suppose you packed a party mask?"

Nicky watches her fit her feet into her shoes. "Mr. Trapp—"

"Sebastian."

"He told me to bring formal attire. Mask included."

"Wear whatever you like. *Comme tu veux.*" Diana glides from the room.

Nicky hears her heels click on the foyer floor, sharp and even, then a quick tap dance. "So sorry," Diana says.

"My bad." Freddy.

A pause.

"Is he . . ."

"He is."

Diana's footsteps fade into the foyer. Freddy's must be soundless. Unless he's lurking.

Nicky pinches the corner of the next page, slowly peels it away. Sebastian as a young man, hunched beneath the yawning hood of a Pontiac Firebird, inspecting its innards. He and Hope, eyes locked over a Scrabble board, smiles quirking their lips, her hand resting on the swell of her belly. A woman in a sundress, bare back and shoulders, either hand in the grip of a small boy. A plump blond girl sitting by a fireplace with a baby cradled in her lap. The baby is very small, the folds of his blue blanket roiling around him like waves; one tiny fist is raised, as though signaling for help. Nicky, who loves babies, feels her heart fill up.

And Madeleine, clasping that hand in hers. She must be five or six here, a whole life ahead of her. Nicky glances at the doorway, in case she reappears, in case Nicky can reassure her.

But Madeleine doesn't, and Nicky can't.

For an hour she tours the Trapps' past, dozens of photographs across dozens of years, watching as acne mottles Madeleine's skin, as Sebastian and Hope wobble atop camels, as Cole and Freddy wash a wild-eyed dog . . .

She wiggles her jaw.

Sebastian won't say much about his wife and son. Madeleine told her as much; *he* told her as much. Yet here in her lap, at his request, Nicky holds a gallery of family portraits arranged by the man himself. *Quite a three-pipe problem,* agrees Sherlock Holmes.

"What, like, bongs?" asks Irwin later on as Nicky shimmies into her pajamas. "Sherlock was into drugs, right?"

"Cocaine. But that's not what I meant. The album: why would somebody who—"

"Killed his family and got away with it then art-direct an album like that? Dunno. Hey, let's ask a real criminologist. C'mere, Potato."

After she says good night and switches off the lamp, Nicky counts six spokes of moonlight slanting through the windows—dim, dimmer, dimmest, down the length of the attic—then studies the galaxy unrolled across the ceiling. C O L E.

Her gaze slides along the C, skates around the black-hole edge of the O, descends the long leg of the L . . .

Rat-tat. Trapp. Keystrokes bump their heads against the floor. She folds one arm across her chest, feels her heart skimming against her ribs.

The fever is upon her.

Do you feel an uncomfortable heat at the pit of your stomach? And a nasty thumping at the top of your head? I call it the detective-fever. It will lay hold of you. Wilkie Collins, *The Moonstone*—the original country-house whodunit. The light show behind her eyes, the riptide in her veins: detective-fever.

Rattarattatrapp-tat-trap.

Maybe she should fold back the blankets, swing her feet to the floor, walk to the door and down two flights and along the corridor and into his study. *You and I might even solve an old mystery or two,* she'd remind him.

And he would smile and say, *Come—come; let's sit by the fire and plot.*

Friday, June 19

17

AGES AGO, A THERAPIST ZEROED IN on Madeleine's Fear of Abandonment—"Possibly because of your mother and brother's disappearance," he suggested. She thanked him for the blinding insight. His next words, however, surprised her: "Which is why you abandon first."

And lo, abandon she had, and abandon she would: law school, her second novel, assorted better-off-without-her boyfriends. But she's never ditched her father.

Madeleine considers this while strapping on today's armor, loose slacks (the more easily she might access bottom shelves without complaint) and a blouse that fit better just a month ago. When Sebastian returned from England, she was waiting for him at home; a few years later, she dropped out of school and claimed the downstairs suite she'd always wanted; and thereafter the two of them made a quiet life for themselves, reading and cooking and every so often venturing beyond the front gate—though neither so far nor for so long that Madeleine thought to remain there, in the wild. She dated a few men, mostly to indulge her matchmaker then-friends; more than anything, she committed herself to the same projects once dear to her mother: an animal shelter, a needle-exchange clinic, an urban farm . . . yet one by one, except for the library (give her time), she's abandoned them. She abandoned her therapist, too.

She never abandoned her father. Now her father is abandoning her.

She grimaces as she buttons her shirt, tells herself to grow up. "He's *dying*," she adds under her breath.

. . . But in the end, isn't it the same? She'll be left alone. What use *is* she, really? *I'm here to take care of you*, she promised her father when she moved in. *I'll fill the void*, she didn't add, has never added, although for nearly twenty years she's tried. But really it's Adelina who cooks and cleans; it's Diana who accompanies him to the yacht club, to the theater, to Scandinavia and the savanna and the world outside this house. And Madeleine? She . . . chats with him, sure, easily and often; sometimes they read the same book or flank-attack a jigsaw puzzle, watch dawn break from their lookout at Lands End—sunrising, he calls it. But she doesn't contribute much to his life except her presence, does she? She's the kid on the team who shows up, observes the game yet rarely plays, and maybe earns a participation trophy at the end of the season. *Congratulations, Madeleine: You were there! You were bodily present!*

What will she do after he's gone?

At the kitchen door, she stops so short that Watson bumps into her ankles. Their guest is lodged in the window seat, in jacket and jeans and earbuds, speaking in a slow, shiny voice to the phone propped in her lap.

"Beautiful girl!" she says. *"You!"* When Watson trots over and squats like a gargoyle beside the window seat, Nicky glances at Madeleine, waves, and tilts the phone to the dog. Madeleine makes out a small, dark child with a bandaged face.

Nicky laughs again, says a happy goodbye. Unplugs her earbuds and unwraps a granola bar. "Hello," she beams, and Madeleine suspects with horror that this is a Morning Person.

"Was that your boyfriend?" she asks, in case Nicky thinks she was peeking.

"That was a fourteen-month-old girl in Boston who just had a small surgery for her cleft palate." Nicky giggles—the woman is a laugh track today; Madeleine wishes she found it more annoying—then, with relief: "My goddaughter. I'm a little . . . giddy. Her parents have been anxious about . . ." Nicky pauses to clear her throat, and *oh Christ no is she tearing up?* "It's their child's face, after all. But she was a perfect patient." She nods, eyes bright, cheeks dry.

"Well." Madeleine turns and pours coffee, leans against the island. Pauses. "Did you make this?"

"Poorly, I suspect. I don't drink it."

"You made it for everyone else? Are you a good person or something?"

Nicky bites into her granola bar. "Or something, probably."

"Ooh—the coffee's really bad."

Nicky chews, shrugs.

Madeleine spots the book in her lap. "That one of my dad's?"

"Mm. *The Crooked Man.* I've read it six thousand times."

"Only six thousand?"

"It's dedicated to you."

"He dedicated four to me. Five to my mother, but she had to put up with him longer than I did. At the time."

The homunculus nods. "What about your brother?"

"That's private."

Nicky's eyes widen. At her feet, the dog grunts as if to console.

But how is that private? Madeleine asks herself. Eighty million copies sold is eighty million dedications printed. "Three, I think?" she says. "Or—maybe two. Definitely one. *Little Boy Blue.* That's the book Dad wrote after Cole was born."

Four to one. She's surprised to find that she's never kept score.

"Readers were angry about *Crooked Man,*" she says instead. "They went in assuming that after a decade Dad would *finally* reveal Jack's identity. And now"—sigh—"we'll never know. Even I don't know who he is," she adds, before Nicky can inquire. "And I've asked. Many times."

"I would've guessed Simon's sister. Until Jack murdered her."

"That did seem to rule her out. My money's on the pharmacist. Mr. Myers. Nobody's that perfect." Madeleine sips the coffee again, swallows with difficulty.

"I read somewhere that he—your father—always works out the end of a story in advance," Nicky is saying. "Do you—"

The kitchen door swings open and Diana enters wearing shocking-white tennis clothes. Instantly Madeleine feels like the Hulk in office casual. "Is that coffee?"

"I can't tell."

Diana waves it away. "No, no time. Nicky and I—good morning there—we're off to see your aunt and cousin. Simone has got lots to say about Sebastian, apparently."

"There is literally no subject about which Simone hasn't got lots to say."

"I thought they ought to meet before cocktails on Monday. Nicky will be attending."

Of course she will. "My parents threw this party every year," Madeleine explains as Nicky rises from the window seat. "I always dreaded it. Still do. 'Midsummer's Eve'—pretentious, don't you think? You don't have to answer. But it is." Nobody protests. "After Dad remarried, he decided it'd be a good way to introduce everyone to Diana. To you. Only he outsourced all the invitations to Simone. Who said, 'Hey, you know a good way to introduce people? Have 'em wear masks.' And it continues thus," she concludes gravely.

"It continues thus," agrees Diana.

After she and Nicky have left the kitchen, Madeleine eyes Watson by the window seat, gazing forlornly at the door the homunculus just stepped through. "Remember you're on my side, lady," Madeleine reminds her. The dog pretends not to hear.

18.

THEY CRUISE SLOWLY OUT OF PACIFIC HEIGHTS in Diana's bulky Volvo. "I wanted a tank," she explains. "Still not entirely comfortable driving on the right."

"I'm not comfortable driving at all," replies Nicky.

"This one shuts off automatically when I'm stopped. Just sudden quiet. Like sleep apnea. I always worry it won't restart."

Nicky would like to ask Diana about her husband—how he proposed, married-life stories, places they've visited—but her chauffeur seems content to sing along with this morning's soundtrack. "'*Girls who want boys who like boys to be girls . . .*'" she warbles; her alto is tuneless and charming. "Like time-traveling back to my teens. Sorry—I can't sing."

"I walk into a karaoke bar and they summon the police," says Nicky. "Do you get back to England much?" Hope was English, too. Sebastian Trapp has a type.

Diana shakes her head. "Sebastian has a home in Dorset—the family spent summers there once upon a time—but I've never been. '*Let's all meet up in the year 2000 . . .*'"

Nicky gazes out the windshield at the low row of storefronts, a sprawl of park. The sky is thinking about rain, but still half a dozen young people lounge on the grass, smoking joints, picket signs leaning listlessly against their shoulders: CAN'T WE ALL JUST GET A BONG? "I'm not sure how much to ask Sebastian about his wife and son."

Even Diana's squint is lovely, she observes—the finest craquelure at the corner of her eye. "This was his idea," she says at last. "This memory book. So ask him anything you'd like to know. He might need a push, might *want* a push. If he shuts up, then you just wait it out. He's bad with silences."

There's a good deal Nicky would like to know. "So these Trapps I'm seeing today . . ."

"Freddy and his mother. Dominic I met only a few times. He was opening a new restaurant that autumn I worked for Hope. And by the time I"—Diana steers into a side street—"found myself back here, he had died. Years earlier."

"Right after *The Crooked Man* was released."

Diana nods. "His car broke down on the Pacific Coast Highway. Then—hit-and-run. That's all we'll ever know. Somebody hit, somebody ran, somebody died." She sighs. "There's a silly notion that Sebastian killed his brother, or had him killed."

A pet Trapper Keeper theory: Dominic had in fact authored the Simon St. John novels, yet ceded credit to his brother . . . until the momentous publication of *The Crooked Man*, when he threatened to reveal the scheme, prompting Sebastian to mow down the disgruntled ghostwriter roadside.

"Simone, his wife—widow—is a force of nature." Diana glances at Nicky. "I'm sure you'll like her," she adds, in the tone of one sure of no such thing.

They roll into the broad driveway of a shy Spanish colonial, stucco walls and a roof of curved tiles. Nicky casts a glance at the sky overhead—brushed metal, flat and glinting—and lifts her bag from the floor. Together they exit the car; together they walk to the whitewashed front door. "You've got Baker Beach there," Diana explains. "And see those trees—that's the Presidio. It used to be a military base, and now it's this rather marvelous wilderness—"

Together they freeze when they hear the shot.

Nicky moves first, flinging wide the door and bursting into a worn living room tinted gray beneath two skylights. "Wait—" Diana calls behind her, but through a far doorway Nicky glimpses motion in a backyard, a cluster of figures, a woman screaming—

"This patio is *brand-new*, Frederick."

Nicky slaps a hand against the wall, checks herself at the door.

"Just *look*." The woman points one plump toe at a scorched flagstone, a six-inch blast radius, gritty with black powder, and twists her head away as though the sight is too much to bear.

"Here we go," says Diana.

Nicky follows her into the backyard. Weeds riot in the grass, stray twigs flail from the hedges, ivy strangles a laurel tree. Across the patio stands Freddy, biting a knuckle, shoulders hopping as he giggles.

Boldface letters across his T-shirt: SURELY NOT EVERYBODY WAS KUNG FU FIGHTING.

Beside him, a shorter man stares contritely at the burn mark.

"I'm sorry. I'm sorry." Freddy scrubs his eyes with his fists. "Can I—rinse it off?"

"No, you cannot rinse it off, Frederick."

She's a stout woman, on the downward slope of her sixties, wearing a ruby-red top, billowy yellow slacks, green sandals. She looks, Nicky thinks, like a traffic light.

"Oh," she says, turning. "You're here. I apologize for my idiot son and his idiot friend."

"Jonathan's not an idiot," Freddy protests. "Not always." He throws one arm around the part-time idiot, whose head tops out at Freddy's shoulder and who has thrust his hands deep in his shorts pockets. He shifts his weight to his heels and knits two streaky brows, eyes wide and guilty and blue. His nose is narrow at the tip but flattened at the bridge. See-through skin and a crown of tousled sandy-blond hair. Nicky would bet anything he's British.

"Most of the time, though," he mutters, and she wins her wager.

Now Freddy rests his hands on his mother's shoulders. "We dug up an old bottle rocket in the attic. Jonathan had never seen one before."

Simone's eyes narrow. "Jonathan had never seen a firework before?"

"Not *this* one."

"And which one was this?"

"They call it the Neighbor Hater," says Freddy with reverence.

"It hates too hastily," Jonathan adds.

The five of them stand in a circle around the blackened stone, as though gathering for a séance. Then Simone sighs, thaws, pats her son's fingers. "What were you doing in the attic, anyway?"

Jonathan raises his hand. "That was my fault. Fred ducked up for—your uncle's old photos, was it? Letters? And he invited me along to see some film props."

"Pretty sweet stuff. Simon's snuffbox, his monocle, a severed finger. Then we noticed the Neighbor Hater. We're sorry, Simone."

She faces Nicky. "My son calls me by my name. And he hates the neighbors. I don't know where I went wrong."

Diana clears her throat. "This is Nicky Hunter."

Introductions, five arms jousting. Freddy lifts Diana's hand to his lips before Jonathan grasps it. "Diana Trapp," Simone informs him. "Sebastian's second wife."

"Whereabouts are you from?" he asks.

"Wiltshire. Originally. Then London."

"Lyme Regis. But I lived in Shoreditch for a while before moving to San Fran."

"No one calls it that," say mother and son in unison. "S'okay, buddy," adds Freddy. "You're still new in town."

Nicky watches Jonathan, his lean body, his busted nose. She likes imperfections; she's drawn to what's broken.

Then, for an instant, he looks at her—and winks, a quick camera-shutter of his left eye.

Automatically, Nicky winks back.

The plot thickens.

"What brought you to San Francisco?" asks Diana. "Work?"

"Oh, the opposite. I came here to be happily unemployed."

Freddy claps a hand on his friend's back. "Jonno joined my soccer league last month."

"Actually, I joined your football league."

"And he kicks ass. And balls. Soccer balls. Human ass."

"We're not here to talk about Jonathan," Simone reminds them. "Or my son, for that matter. Diana, you aren't staying, are you?"

"Errands, I'm afraid." Diana retreats to the patio door. "Jonathan, I hope you enjoy your footie. Go easy on the Americans."

"I'm not quite World Cup material."

"Bullshit," says Freddy. "Sorry, Simone. But I bet he's really ex–Premier League. Maybe he's playing the long con!"

"I could be anyone," agrees Jonathan.

19

WHY DID SHE WINK? Nicky feels as though she scanned a checkout item without wanting to. Or without meaning to, anyway.

And why has Jonathan joined them in the living room? It's not as though his hosts are too polite to boot him out. ("Jonathan, dear, are you a caveman?" calls Simone. "Use a napkin.") Yet here he is, draped along a rocking chair by the fireplace, looking very much at home. Maybe Freddy wants an ally.

Or perhaps he's a fan. "Do you read the St. John books?" asks Nicky when Simone bustles into the kitchen.

"I don't, I'm afraid. I mainly read books on finance. Also self-improvement, self-help."

"Better read some more," says Freddy.

Again Nicky surveys the room: bohemian shabby, worn upholstery, shag rug cloudy with wine stains, coffee rings scarring the table. Vases flank both sofas, spouting fountains of peacock plumes. A pile of cats stirs upon the cold hearth, tails wrapped like twine around themselves. Overhead, between the skylights, a sulky fan circles, pushing the air but not happy about it.

She feels Jonathan's eyes on her like weights. Feels a blush stalk the length of her neck. Feels her phone buzz in her pocket. Checks the screen. She'll call Irwin back later.

The far wall is paneled with photographs, rich black-and-white beneath gleaming glass. Sebastian appears in many, even most, alongside a man like his distant echo. Arms slung around shoulders, grins toothy and wide, the odd headlock. Dominic's head.

"Oh, there's my husband!" exclaims Simone, lemonade jug in hand. "He's the one getting beaten up. He died in a highway hit-and-run, you know." Nicky nods in consolation.

Simone gazes at the photo. "Wouldn't it haunt you?" she asks darkly. "Taking a life. *Blowing* past the—like he was a bump in the road. Never coming clean. Who could do it?"

"*Cui bono,*" murmurs Nicky.

"I don't speak Spanish, dear."

"It's—Latin. I'm sorry." She *is* sorry. The woman is mourning her husband and here's Nicky offering a lecture. She should shut up—but they're all looking at her, and hey-ho, she's talking again: "It's sort of a crime-fiction precept. 'Who benefits.' When investigating a crime, pay attention to . . . well, the beneficiaries." *Touching apology, Nicky!*

"Cicero said it," says Jonathan. "I read classics at university," he adds.

Simone pours herself a glass of lemonade, pulp like flotsam on the surface. "What an education I'm getting today. And who benefited from my husband's death?"

"Nobody," Nicky assures her. "Of course. I'm so—I was showing off. I—"

"Don't be sensitive, you." Freddy reaches from the sofa, kneads his mother's hand. "We're not here for Dominic. It's Sebastian Day. My dad was a good brother, though," he assures Nicky as Simone tops him up. "When Cole and Hope disappeared, he was first responder."

Finally—those words in that order: *when Cole and Hope disappeared.* Nicky taps her phone, readies her notepad, and, having already offended, doubles down. "What was that *like* for you?" she asks. Very forward, but she's very curious.

Freddy shrugs. "At first I hoped he might've run away. Who could blame him? But—"

"How do you mean?" When Jonathan furrows his forehead, his eyes narrow, his brows slant; he looks both confused and concerned. It's cute, thinks Nicky. It's distracting.

"I mean—I've worked in schools for thirteen years now, and I've still never . . . just, the *bullying.*" Freddy pushes one hand through his hair; Nicky hears the crackle of dried pomade. "The name-calling. The pranks—the 'pranks.' The regular kickings of his pale ass: hitting, spitting, the kid who *bit*—"

"I'd forgotten about the biter," murmurs his mother. "Primitive little bitch."

"And Cole couldn't defend himself. Too sweet. Too small."

"Which we could never understand," Simone says. "His father is six-five. My husband was a bit shorter than that. And Frederick is a bit shorter than that. But Cole would've been *much* shorter than that."

"Maybe he is," suggests Jonathan, as a cat scales his shin.

They all stare.

"I mean—oi, mind the claws—he might be out there, no? Both of them, even."

Nicky looks at her hosts.

"Jonathan, should *you* be *here*?" asks Simone.

"It's fine," her son tells her. "He's interested."

"Well, no—I mean, I'm not interested in the *books*. But it's an interesting story, is all. Happy to leave, if you like? Might take this little guy with me."

"You're fine, dude. What were we saying?"

"Cole," Simone says. "Getting gnawed on. It so upset Hope. She was *very* devoted to her boy. Moved him from one school to another, didn't she, Frederick?"

"Like he was a chess piece. Private school, Catholic school, that all-boys academy . . ."

Jonathan frowns. "Did anyone consider public school?"

"They were trying to *keep* him from getting murdered," explains Simone.

"What about Sebastian?" The other three swivel toward Nicky as if surprised to find her still present. She leans forward, fingers knotted beneath her chin. "He hasn't said much to me about Cole."

Simone stands, hand on Freddy's head, and crosses to the kitchen door. "Cole *puzzled* his father," she calls. "He didn't like sports. He didn't like video games, or—what else do teenage boys like?"

"Mostly video games," says Jonathan.

"Cole liked *real* games. Board games. Hide-and-seek. Liked drawing, too." She returns, bearing hummus and celery. "And—I can never pronounce it: oregano?"

"Origami," Freddy says.

"Chinese paper-folding. Not a good reader, though. Dyslexia, or such." She has dropped her voice, as though discussing a grim prognosis. "Which did not please Sebastian."

Hardly his fault, thinks Nicky. "Hardly his fault," mutters Jonathan.

"I wouldn't say he *disliked* Cole." Simone settles beside her son. "It was more—oh, how would you put it, Frederick?"

"I'd put it as he disliked Cole."

"No, no . . ." Simone flutters one hand. "He *tried*. He took you boys to soccer every Saturday, remember?"

"Cole hated soccer."

"And Scouts! Your fathers signed you boys up for Scouts. You were rugged outdoorsmen!"

"Most nights Cole would wake up to someone pissing against his tent. But his dad refused to bail him out."

"You were there for him, anyway. You were a good friend."

The moment squeezes past slowly, like a lump in the throat, until a raindrop pops on the skylight. Simone leans toward the table, strikes a long match, lights two pillar candles. When Freddy speaks, it's as though they've huddled around a campfire.

"We went to a spin-the-bottle party once," says Freddy. "Bunch of us in the basement, Mario Karting, guzzling Coke, playing with this slobbery French bulldog—that's why Cole tagged along; some Watson or other had just croaked—and amping ourselves up for the main event. But the dog ignored Cole, and everybody else did, too. So he camped out in the bathroom.

"You know the drill. The blindfold, the bottle, oohs and aahs, then the kiss. I was desperate to kiss Alice Poor."

"She grew up to be quite the slut," recalls Simone.

"A couple kids dragged Cole over." Eyes searching, back in the basement. "He was shaking so much that soda slopped onto his shirt. They blindfolded him, he spun the bottle, and . . . Alice Poor. I couldn't watch." Freddy's jaw tightens. "When I peeked, Cole was leaning into the middle of the circle, handkerchief over his eyes, everybody staring. Because—" His nostrils flare. "Alice had scooped up the French bulldog, hind legs dangling, and she was pushing it toward him.

"Before I could say a word, Cole had kissed the dog. And there was silence." Rain drums overhead. "Then the dog licked him."

The flame wiggles, embarrassed. Nicky winces.

Freddy rubs his neck. "Mayhem. Screams, shrieks. Cole pulls off the blindfold, sees this Frenchie drooling at him."

Nicky bows her head gently, as if urging him on. "What did he do?"

"He smiled and said, 'I guess that was a French kiss.' Nobody noticed. 'Dog-fag, dog-fag,' they're chanting, because the dog was a boy, a male. And Cole just sat there, looking confused and stroking the Frenchie's head. So I marched him upstairs and brought him home. And that was Cole's first kiss."

A silence. "Frenchies are such ugly dogs, too," observes Simone.

Freddy eyes her. "The breed doesn't really matter."

"I suppose not."

"I top-bunked whenever Cole slept over; he was scared he'd roll out of bed. And most nights he would force himself to read twenty pages before lights-out—he was working his way through the collected works of Sebastian Trapp, even though they were difficult for him."

"Dyslexia," Simone reminds them. "Or such."

"But that night he just switched off the lamp. And then I heard him start to cry." Freddy nods. "For an hour he just . . . wept."

Nicky imagines the little body crumpled beneath the blankets, imagines Cole pulling the sheets taut over his face; imagines Freddy overhead, listening.

"He sounds like a lonely little boy." Jonathan's voice is heavy.

Simone squeezes her son's fingers. "But you *did* take good care of him."

The skylights shudder, rippling with water. As Nicky looks up, Simone adds, "This will blow over in three to five minutes."

"Looks biblical," says Jonathan doubtfully.

"I've had a lifetime of Bay Area weather, young man. Three to five minutes."

"Nicky," says Freddy, face lit above a bashful smile, "I'm an ass."

"First step's admitting it, mate."

"Shut up, Jonno. We've just spent half an hour talking about Cole, and Nicky's here to talk about Sebastian."

"I'm in no rush," she says.

"Oh, goodness." Again Simone struggles to her feet. "The photos! I made a list—where was . . ." She exits, pursued by a cat.

"I'm going to scarper," announces Jonathan, rising. "Leave you to your business."

"Dude." Freddy points to the rattling glass, but Jonathan waves him away. "Beach day for me," he says. "Besides, your mum predicts—"

And even as he speaks, the downpour dies, as though a spigot has been clamped shut. All three of them look up at the skylight. "Is she a witch?" whispers Jonathan.

"Sometimes I wonder." They bro-hug, one arm apiece, each slapping the other man's back as if to dislodge an obstruction in his throat.

"Sorry to dash. I meant to take off earlier"—Jonathan looks at Nicky—"but it was all so unexpectedly interesting." As he crosses to her, she stands. "May I give you my number? Neither one of us belongs in San Francisco just yet. Perhaps we might compare notes."

"Or you could go for someone less handsome," suggests Freddy, hoisting a one-eyed tabby. "Comes with cat."

Nicky looks at Jonathan, at his blunt stubble and his shaggy brows, and assesses him as she would a novel: does the tale of the mysterious expat intrigue her? She feels a faint heat radiating from his skin.

She offers her phone. "Ring me," he says, tapping in his number. "Or call me, if you like."

"Leave this house," shouts Freddy.

They walk out. Nicky steps to the gallery on the far wall: Dominic and Sebastian, and Simone, and the children aplenty, all of them various ages, dressed in the fashions of various decades.

Hope is missing. Art imitating life.

Phone call Nicky dial phone

She sighs at her screen, smiles, dials her aunt. "Can't talk right now, Aunt J—"

"Plainly you can."

"—but today's word was *sanguine*. As in 'optimistic or positive.' I am feeling sanguine about my interesting errand here. I hope you are, too."

"The root word for *sanguine* in Latin means 'blood.' Take it from a teacher. So no, I don't feel particularly positive. Where are you?"

"I'm at—" A shimmer in the glass of the picture frames: Nicky watches Freddy return behind her, cat cradled in his arms. He pauses in the doorway, silent and still.

"You're at . . . ?"

She doesn't want to answer her aunt—it feels rude, somehow, in front of Freddy. "I'll call you later."

Slowly he approaches her. Sebastian has mentioned Freddy a few times over the years, not without asperity (**His is an intellect rivaled only by bait**), but she likes him. Goofy, and he tries far too hard—but Nicky can be goofy. Nicky has tried far too hard.

Before she can turn, he's spoken: "Thinking deep thoughts?" His voice closer than she expected.

The blood is fizzing in her veins; questions clamor in her brain. *Do you feel an uncomfortable heat at the pit of your stomach?* She does. The first symptom of *that irresistible malady*: detective-fever.

She faces him. "You want some of this action?" he asks, stroking the cat, and Nicky, not one to resist an animal, particularly of the monocular variety, rubs the downy tummy until the cat is writhing.

"You've done this before," says Freddy, and she laughs.

Then she says, "About Cole and Hope—"

"Enough about Cole. And Hope." Simone has blown back into the room, a thick wedge of photographs in either hand, papers pinned beneath one arm. She shoos Nicky and Freddy back to the sofas—"Tsst, tsst"—and, seating herself beside her guest, promises, "I've got so many stories to tell," with an intensity that the audience finds almost unnerving. "All these memories! Where to begin?"

"Why don't we just let her take a look, Simone." Freddy reaches for the lemonade.

"Yes, yes," replies his mother. "Of course. We have no secrets in this family."

20.

TODAY MADELEINE LEADS STORY TIME at the library, feeding *Green Eggs and Ham* to a gaggle of toddlers, most of them calm and quiet, a few who wouldn't fare well at a custody hearing. At lunchtime, she slumps on the floor in the plant-sciences section, where no one will discover her, possibly for years.

With every spoonful of yogurt, she thinks of that stranger in the attic, this woman making an unwelcome cameo in the final act of her father's life.

In the early afternoon she shelves, squatting and stretching, slow-motion aerobics; and now, crouched barefoot in the picture-book aisle, she hears her name, dipped in honey and light.

"Maddy Trapp! Get up—get up and let me hug you!"

"Bissie," beams Madeleine, wanting one of them to vanish.

Bissie Bentley is vacuum-sealed in what people Madeleine hates call "athleisure." Face gently rouged—of course Bissie makes herself up for the gym. Madeleine knows she's being unfair; Bissie means well, has always meant well, ever since high school, where she was voted Most Nice ("Who the hell is teaching you kids English?" Hope wondered). Sometimes, in a light breeze, you can detect the faintest hint of a personality.

"Look at you, dusting down there like Cinderella!"

Madeleine glances at her flushed feet. "Well, shelving. Working," she adds, with dignity.

"It's so funny," says Bissie, and Madeleine knows that whatever it is, it definitely isn't funny, "Ben and I were just talking about you. And the party. And your dad. How is he?"

"Oh, he's a goner."

Bissie blinks. "We're so sorry."

"I'm afraid that won't help."

"You know, I haven't forgotten about our hug!"

Madeleine rises, book in hand (*Everyone Poops,* naturally), steps into Bissie's arms. She smells of rainbows. "And what about that Frenchman of yours?" Bissie asks. "Jean-Luc, is that right? Will we finally get to meet him?"

Jean-Luc is Madeleine's off-again-on-again boyfriend of three years, a Parisian she met at a dinner party in Marin County. Jean-Luc is handsome. Jean-Luc is an architect. Jean-Luc is imaginary.

"That's over," says Madeleine, surprising herself; she hadn't meant to end the relationship today. Maybe ever. "I broke up with him," she adds. *Nice, Madeleine.*

"Oh! Well, you know who you ought to meet?" *Whom,* Madeleine thinks. But also: who? She feels genuinely curious.

Bissie's expression stalls, her smile on autopilot, and Madeleine realizes that the poor woman has spoken as a reflex, can't actually come up with any contenders. "I'll think of someone!" Bissie assures her at last. "Must run. Just signing Benji up for story time. He'll be five in August, if you can believe it." Madeleine can and does believe it. Benji is Benjamin Bentley the Third, son of Benjamin Bentley the Second, former boyfriend of Madeleine Trapp the First. Five years ago she walked home from the baby shower in the summer rain, a pastel-blue cupcake melting in one hand, wondering whether she and Ben should have married, if only . . . well. Probably not, because Ben was a whopping ass. Good cupcake, though.

Madeleine watches Bissie disappear in a cloud of pixie dust, feels her heartbeat slow.

At three, she punches out, escorting a homeless gentleman from the building—one of the regulars, a late-in-life Vietnam vet who camps out most days in a remote corner of the library—and drives him to the shelter four blocks away, her seat belt drawn tight across her chest.

She's in the dining room, chewing on a sandwich and staring at her laptop, Simon St. John explaining to Inspector Trott the whereabouts of a murder weapon ("It is not *missing* but *melted:* our friend the albino was stabbed with an *icicle!*"), when—

"I've got *so* many stories to tell!"

Madeleine nearly chokes.

He's speaking in his whitewater voice, that full-boil roar that rushes around corners and bursts through walls. He could be anywhere in the house; when Nicky replies, she sounds far distant.

Now Madeleine hears their footsteps in the foyer; now she glimpses him as he strides past the doorway, Nicky in tow. And after her, at a silent trot, Watson, who halts, looks inquiringly at her mistress.

Madeleine stays still. The traitorous dog moves along.

Through the window, through the leaves of an unruly dwarf willow, Madeleine sees the party enter the courtyard maze, sees her father screw his eyes shut for his guest's amusement before he guides her through the lanes. Back when the yard was wild lawn, Madeleine and her brother would run toward each other with croquet mallets aimed like lances; the maze they liked even better: she would blindfold Cole, or Cole would blindfold her, or their father would blindfold both of them, and half an hour they would spend lumbering between the hedges. Sometimes through the hedges.

Sebastian and Nicky arrive at the sundial on its stone pillar, the blade of metal jutting from its face like a shark's fin, and he gestures to the small iron table beside it.

In another maze, the pillar would sprout from the center. But there's no center here, just a tangle of alleys. Why had he plotted the hedges like this? Madeleine once asked. "What we all dread most is a maze with no center," her father had replied.

So why situate within his walls what he dreaded most? To water and prune it, tend and protect it?

He had cast his eyes down at his desk, and for a moment simply studied the ranks of butterflies beneath the glass. "I think it's good to learn to live with fear," he said. "Fear and failure. And the unknown."

That was a quarter century ago. She wonders what he fears now, now that the worst has already happened.

Quietly Madeleine stands. In the parlor, she crosses to a narrow bookcase and touches a finger to a spine. Then she tilts the book forty-five degrees from the shelf.

Soundlessly, the wall swings toward her, and Madeleine steps into the room concealed behind it.

21

FOUR YEARS AGO, a disused alcove, eight by twelve feet, had been un-covered behind a parlor wall during an earthquake-resistance survey. No windows, no apparent purpose; a vault (suggested Diana), or a priest hole (insisted Simone), or a sex dungeon (this was Freddy).

"And soon it'll be Mrs. Trapp's sketching studio," announced Sebas-tian, who had greeted the discovery like an archaeologist stumbling upon a hidden temple.

"It'll be a hangover room," replied Mrs. Trapp, "for anyone who needs a quiet morning after." This has been its primary function, and Madeleine its primary tenant, ever since, although Diana did get to select the open-sesame book on the shelf. *Rebecca*.

Two lamps blush with shy light as Madeleine enters. Botanical prints on the walls; vintage maps, too, exotic cities of Eastern Europe; and a half dozen charcoal drawings on rough paper—Diana's still-life sketches. The scallop shell is good, Madeleine concedes. The tulip is better. What can't her stepmother do?

She sinks onto a bottle-green chaise longue, the only furniture in the room. Folds her legs, leans forward, velvet fizzing beneath her, her hair slipping over her shoulders.

Fitted into the baseboard by her foot is an old ventilation grate, slot-ted bronze. The gaps in the grate, as Madeleine discovered one day while chasing the dog, admit not only air but sound—sound from the courtyard.

Now the burble of pondwater washes in, and so does his voice, far-away but clear: "Let's keep it jolly this time, shall we?"

Madeleine listens.

He relays some amusing stories, most familiar to her, of his various international tours: the morning at the Sydney zoo when a pugnacious mother wallaby dislodged his molar with one vicious kick; the night a nonagenarian barman in Rio de Janeiro taught him the secret of the perfect caipirinha (a secret Sebastian refuses to reveal to Nicky: "I gave that man my word," he explains solemnly); that New Year's Eve when the last ferry from Tallinn to Helsinki stalled in the Baltic, and her passengers—most of them Finns importing inexpensive liquor—

unzipped their clanking duffel bags, opened their clinking backpacks, emptied their bulging pockets, and toasted the year to come.

"Probably the most unexpected New Year's Eve of my life," says Sebastian. And then: "Well, second-most unexpected."

Madeleine feels her eyes go wide. He moves on briskly to a bullfight in Argentina; she slides to the floor, sits beside the grate, back to the wall.

He names his hobbies: swimming and sailing and playing of squash—pre-dialysis, anyway. He describes his butterfly specimens and how each came to be pinned to the spreading board in the library. He has collected all manner of curiosities—many on display in the attic, he notes, with still more crowding the guest bedrooms: centuries-old keys, Victorian silhouette portraits, an orchestra of exotic musical instruments ("My wife's one rule was 'No bagpipes'").

Above all, however, he loves to read. "Most of my favorite authors are dead. I know too many of the ones still alive." Women, he adds, make better crime writers than men; "I think it's because every day they must contend with sinister forces." Nicky answers unintelligibly. Sebastian speaks again: "Men."

Blackout. Madeleine doesn't flinch. A wave of her hand will light the lamps again, but for now she keeps still in the dark—deep-sea dark, her ears brimming with the sound of water—and listens to her father.

He has amassed thousands upon thousands of crime novels, some bought at shocking expense from rare-book dealers, others picked up for pennies at used bookstores. Also in his possession: certain personal effects of their authors—Ngaio Marsh's opera glasses; Georges Simenon's cufflinks; a tumbler from which Anthony Horowitz once tippled whiskey; a fountain pen stolen from Louise Penny; David Handler's umbrella. As he catalogs his treasures, his voice brightens; Madeleine thinks of show-and-tell hour at the library.

"Frantic for a dog growing up. We planned to name him Watson— our sidekick. No dogs were allowed on the base, alas. *Keine Hunde.*"

Madeleine can practically recite the monologue that follows. It's a tale he used to tell in interviews and on television: how he and Hope returned from their Mexican honeymoon one wet spring evening to find their asbestos-trap bungalow in Twin Peaks thoroughly burgled. After Sebastian dialed the cops from a corner pay phone, he and Hope sank to the sidewalk, in the drizzle, his head flopped upon her shoulder, her cheek pressed to his hair.

Then a breakably small chirp sounded nearby. They looked: Off the curb, in the street, a tiny creature—the size of a small potato, speckled pelt fine and slick—staggered against a current of rainwater pushing it toward the storm drain. Its face was crumpled, its body quaked. One ear erect, the other drooping; one eye wide, the other just a puckered socket.

They never did learn how she lost an eye, nor who abandoned her. But before the cops arrived, they'd christened her Watson.

His stories burst like fireworks, one after another; they pop and dazzle. As he tours his past, resurrecting the dead, Madeleine nods; then she grins; at one point she laughs so hard, eyes screwed shut and shoulders quaking, that the lamps burst into light again. And now, for the first time, she understands why her father has recruited a biographer: He wants a new audience. In print, yes, but in performance as well. For Sebastian Trapp, the joy is in the telling.

The first Jaguar he ever repaired. Strangest fan letter. His second honeymoon. Murder.

Madeleine sits up.

"People think I got away with murder," he'd said, easily.

She presses her palms to the floor, puts her ear to the grate.

"Who can blame them? I suppose I . . ."

Cool air haunts her face.

"Sometimes I wonder if Diana ever asks herself . . ." His voice crumbles away.

Madeleine holds her breath.

Pondwater.

He shouldn't be going here—it'll upset him. Abruptly she stands, pushes her hair back; she walks to the wall of maps and presses a lever fixed just below 1906 San Francisco. The door sweeps open and she steps into the parlor.

"I've got a surprise for you," says Freddy.

Madeleine nearly screams. "Christ, Fred. Were you just *lurking*?" The door swings shut behind her.

"I was heading outside—" Jerking his head at the wide-open French windows. Madeleine glances at the courtyard, at her father's back, silver hair brushing his collar; opposite him sits Nicky, eyes bright, listening.

"Methods of murder!" Sebastian booms. "*Here* are a few that Simon's never seen—"

"Special delivery." Freddy again. "Found it at the front door."

He holds a box: a small cube, wrapped in pink paper and a baby-blue ribbon. Madeleine takes it; nearly weightless. No note, no postage. In one corner, neatly printed, the letters ST.

She frowns. Fans used to tape letters to the postbox at the bottom of the driveway, or leave packages on the steps—manuscripts of their own, oftentimes, but also . . . oh, a dog collar for some Watson or other, or a vintage poison bottle (poison not included). And later, of course, concerned citizens littered the sidewalk with death threats and vandalized copies of Simon St. John novels and, in one instance, a plastic bag of feces, although eventually they ran low on ire, and perhaps on feces.

"Madeleine?"

"I'll give it to him." She holds the box to her chest. "Did you see Adelina?" A clattering of cookware from the kitchen, right on cue, and an Italian oath.

Freddy loves their housekeeper, whom Simone appointed more than a decade ago, nudging Madeleine that much closer to redundancy. Not that she'd cooked especially well for her father—more often than not, he insisted on cooking for her, possibly as a preemptive strike—and not that she cleaned very thoroughly, either, so she hadn't really been much use to Sebastian anyway. Adelina seems slightly afraid of him, but she dotes on Freddy, who sings as he hurries away. "Gonna get me *(sì!)* some arancini *(tutto bene!)* . . ."

Madeleine turns to the courtyard. Nicky's lips are closed. So many people listen with mouths ajar, eager to seize their chance to speak. This woman seems content to wait. It's an appealing quality, allows Madeleine, who could stand to shut up more often.

"Now," her father says, "an electric eel's voltage isn't sufficient to kill a human. But it hurts like hell, as I learned in Trinidad . . ."

In the kitchen, Adelina swears again, lustily, as water smacks the floor. Madeleine grips the box and leaves the parlor, her fingers worrying at the ribbon.

22

"DO YOU BELIEVE HE KILLED THEM?"

Madeleine watches Nicky across the dining table, where glades of candles sprout and the platters steam. Adelina has prepared a Sicilian feast in honor of their guest: pasta 'ncasciata, sheep's-milk cannoli— "*Bellissima*," her father cooed—and Sebastian has just proposed a round of tabletop bocce ("Let's play with our food") when Madeleine feels her lips shaping the words.

She doesn't breathe them to life, though. Not here.

"Tell us about yourself," says Sebastian, rolling a rice ball down the table. "Your parents died, yes? Orphan child?"

"She's too old to be an orphan, Dad," Madeleine sighs.

"One can be an orphan at any age, I'd have thought," says Diana, who is herself without parents, Madeleine recalls. An orphan, if you will.

"I *feel* too old to be an orphan." Nicky whisks her arancini toward Sebastian; it skids off the table and Watson pounces.

Diana eases wine into Nicky's glass. "Have you got brothers and sisters?"

"Only child. But I have an aunt and cousins—"

So do I, thinks Madeleine.

"—and a goddaughter and my students and more friends than I deserve, really."

Oh, shut up, thinks Madeleine, who softens slightly when Nicky mentions a dog.

They empty a bottle of vermentino, then another. Sebastian seems to have tired of time travel; the conversation remains firmly fixed in the present. (The future goes unmentioned.) At intervals, like a concertgoer making a request, he'll suggest new topics: Has Nicky slept in many attics? ("Just this one.") Which Watson does Madeleine miss most? ("Watson the Fifth was a psychopath, but I loved all the rest.") And, by the way, what did Diana make of Freddy's new playmate? The Englishman Nicky told him about this afternoon? ("He's from Dorset"—news Sebastian receives with mild interest.)

Nicky giggles—that same sweet giggle—and proposes a toast: "To all of you, for making me feel so at home."

Madeleine smiles at her, raises her glass. *But do you believe he killed them?*

By nine o'clock, the flames are trembling, icicles of wax drip onto the tablecloth, and snores gutter beneath Sebastian's chair. "Watson has got the right idea," he says, bending with a grunt—"C'mere, darling"—and rebuilding himself until he stands, arms laden with bulldog. "Thank you all for a charming evening. Nicky"—bowing to her—"be kind at your keyboard. Lie if and as necessary."

Nicky bows in return. "'A woman who doesn't lie,'" she replies, "'is a woman without imagination and without sympathy.'"

Those must be somebody else's words. *Fucking hell,* thinks Madeleine. *We've got another one.*

Once the plates and cutlery are filed in the dishwasher, the napkins tucked away, and the bottles chiming in the recycling bin, Nicky and Diana disappear. Madeleine returns to the dining table and blows out the candles, one by one, the room dimming with each breath, until at last she finds herself alone in the dark.

In her suite, she takes the pink-and-blue box from the desk. Brings it to her ear, as though it were a ticking bomb.

Nothing. (Of course nothing.)

Upstairs, his door is ajar. She steps over the column of light toppled across the hallway floor, pauses at the threshold.

From here, she can see the vast four-poster bed within its canopy of rose-red velvet drapes. (Her father even sleeps dramatically.) She sees the dresser, too, and the mirror crack'd from side to side—"It's broken," Diana once observed; "It's perfect," Sebastian replied—and an Edwardian fainting couch in egg-yolk yellow, tufted cushions and curlicue arms (Madeleine has never met a man less inclined to faint). She sees the bedside chair where Diana sometimes perches, politely, during Sebastian's treatment.

Opposite the bed in which he dreams alone, gazing into the mirror that once reflected his previous wife, her father shucks his jacket.

Madeleine haunts the doorway like a ghost.

He glances at her reflection, his fingers attacking the buttons of his waistcoat. "Hullo, fruit of my loins." He winks, then cuts his eyes to the box in her hands. The fingers pause. "Really, you shouldn't have."

"I didn't." She crosses to his side. "This was at the front door."

He takes the box from her, cocking his head. "I do like surprises," he says, impish, like a child about to play a new game.

Madeleine's smile is uneasy.

The bow collapses when he tugs the ribbon. He peels away the wrapping paper, lifts the lid, and peers into the box.

He stiffens.

She steps closer.

Inside, flat on its back, is a crimson paper butterfly.

Creases and folds, planes and edges, clean lines, tiny flourishes: the crimped thorax, the tendril curling from the base of either wing, twin spikes crowning its head.

Inked in black upon the left wing, in a strangely childish hand:

CHERCHEZ

Inked upon the right:

LA FEMME

Madeleine glances up, confused. Her father is frowning, his forehead grooved, lips parted. He dips his fingers into the box and excavates the butterfly, carefully, as one might a live creature.

It's lovely and dangerous, sharp as a ninja star. Sebastian lowers and raises his hand, a curator weighing a specimen. He tips it into his other palm, inspects the back. Tips it again. Then he considers the box, the inscription. ST.

"I do like surprises," he murmurs.

Madeleine feels a quiet urge to touch the paper, the way she might a jewel. But Sebastian peels off the left wing, then the right, dropping them into the box. The crinkled body he presses between his palms; Madeleine hears the paper rasp, like a living thing crushed in her father's grip. When he opens his hands again, the butterfly carcass is a scrap of red paper. He tips it onto the broken wings.

"I don't understand," she says.

"Well, neither do I." Balling up the wrapping paper and ribbon, tucking the wad into the box, pressing the lid shut. "An odd little prank. Some cave-dweller from the Baron, I'm sure." He grasps the box, places it in Madeleine's hands. "Just a joke."

"A bad one."

"Certainly. So let's not bother Diana with it." He bows his head to kiss her own. "And now, daughter mine," he says, retreating to the bureau, "it's bedtime."

Madeleine thinks of her queen-size downstairs, its sheets rough with dog hair. Too big by half.

She turns, walks to the door. When she looks back, she sees him standing before the mirror again, fingering the buttons of his shirt until it parts like a stage curtain, pale flesh beneath, the seam of his appendectomy scar faint in the lamplight.

Madeleine leaves the room. The box—just a flimsy cardboard square, a few shreds of paper rattling within—feels heavy in her hands.

23.

IN THE ATTIC, Nicky parks herself at the desk and unfolds her laptop, yesterday's transcript bright on the screen. Tonight she'll start to write, editing and compressing, braiding his words with her own—the approach they'd agreed on that afternoon.

"You needn't preserve my every syllable, young Hunter, but remember that I'm the authority on my own life. And (forgive me) no one's going to pick this up thinking, *Forget what the man was actually like—I must know what the* writer *made of him!*"

"Who *is* going to pick this up, since you mention it? Just the family?"

"Do you know, earlier today, as I was devising escape routes for our party next week, it struck me that perhaps I might circulate your scribbles a bit more widely. Well, *I* won't circulate them. *I'll* have joined the great majority."

She loads a classical-piano mix on her phone. The wine in her blood burns hot and sweet. Her fingers flex, cats stretching before the nightly hunt.

Nicky writes well when she's had a drink, and tonight she feels more sure of herself, of her mission. He seems to like her. Her! Liked by Sebastian Trapp! And the family—she's read about these people, of course, but she hadn't expected to react to them with such . . . wonder, really. Affection, too.

In the breath between songs, she remembers that shadow in his eyes. She saw it in his library, saw it at the Baron Club; saw it today, in the courtyard. "People think I got away with murder," he'd said, easily. "Who can blame them? I suppose I ought to take it as a compliment. Sometimes I wonder if Diana ever asks herself . . ." Then the shadow passed. "Oh, let's not dwell. Let's talk about *methods* of murder! *Here* are a few that Simon's never seen . . ."

Nicky sighed.

Now, scanning the transcript, she selects a first line: "Life is hard. After all, it kills you."

In the glow of the task lamp, before the glass eyes of six dead dogs, she begins to type.

THREE FLOORS BELOW, in the parlor, on the sofa, bulldog grunting at her feet, Madeleine sits quietly—a shade among shades, one hand cradling a wineglass, the photo album unfolded in her lap. In the dark, the faces are faint as ghosts: Sebastian, a cigarette jammed between his teeth; Hope and Cole, shucking corn and wagging their tongues; Madeleine herself, head bowed over a jigsaw puzzle.

Rat-a-tat-ting. Hail on the roof—one floor above, her father is battering the Remington. Madeleine closes her eyes, listens to the keystrokes falling upon her. What *is* he writing? It's been more than a week since these storms began—keystrokes raining night and day, dropping onto the foyer floor, washing into her bedroom, the kitchen, wherever she—

On the coffee table, her phone shudders.

She sighs, hinges herself forward. Flips the phone over.

Catches her breath.

Hi, Magdala.

She twitches like an exposed wire.

That's impossible.

Three bubbles pulse.

It's me. Magdala.

Saturday, June 20

24.

OUTSIDE THE DINING ROOM, bag slung over one shoulder, Nicky checks the time: ten o'clock. Already this morning she's reassured Julia, chatted with Potato, watched her goddaughter open birthday presents, and gently advised a summer-school student to reconsider his werewolf novel. Now she observes Diana at the table, spearing melon on a fork.

Nicky lingers. She's a patient person—but then so is Diana: patient with her stepdaughter, patient with her sister-in-law. And the fifteen years between Hope's disappearance and Diana succeeding her as Mrs. Sebastian Trapp: had they required patience, too?

The lady of the house looks up from her laptop. "Join me. Enough to feed an island nation," she says, nodding at the dining table: omelets folded crisp as napkins, wavy strips of bacon, a basket of fruit. "He's up in his room. Treatment today."

Nicky seats herself. She's wearing a skirt, a dusting of makeup, too; yet opposite Diana in her sleeveless blouse, with those perfect shoulders, she feels lacking. "Am I interrupting?"

"Oh—" Diana closes the laptop, as though it's an underwear drawer she's left open. "Just—writing to a friend of mine in England."

Nicky is scraping meat and eggs onto her plate. She can't quite imagine Diana having friends.

"She's got a daughter called Pandora. Goes by Panda." Nicky grimaces. "Well, quite. You're seeing Isaac Murray today, I think?"

"Anything I should or shouldn't say?"

A smile breaks slow on Diana's lips. "He kissed me once," she says, shyly. "At a warehouse party, of all places. I remember his—those Year 2000 specs. You know, the first two zeroes circling either eye." Her cheeks color. "'Hungry Like the Wolf' was blasting, and Isaac was singing, '*I'm on the hunt, I'm after you.*' Perfect gentleman, though."

Nicky smiles, sawing at her omelet. "Was that New Year's Eve?"

The color drains. "Yes."

"Was what New Year's Eve?"

Nicky turns to find Freddy in the doorway. He knows how to pose, she admits, chest flexed beneath his crossed arms, biceps bulging in his sleeves.

"Sebastian's upstairs," Diana tells him.

"Cool." Freddy aims two fingers at Nicky, gunslinger style. "Whoa—what are you eating?"

"Breakfast," she answers, mouth full.

"Whose? That's, like, five breakfasts on your plate."

"Don't feel threatened just 'cause my breakfast is bigger than yours."

"Glad to see everybody getting along," says Diana.

Freddy beams. "Grab you in thirty, Nicky."

She blinks. "Am I to be grabbed?"

"I thought Fred might drive you to Isaac's," explains Diana. "Do you mind?"

"Looking forward to it."

"Cool. Mad here?"

"She's at the library Saturday mornings."

"Car's outside. Could I grab an apple?"

Nicky tosses him a Granny Smith. Freddy catches it one-handed, bites, leaves.

When she looks back, Diana is staring into her teacup. "Dialysis days are hard," she sighs. "I can feel him fading. Like a lightbulb burning out. Slowly getting dimmer."

"Seems better than a sudden death," says Nicky.

Diana lifts her eyes to Nicky. "I don't know that it is."

And she tells her story.

SHE'D FOLLOWED A BOY TO SAN FRANCISCO. They split almost overnight, but already Diana loved California, so she tutored students for a while until Hope Trapp, fellow Englishwoman and champion of the downtrodden, saved her from deportation. Diana assisted her for six months; then, shortly after Hope and Cole disappeared, she returned to England, found herself a proper teaching job in London: ten years in sixth form, training sweaty boys and anxious girls for their French and Latin exams, bumper crops of acne and a fusillade of propositions (*Voulez-vous coucher avec moi ce soir, Mademoiselle Gibson?*). At last, on her thirty-fourth birthday—a decade after San Francisco, a decade of desultory dates and mounting loneliness—she met Ewart at a wedding.

His name didn't bother her. ("It bothers *me*," he complained.) Neither did his Bermondsey flat, with its vacant refrigerator and its ashtrays and its drifts of papers on the floor. Ewart was a graphic designer, a job he loved, although within a month, he loved Diana more.

Three years and three miscarriages later, she was pregnant. She, not they—"I'm the one vomiting at dawn," she reminded him, after he cheerfully informed a friend, "We're with child!" But he gathered her hair as she bowed before the toilet, stroked her back, promised to spank the brat in due course.

They didn't want to know the baby's sex. Diana didn't, anyway; the suspense was undoing Ewart. "Have the doctor whisper in your ear," she suggested, but her husband refused.

"You can keep a secret," he grinned. "I can't."

Together they painted the nursery walls, wide bands of pink and blue. Her belly swelled. He took to tapping it with two fingers—"Morse code," he explained.

And then, one drizzly morning at the beginning of her (not their) third trimester, as they drove away from the baby shower beneath a sky like wet wool, their SUV loaded with cotton booties and hand-stitched quilts and a onesie printed with the words HERE COMES TROUBLE!, a lorry burst through a red light and T-boned their car and killed Ewart instantly.

By the time the paramedics arrived, Diana had gone into labor. As they loaded her into the ambulance, she glimpsed Ewart still in his seat belt, the passenger airbag wilted against his chest. The doors slammed shut. Scenes strobed in her eyes: A wheelchair. An operating room. An epidural. A push. A cry.

The baby was a girl. The baby was dead. The cry was her own.

Two years passed before Diana wrote to Sebastian, a widow still grieving. Strange, it felt, to print that address on an envelope; stranger still to narrate her story for someone she'd known so long ago, even if he and he alone might understand. How had he survived the loss of his wife and child? she asked. How could she heal?

Come to California, he answered.

She had nowhere to be—not at school, where every girl reminded her of her own daughter; not at home, the somber one-bedroom where she slept alone every night, on those nights when she slept; not with her parents, who had died years earlier, nor with her friends, whom she never saw anymore.

So Diana came to California. Her first morning in the city, Sebastian invited her to tour the house she had left fifteen years earlier. "Doubled the library," he bragged. "Installed a koi pond. The koi are plump as plump can be. One day I'll scoop them up like a bear and wolf them down, bones and all."

That week, they met twice; the next week, two dinners and a drive. Diana found herself postponing her return: a fortnight, then a month, then three months. She liked San Francisco, liked its multiple personalities. She liked her rented apartment in Russian Hill. And she enjoyed Sebastian's company, after all these years. After all these many, many years: Diana was now tiptoeing toward her fortieth birthday. Middle age.

"You're not middle-aged, you toddler," he scolded her. "We're just getting started, both of us." That was the night of his sixty-fifth.

He showed her yellowed letters from his favorite authors, fanned them out on the floor of the library, analyzed their penmanship, their signatures, even the postage on the envelopes. "Look at those loops!" he would exclaim, indicting the L's of a British national treasure. "She was a horny one."

She showed him photographs of Ewart, her throat tight. Showed him her baby's birth certificate, her eyes wet. Showed him the few condolence cards she'd kept; showed him the journal in which ever since she'd recorded her depthless despair and her hatchling hopes.

They married at city hall, with Madeleine and Freddy as witnesses (Simone backed out an hour before the ceremony, complaining of allergies). Diana, in a quiet gray dress, faced Sebastian, in a charcoal suit—"We look like a pair of shadows," he said—and vows were pronounced, and four hands clapped, and the lightest of kisses at the end. They returned home, where Sebastian carried his bride up the grand staircase and invited her to survey her domain.

(He carried her up to the next floor, too, before announcing that he could never marry again, because he didn't have the back for it anymore.)

And so Diana sat here at the table where Hope had once sat, walked the same corridors, slept in the bed Hope had made. A new life, or perhaps a hand-me-down life, thousands of miles from the wreckage of her past.

"Has it been a happy marriage?" asks Nicky.

A nod. "Different from Ewart. Different from Hope, too, I'm sure. But happy. We've toured the world, we've . . ." Diana trails off, looks at the window.

Nicky waits.

"You're wondering if I ever suspected him."

Nicky is wondering precisely this.

"I haven't. Truly." A slow shake of her head. "I cannot picture him doing violence to another person. Let alone two. I can't. We've never spoken of it, but—no, never."

Nicky's lips have parted in surprise.

"And I know that's unusual," Diana continues. "But in any marriage—you're not married? I didn't think so—in any marriage there are places you don't visit. Like plots of acrid land."

This plot just happens to be six feet deep and two bodies wide, Nicky thinks.

"Life is loss," says Diana, very softly.

After a moment, Nicky shrugs. "Life is change. And—discovery."

"But I've had enough change. I've discovered too much already."

"What do you mean?"

"Oh—never mind. You're here for Sebastian, not for me. Sebastian, whom you've *jolted* back to life." Nicky smiles. "Truly! He's dusting off his old material, he's curating photographs, he's visiting his club. The man is *excited*."

"But why?"

Diana squints at the windows. "I've wondered. Sebastian loves to learn. Perhaps he's learning from you."

"I doubt I have anything to teach him." A pause.

"You look as though you're about to say something," observes Diana.

Nicky shifts in her seat; she wants to phrase this just so. "I've—he's sort of glanced sideways at Hope and Cole without saying much. I don't know how to describe . . . what they were like. What *were* they like?"

Silence. Nicky holds her breath.

Then Diana pushes herself from the table and stands and says, "I'll show you."

25.

"THIS IS A FOSSIL," declares Diana, sliding the VCR beneath the television. "Jurassic." She snakes a fistful of jungle-vine cables behind the set; the machine grumbles to life, annoyed at being woken, and the screen fizzes with static.

Nicky peers inside the console cabinet: a bulky video camera and a dozen cassettes, each scored with strips of masking tape, neatly hand-lettered—*Mad First Ski 1985, T'giving/Xmas 1987, Library 91 (4 mins).*

"Let's see . . ." Diana pries loose *Soccer + Dance Show Autumn '95.* "Cole would have been ten here. Or nearly ten. Shall we?"

She pushes the cassette into the mouth of the VCR, gently but intently, as though spoon-feeding a stubborn child. At last it relents, swallows the tape—and abruptly, the screen flares grass-green, hues molten. "These new camcorders are so heavy," laughs the cinematographer. Her voice is like soil, deep and warm.

Next to Nicky, Diana shifts. "Strange to hear her," she murmurs.

Morning sun, soccer field. Children in uniform—some red, some blue (the uniforms; all the children are distinctly white). Ponytails flag from the girls' heads. The boys have pasted stickers on their cleats. Hope's lens examines the goalie.

"What's on all those shoes?" she asks.

"Ninja Turtles." Dry, distant. Madeleine.

"Where are Cole's?" Hope wonders. "Where are his turtle ninjas?"

The camera swings to Madeleine, solid and sullen, acne clouding one cheek. She chews on a coil of hair, eyes cast low, as Hope rappels down her body, past the book in her hand, settling on her sneakers. "Where are your turtles?"

Madeleine shuffles out of shot. The camera roves the field.

"And where's your brother?"

"Where indeed?" Enter Sebastian, paper cups in hand, looking to Nicky much as he does today, tall and jagged, hair swept back in a rough wave. His eyes narrow. "What is he *doing*?"

Hope finds him in a far corner, blond hair blazing in the sun, small in his red uniform, staring at the grass, limbs jostling like wind chimes as he sways. Hope zooms in on his footwear, bereft of reptiles, and then lifts the lens to his face. His lips move slowly.

"Is he watching his *shadow?*" Sebastian balks.

Cole is in fact watching his shadow, long in the morning light, straining from his shoes as though trying to detach itself. He pulls his arms into his jersey, making empty sockets of the sleeves.

Roars. The camera swerves downfield, startled. "The other team just scored," rumbles Sebastian. "Can—get his attention, will you?"

"Seriously, Mom."

"Knock it off. You and you." Hope pans back to Cole, limbs regenerated, hands busy with a slip of baby-blue paper.

Nicky watches with interest. This is the first time since arriving here that she's seen Cole in motion.

Now he kneels, folding the paper, flipping it, folding it again. "He's entertaining himself," says Hope.

"The *game* is the entertainment!" Sebastian steps into shot, cups a hand around his mouth. "Cole!" Louder: "*Cole!*"

Hope ("Stop that") and Madeleine ("Jesus, Dad") object, but Sebastian shouts them down. "They scored! A *girl* scored!"

"How far we've come," says Hope.

"While he's playing with *dolls.*"

Hope pushes in on Cole. "It's a butterfly."

"I can't watch this," sighs Sebastian, stalking off. "Give my regards to Pelé."

"Gaylé," mutters Madeleine.

"Careful there." Hope's voice is dry ice.

"It's embarrassing. Like, you need to do something about him. Do you know what Misty said?"

"'Why the hell did my parents name me Misty?,' I expect."

A smile twitches on Nicky's lips. Cole pinches the tips of the paper wings.

"Her sister Aspen told her everybody at school calls Cole the Dickless Wonder. And the teachers don't let him read aloud because he's illiterate. Aspen even formed a Cole Patrol, and every day they—what are you doing?"

Hope has pivoted to her daughter, whose face fills the frame, powdery with concealer. She wears a hoodie and a frown.

Diana frowns, too. "Perhaps we should choose another video," she murmurs.

"Tell me about this Cole Patrol," says Hope. "I simply must know. Every day they what?"

Madeleine hesitates. Then, glaring: "Every day they tell him to kill himself. They write suicide notes for him to sign and tape them to his locker. He skips class to sit in a toilet stall."

The camera has tipped a few degrees to one side.

"Cole and Aspen were partners on some invisible-ink science project, and after they wrote down their names and the teacher shone a light on the paper, it turned out Aspen had spelled out *I'm a fag* and Cole had just written *Cole,* like he'd signed it."

The camera tilts further. Nicky and Diana now see Madeleine's arms, folded across her chest. One hand clutches her book; Sebastian Trapp gazes sternly from the back jacket.

"Her friend ran for class president and made a campaign promise to buy tampons for Cole. And if they catch him making origami, they force him to eat it."

Shrieks in the distance. The camera rushes up Madeleine's body, peers beyond her at her brother, who has sculpted another butterfly, posed at his knees beside the first. He lifts his arms, waves them overhead.

"And how did you respond," says Hope, quietly now, as Cole mouths a cheer, "when—Misty, was it? When Misty shared this with you?"

Madeleine suddenly finds the ground very interesting. "I just said Cole was a spaz and to ignore him."

"I see, I see. Pass a word along to your friend and her sister for me, if you please." Hope's tone is calm but dangerous; Nicky pictures a crocodile cruising toward a riverbank. "Tell them that Misty is what a stripper calls herself, and Aspen is what a stripper calls herself when she thinks she's too high-class to be a Misty."

Cole claps for his teammates as Hope continues.

"And if young Aspen even *thinks* about *thinking* about your brother again, I will visit Leys Academy, and I will haul her out of the cafeteria by her training bra, and come graduation that knuckle-dragging little bitch will be voted Most Likely to Get a Handicapped Parking Space."

Madeleine's mouth unhinges.

"*And* if you *ever* hear someone say that another person should commit suicide, remember your father's father—"

Instantly, three girls in turquoise leotards strut onscreen, thrashing in the footlights of a small stage. The dancers on either side beam at the audience; between them, almost a foot taller, Madeleine glowers in concentration, her steps half a beat off the clop of percussion. It takes a moment for Nicky to recognize the music: George Michael, "I Want Your Sex."

"The talent show, I presume," Diana says. "Madeleine probably wouldn't want us to see this."

They watch for a few minutes before Diana switches off the TV. "That wasn't the heartwarming home movie I was expecting." She twists her wedding ring. "I don't think he's ever mentioned his father in public. For all I know, that was the first Madeleine heard of it." She frowns. "In fact, did he—"

"He told me." She can see him: sipping a beer, voice light, one foot wagging in its loafer.

Diana nods, clears her throat. "I saw students bullied as a teacher. Sometimes the abuse was physical, but far more often it was psychological, or social, and so insidious that even I couldn't make out its exact shape. Although it shapes the person who's bullied."

Nicky nods.

"I don't think it's true that bullies always hate themselves, or that they necessarily hurt others because they're insecure. Some Aspens genuinely believe they're special, they're better. Common thugs and cowards is what they are, the shits."

It's gratifying to hear Diana swear. Nicky studies their reflections in the television, gray ghosts haunting the screen. And she hears herself asking, "You last saw Cole . . ."

"The night he—New Year's Eve. I drove the boys to Freddy's house after Hope's birthday party."

"Speak of the devil." The women turn to find Freddy in the doorway once again. *Does the man ever just enter a room?* wonders Nicky. He's like the cat in a slasher flick, springing into frame for a cheap scare.

"Ready to roll?" He pushes himself off the door frame and grins, and Nicky grins back, despite herself; and then he says, "We're on a mission to the Mission," and she wants to kick him.

She hitches her bag onto her shoulder, follows him from the room. When she returns a moment later, she finds the lady of the house gazing at the television, at the phantom trapped within it. She has lifted a hand, as if to say hello, to be greeted in turn.

She starts when Nicky speaks her name.

"Thank you for telling me your story," says Nicky, and she means it.

26

MADELEINE HASN'T SLEPT, hasn't tried. She's a ship in a storm, pitching back and forth, the past washing across her decks like seawater.

Who knew?

For a while last night—maybe a few minutes, maybe an hour—she stared at the text in the dark of the parlor; when the screen fell asleep, she mechanically tapped it back to life. White wine warmed in the glass in her hand. Watson snored upon the rug at her feet. Madeleine noticed nothing.

Who knows?

A mob of caller ID websites clamored for her to pay forty dollars to trace the source. The first revealed only that the number was registered to a burner app. The second and third—under other circumstances, whothefuckiscallingme.com would have amused Madeleine—reported nothing further.

Who could possibly know about Magdala?

She checked the Internet for any mention of the name in connection with her family. The Internet reminded her that in *Roses Are Red,* the ninth St. John mystery, which pitted Simon St. John against a charismatic MP whose wives tend to vanish, the killer turned out to be a lesbian suffragette named Magda Smack. It was not one of Sebastian Trapp's finer efforts. So on Madeleine tumbled, down rabbit hole after rabbit hole, chasing Magdala.

. . . Cole might've mentioned it to Freddy. Maybe Freddy told somebody? Or her aunt? Possibly—Simone would share her bank codes if you made eye contact—but that's assuming either knew to begin with. It was a name used only in secret moments, breathed into her ear when he was frightened, pronounced with feeling while playing spies at Fort Point. It was a name impossible to discover.

. . . although apparently not.

Madeleine shed her clothes, stepped naked into bed. The drapes were slightly parted, as though about to whisper; to one side, advancing through the haze, the dog approached like a deep-sea monster in submarine light, then flopped tragically against her shoulder.

Hi, Magdala.

It's me. Magdala.

All night, she holed up in an interview room deep within her brain, interrogating a vast cast of suspects: friends, acquaintances, this ex, that classmate . . . She listened to their alibis: *Magda-what?* and *How could I have gotten your number?* and *Remind me who you are?* At some point, she heard her father ask Diana for a three-man breakfast ("Three *lumberjacks*") and then call her name ("Maddy? Are you feeling lumberjackish this morning?"). Later, Freddy knocked on her door, asked what she was up to. When he and Nicky left the house, Madeleine whisked Watson outside, whisked her back in, let her trot away toward the kitchen. They both could use their space.

And now it's 10:53 A.M., and she's bird-bone hollow with fatigue. Her stomach is angry. So is she. She swipes her phone to life, scans the message again.

Who could *possibly* know about Magdala?

Her fingers quick-step across the screen. Prove it, she types, and then she hits send.

27.

"Sebastian's high." Freddy's jaw works a wad of gum as the Nissan rolls south, past low-slung condominiums and trees with branches thrust toward the blue sky, as though rejoicing. "That's Japantown over there, if you like sushi," he tells Nicky. "Or even if you don't."

"He's high?"

"I slip him an edible before hooking him up. Cherry gummy bear. Chef's special. He'll be groovy."

Nicky can't picture Sebastian groovy. "Mind if I DJ?"

Freddy offers his phone. "Surprise me."

"Man, Freddy," she winces, scrolling through pre-millennial album art, "you are one white male aged thirty-five to forty-four."

"You don't like my music?" He's grinning.

"Look at the tattoos on this guy. Like a road map of the Kingdom of Douche. Would you get a tattoo?"

"You've met my mother. She would burn me alive."

Nicky pauses. She hadn't even meant to trap him—but he *does* have a tattoo. She saw it that first night: text inked near his elbow. Why would he deny it?

"So what's it gonna be?" he asks.

She taps the screen and Freddy turns to her, blue daubed beneath his eyes, lips pale and chapped and smiling. "Now, *this* is a deep cut. '*I get knocked down . . .*'"

"*But I get up again . . .*'" she shouts. They get knocked down and get up again several times before he observes that she can't sing. "Forgive me, Pavarotti," she replies.

"So you liking the city? You miss your friends?"

"Well, it's only been four days. I'm holding up." She smooths her skirt, looks at him. "Have you ever thought about leaving?"

"Jesus—is it *that* bad?"

"No," she says, laughing, "just—"

"Nah, I've got a life sentence. Gotta stick with what's left of the family." And for the next quarter of an hour, with the car scooting fitfully through morning traffic, with late-nineties music on tap, Nicky listens, her smile dimming, as Freddy narrates his life, present and past: coaching, girlfriends, the inexorable migrations of his buddies to altars and suburbs . . .

"I'm not boring you?"

"You're not boring me." Nicky likes people, likes to hear their stories; she likes Freddy, too, despite his swagger—likes him all the more now that he's described what sounds to her (although he doesn't say it, although he might not think it) like the steady erosion of opportunity and hope. Like Madeleine. Is she condescending to them? She hopes not.

And the weary face, the weary voice: rough night, maybe, but—it's as though something has *marked* him. Before last night. Long before, perhaps. Even his taste in music stopped developing in the mid-aughts. And that was not a good time to stop.

Suddenly she's sure of it: there's something he's not telling her.

Do you feel a nasty thumping at the top of your head? It will lay hold of you. The detective-fever is breaking out across her brain.

He cuts his eyes to her. "I've got a secret for you."

She leans in. "What?"

He draws up along the curb, leans close, and whispers, "We're here."

28

HERE IS A NARROW TWO-STORY VICTORIAN TOWNHOME, Caribbean blue, rubbing shoulders with two houses in sunburnt red, and Isaac Murray himself is stricken with a summer flu. The threadbare floral-print bathrobe he wears favors few of his angles; "Nothing else is sanitary," he croaks, ushering Nicky inside.

His forehead and hairline are negotiating a surrender; his beard is overseasoned with salt, and a faint sweat flushes his skin. Yet sitting at his kitchen table, drenched in the light of a bay window, Nicky understands Madeleine's "foaming-at-the-mouth crush," even twenty years later. It's those poet's eyes, she decides, dark and deep, gazing soulfully through tortoiseshell glasses.

"The Mission is situated in a microclimate," he says now, squeezing lemon into his tea, "so I always get my summer flu before the rest of the city. Homemade honey, by the way. Apiary out back." He taps a jam jar. "Care for some?"

Nicky nods.

He stirs a spoonful into her teacup and settles onto the cushions opposite. "Clean forgot about you. All these antihistamines." Sniffling. "I'm bummed about Sebastian. Surprised, too. For a second I wondered why he hadn't asked me to help. With the writing, I mean. I ghostwrite celebrity memoirs." Uncomplaining.

"You're overqualified. I'm just collecting some stories. For the family."

Isaac sips. "Not to sound cynical—needs more lemon—but it's a smart way to soften his image. 'According to a private volume published for his loved ones,' et cetera. You can't Trojan-horse that kind of material into a press release. It's too human."

Nicky considers this, her gaze roving the kitchen, bright cabinets and scuffed floors. *I might circulate your scribbles a bit more widely,* Sebastian said—but if he hasn't tried to reshape his public image before, when he might have benefited, then why now?

"Hope and Cole are gonna loom large out there. In the obits and for a long time afterward. Like William Burroughs—I bet most pieces running beyond a sentence let slip that he shot his wife in the head."

"Accidentally."

"Made no difference to the wife. Point is, if you're a writer—especially a crime writer—with blood on your hands . . ."

"Nobody knows if there's blood on Sebastian's hands."

"Probably isn't." Isaac plucks one, two, three tissues from a box, blows his nose with hurricane force. "Think I lost weight just now. As I was saying: Sebastian could be an almighty pain in the ass—maybe don't quote me on that—and he and Hope were fighting like warriors—don't quote that either—but can I picture him *doing away* with his wife and son the way villains *do away* with victims in his books?" He grimaces. "Doesn't matter now, anyway."

Nicky taps her phone. "You were—I'm recording, if that's okay—you were his research assistant on his nonfiction book."

"*The Nerve and the Knowledge,*" Isaac proclaims. "In which we observed that crime fiction is a form of moral education, and the detective—you've read it?"

"The detective restores order and upholds justice."

"It's irreducibly ethical. Aristotelian, even. Sebastian liked my research experience, but—this being pop philosophy—he especially wanted a skeptic. Somebody to win over." Sponging his forehead with a sleeve. "And I liked him, liked the family. We'd moved on to his next novel when the new millennium rolled in."

Nicky nods.

"Hey, top me up. I'm gonna grab my props."

These amount to six or seven items that feature in six or seven stories about Sebastian: a speeding ticket, a champagne cork, a pocket square ("He taught me five different ways to fold this"). Isaac knows how to tell a tale, and how to flatter his subject, and as the noonday sun creeps across the tabletop, the jar of honey glows like a lantern.

At last he sits back. Nicky scribbles a note in her pad, looks up. "Is there anything else I should ask you?"

He pauses, swirls his tea. "Philosophy," says Isaac, slowly, "teaches you how to highlight the strengths of an idea while hiding its weaknesses behind your back. Creative writers—you; me, in my way—we do it all the time when we're crafting a story. And this . . ." Eyeing her phone, his mementos. "The weight feels off." He begins mopping his lenses with a tissue. "Do you know what I mean?"

A slight shake of her head.

"Hope and Cole." Those eyes gleam. "The greatest mystery in Sebastian's life, right? Why isn't he making a public appeal in his dying days? Trying to smoke out the truth? Must be a reason."

"Are you saying he already knows?"

"It's a possibility."

"But you told me you can't see him—"

"I said I don't think I can."

"If he knows, then why wouldn't he say?"

A shrug. "It's like when a magician waves his right hand so you don't notice what the left is doing." He pushes his glasses back onto his face. "Has he talked much about them? None of my business, I know. I'm only human."

"Hope, yes. Cole, not so much."

"Not so much." A sigh. "Cole wasn't . . . well, put it this way: he wasn't Sebastian Trapp. Never would be."

"Never had a chance."

"Fair. All the same, he frustrated Sebastian. Especially 'cause his brother's son was such a scrapper. You've met Freddy?" She nods. "Bought him beer when he was fifteen. That kid owes me twenty dollars."

Then, cutting his eyes to her phone: "Kill the recorder, would you?"

She taps the screen. A moment later, he clears his throat and continues.

"A couple months after I started working for his dad, Cole hurt himself. Deliberately," he adds as her eyes widen. "I walked in the front door as his mom was running out, with Cole in her arms wrapped in a bath towel. 'Tell Sebastian his son just cut his wrists,' she said, and then she chucked the kid into the car and floored it. That's all I got. Never found out why." He turns to the window, winces. "I caught his face over her shoulder for an instant," he says. "He looked . . ."

Nicky waits.

"Defeated," decides Isaac. "Utterly defeated." Again he sighs. "I saw his bare arm a few times after that. If I looked close I could make out the scars, a little ladder of 'em."

She says nothing, merely studies the honey jar. *How very sad,* she thinks. *How sad to feel so helpless.*

They both flinch when the front door screeches, smashes shut. "I'm breaking and entering," a woman calls. "You still alive? 'Cause if not, I'm taking your wallet—"

She enters the kitchen, tall and trim in jeans and jacket, eyes quick beneath a helmet of glossy blue hair.

"I give you the greatest sleuth of all," Isaac says to Nicky. "My wife, Detective B.B. Springer."

29

"I'm sorry—no, stop it"—as Nicky stands, struggling against the table—"sorry to interrupt. Just checking on the patient. Brought some sourdough." B.B. Springer drops a paper bag on the table, a rump of bread poking from the top.

"I won't kiss you, but know that I'd like to. Where's Tequila Sunrise?"

"Cop shop. My new partner is a fair-haired man with a Latin name," B.B. explains to Nicky, rounding on the fridge. "Also known as Antonio Blonderas." She harvests a bag of baby carrots. "You get to the part where you met me?"

"B.B. was one of the detectives investigating the Trapp case," Isaac explains. "First time I laid eyes on her, we were in an interview room."

"And about twelve months later, he calls and asks, 'Am I still a person of interest?' And I say, 'No,' and he says—"

"'Can I be?'" they drawl as one.

"I was drunk," adds Isaac.

"At least something good came of that business." B.B.'s smile fades; she bites into a carrot.

Nicky inspects her phone. "I should get going. Thank you for your time."

"Please give my best to Diana," says Isaac.

His wife grins. "Yes, Isaac *fancied* Princess Diana."

"I like to think we fancied each other."

"And yet twenty years later she's married to Sebastian Trapp."

"Only because I married you first."

"I would've guessed the sister-in-law. As the sequel wife." B.B. kills another carrot, eyes Nicky.

Isaac paws at the empty tissue box. "Be right back," he says, hurrying from the room.

The women regard each other in silence, B.B. chewing, Nicky fidgeting—face-to-face with a flesh-and-blood detective, she feels like a specimen pinned to a dissection table.

Suddenly B.B. crosses the kitchen and crouches. She leans in, pushes a lock of blue hair behind her ear. "You know, if at any time you'd like to talk about Sebastian Trapp—"

"Nicky isn't a mole, babe." Isaac, in the doorway, trumpets into a tissue.

B.B. stands, hands spread in surrender. "No case is ever too cold to touch." She moves to her husband, kisses his forehead. "You look better in this robe than I do. Nicky," she calls, walking backward out of the room, "take care."

Isaac pulls a jar of honey from a cabinet. "Would you pass this along to Sebastian? Always felt rotten I never got to say goodbye. Or I'm sorry, for that matter. I wrote him a few letters."

He leads her into the hall. "Never spoke to Diana again, either. After that night. Not until she called the other day. Last time I saw her was at the precinct, giving a statement. Is she good?"

Nicky smiles. "I think she is."

They step out into the sun. "Do you know him?" asks Isaac, glaring at the Nissan on the curb.

"That's Freddy Trapp. He's my ride."

"Your ride just took a picture of you. Of us." Squinting. "Or maybe he was texting in our direction. Ignore me. Living with a cop makes you paranoid."

He waves her hand away—"Still contagious"—and then, to her surprise, he draws close, as though afraid Freddy might overhear.

"My wife has always believed that someone in the family knows more than they've said."

Nicky pauses. "Who?"

"She's not sure. Just a feeling. But watch your step in that house," he tells her, speaking low. "Too many rooms, too many stairs. B.B. says it was the kind of place where at any moment someone very dangerous could be standing right behind you."

Nicky waits.

"Enjoy San Francisco," he adds, and retreats inside.

After a moment, she descends the steep steps to the sidewalk. Approaching the car, she glances at Freddy's hands, thumbs busy on his phone. He doesn't notice her. Nicky tilts her head, tries to read the screen.

"Got you coffee," he reports, without looking up, and she steps back, so startled that she almost fumbles the honey.

30.

"I THINK I OWE THAT GUY TWENTY DOLLARS," says Freddy, jerking away from the curb as the speakers boom the song from earlier. "Here's your Americano."

The cup reads BREWED AT BETTY'S. Nicky chooses not to tell him she doesn't drink coffee, just pretends to sip while discreetly eyeing her driver. *His brother's son was such a scrapper.*

The scrapper swats the turn signal. "We're getting knocked down and getting up again," says Nicky. "Again."

"Ah, sorry."

"Not a complaint."

"Cole liked this jam, I remember. Which got me thinking." He clears his throat. "Yesterday I mentioned that party."

"Spin the bottle."

"And how later I heard him down below. In the bottom bunk."

Nicky waits.

"The only time he *ever* slept up top? The night he disappeared."

She feels the hairs on her neck begin to stir.

When Freddy turns his face to hers, his pupils are bright and quivery. "I never—that hadn't occurred to me before. Nobody asked, I guess. Besides, there were no more sleepovers."

As they approach a stop sign, he ceases talking, as though the sign were shushing him. He crushes his eyes shut for a moment.

"He wanted that top bunk that night."

"Why?"

"Why is right. He said—it's been *years* since I . . ."

His fingers are flexing on the wheel. Nicky listens.

"He hoped it was gonna be a better year. Guess that didn't work out." Freddy grimaces at her as the car idles. "Why'd he want that bed?"

Behind them, the tap of a car horn. He ignores it.

"And how could I have slept through whatever happened?"

Since this morning, Freddy seems to have slowed, darkened. Nicky shakes her head.

His voice is squeezing through his throat. "Simone said I was his friend. But I—" He claps one hand to his brow, winces, and now he caves in; now tears roll down his cheeks. "I wasn't always." Another tap of the horn. Freddy raises his middle finger, keeps talking. "That dog he kissed? That—"

He chokes. Nicky waits.

"Christ, that was my idea. Just a gag, but—I hoped I could, like, *manage* the guilt by telling it the way I did. I made fun of him sometimes. Oh, hell." The sobs are seismic.

Her seat belt retracts with a hiss. She wraps her arms around his body, her chin hooked on one wide shoulder and her hair pressed against one rough cheek. After a moment he calms, quiets down.

At last he drags a hand across his face. "I should've fought everybody beating up on him." Narrowing his eyes. "Especially his dad."

"You've still got your finger up," she tells him after a moment.

"Oh." Exhale. "Ignore me. I'm a mess lately."

"Do you want to talk about it?"

"*No*," he splutters, laughing. "Personal shit. Shouldn't be telling you all this."

She picks at a thumbnail. "Why *are* you telling me all this?"

Freddy checks his rearview, pats his cheeks ("Christ—look at me"), then squints at her. "Why? I guess you're easy to talk to." A bleary smile, and the car eases ahead.

His knuckles are blanched on the gearshift.

"So what's your theory?" he asks. "Hope. Cole. Once upon a time."

Nicky watches telephone poles ticking past. "I mean, I know the story, but it's not—I'm here to write about your uncle. His books." Mostly true.

"Scenario one," says Freddy, as though he hasn't been listening. "They ran away. In which case somebody would've spotted them sooner or later. Within twenty years, anyhow."

Nicky goes with it. "Agatha Christie went missing once. Just up and left, no abduction or anything. National manhunt, media circus, the works."

"How long until they found her?"

"Eleven days. She was identified by a banjo player at the hotel where she'd holed up."

"Where's a banjo player when we need one? Scenario two: kidnapping. Only—no notice? No ransom? No nothing? No, ma'am." Wiggling three fingers. "Scenario *tres*: UFO. Believe it or not, some people buy that."

"I believe it."

"There's, like, chat rooms and comment threads where people swap conspiracy theories. Trapper Keepers, they call themselves. It's messed up. You have no idea."

Nicky has a very good idea.

As they cruise through Hayes Valley, Freddy's phone bleats. "Oh, Simone," he mutters, and it rings out. Nicky remembers B.B.'s words: *I would've guessed the sister-in-law. As the sequel wife.*

She drums her fingers atop the honey jar between her thighs. "Were your mother and your aunt close?"

"Not really." He brakes. Nicky turns to the window; how did a house so vast sneak up on her?

"Thanks for the ride," she says, climbing out of the car.

"Thanks for the hug."

"You'll get my bill in the mail."

"You forgot something."

Nicky inspects the passenger seat, slaps her pockets.

"Scenario *cuatro*. And, if you ask me, the real story." Rippling four fingers. "They died."

Even in the early-afternoon sunlight, Nicky shivers. "How?"

"That," says Freddy with a shrug, "is the mystery."

31

IT'S HIM.

Throughout the long hours of the day, fitfully but ineluctably, he builds his case text by text, with Madeleine huddled on her sofa in the dark.

Two dozen stories—vacation adventures, childhood games, miscellaneous Watsons. Decorating a sign for Madeleine's first junior-high locker, her name almost indecipherably misspelled; sipping mugs of Russian tea after school while *Remington Steele* reruns played on television; the hours he would sit in her bedroom, patient and placid, as she troweled makeup onto his face.

A dossier of family secrets, including their parents' tussle over growth hormones, which Hope forbade, arguing that Cole should "mature naturally." The floor plan of their house in England; their grandfather's suicide.

Your friend Patti fed Watson III white chocolate to see if it would poison him. After he threw up in the solarium, you told Mama and Dad that it was me. Patti would know this, too, of course, but she's serving four years for graft.

You thought you were pregnant on Christmas Eve 1996. Senior year, Cameron Dunlop, his brother's waterbed, and two weeks later, she drove Cole to the drugstore and begged him to buy a pregnancy test. ("Shoplift it if you have to.") He spent months inside; "I wanted to choose the best one," he explained, climbing back into the car with a pink cardboard box and a bag of M&M's. "The candy is in case you're sad there's no baby." Back home, after a curt NO materialized on the test wand, Madeleine split the M&M's with him.

Once we biked to Fort Point and played hide and seek in the catacombs and you couldn't find me for an hour. When I showed myself, you slapped me and hugged me. He loved biking, especially to Fort Point: a brickwork bayside gold-rush-era citadel (unmanned), topped with a lighthouse (decommissioned), commanding a fine view of Alcatraz (vacant), fixed forever beneath the Golden Gate Bridge. When he was twelve or so, he began riding there on his own, three miles from Pacific Heights, with a sandwich and a sketchpad in his backpack.

I miss playing hide and seek with you, he added.

Theirs was a language. The person on the other end of this line is a native speaker. The person on the other end of this line is Cole.

Her hands shake. She always hoped he was alive, of course. Believed, even. But this is overwhelming.

Her eyes ache. She switches on her desk lamp ("Don't you want a softer bulb?" her father had asked. "You could summon Batman with that thing") and floats to the sofa, mouthing his name, shaping her pale lips around it. *Calm down,* she tells herself. *Rejoice!* she adds, suddenly ecclesiastical: Rejoice for Cole, her flesh and blood, made warm again. Rejoice for this lost child, star of a famous vanishing act, who could now explain so many mysteries. Rejoice for . . .

. . . how *many* mysteries, precisely? What can he tell her? Why the invisible-man approach?

> Why now? It's been a long time!

> Magdala. I need your help.

Ninety minutes since his last text. She stabs at the screen.

> Anything.

> Where are you? Can I see you?

She holds her breath.

Dots sequence in his text bubble like Morse code. Then the bubble pops, dots and all.

Madeleine's fingers wobble on the glass.

> I am overjoyed to hear
> from you
>
> Please can we meet so you
> can tell me every thong
>
> Every think
>
> Ship
>
> Shit

How do people in films text so flawlessly, even when they're saving the world? Are Cole's fingers trembling, too?

> This is about dad.
>
> I know he's dying. I need your
> help before he's dead.

Not *gone,* but *dead.* Madeleine winces.

> Don't you want to know what
> happened to mama?

She blinks.

> Do you know?
>
> Maybe. But I need your help.

She wants to ask what he knows, of course, the same way that bony Disney princess wanted to touch the spinning-wheel spindle: it'll hurt, but what if he's right?
(But what if he's wrong?)

> How can I help?

Tell him you wish you knew
what happened to her.

He can tell you.

I wish I knew what happened
to YOU, and you can tell me.

Does Dad know about you?

No idea. Be careful.

Their father has no idea that Cole is alive? Or Cole has no idea if
their father knows? And what exactly *does* Cole think that Sebastian
knows? And—

Oh, it's a knot. Madeleine rubs her forehead, as if to smooth it
out, but still the question surfaces in her mind, like a weighted
body that won't stay submerged: is there something her father has
kept from her?

She won't ask him. She doesn't want to know.

Again her phone shudders.

I'll see you soon.

And she shudders, too. Doesn't hear the door creaking open.

32

"Madeleine?"

The phone clatters atop the desk. She says something unprintable.

"Sorry to intrude." Diana steps inside. "Watson was plopped outside the door. Grunting a bit."

"Ah." Madeleine clears her throat, peels her hair from her cheeks. "Sorry."

"I'm sure she doesn't mind." Madeleine was not apologizing to the dog, who now trudges into the room with the air of one who minds very much, but whatever. Through bleary eyes she beholds Diana, in sleeveless black blouse and cream slacks, shimmering like a mirage.

"Quite dark in here," she says. Madeleine glances at the room, beholds a little theater—walls and shelves dark, draped in shadow curtains, and windows draped in actual curtains; the mirror in the corner is black glass. She sits in the spotlight of the desk lamp. Diana stands just beyond it. "You all right?"

"Everything's great," Madeleine replies. "It's so great."

"I was just unhooking your father. Freddy hasn't come back." Madeleine winces. The nephrologist had trained each of them—caps, clamps, tubes, valves; not especially complicated, he said, but Madeleine couldn't manage it, couldn't bear it.

"What will you do after he's gone?" she hears herself ask.

Diana tilts her head. "Do you mean how will I cope? Or where will I go?"

Madeleine, to her shame, hasn't really considered how Diana will cope. "Both."

Diana steps into the light, leans against the rolled arm of the sofa, and now the two of them are playing an intimate scene. "Well. This isn't my first loss, you know."

On the night before he proposed to Diana, after Madeleine asked him why he wished to remarry, her father told her the story: the young husband, the accident, the stillborn baby, the life that disintegrated around Diana like a house in flames. "She knows loss as well as we do," he explained. "I think we can help each other."

Madeleine inclines her head very slightly. She and Diana have never spoken of it.

"That loss was different, though," says Diana. "Your father has lived. He's lived a whole life! And when he dies—I *do* use that word, because that *is* what's going to happen . . ." Her eyelids drop, and she folds her hands against her chest. "I shall *miss* him. Oh, I shall miss him terribly. But"—looking at Madeleine again—"I've got a whole life to live, too. I don't know what it will look like, but I *do* know that I'll owe it to your dad.

"A lot of me is gone." She says it very simply. "A lot of bits are missing. For a while I waited, thinking they'd be restored to me in time—but no: They were gone. Like jigsaw pieces you've lost. You've still got the borders, you know, the clean edges on the outside, but the picture isn't complete. And it never will be."

Madeleine has never heard her talk like this. Never heard her talk as *much* as this. It's part of why she never entertained the notion—popular in certain chat rooms—that Diana and her father had paired off before her mother's disappearance. Back then, Diana spoke even less, and Sebastian wouldn't have taken the remotest interest in a quiet woman. Even as he and Hope waged cold war, they still *spoke*, still took pleasure in sparring. Much later, of course, after those blighted years, he would find a quiet person ideal company: someone to listen as he regained his voice. Enter Diana. Or reenter Diana.

Whose eyes are bright. She's shining.

"But there's enough of me left. And . . . oh, I've a notion that I might move to Provence." She smiles. "Brush up on my French. Or perhaps the Middle East—that would be an adventure, wouldn't it? I feel like Death keeps aiming darts at me, keeps hitting those I love. Perhaps he'll catch up with me abroad. An appointment in Samarra." Her smile fades. "But what I won't do is remain in San Francisco."

To her horror, Madeleine's ribs squeeze her lungs. She is going to be alone. She hadn't assumed Diana would stay—hadn't even wanted her to, really—but now she feels electric with alarm.

"I haven't seen the will," says Diana. "In case you've wondered. But I don't want the house. Either house." Madeleine's heartbeat quickens. "I want nothing. Your father is very aware of this. Oh,

Watson"—who has wandered toward her, snorting—"I shall miss you terribly, too."

Watson sighs.

"Madeleine." When Diana says it, Madeleine realizes how rarely she speaks her name; it sounds faintly exotic, clothed in that lovely low voice. "You're the last one left, and this is your home. I don't plan on staying very long"—again that spurt of panic—"but if you'd like to escape for a while, you're welcome to join me."

They both know she won't, or at least Madeleine knows it, but now the front door clacks shut. "Our guest," murmurs Diana, and as she stands, she steps from the spotlight. Their scene is concluded.

"About that," says Madeleine. "About her. I—knock it off." The dog is chewing on a cigarette packet. "Why not me?" Anger in her voice; suddenly her vision blurs. "Why didn't he ask me?"

At the door, Diana turns.

"I wasn't a good enough writer?"

"Oh—of course not. Don't . . ." Diana pauses. "I think he didn't wish to preoccupy you with his death," she says. "I think perhaps he didn't want you to relive what you've already lived."

"Did he say that?"

"I'm saying it. Because I believe it."

After she leaves, Madeleine draws back the curtains; tired afternoon light crawls in, gives up and dies by the sofa. She returns to the desk, checks her phone for trespassers.

So she's to be abandoned. So she's to live alone in this house. Except for Freddy, she supposes, and except for Simone. Except for Simon St. John, if she can project him out of the past and onto the screen.

And except—possibly—for her brother, twenty years older, equipped with an anonymous number and what feels like a plan.

33.

SOMEONE IS WATCHING HER.

Nicky doesn't notice it all afternoon—not as she types at the desk, transcribing Sebastian's stories; not as she writes on the floor, in a patch of sun, shaping and refining them; not as she lies on the bed, reviewing her grammar. Not when her hostess knocks on her door bearing printed pages and takeout sashimi.

("Isaac keeps bees?" Diana asks, inspecting the honey jar. "How unexpected.")

Afterward—after waiting in the corridor, bracing herself in vain for the skitter of typewriter keys—Nicky slips the pages beneath the library door. Nine thousand words, his voice in duet with hers. She's surprised how much she hopes to please him.

Now, though, in the weak moonlight, the weight of a stare is like a tap on her shoulder. She turns to the stuffed-bulldog platoon, in nighttime camouflage mode, but they gaze straight past her with military focus.

No: The eyes on Nicky, she sees, are fixed in the face of a child of indeterminate sex, finely painted and framed in gold, propped in the sagging seat of a rocking chair. The portrait is at least a century old. The child is unusually ugly.

Nicky treads the length of the room, advancing slowly on the androgyne in oil. She hasn't noticed her or him before. The plate at the bottom of the frame reads, unhelpfully, *A Child*.

Nicky goes still, then rocks back. The plank beneath her heel gently gives.

She steps away. *A Child* watches her.

Nicky kneels, presses the plank into the space under the floor, dislodging a shot of dust.

Holds her breath, peers into the darkness, makes out a . . .

. . . red butterfly.

She blinks.

Then she dips her hand into the floor. The butterfly is smooth to the touch, the dark around it soft as an animal's pelt. She flinches, presses her fingertips against the fur, traces the long edge of—

She lifts it from its lair.

A book, short and thick and floury with dust, butterfly decal pasted to its plum-purple cover.

Nicky opens it.

The first page is inscribed in Magic Marker, tropical colors, careful block capitals:

THE DAIRY OF COLE TRAPP

Below, in small print:

COPYRIHGT MCMXCVII

Cole Trapp's diary, wearing twenty years of dust. Imagine that. She turns to the next page.

> *December 31 1997. Please dont' read my dairy!*
> *Thank u and Happy New Year!*

Clumsy cursive, smudged ink.

Nicky catches *A Child* looking over her shoulder and retreats to the bed. Where, by lamplight, she begins to read.

DYSLEXIA, OR SUCH, Simone had sighed, and sure enough, Cole was a poor if conscientious speller, a few words on each page struck out and remodeled. Yet still he chose to write. *Good for him*, thinks Nicky.

His diary, like most young people's, was plainly maintained for an imaginary audience, at least at first: perfunctory recaps of meals or math tests, his adventures at the zoo. He transcribes an extremely vulgar joke overheard in carpool (*I dont' get it!*). He tracks his height and weight for half a year, neither changing much. Every other month, he and his mother jaunt off for a weekend: grape-stomping in Napa, Puget Sound whale-watching, Disneyland. Badly sketched flowers garland the margins, bees and butterflies hover between the lines.

Toward the end of eighth grade, however, the entries darken, deepen; even the ink on the page appears blacker. *There is something about me that other people don not like,* Cole concludes on the last day of school, reporting a bloody lip (*Teddy locked me in my locker so that in Setpember a student would open it and see a pial of bones*) and a firing line of classmates who shot insults at him during morning assembly.

Nicky skims through that summer: afternoons caring for baby turtles and wounded birds; regular visits to his godparents' swimming pool. Hope appears frequently, of course, and Madeleine, too, in the months before her sophomore year at Berkeley—on one page, Cole has pasted a postcard she sent from Belize; on another, she mocks him for fleeing *Saving Private Ryan* (*She was supposed to take me to "Mulan"*). Freddy, in Berlin for two months on a study-abroad program, had written a letter, beneath which Cole translates the message into English: *Dad says this means I AM A BOTTOMLESS BEER HOLE AND I LOVE TO PUT MY TOUNGE IN THE FACES OF MANY GERMAN WOMEN.*

Sleep tugs at her eyelids. Nicky reads on.

Sebastian has spent early 1998 on tour—in February, Cole catalogs the gift of a boomerang shipped from Perth, accompanied by a note reading *Give this to your sister if you don't want it*—but when he returns, he blows through the journal like a spring wind, so brisk and biting that the pages nearly ruffle. March: *Dad told Mama it's embarasing that a writers son cant' spell.* April: *Dad asks why can't I be more like Freddy.* Mother's Day: *Dad says I spend too much time with Mama.* Father's Day: *Dad said thanks for my drawnig but Maddy told me he threw it away.* The Fourth of July: *Fire works night. Dad says not to plug my ears, he says not even Watson mind the noise and his ears are bigger.*

And then, a month after school resumed, on his fourteenth birthday, those same words: *There is something about me that other people don not like.*

Nicky feels cold.

All morning, students had flocked to him, hands raised—*They said Happy Birthday*—and Cole eagerly crushed his palm against theirs. (*Misty gave me a double high five.*) Only at lunch did he learn, from Freddy, that someone had taped a sheet of looseleaf to his back: *HIGH-5 THE BIRTHDAY FAGGOT.*

I walked home Dad was here. He got mad and told me to be tougher.
Isaac drove me back to school. He said our car is very burjwah and
that bullies don't like themselves. I'm sorry they dont' like themselves
becuase I dont' like myself either and it feels terible.

Suddenly Nicky needs to look away from Cole. She swings her feet
to the floor and stashes the diary beneath the portrait, thinks of the
postcards in her bag, his clumsy handwriting. *A Child* regards her with
conspiring eyes.

Sunday, June 21

34.

ONCE HE'S PILOTED THE RENTAL BOAT into open water, Jonathan invites Nicky to skipper. It's been years since she sailed, and she's certainly never helmed a forty-six-footer.

The *Bavaria* cruises through a light chop. Nicky scans the waves scrolling across the bay; islands to the north, east, and west; further south, the curve of the waterfront, and the city stacked behind it on steep-raked slopes; in the distance, the Bay Bridge threaded between San Francisco and Oakland. All of it—all the seawater and skyscrapers and even the sickly stone of Alcatraz—all Technicolor-bright beneath a white noonday sun.

"Arr, matey," she mutters.

As Nicky steers past the prison, sails swollen with wind, Jonathan reads aloud from the marina brochure. "'Angel Island State Park'"— his finger draws a circle in the air until it finds a rugged bulge of greenery—"'is the largest natural island in the San Francisco Bay. During World War II, Japanese and German prisoners of war were detained on Angel Island before being sent to inland internment facilities.'"

"Delightful."

"And that"—a floating city straight ahead—"would be Treasure Island. Built for the Golden Gate International Exposition in nineteen thirty-nine. Some human sacrifices in the fifties, too."

Nicky awoke this morning to find an envelope beneath her door, like in a spy story. Sebastian hoped she might excuse his absence—he must visit his `quack doctors` today—but Nicky should `have yourself a jolly adventure`. Tomorrow, he would bring her to `a place that will amaze you`. And below his blue-ink initials:

> `If you find my body outside your door, the climb has`
> `killed me.`

She smiled. Inspected the landing, just in case. And not a minute later, as though sensing an opportunity, Jonathan called to invite her for a sail.

They've chatted easily since meeting at the wharf: his years in London finance, her years in New York classrooms; his classical studies, her MFA; his friends back home, her friends back home.

"Lately I've been going through classic books translated into Latin. My ancient Greek is gone, but I like to keep up-to-date on my Latin."

"Up-to-date on your dead language," Nicky says.

"Look, if ABBA can come back, so can anything."

Only as they clear the shadow of the Bay Bridge, and the sails flush again with sudden light, does she ask him why he's come to San Francisco. He's standing atop the cabin, mainsail aglow to one side and pure blue sky to the other, so that she can't quite see his face.

"I spent some time here ages ago," he says. "Don't remember loving the place, really, but . . ." A shrug. "Here I am. Two months now."

It's not much of an answer. Gently, Nicky rolls the wheel, so that the shadows slide off of him. He stoops to release the mainsail. "It's a strange city. You've got aging hippies, local aristocracy, tech bros stepping over homeless people on the sidewalk—oh, man: some of the startup blokes on my football team . . ."

Nicky steadies the wheel, pushes her sunglasses onto her face.

"One guy—Chad, he's called—"

"Of course he is."

"—Chad created an app that matched bros with bro-friendly employers." Jonathan leans against the mast. "You could search companies by hotness quotient of female workers, or frequency of office parties, or whatever. And then you'd network with other users—*brofessionals* was the term—and wangle yourself a job."

"What could go wrong?"

"What went wrong was that Chad and the other brogrammers named the app without thinking it through."

"What was the app called?"

"BroJobs."

They slice across the bay, pinballing between the islands, swapping shifts as the waves roll and the sails hum. Nicky feels giddy with oxygen. She releases the wheel, hugs herself.

At the same moment she cuts through the wake of a powerboat, Jonathan emerges from the cabin bearing two tumblers of merlot; the glasses jolt from his hands and smash on the deck, bloodying the fiber-glass. He stares forlornly at the carnage. "Looks like a crime scene," he mourns.

So they swig wine from the bottle, Nicky sitting cross-legged, Jonathan clasping the wheel with one lazy hand. She watches the muscles in his throat shift as he drinks, swallows. "How long will you stay here?" she asks.

"Unknown. I fancy a cool summer. London hit triple digits last July." He grins. "I speak Fahrenheit."

"And after the cold, gloomy summer," says Nicky, rising, "where will you go? Where do the other—what's your last name?"

"Grant."

"Where are your fellow Grants? Your Granti?"

Jonathan swivels his head toward her, the lenses of his glasses like high beams in the sun. The movement is so sudden, and the light so intense, that Nicky edges back, the wire rail flexing against her shoulder blades.

"Hither and yon," he replies, spinning the wheel, driving the boat closer to the wind. "Shall we head south?"

He wraps line around his knuckles, hauls in the mainsail. As Nicky steps to the bow to uncleat the jib, the craft gains speed, sails smooth and tight as skin except for the very edges, trembling like nerves. She slips on the deck, breaks the fall with her palms; "Wait," she calls to him, but already they're swerving into the wind, and a snap cracks the air, gunshot sharp, and the mainsail rushes toward her in a vast wave. She ducks beneath the boom as it swings across the boat, dragging the shadow of the sail after it, so that when she stands, the sunlight dazzles her. She narrows her eyes and pounces on the jib cleat.

"Sorry," bellows Jonathan over the roar. Nicky, breathless, hurries to the opposite cleat, fastens the jib, and retreats to the wheel. "I fear I'm sailing drunk."

"I'll steer," she tells him.

Later, as they scud toward the Golden Gate, Jonathan sits in the cabin doorway, hugging his shins; he looks almost adolescent, thinks Nicky, limbs folded like a disassembled tent. "So Fred's uncle must be an interesting specimen."

"You said you haven't read his books?" asks Nicky.

He inspects a scab on one bald kneecap. "As I told Fred, we don't much like American authors playing dress-up in our past."

"I think he's pretty popular there."

Jonathan shrugs. "Give me a good biography." He tilts his head as the boat tilts, too. "That's what you're working on, no?"

Nicky braces her feet, unwinds the mainsheet a few inches so that the sail spills wind and they even out. "Just collecting some reminiscences. Then setting them down."

"Can't the famous writer set them down?"

"Better things to do, I suppose." She thinks of those keystrokes fizzing in the dark, in the morning, at all hours. *Rat-a-trat-trapp.*

Jonathan stands, gazes beyond the bridge to the blue horizon. "Imagine sitting on your mum's lap as she blows out her birthday candles, and then just hours later . . ." He turns to Nicky. "That's correct? A birthday party?"

"A birthday dinner, early, then a New Year's Eve party. He was probably a bit old to be sitting on her lap."

Jonathan shrugs. "I guess they died. Somehow. And were never found." A sigh. "Or maybe they don't want to be found."

Nicky looks past him at the Golden Gate, radiant in the afternoon light. Tonight, fog will pour across the bay, across the bridge, only the peaks of its towers and the swoops of its cables rising above the vapor; for now, under a sun rolling slowly down the sky, all is clear, and bright, and diamond-edged. They could stay the course, glide into the ocean, never to be found. So easy to disappear.

35

So EASY TO DISAPPEAR, thinks Madeleine, sheets drawn clingfilm-tight over her head. She could simply linger here in bed, out of sight, erased from the world and its mysteries and the thousand natural shocks she seems to be heir to. "Didn't somebody used to inhabit this room?" they'd ask years from now, but she would remain huddled where she lies, not somebody, not even a body, just a distant memory from the distant past.

Like Cole.

Her father and Diana are visiting the nephrologist this morning. She can hear Adelina and her two nieces readying the house for tomorrow's *fête*, as Sebastian calls it, mostly to annoy Madeleine. She enjoys hearing them call to one another in musical Italian. Like birdsong: a language she can't speak yet likes to listen to.

When their voices fade, she opens her bedroom door and spies Watson across the foyer, in the jigsaw room, dozing beneath a table.

"Mad!"

Her stomach drops.

It's a woman's voice.

It's her mother's voice.

Her heart stalls. She stands at the threshold of her room, wavering.

"Mad! Come here!"

First her brother. Now her mother. She can't breathe.

Watson awakens, chugs toward the living room. Madeleine feels herself sleepwalk after her.

"*Madel*—right. Count of five. Four."

Voices rustle like leaves. Madeleine's feet slap the marble, moving faster.

"Three. Two."

She trails the dog through the doorway.

"Lo, she appears," says her mother.

Madeleine finds her in the living room—in the television, specifically, crouching beside Cole, who sits at the head of the dining room table. Candles poke from the cake before him. Madeleine flinches: she hasn't seen Cole in motion since . . . 1999? It must've been 1999.

She watches herself barge onscreen, take a seat beside her father, opposite Freddy and Dominic. Dom is more handsome than she remembers, a softer Sebastian, his black hair shot with gray at the temples. He looks happy, easy, chatting with his son, until the cinematographer calls for everybody to "shut up and sing before the candles melt."

"Thank you, Simone," says Hope, and Madeleine catches her breath: How young her mother is! How healthy, in her popped-collar polo and tortoiseshells! Madeleine squints at Cole, at the cake, tries to date the occasion—but he was so small, her brother, and for so long, that it could've been his ninth, could've been his fourteenth.

Colors shift in the corner of her eye. Diana, in tennis kit, sits perched on the sofa, remote in one hand. Like some fairy-tale sorceress: the white costume, the wand that summons the past.

What are you doing and why? Madeleine does not ask. Instead, she withdraws into the recess between the door and the wall it cracks against when opened with force. As a kid, she used to stash herself here playing hide-and-seek; the fit today is somewhat more snug, especially with Watson parking herself at Madeleine's bare feet, staring up at her in search of answers. But she can still see the screen, still hear the family massacre "Happy Birthday."

Twelve candles. Nineteen ninety-seven. Cole huffs at them until Simone recruits Freddy. "Shouldn't require a tag team," Sebastian says. Freddy laughs. Cole, too.

Madeleine strains to peek around the edge of the wall; she can see Diana's hands in her lap, fingers knitted, but her lovely face remains out of sight. She's rested the remote beside her. Settled in for a proper viewing.

The camera presses in on Sebastian, watching him watching his son. Blue suit, red tie knotted in a bulb at his throat; he appears ill at ease.

"Smile, birthday boy!" calls Simone, in a tone common among hostage-takers. Birthday boy obeys, braces bright, as he and birthday mother sink a knife into the cake.

And then the camera drifts back to Sebastian, who pops a champagne cork as Simone demands that he toast his son.

"To Cole," he announces. A pause. Then: "You're becoming a fine young man, and one day you'll make the family proud."

Madeleine rummages through the attic of her brain in search of this moment. Down below, Watson scratches at her ankle.

Silence in the dining room. Discomfort, too; she can feel it radiating through the screen. The camera glances at Cole, an uncertain smile pasted on his face.

"Shoot," mutters Sebastian. "Should've poured drinks first."

Hope spears a chunk of cake on her fork. "Darling Cole, you already make us proud." Her voice is ringing. "You're kind, and generous, and sensitive. You have the strength to be yourself." Cole beams at her; decades later, Madeleine feels herself nearly beaming at him.

"And now you've got your spanking-new bike!" says Hope, pointing offscreen. "Who knows where it'll take you? You're in for some great adventures, darling, and I—we—all of us here, we're so lucky to be your family." She aims a look at her husband, who nods.

"Let's eat to Cole!" she says, and five voices echo her as five forks airlift cake to five mouths (Cole's slice has tumbled to the floor). The camera tracks Sebastian to the credenza.

And in the living room, the door beside Madeleine suddenly pushes against her shoulder.

36

"What're you watching?"

The voice has ambushed her from the other side of the door. She scuttles back into the corner, thudding quietly against the walls. The dog snuffles.

"You startled me," says Diana.

Again the door presses into Madeleine. Freddy must be leaning on it now, per his custom. Doesn't the man ever just enter a room? And he's clouded himself in that body spray he likes—Arctic Douche or something.

Now he swaggers in, blocking her view; a nimbus of digital light edges his head and shoulders. The man is an eclipse.

"What are you doing here?" asks Diana.

"Helping out, I thought. But Adelina says he left hours ago."

"He did. We did. He's still out." Diana's hand grasps the remote. "I'm sorry. I forgot to tell you."

Madeleine takes a breath. Last chance to make herself known— *Heard the TV, didn't want to disturb you, oh hello Freddy!*

"Hey!" he says, stepping toward the TV. "Look at young Fred Trapp before he got all famous! What's in that box I'm holding?"

"It appears you've got a birthday gift for your cousin."

"It *does* appear," agrees Freddy in wonderment. "No, don't pause, don't pause! What's in the box?"

The screen freezes. Diana enters Madeleine's view.

"I've got a tennis game." She offers the remote to Freddy. "You can—"

He gasps; a cracked lightbulb sparks above his head. "Hey—what was in that *other* box? Not *that* box"—thrusting the remote at the TV—"the one at the front door. The *mystery* box."

"Mystery box?" says Diana, crossing her arms.

"I gave it to Mad. Special delivery. Pink box, blue ribbon. Or blue box pink ribbon. Initials ST on it. So maybe for my mother," he giggles, "but—unlikely. Nobody told you?"

"Are you all right, Freddy? You seem a bit high-spirited."

"I'm awesome." He turns back to the television. "Who's shooting this?"

"Your mother, I believe."

The dog grunts. Madeleine looks down, mouths a *shh*.

Now Freddy sidles toward Diana. Between them stands Sebastian, hands bristling with glassware. "It's like *The Sebastian Show*. She got a thing for him?"

"Of course not."

"Maybe not today, but back then?"

"Freddy, you can't expect me—"

"It's natural." His tone is not; he sounds silky, hungry. "Women yearn. Don't they?"

What balladeer twaddle is this? Again Watson grunts. Madeleine smiles reassuringly at her, whispers, *"Shut the fuck up."*

"I've got to go, Freddy." As Diana moves past him, he clasps her shoulder; she drops her eyes to his hand.

He releases her, but leans in close. "She wanted him then," he says, "even with her husband and his wife in the mix, and she probably wants him now."

"You're talking about your mother."

"Don't I know it. The wife disappears—the kid, too—and then Dominic, one dark night . . ."

"Are you suggesting that your *mother*—"

He steps forward, his voice softer. "And then *you* showed up."

"Why are you saying this?" she asks, eyes narrowed.

"Just . . . beware. You know? Beware. It's the last-chance dance for Simone. Like I said, everyone yearns." And he kisses her.

Quick—so quick that Madeleine barely has time to catch her breath—but intense. And though Diana presses her palms against his chest, she hesitates for an instant before pushing. Or so it seems to Madeleine.

Freddy rocks back on his heels; she steps away. "I've wanted to do that since forever," he says, suddenly shy.

"Please leave."

He blinks, then surrenders. "Sorry. Sorry."

"Just go." Cool, but Madeleine can see Diana's hands trembling.

For a moment, Freddy works his jaw, taste-testing replies; at last he turns, politely places the remote on the sofa arm, and walks to the doorway. A blast of Tropical Assault or whatever and Freddy is offstage.

Madeleine seethes—for Diana, perhaps, but quite unexpectedly for Simone. Impossible that she would have killed her husband. Or her sister-in-law, for that matter. Who could imagine it? Aside from Freddy, it seems.

Diana stands in the spotlight of the TV screen. Madeleine watches her, wondering.

Then she bends, collects a tennis racquet from beside the sofa— Madeleine hadn't noticed it, and Freddy hadn't, either, she'd bet, or else he might've behaved himself—before she exhales, dabs at her eyes, and leaves the room by the far doors.

Madeleine counts sixty before emerging. (To think her mother lured her in here!) Across the room Sebastian fills the television screen, face angled toward her, witness to the kiss.

And now, as Watson wobbles from captivity, she spies Cole at the table, beaming at his father. She approaches the TV to get a better look at him: the little prow of his nose, the blond hair brushing his eyebrows. So young, a work in progress—no telling how time would sculpt his face, or to what depths his voice would drop, or whether he would grow tall like his parents. Like Madeleine.

No telling who he might become.

He could be anyone.

37.

NICKY BALMS HER LIPS and rakes her hands through her hair (straw-dry; all that sea air). It's nice to primp for someone. Been a while.

Mouth glossy, hair swinging, she emerges from the powder room. Jonathan lives in a converted church near Dolores Park; his loft is all concrete floors and steel kitchen, but the architect has preserved elements of its past life: brick walls and stained glass, arched windows leaping two stories tall, even twin pews by the front door. "Where guests sleep," Jonathan explained when they walked in.

Now he sits before two mugs on the coffee table. The furniture, spare and modern, belongs to the landlord; Jonathan's personal inventory, he told Nicky, amounts to his clothes, toothbrush, and two dozen unopened boxes. ("Jury's still out on San Francisco.")

He invites her to the sofa. "I thought we might watch a film. If you fancy." Thumbing his phone, glaring at the television.

"Sure." Nicky lifts a mug to her lips.

"To be clear, this was my evening's entertainment already sorted. That's why I had your boss on the brain. Fred does like to talk about Uncle Sebastian." Graphics load onscreen: a painterly long-ago London, a man in long coat and top hat casting a shadow down a cobblestone street. Deep blacks and jade greens and golden script: SIMON SAYS.

"Guessing you've seen it?" asks Jonathan.

"Only once. Book is better."

"Books usually are—bollocks." He has knocked her bag from the sofa. It bursts on the floor like a piñata. "Bollocks. Sorry." Hands scrabble on the concrete, collecting pens and hand-sanitizer bottles and a slim pepper-spray tube, which Jonathan presents to her with neither comment nor blush.

After restocking, she folds her legs lotus-style—"Ready?" he asks—and the film begins.

This second viewing again fails to enchant Nicky, but Jonathan is delighted, gasping and laughing at intervals. Shyly, she studies the shadow and light playing fast and slow across his face, the maybe-broken nose, the pale eyes. She likes this man, finds him almost gravitationally attractive.

Now and then, she notices his left hand as it idly fingers a button on his shirt, as it discreetly adjusts his crotch, as it advances a few inches across the sofa and then withdraws to the safety of his lap.

"*Whoa!*" he shouts when Spring-Heeled Jack leaps from an alley in his mask. "*Whoa!*" Slapping his thighs in excitement.

Nicky can barely look at Jack in his mask. Still horrifying, the fleshy molding, the tiny black eyes. She smiles, shudders.

Just after St. John discovers the second corpse—that of a fishmonger, stashed in a telephone box—thunder cracks the sky outside, hard enough that both Nicky and Jonathan hop where they sit. Beyond the window, beyond Dolores Park, a jagged seam of lightning.

As she consults her weather app, he turns to her. "I meant to ask earlier," he says. "May I kiss you?"

She looks up, startled. "That's—that's very attractive."

"Me asking if I may kiss you?"

"You using the appropriate auxiliary verb."

Jonathan grins, mussing his curls. "I wouldn't like to make you uncomfortable. Strange man. Deconsecrated church." Onscreen, violins shrill as Simon deciphers a rebus tattooed across the victim's shoulder.

Nicky smiles back, tilts her head, and surprises herself. "No."

When he starts to apologize, she talks over him: "Only because I need to leave. There's a storm a-comin'." She taps her screen, streaked with digital rain.

"Quite." Jonathan rises. "Shall I summon a car for you?"

"I've got it, thanks. You should finish the movie."

"Do you know, I think I will. Curious to see who the baddie turns out to be."

Nicky doesn't warn him that Jack remains, as of this viewing, unidentified. Instead she stands, shoulders her bag. "Any guesses?"

"Oh, I'm no good at guessing. But I know it's never who you think it is."

Nicky walks out of the church and into a wet early-summer night.

By the time her Uber plows through a curbside river to deposit her at the foot of the Trapps' driveway, sheets of water are billowing over the city, and the streets seethe. She hikes up to the house; at the door, she crouches, rummages through her bag beneath the glare of the phone.

It must be on Jonathan's floor.

"I lost my key," she explains when Madeleine answers the doorbell, Watson dancing a jig at her feet. "I'm so sorry."

Madeleine steps aside.

In the dark basin of the foyer, single sconces glow on either wall. The hiss of rain fades when the door closes behind Nicky, but she can still hear it outside, whispering.

Madeleine is bled of color: skin white as the marble floor, hair tinted gray, the hollows of her eyes bruise-dark. Even her nightgown—who would've pictured Madeleine in a nightgown?—is merely a shadow draped from her shoulders.

"I look like hell, yes," she grunts.

From the depths of the foyer, a ghost approaches. Diana, in her tennis whites, stares at them blearily; then, as she nears, livid lightning blazes beyond the twin windows at the top of the staircase and strobes across the walls, the floor, the staircase, all wiped bright for an instant, and for another.

Oh, stop, Nicky thinks. This is a hoary Hammer horror film, or the death-trap house on Soldier Island in *And Then There Were None,* cowering with its ten guests beneath the tempest. The second wife, the spinster daughter, the stranger—and the riot in the clouds, the rain against the glass. Her eyes glide up the stairs, all the way to the portrait. It flickers in the lightning like a sputtering bulb, those four faces spectral as skulls.

It was a dark and stormy night.

Now thunder growls. The three women watch the ceiling, as though a predator is passing overhead. Nicky holds her breath. Nobody moves.

Then the noise slinks off, and in the quiet Watson sneezes, and the spell is broken.

"Nicky's lost her key," says Madeleine.

"I know where it is." Stamping her waterlogged sneakers. "Which isn't helpful just now."

Diana blinks. "I keeled over"—she gestures toward the living room—"in front of the television. Old movies." A vague smile.

"C'mon, Watson," beckons Madeleine, retreating to her door.

As Nicky walks toward the stairs, she hears a little rainfall of quick clicks at her back: the dog is trailing her across the marble. "Wrong way, baby," she says, pointing to Madeleine. Watson considers her mistress, then drops her bottom to the floor, liquid eyes bulging.

Nicky glances at Madeleine. In the recess of the doorway, her shoulders are slumped, her arms dragging at her thighs. This is a woman in need of a dog.

Nicky crouches to scoop up Watson—"Back to bed with you"—and stands to find Madeleine's door closed and Diana vanished. For a moment she waits there, thinking sadly of her hostesses, wondering if she ought to offer tea or toast; instead, she begins her trek up to the attic, where she'll confirm to Aunt Julia her status among the living.

38

WHY HAD SHE SURRENDERED WATSON? Tonight of all nights?

"I'm lonely," says Madeleine, throat tight. Saying it to herself somehow feels much sadder than saying it to somebody else.

"I don't want to be lonely," she adds. Then she kills the bedside lamp as the storm torches the walls.

Cole used to steal into her room on nights like this, and she'd stage a little drama—rumbling and muttering, *oh come on*-ing—before rolling back the blankets. In the morning, she'd complain at breakfast and vow to lock her door forever after.

Sebastian: "Don't leave your room, Cole."

Hope: "Don't be a bitch, Mad."

"I wish I'd been better to you," whispers Madeleine, so quiet it sounds more like a thought. She wishes Watson were lumped beneath her sheets, not upstairs with—

—*l'usurpateuse*. She hasn't told Cole about Nicky, has she? The girl their father is . . . well, using, isn't he? Manipulating? To *shape his legacy* or something?

In the dark, Madeleine frowns. She hadn't known that's what she was thinking. Yet it's true. Partly true, at least. Why else would he allow anyone to sift through the past?

Cole ought to know about this.

She taps her phone awake. Attacks the keys with her thumbs, as balloons swollen with text float up the screen. Tells him about their guest, her assignment, how Sebastian has installed her in the attic—Cole's attic—like a boarder. How she's stirring up the past without even meaning to.

And he INVITED her here

I think she should leave

After a minute, Madeleine glances at her phone. Dark and dreaming. She peers through the gloom at the framed illustration above her dresser, the blown-up German postcard: a sepia-toned young woman, illustrated from behind, a thin band around her throat and a tumble of hair down her back and a white cap atop her head. YOU SEE MY WIFE . . . BUT WHERE IS MY MOTHER-IN-LAW? wonders the text below. Adjust your vision, Madeleine knows, and you can locate the fugitive matron in the same image, in the same body, the daughter's fragile cheek now the mother's fleshy nose, that band at the girl's neck suddenly the grin of a crone, a smile like a slit.

Both women wear the same hat. Madeleine has always liked that. She and her own mother could never share clothes: different sizes, different styles.

When light tints her eyelids, she glances toward the window—but it's her phone glowing.

Name?

Nicky Hunter

His next text is Nicky's faculty headshot. She looks sunny and bookish and not at all like she's about to make Madeleine's life very uncomfortable.

She smiles a lot in person too

What's she like? What's he telling her?

His greatest hits as far as I can tell

A pause.

Then let her stay

Keep your enemies close etc

Is she an enemy?

Depends

Why would he invite an
enemy to live here?

Dad loves games remember

Maybe this is all a game
for him.

Monday, June 22

39

NICKY THRUSTS THE JOURNAL beneath the sheets, cuts her eyes to *A Child*. "Come in."

A Child watches expectantly.

The door opens, and Sebastian fills the entrance. For the first time since her arrival, he isn't wearing a suit; today it's a mohair sweater in pale lilac, gray collar at his neck, gray cuffs rucked elbow-high. Trousers, white flannel, and boots, sturdy leather. Stripped of his pocketwatch and necktie, his lines and angles sanded and smoothed, he looks nearly mortal, somehow flesh-and-blood.

"May I enter?" he asks as he enters. "You don't lock your door, I see."

"Should I?"

He shrugs, advancing slowly through the slanted light of the dormers, appraising his museum exhibits. Nicky watches his slideshow face—the smiles, the squints, the occasional blank stare—and when he approaches the lineup of Watsons past, he laughs in delight.

"Each time I visited a new country," he says, "I felt sure I'd never be lucky enough to return. So I shipped mementos back home. That octopus was a challenge. Did one of you just grunt?"

Nicky points a finger at Watson present, sitting at the foot of the bed.

Sebastian moves to the dog, grasps her paws with two hands as she rears to greet him; they begin to dance an unwieldy waltz. "Today I'm taking you someplace amazing," he tells Nicky. "As promised."

Strange to find herself alone in a bedroom—Cole Trapp's bedroom, no less—with the man. As though he's a parent rousing his child for school. But now she recalls the words she just read, written in that same shambling script, even if Cole no longer dots his *i*'s with stars: *I feel like I am being punished. I want to hide.*

Cole is hidden now, pressed shut and buried under a snowdrift of white linens. She'll keep him safe.

"I," says Sebastian, attempting to dip the dog, "have come up here to *cherchez la femme*." He scoops Watson from the bed, strides to the door, his voice streaming behind him like a banner. "We set sail in ten. Dress warm." And then, framed in the doorway, he turns. "I do hope you feel at home with us," he says.

"I promise I won't overstay my welcome."

Sebastian melts into the shadows of the staircase. "Stay as long as you like," he calls. "Die here."

40.

He treats Nicky to "the scenic route," curving the Jaguar through the wilderness of the Presidio, beneath Monterey pines walling them in on either side; they snake past vacant military barracks and a cemetery and what once was a derelict airfield, rehabilitated in the nineties as a sprawling park. "Hope was on the committee," he adds. "A real do-gooder, my wife."

Up a hill, crowned with a beaux arts palace—the Legion of Honor, he tells her, a fine-arts museum—and then down again, another tunnel of trees, the road ahead of them clear as a bowling lane. "Just you and I," he says as his window slides down, "out here at the north-westernmost ends of the earth. No cares . . ." The breeze whips his hair. "No worries . . ."

"No witnesses," says Nicky.

Sebastian pauses, then laughs, and they coast into a desolate parking lot, past a weathered wooden sign: LANDS END.

"When I took my children here, we'd stash the car in a hiding spot by the Legion. But I fancy a little wander along the beach today." He kills the engine, rolls a peach into Nicky's hand. "Breakfast is served."

When Nicky exits the car, distant thunder rumbles in her ears: the sea, just beyond a tall fence of pines at the edge of the asphalt. "Listen to that slosh!" Sebastian sighs, slapping shut the driver's door and stretching his arms overhead. "Oh, to be a merman today."

He strikes out for the far end of the lot, and Nicky hurries after him. A white-dirt path leads them through the trees, the rasp of seawater ever louder, until finally Sebastian arrives at an overlook, where he rests his hands on the low wall.

Nicky catches up—and the scene beyond her guide erupts into view, sudden and vast, pushing forth to meet her even as she approaches. This is a slow-motion moment, she thinks: the ocean waves, chapped with sunlight, green-screen pristine; the scuffed clouds floating above them, plump enough to pinch; and below, just over the edge of the wall, a steep cascade of rock that topples into the boiling surf. All clear and sharp as though engraved.

Nicky and Sebastian stand in silence. Possibly they levitate, for all she knows.

A few moments later, when she sinks to earth, she wonders what he's thinking, his eyes narrowed against the sun and sea. Can he hear the ocean over the hiss of sand seeping through the hourglass? Would he gaze at that infinite sky and imagine his soul rising into it? Nicky isn't religious, but the moment feels almost holy.

Abruptly, he turns right, and she follows him along a path sign-posted COASTAL TRAIL. Perhaps she should scurry forward, walk by his side, but he's striding down the middle of the lane, with little room to right or left, and she'd rather not trot beside him like a terrier. Better to trot behind him, she reasons. Also like a terrier.

The man's paces are boundless.

Sea wind pushes the waves onto a fringe of rocky beach. Across the water, those same headlands that scrolled past her boat yester-day, and further east, the Golden Gate strung from coast to coast. Now and then, they pass a cypress swaying on the cliff, its branches flung wide as though desperate for rescue.

The path bends into a dense grove of pine and eucalyptus. The air cools, the light dims. Nicky shivers in her sweater. She senses that they're escaping from the present, retreating in time—years, decades, more.

Moments later, Sebastian turns left, where a flight of steps trickles down the bluff. They emerge into sunlight, the beach at their feet scattered with seaweed. Beyond the surf, hunched against the tide, boulders glisten.

Water is rolling up the bronze sand like a rug unfurled. Sebastian tugs off his shoes, hitching them from two fingers—"I shall wear the bottoms of my trousers rolled," he declares, walking north. After twenty minutes of silence, the words sound like a new language.

Nicky steers herself between him and the sea. "Can you swim?" he asks.

Why does he want to know? She casts a glance over her shoulder. "I sure can."

"Well, let's hope it doesn't come to that. Your phone won't work here," he adds as she taps her screen.

"Just checking how cold the water is." She's checking for reception.

"Never colder than in June."

Nicky slides the phone back into her pocket. Why has he brought her here?

They proceed, Sebastian marching confidently ahead, the soles of Nicky's sneakers slipping on stones. "Do you dare to eat a peach?" he asks, biting into his; as she dares, he starts to talk again, recalling how, in interviews past, he claimed that a boyhood love of military history had inspired his novels.

"The truth is a bit more personal. As the truth often is. My wife got me interested in postwar England. Her grandfather survived the Somme, though his leg didn't. And yet he came home jolly and relaxed, at peace with what was left of the world and of himself. No tinnitus, no shell shock, no night terrors.

"When Hope told me about him, I thought of the mystery novels I loved: how their veterans always seemed so well-adjusted, so sane, as though war had merely built character. Sometimes Poirot or Alan Grant or whoever would unmask one of these fellows as a killer— quite often, in fact—but even then, the murders were for profit. Rational, I mean. If murder's ever rational.

"Years later, I decided to set *Simon Says* in the early twenties, when the world—or that world, anyway, the English world—was struggling to hide its wounds. And I cast a hero much like Hope's grandfather: a pleasant, chatty type, fancier than Grandpa Percy but still folksy, who—despite digging trenches and scarring himself on wire and watching friends explode—who made it back sound in mind and mostly sound in body." He pinches his left earlobe as Nicky pinches hers. Simon St. John's had been clipped by an enemy bullet.

"He couldn't be, though. Compos mentis. Not totally—not after what he'd witnessed. Hence his moods, the wild highs, the crushing lows. Hence the chats with his friend's ghost." Suddenly his arm wheels, once, twice, and for an instant Nicky knows he's going to strike her; then he looses the peach pit over her head, into the sky. She watches it float above the water. If it lands, she doesn't see it.

"I thought—and I think I thought rightly—that escapist readers might reject a psychological mystery," says Sebastian. "Too grim. So we played up the historical angle and smuggled the psychology in undercover." Sweeping his heel along the beach, gouging a furrow in the smooth sand. "We say 'She's full of heart' or 'He's got guts,' but the fact is, most of us are made of not a little scar tissue. I'm interested in the wounds a person keeps secret. Even the madness. Why do we hide them?"

"Why would we show them?"

He looks down at her, but without her sunglasses, she must squint. "What secrets might you be hiding, young Hunter?" His voice is inviting.

She laughs. "I dance alone in my bedroom all the time. I hid an injured pigeon in my apartment for three weeks while it recovered, against building rules. I'm not interesting enough to have real secrets."

As he leads her up a scrubby hill, his shadow spilling from his heels, she senses she's disappointed him. At the top of the trail, they rejoin the cliffside path and stand together.

"I can't have children." She's surprised herself; it's more than she meant to say. But she'd like him to know. Or at least she doesn't mind if he knows. "And that's a little sad for me, because I—because there's enough about me that I like that I'd want to give it to another person. A friend of mine is in the same boat, so she and her husband are adopting. I'd like to meet someone first, but I don't need to. I like my life. Sometimes I feel I should keep *that* secret: I like my life, I've got few complaints."

Suddenly Nicky feels shy. But then Sebastian nods, smiles kindly at her. "If childbirth is all you miss out on in your life, then you can die happy."

The breeze blows her hair across her face. She looks at the sea, at the slope dropping away behind her. A slip could break a person's neck.

A push could break a person's neck.

She turns back to Sebastian, who still wears a faint grin.

"Your secrets are safe with me," he says, and turns away.

She exhales, follows him down a slope toward a broad, flat bluff bulging into thin air, a shelf of grit and loose stones. Beyond and below booms the dark sea.

Until suddenly it fades. The wind holds its breath. Clouds scuttle across the sun. A labyrinth appears before them.

Seven concentric circles radiate across the ground, each a hoop of rocks, the outermost skirting the very edge of the bluff; within the rings, byways and blind alleys swirl around a vacant center. Fifty feet wide, its routes just broad enough to navigate on foot. The rocks rise only a few inches, but to Nicky, they seem almost forbidding.

"Didn't I say this place would a-maze you?" he cries as the ocean recovers its voice.

Nicky grimaces (dad jokes sound misshapen in Sebastian Trapp's mouth), stops at the first ring. "Madeleine and I used to go sunrising here. Our little daddy-daughter ritual. Arrive before dawn, doughnuts and coffee."

"Why here?"

"What place could be more interesting than a maze?" Thrusting a finger straight ahead. "I proposed to Hope right there in the bull's-eye. One evening in the winter of seventy-six. Hours later, some drunk college kids chucked every last stone into the sea."

He lifts a foot, ready to swing it into the labyrinth; then he sets it down again.

"Been rebuilt over and over since then. Different map every time, different number of circles. Some years after that, my wife and I returned. And there"—the center of the maze again—"we made Cole."

Nicky blinks. "You made—"

"April of eighty-five. Some advice, young Hunter: Don't get naked here in April. Of any year."

She steps over the stone perimeter and into the seventh circle. Glances both ways. Slowly walks clockwise, face turned to the sea. Outside the circle, Sebastian walks with her.

"Made in a maze," he says to her back. "Was Cole. Although he never much liked it here. Too much drama, too many . . . elements, I suppose. He liked the house. Liked hide-and-seek. He *loved* Fort Point.

Over yonder," he adds, pointing northeast, to the Golden Gate. "Just beneath the bridge on the south side. Old military outpost, never used. Then or now. Good place to stumble upon a body, I always said."

Nicky dead-ends against a row of rocks, quarter-turns into the next ring, proceeds in the opposite direction. Sebastian keeps pace just beyond the circle, like an animal unwilling to cross a line of fire. Is this why they're here, at the point of origin? Is this where he feels closest to the wife and child he lost? She halts, frowns at a stubby light-house poking from the waves.

"What else did Cole like?" she asks.

At her back, Sebastian sighs. "Oh—long weekends traveling with his mother, I remember. Every few months, they'd drive to Disney-land, or Yellowstone, or take the train anywhere they pleased. Neither of 'em cared for planes."

Nicky has read about these trips in Cole's postcards. "I can't fly with-out sedatives," she says.

"Well, thank you for toughing it out all the way to California. So what do you suppose happened to my son and his mother?"

It's like hearing him cock a gun. She tries to think.

"Do—you know?" she replies, speaking to the water.

"If I knew, would I ask?"

"If you knew, would you say?"

"Depends what, exactly, I knew."

"We're talking in circles."

"You're *standing* in circles."

Nicky breathes deep, looks at the edge of the cliff, the plummet to the sea.

And then she remembers Isaac's words: *Someone very dangerous could be standing right behind you.*

She whips around. Sebastian's eyes are shut, his head tilted back, the wind blurring his hair; he smiles at the sky, hands slid into his pockets. "I told you that I nearly died, you'll recall. More than once. More than twice."

Nicky exhales. He's packed the game away for now.

Sebastian begins to walk, unseeing but surefooted, hugging the rim of the maze. "Before my mother died, I had never felt unhappy—

not *really* unhappy. Even my dreams were sweet. For a long while afterward, too. Then one night years later—" He waits for the waves to retreat. "I climbed into bed and found myself in a forest clearing. I'd never visited this place, in dreams or in life: bare white birches, a rug of brown leaves on the ground. In the corner of my eye, something flickered."

He stops. His eyes quicken beneath the lids.

"I turned"—he turns—"but it was gone." His boots stay in place as he steps blindly into the past. "But a few seconds later, I saw it again, just its bushy tail. And then I heard the snicker-snack at my back. I twisted round and round: between the trees I glimpsed golden eyes— six of them, a dozen, a score, then more—and stalking legs, a low whirl of sleek dark smoke circling the glade. And all the while the leaves biting, biting underfoot. As though the forest were gnashing its teeth.

"The smoke thinned. The wolves were emerging from the woods, eyes brilliant, coats black. They had surrounded me, and now slowly they closed in, like a knot drawing tight. My breath dragged in my throat. I stepped backward, stumbled. As I struggled to my feet, a chorus of soft growls echoed in the clearing. Yet now I sensed that the wolves were looking not at but beyond me, and when I spun around I tripped again—this time over a body on the forest floor."

Sebastian pauses. His eyes remain closed.

"The skin was pale, the uniform was filthy, and the hole at the back of the skull unexpected, but I recognized him. Of course I did: he was my father."

Nicky's eyes are wide open.

"Before I could listen for his breath, before I could shake him awake, the wolves surged past me in a rush of fur and fangs and swarmed him." At last Sebastian looks at her, sadly. "Then I awoke. I lay there, my heart detonating in my chest. I plucked wolf hairs from my sheets. And later, while I stood in the shower trying to scrub the night away, trying to cheer myself up with a song, the Sergeant ate a bullet for breakfast."

Down tips his head, slightly, as he retraces his steps. She walks beside him.

"You dreamed your father's death before it happened?"

A shrug. "I don't go in for that sort of thing, but—it would appear so. And then, night after night, I dreamed of wolves. Watched them pick clean the body on the ground. Each time I woke up in a blacker mood. Exactly one year after the Sergeant discharged himself, alone in my tiny Tenderloin apartment, I slipped a trash bag over my head.

"As the air thinned, I remembered a story I'd heard about a man discovered hanging in his basement with a frenzy of fingernail scratches at his throat. I clawed my way to air after forty seconds, I suppose. Vowed never to try again. Tried again four months later: another bag, then pills and whiskey, then . . ." A sigh. "After I met my wife, I stopped dreaming for a while. The night of Maddy's second birthday, she found me in our garage with a hose plugged into the station-wagon exhaust."

He squints past her. Nicky turns to see a distant yacht battling the waves.

"She'd seen me low. Seen me high, too. Seen me talk in a blur, laugh and lie and lash out. Dazzle and bore, charm and annoy. Head foamy as beer. Reckon with the hangover in the morning. But after the garage, she frog-marched me to a psychiatrist who prescribed lithium. And I vowed to her that, for the sake of our daughter, I would never take my life. She forced me to swear at knifepoint, which sent a confusing message."

Nicky faces him again. "And if it's been a hell of a life," he says, "at least I won't end up like that corpse on the forest floor. A hole in my skull and my child beside me."

He's seesawing one foot atop a rock, as though still forbidden entry. "Yet almost every day I hear the wolves. In my waking hours, I mean. A mutter in the hall, or claws grazing the stairs. Perhaps a dry red tongue lapping at the pond. Some mornings, I swear I wake up with teeth marks on my throat. There's a leader of the pack, a massive brute curled up beside the fireplace in my head. My head resembles my library," he explains, "all bright colors and deep shadows. And weapons. And that eternal fire burning in the grate." He gazes at the sea. "That's where the wolf king lies, waiting. Waiting and hoping."

Wind hurries past. "'All human wisdom,'" says Sebastian, "'is summed up in these two words: wait and hope.' *Monte Cristo.* One of my favorites. The original psychological thriller, I'd say. The gamesmanship! 'Do your worst, for I will do mine'—imagine saying that to someone!"

"Imagine hearing it," replies Nicky.

He smiles at her, one eye crinkled against the clouds. She looks at him across a trio of tiny mountain ranges. Behind her, waves thrash the cliff; behind him, wind rakes dust over the ground; yet the air between Nicky and the dying man seems curiously still.

"Your wife and son," she says carefully. "You said—at the end of our first talk, you said that we could solve a mystery together."

"I said we *might.* And I said a mystery *or two.* I never forget my own dialogue."

"Any theories?"

Again he looks at the crease of the horizon. "You're not making this easy, are you, Miss Hunter?"

Suddenly Nicky wonders if he'll ever return to Lands End—if, here and now, Sebastian Trapp is saying goodbye to the sea, and to the cypress trees, and to the born-again (and again, and again) labyrinth coiled at the brink of a cliff, where both his marriage and his son began. Perhaps this is why she's here today: as witness to his leave-taking. And suddenly she hears herself asking:

"Do you think they're still alive?"

Maybe the rising wind blew the words away, over the bluff and out to the ocean, where someday they might float into the ear of a passing mariner; or maybe Sebastian is barefoot on the beach a quarter century ago, or weaving through the labyrinth in 1976; or perhaps he's deciding whether to piss before they head back to Pacific Heights. Whatever the reason, he simply peers beyond her.

Finally she turns away, to watch those dark swells froth and charge like horses.

"I wait and hope," says Sebastian.

41

ALL MORNING LONG, Madeleine monitors her phone like it's a pulse. Four hours at the library: no Cole. Home by lunchtime: no Cole. She unwinds her noose of pearls, swaps her shapeless dress for a shapeless robe, inspects tonight's party gown, a wine-red wrap (in case she spills red wine). Twists the tub faucet. Water rushes.

Then she twists the faucet the other way.

In the foyer, caterers assemble cocktail bars and a fondue station and, by the stairs, a pyramid of champagne flutes. Madeleine ignores the caterers; they ignore Madeleine.

She enters the den. Warily, she approaches the VCR as though it's a beast in chains. Waits for it to thrash free of its cables, to roar at her through its flap.

It appears to be sleeping. She pulls open the drawer beneath.

Madeleine hasn't viewed these tapes since . . . ever, probably; her parents were not instinctive documentarians. She scans the labels on the cassettes ranked against one side of the drawer. *Cole at zoo. Mad tennis 96 & COOKING.* Birthdays and anniversaries and random dates.

But not the date she's looking for.

December 31, 1999.

Would they have filmed it?

Prom 97. HT Surprise 45 1994. No, nothing else to see here, save the camcorder itself, the size of a station wagon. A red eject button bulges from the cassette hatch.

Madeleine swallows.

Pushes the button. The hatch springs open.

Lodged within is a tape. No label.

But she can guess what's inside, printed on its film, furled around its reels, long forgotten. She pries the tape free and feeds it to the VCR. The machine clears its throat. Madeleine steps back from the television.

Again the family is assembled in the dining room, candles tipped with steady flames, voices mutilating "Happy Birthday"—but in this scene, the windows are tinted nighttime, and the seating arrangements have changed: Freddy is between his parents, both dressed to impress, with Sebastian across from them, suited and booted. At the head of the table sits Hope in a citrus-red jumpsuit, the bloody tint of ripe grapefruit, with Cole—still small, still blond—leaning against the arm of her chair like a handmaiden.

After the song expires, after Hope blows out a forest fire of candles atop a cake, the camera locates Isaac at the credenza, pouring Krug into a line of flutes. "Jam a spoon in the bottle, Isaac," calls Simone. "Keeps the champagne cold."

"I don't think that's true, Simone," sings Isaac pleasantly. He's wearing jeans and a denim jacket and wearing them well.

As the camera travels past a mirror, Madeleine glimpses Diana in an exercise leotard, aquamarine, and leg warmers, fuchsia. Impossibly, it's becoming.

New Year's Eve, 1999: The night of the eighties-themed warehouse party. The night the Trapps hosted their final jaw-dropping ball-dropping gala. The night two people disappeared.

"I'm back."

Madeleine spins around. Her father stands in the doorway, hair tousled, skin tinged pink. "What's this?" he asks.

As she gawks, her brother's voice pipes through the speakers: "Can Watson have a slice of cake?" Still soprano, age fourteen.

"I was . . ." Madeleine lets the sentence sink. To be approached by Sebastian Trapp—all six feet of him, and every last one of those spare five inches—is like watching a wave advance.

"Let Watson eat cake! Let us all eat cake!" he shouts, twenty years ago, as Cole scampers to the wall and flicks the light switch, while Hope cuts dessert and Isaac serves champagne and Freddy drains his glass before his mother can object. "Diana," Sebastian calls to the camera, "give that to Isaac. Let you eat cake."

Now he simply towers beside Madeleine, gazing at the television.

"Make way for the auteur," says Isaac. Then the lens wobbles, and Diana moves into frame, tugging a slim packet from her back pocket, and crouches beside Hope, who unwraps a red leather hip flask. She roars with laughter, unscrews the cap, shakes the flask above her open mouth. Cups the back of Diana's head as they hug.

This century's Sebastian leaves the living room. Madeleine continues to watch.

Just as Simone informs the table that their guests will arrive in "thirty-nine minutes, ladies and gentlemen," she hears footsteps behind her again, from the other entrance; Diana this time, dark beneath the eyes. She looks exhausted; she—is she wearing her shirt inside out?

Diana catches her breath. "This was the night . . ." Her voice wanders off. Madeleine doesn't go looking for it.

Instead, they observe as Cole arranges gifts before his mother like silverware. From Isaac, a copy of Kant; from the in-laws, a diaphanous shawl ("You're too pale for black," explains Simone, "but it was all they had"); from Cole, a murmured "Happy birthday" and a fine silver necklace, small pendant dangling from the chain ("Inscribed!" Hope marvels); from Freddy, a bottle of Diavolo by Antonio Banderas. "That's for men, son," notes his father, at which Freddy balks and insists that men don't wear perfume. "'Diavolo is a sensual dance to a wild and crazy tempo,'" he argues, reading the box.

Hope mists her neck with cologne, beams at her nephew. She drapes the shawl across her shoulders, fastens the necklace around her throat, tucks the flask into her cleavage, and pretends to read *Critique of Pure Reason* ("Epistemology forever, bitches!" hoots Isaac) as the family applauds.

"She wore that to the party, I remember," Diana says to Madeleine. "All of it. The shawl, the necklace. The cologne."

Hope turns to Cole, spritzes him with the sensual essence of Antonio Banderas. He sneezes. He offers her a red paper butterfly.

Now Madeleine's breath catches.

Hope oohs, and Isaac aahs, and Sebastian mutters, "Fucking hell," pinching the bridge of his nose. Nobody notices, or at least they pretend not to, as Hope flutters the fine-edged wings.

"Fucking *hell*." The chatter ceases as though unplugged.

"Is there more to that sentence, Basher?" asks Hope, kissing the butterfly to Cole's nose.

"In fact, there is. 'Fucking hell, fourteen-year-old boys don't make origami.'"

Cole says, quietly, "In Japan they do."

"Turn that off, Isaac," snaps Sebastian, glaring at the lens.

The camera descends to the tabletop and rolls onto one side, so that the family is rotated ninety degrees, like passengers on a capsized ship: Dominic, Simone, Freddy, and Diana at the bottom of the frame, Hope and Cole suspended in midair, with Sebastian spitting from the ceiling.

"Do you know why people don't like you, son? Because you're weak."

Hope guides the butterfly to Cole's palm. There it rests, quaking.

"You can't soldier through one night outdoors in a tent," says his father. "Halloween scares you. Thunder *terrifies* you. You can't throw, you can't swim—you can't even thumb-wrestle."

Dominic, calm: "Bash, let's—"

"Your boy doesn't play with colored paper." Sebastian, calmer still. "If you sent your boy a boomerang, he'd find a field and heave-ho, right, Fred? You wouldn't paint it with your sister's nail polish, I assume?"

The tilted room seems to darken. The flames of the candles claw at the air.

"I can sail," says Cole softly.

"Oh, yes—and what did they call you that day on the bay?" asks Sebastian, leaning forward. "Your classmates on the field trip—what name did they give you when you took the wheel?"

Cole stares at the butterfly in his hand. "The Pirate Queen."

Sebastian sighs. "Chaperoning a dozen kids on my own goddamn yacht, and they're calling my son . . ."

Isaac, Diana, the cousins—all aghast. Only Hope is studying Sebastian neutrally, cold and white as marble.

A tear drops from Cole's chin and onto the butterfly, tapping one wing.

"You won't make it through life this way, Cole." Fists on the table, fingers laced tight, a ridge of sharp knuckles flexing at his son. "So no more little-girl crafts. No more clutching at your mother's skirts. You can't keep chasing her forever. No more bubble baths, no more nightlight, no more crying." Cole hiccups. "What did I just—no more *crying*." He sits back, grasping his champagne.

Madeleine turns. Diana's perfect teeth are tugging at a thumbnail.

After a moment, Simone stands and raps her spoon against her flute so sharply that it shatters the crystal. The table jolts, electrocuted—even Cole's butterfly skydives to the floor—yet Hope and Sebastian simply lift their glasses and drink, long and slow, regarding each other coolly over the rims.

Simone blots her dress as Freddy informs her that "you've got Hulk strength."

"I don't know what that means, Frederick. I was just announcing—don't cut yourself, Isaac—that guests will arrive in half an hour."

Sebastian stands, smoothing his shirtfront. "Half an hour!" he calls, striding out of frame. "The show begins in T-minus thirty minutes!"

Madeleine wants to see how the room recovers, but just as Diana bends to speak to Cole, just as Hope starts to idly wind the necklace around her finger, Isaac glimpses the camera and scuttles offscreen. His fingers patter on the camera casing until the image cuts to black. A twenty-year black.

Madeleine shuts her eyes, presses her palms against her ears, eyes crumpled shut; she wants to aim words at her—their—father, loose a hail of arrows at him. Saint Sebastian.

She'd heard about a scene; Simone had mentioned it once, maybe Freddy, too—"Your dad really went off on Cole that night"—but her dad had really gone off on Cole plenty of times, so Madeleine paid no attention. Now she smears a hand across her cheek. Gulps down anger. Wonders how clearly Cole remembers this.

"I'd forgotten that." Diana's voice is low. "I watched a few tapes yesterday, but that—was very upsetting."

"Why were you watching them?"

Slowly Diana shakes her head. "At first just to see them again. Your mother. Your brother. I hadn't really counted on seeing your father. Not like *that*. I don't remember him that way. Even though I was—I was *there*." She points to the television. "Perhaps it got buried under the—all those years in between. But who . . ."

Madeleine waits. *But who speaks to his child like that,* maybe? *But who is your dad, really?*

Back at the thumbnail. "You've never fully solved somebody else, have you?" Diana says, slow, thoughtful. "A person can still surprise you. A person can remain a mystery." Then she turns to Madeleine, and her eyes sharpen, as though she's just remembered something. "What was in the mystery box?"

"What mystery box?"

"The box Freddy found outside. What was in it?"

The kiss had blown it clean from Madeleine's head. "A red butterfly," says Madeleine, folding her arms across her chest. "Origami. With writing on the wings. *Cherchez la femme.*"

Diana is silent.

"Dad says it's just a prank."

"Is that what he says?" answers Diana, and there's something unfamiliar in her tone.

Madeleine rubs her palms together as if she's trying to kindle a fire. "Kickoff at six thirty, I think? I'm going to take a nap and a bath and a Xanax. Before the show begins."

Soundlessly Diana leaves. Madeleine faces the blank television screen; then she fast-forwards until the cassette grinds and clicks. Minute after minute of darkness, a starless sky, her mother and her brother nowhere to be seen, lost in space.

Post-bath, pre-Xanax, she blow-dries her hair. Examines her soft jaw, her sloping shoulders ("Built like a linebacker," somebody once tittered). In the mirror, her eyes find the postcard illusion, the leering hag. For a moment she stares. But the woman refuses to transform.

The phone trembles on the sink. Madeleine drops her eyes. Drops the blow-dryer.

It writhes on the floor like a snake, propelling itself in circles at her feet, as she stares at the screen.

See you tonight.

42

"A MASKED BALL, EH?" says Irwin. "Lemme see the hardware."

"You mean the mask, right?"

"I don't *really* care about the dress. Unless you want me to. In which case I care deeply."

"You know I don't care either," says Nicky—although she cares more than she expected. Today Sebastian Trapp saw her windswept and sunlit; tonight she wants to impress.

The mask is a simple Lone Ranger in violet velvet, ribbon sash, eyes wide like Nicky's own. "Exactly what I would've chosen for myself," says Irwin. "Oh—nobody's heard from you in days. I told them you're only checking in with me because of the dog."

Nicky winces. "I'm sorry—please tell them I'm sorry. I'll tell them, too. It's a bit—it's overwhelming out here."

"Are you safe?" Suddenly he sounds very serious.

"I think so," she tells him.

"That's not quite good enough."

"Let's talk tomorrow. I've got to get back to work. I've got a mask to put on."

When they hang up, she returns to the diary.

Nineteen ninety-nine. Nicky speeds through Valentine's Day (*Someone put a card in my locker and inside was a pitcure of a pug, a pug is not a French bulldog you fools!!*), past a ski trip in March (*Dad told me to try a "black dimond" I fell and jammed my thumb*), before stepping into the shower. All April she blow-dries, as Cole tackles a novel that his father recommended, and on the final day of eighth grade, she pauses to zip herself into her dress.

In May:

> *Dad grabbed me today. He acidently dislocated my sholder so he took me to the hospital becase Mama was in Berkley. He did'nt tell me what to say so when the nurse asked I told her I fell playing scocer, I thoght dad would like that but he looked sad and said Im sorry and I said Im sorry too even thog I don't know why I was sorry.*

He quotes the book his father has assigned:

"I have suffered enugh surely. Have pity on me, and do ofr me what I am unable to do for myself!"

. . . and then, in small print below:

<u>*The Count Of Monte Cristo*</u>
(I will finish it)

Absently, Nicky pushes one foot into a new pump. By the next entry, Cole has recovered:

Something exiting is hapening!!

When she hears the knock—then "You decent?"—she snaps the diary shut, stows it beneath the pillow. Maybe Madeleine wouldn't recognize it; maybe she would. "Yup," she calls.

Madeleine steps in, hesitantly, red dress hugging her body, slender silver figure-eight mask hugging her face. Her arms are folded across her middle in a posture Nicky recognizes from that spell five years ago when she herself weighed too much for her size, just after her father died, just in time for wedding season. The grip of her gowns, the flush of her skin . . . She didn't like feeling that way, didn't like caring.

"Well, well," she says.

Madeleine takes a step back, defensive. "What's wrong?"

"Nothing at all. You look wonderful."

When Madeleine replies, her voice is small. "Please don't make fun of me."

She seems to have surprised herself. Nicky wants to hug her. "I mean it," she says, sitting up. "The dress, the hair—red and gold. Classic. You look classic." Madeleine dreads this party, she'd said as much, and nobody should feel bad about their looks.

Madeleine smooths the fabric at her hips. "Thank you."

Nicky smiles.

"I wanted . . ." Madeleine begins; then she pushes the mask onto her forehead.

Nicky watches her scan the room: the cracked floor mirror, the wheat-sheaf bundles of Zulu spears, the faux topiary in a copper tub. She pauses at the line of stuffed Watsons. "I can't actually recall when I last set foot in here," says Madeleine, sweeping her eyes across the bed, the desk, the paperbacks filed on the floor. "I was afraid it'd feel like . . . a tomb, I guess." Nicky waits politely.

"I remember that." A Victorian pram in greasy black satin, hood down. "When my brother was little, I'd wheel him around the house. And one day, as I was lugging him up the back stairs from the kitchen, I tripped, and—down went baby. Carriage and all."

Madeleine looks at the pram as if regarding an old foe. "It didn't tip over. Just bumped from step to step. So I chased it to the bottom, wondering where I could hide the body, and when I peeked inside . . ." She pauses; Madeleine has her father's flair for drama, thinks Nicky. "He was fine. No tears, no screams, even. He's tougher than I thought."

"Is?"

"Was." Madeleine coughs. "Dad asked me to summon you. Might be warm in long sleeves."

"Forecast calls for midfifties and fog."

"Got a mask?"

Nicky lifts it from the pillow, fits her bare foot into her shoe, follows Madeleine to the door.

They leave the attic, drop down, down into the dark. The staircase zigzags one story, then another, as below them sound rises like a tide, until they stand at the top of the grand steps, where string music bounds up to greet them like an eager dog.

The foyer shimmers white and gold, the marble floor bright as mirror. On a table by the stairs rises the champagne-glass pyramid—five square tiers, raked up to a single flute, bracing itself for the downpour but full now only of pink evening light. Already, guests stream in, women wearing summer-garden colors, purple and yellow and, on one lady, spectacularly ugly chameleon green; men in linen suits, white and dove gray and, on one gentleman, spectacularly ugly chameleon green. And the *masks*! A woman's face is a flock of doves; a man wears a plague-doctor beak, eyes round as spectacles. A skeletal creature in midnight blue, white crescent moon cradling her cheek; an elderly specimen waving a scrap of lace before her eyes; a guy in a rubber Reagan mask.

Caterers pilot hors d'oeuvre platters across the floor. Nicky, who hasn't eaten much today, is relieved to note that San Francisco's finest seem partial to egg rolls.

"When my parents hosted this, it was a cocktail party," says Madeleine. "Now it's *Eyes Wide Shut*. Thanks, Simone." She tugs her mask back in place. "Here we go."

Nicky lifts her own mask to her face and knots the ribbon behind her head—but she waits before trailing Madeleine down the stairs. Her breath is shallow; she feels as though her blood is circulating in reverse. *Something exiting is hapening!!* she thinks, as she takes a moment and takes a breath and takes a step.

43

"Barely a mask," her father says, tut-tut, when Madeleine finds him in the center of the foyer. His own is sky-blue silk, skirting the bridge of his nose, with spokes of gold erupting from the upper rim. The crown of a sun god.

"My mask has nothing to prove," she replies. "It's confident in its body, and it plays by its own rules. Same with hers." Nicky has joined them.

"Well, welcome to *la fête*. That one of Maddy's?" Eyeing Nicky's dress.

Madeleine sighs. "Yes, Dad. From when I was eighty pounds lighter and a foot shorter." She whisks two champagne glasses from a passing waiter, hands one to Nicky. "Where's our hostess? And where's Freddy?" Mustn't forget Freddy, manhandler of wives.

Her father tugs the pocketwatch from his waistcoat as a waitress presents hors d'oeuvres. "Not seen Fred. Perhaps—why, thank you— perhaps I'll hunt down Diana in a moment. This suit is tighter than a Chinese finger trap." Jamming a finger beneath his collar.

He appears healthy, Madeleine decides as he chews a date wrapped in bacon; his skin is kissed a faint pink, and his hair surges back from his forehead in a full wave. (Will he need a trim before the end?) His suit is linen, soft gray. He wears socks but no shoes.

"Couldn't find my bloody cufflinks. Literally bloody. Shaped like tiny droplets of gore. Seen 'em around?"

"No," answers Nicky dutifully.

Madeleine scans the room. "Anybody interesting here?" Ninety guests already, two hundred more expected.

And one rather unexpected.

Sebastian tips his head. "Interesting how?"

"Like—anybody new."

He chews. "Miss Hunter's new. Miss Hunter's interesting."

Madeleine glances at Miss Hunter, who seems unsure how to look interesting mid–cheeseburger slider.

"Are you waiting for someone, daughter mine?"

But suddenly the pocketwatch tumbles through his fingers, jerking and twisting below his hip like a man dropped from the gallows. Sebastian stares. Madeleine and Nicky turn together.

Across the lake of marble, at the summit of the staircase, beneath the family portrait, stands a woman in sunset red—so vibrant it dims the lights behind her, eclipses the painting between them. She presses her hands against her hips, then—carefully, as if unaccustomed to moving this way—she descends the staircase, gown luffing at the hem, hair loose around her shoulders.

Bodies drift across Madeleine's vision like tropical fish; through the wash, she tracks Diana down the steps. And when finally she sets foot on the floor, a hush muffles the room.

Her stepmother is a very beautiful woman. A very beautiful woman also wearing red. Madeleine wonders if she should change clothes, or just hide.

Now Diana draws closer, flickering barefaced among the guests, until at last she arrives. She appears dazed.

"You're a vision, dear wife," her husband says. "Matchless. Maskless."

Diana pats her cheeks with both hands. "I forgot it upstairs," she frets.

"Why cover up that face?" asks Sebastian.

Madeleine turns away. Who will visit the house this evening, stroll past her bedroom door? The parents of her former friends? ("Poor Madeleine—life hasn't quite worked out, I suppose.") The friends themselves? ("Tell her she looks gorgeous. I *know*, but tell her.") Strangers? ("Oh—there's the daughter. Lives at home. Possibly lesbian.") They'll say much the same, presumably, a few months from now at the funeral.

See you tonight. Will she recognize him? Will anybody? What does he want? And—here Madeleine brakes to a stop, eyes wide—what will her *father* do if Cole appears?

"You okay?" asks Nicky. Madeleine feels grateful; then Madeleine feels angry. And now she sees her aunt bearing down on them, black dress and silver jewels.

Madeleine swigs her champagne, wipes her hand across her lips. "I wonder if they're serving beer," she informs nobody in particular, and plunges into the crowd before her aunt can reach them.

44

NICKY WATCHES MADELEINE ESCAPE. "Now, where *is* that girl stalking off to?" calls Simone. "Oh—and Nicky is still here," she adds, as though Nicky were a stubborn stain.

"The house is more interesting with her in it, I find." Sebastian turns to his wife. "Don't you, bride?"

Diana nods, vaguely, pushing her hair from her eyes.

"They sent me the wrong mask." Simone is glaring. "I ordered a very colorful *Thalia*—muse of comedy, you know, the laughing mask—to pair with a black dress. Do you follow me? I didn't want the *body* to upstage the *face*. But they sent me an alabaster *Medusa*. Just this hideous white woman *screaming*, with an orgy of snakes writhing on top. If I wear it, I look demented, but without it, in just plain black, I look like a widow. An *indignant* one. Do you understand?"

"I understand," Nicky assures her, because no one else is doing so.

"I stole a few sparkly *relics* from one of the spare rooms." She waves her fingers, hands hovering over her chest, her ears. "And from Madeleine's. Like a cat burglar. Is that why she's in a huff? Perfume, too. Something called French Lover. Which reminds me: whatever happened to Jean-Luc?"

Who? wonders Nicky. "Who?" asks Sebastian.

"Jean-Luc. The architect."

"You know, from France." Freddy has materialized behind his mother like a time-traveler from a later hour: his eyes are glazed, dark hammocks slung beneath them. Long day, Nicky guesses. Long weekend, even. "Plays guitar in a band. Kite-surfs. Right, Simone?"

"He's vegetari—never mind. What's wrong with Madeleine tonight? Why was she crying?"

Crying? wonders Nicky. "Crying?" asks Sebastian.

"I spotted her through her bathroom window not half an hour ago. Wandering through that useless maze, drinking and smoking and sniffling. I hope that's not a typical Monday evening for *you*, Frederick."

"No, my backyard maze is being redesigned at present."

Sebastian's eyes roam the room. "Leave Madeleine to me." He turns to his wife. "And you—you're positively ablaze, darling."

Diana glances across the foyer at the grandfather clock, looming above the string quartet like a stern maestro. "Oh, fine," she answers tersely when Freddy asks her if all is well—but then, tilting back her lovely throat, she murmurs in her husband's ear, "Sebastian—"

His name echoes behind Nicky, then to one side, then to the other: strangers are spouting through the front door in flood, streaming toward their host.

Hurriedly Simone briefs the family. "Her husband was crushed by a whorehouse vending machine on *Christmas Eve,* so whatever you do, don't mention Christmas, or vending machines, or whorehouses— well, I'd say there are plenty of other things you could talk about, Frederick—and that's Pam Dolara; everybody likes her, which seems suspicious . . ."

Diana paws helplessly at her husband's shoulder. "Sebastian . . ."

"Darling, won't you chaperone Nicky here? Might be some good copy in this lot. Just look at 'em! The madness of crowds."

And as the newcomers throng around Sebastian, fastening themselves to him until he's a magnet feathery with iron filings, he catches Nicky watching and winks at her.

She senses that a curtain is rising. Ladies and gentlemen, please take your seats. Act 2 is about to begin.

45

MADELEINE HAS STATIONED HERSELF by the string quartet, strangling a bottle of Hoegaarden in either hand; the racket here should discourage well-wishers. From behind her mask she glares at the guests pouring in gouts through the distant front door, glares at the caterers who approach her with finger food, glares at the stepmother who can stop time just by flowing down some steps.

Strolling toward Madeleine on tasseled loafers is a man like a golden retriever, blond and shaggy and visibly eager to please; years ago, every time they slept together, she had to resist the urge to tell him he was a good boy.

"Beer o'clock already?" asks Benjamin Bentley the Second. She offers her cheek, mostly to keep his mouth busy. "How's the ol' dude?"

"Oh, you know the ol' dude—tough nut to crack."

"Runs in the family." Chuckling. "I'm always telling Biss, Maddy Trapp should come with a manual."

"Like you could read it without pictures," she replies. He chuckles again.

As Ben updates her on married life, Madeleine resumes surveillance, scouting the roily crowd like a whale-watcher on deck. Maybe Cole isn't blond anymore. Perhaps he's filled out, shot up; taken those growth hormones, even. She bites her lip.

Ben pries a bottle from her grip and swigs, placing a brotherly hand on her shoulder. "Mad, you need a man."

"First time for everyth—" Then she sees, cruising toward her, exactly that: a man—angular, pale, not too tall, Zorro mask, tousled hair.

Tousled, toasted-blond hair. Watson cradled in his arms.

Madeleine steps forward.

Suddenly, Freddy, harasser of stepmothers, bursts from the scrum. "My buddy here saved the dog from certain doom!" he squeals, wild-eyed.

The stranger smiles. "Spotted her chasing a meatball under-foot." Crisp English accent. "I've picked up worse at parties."

Freddy makes introductions as Madeleine inspects Jonathan Grant—the steep cliff of his brow, the curve of his lips. The pale blue eyes. "You're British?" she asks.

Swallowing champagne. "It is my curse."

"What brings you—oh, you can set her on the floor."

"Really? Looks dangerous down there."

"Then she dies doing what she loves. What brings you to San Francisco?"

Freddy answers for him. "He came out here a couple months ago to find himself."

"To eat, to pray, to love," agrees Jonathan.

"A little young for a midlife crisis." Madeleine smiles tightly at him. "Are you even thirty-five?"

"So where's Nicky?" asks Freddy, clapping his hands. "Jonathan's girlfriend, you know."

"Nothing of the sort," mutters Jonathan.

"You took her *sailing*—"

Madeleine frowns. In order to take Nicky sailing, you'd have to notice her first.

"—so you won't mind chatting with my fetching cousin here while I show your non-girlfriend what she's missing?"

He grins, Jonathan flushes, Ben gulps his beer, and Madeleine reflects that the accent would be a bold touch indeed.

As DIANA LEADS HER across the foyer, Nicky hears words hiss through the air like arrows, feels them quiver in her back:

Stranger.

Stories.

Dying.

"Have you seen any butterflies about?"

Diana has turned to face her, the skin beneath those lovely eyes a bit dark. "Well—several," Nicky says. "In Sebastian's desk, on the wallpaper in the—"

"Butterflies in boxes. Freddy found a box at the front door, and inside was a red . . ." Nicky watches the sentence float away. Diana is not herself.

"Butterfly?" she suggests.

"*Cherchez la femme* written on the wings."

A shiver drags itself up Nicky's spine, places its hands on her shoulders.

Diana bites her lip. "Sebastian says it's a prank."

Writer.

Attic.

Disappeared.

A champagne flute appears in Diana's hand. "Are you learning lots about Sebastian Trapp?" she asks.

"Sure. He's quite a guy."

Diana nods, as though Nicky hasn't yet supplied the correct answer.

"And his stories are just—well, just like his books. Very engaging. Full of surprises."

"I find he continues to surprise."

The crowd jostles, and Nicky and Diana with it, so that Diana's mouth is suddenly at Nicky's ear.

"I told you I couldn't imagine him doing violence to another person. You remember? I said so right before we watched that football game. Well, I've watched a lot since, too, and it was violent. Not bruises and blood, but brutal all the same."

Then she steps back—she's said too much, Nicky sees. "Let's find someone for you to talk to," says Diana, slipping through a crack in the crowd.

Widow.

Wife.

Murder.

Dollface!

This from a man in a glowering kabuki mask who has clamped a hand on Nicky's shoulder. "Saw you at the Baron last week, didn't I? You're the little lady writing—"

"Yes." She searches the crowd, catches a jewel-red glimmer.

"Dangerous assignment! Now, I've got some *information* . . ."

A tray of glasses crashes to the floor; a wave of guests crashes through the door. When Nicky glances back, Diana has been swept away.

MADELEINE IS CASUALLY INTERROGATING Jonathan Grant.

Previous residence? "London."

Current residence? "Dolores Park."

Profession? "None at present."

Previous profession? "Finance."

Connections to San Francisco? "None." ("Aw—you got *me*, bud," says Freddy, who then leaves.)

Family life? "Only child." Is he fidgeting?

Favorite film? *"The Lady Vanishes."* He smiles mildly.

. . . And you know Nicky how? "We've *met*. At Fred's. Sailed the bay at the weekend. Do you sail?"

Used to. Where's home? "Lyme Regis. Dorset coast. But I've scrubbed away my West Country accent."

"My mother was from Dorset," says Madeleine.

"Ooh arr!" He grins.

"You two getting to know each other?" Ben, faintly lewd.

"Well, Madeleine's getting to know *me*," says Jonathan pleasantly, adjusting his mask.

"Give me your number," she blurts.

"Down, girl!" says Ben.

"No, I meant—I'd like . . ." *I'd like to know more.* "I'm hosting a party for Fred next month. It's the last thing she would do right now."

"What? His birthday's in May, same as mine."

"Shut up, Ben. It's not a birth—I'm inviting his friends. You're not invited."

"If you're inviting Fred's friends," says Jonathan, tapping in his number.

A nymph flits into the circle, skin rose gold against a green dress. Madeleine feels fucking enormous. "Twice in one week!" says Bissie, offering Jonathan a nice-to-not-meet-you wave as he excuses himself. "Madeleine, you are the most gorgeous hostess." Lifting her glass.

Madeleine's phone shivers.

"To Madeleine . . ." says Bissie.

"To Madeleine," says Ben.

Madeleine smiles weakly, sips her Hoegaarden. Glances at her phone.

> Don't look so nervous.

> And don't look for me.

When the bottle smashes on the floor, the music falls silent, and for a moment all she can hear are the suds hissing and popping amid the wreckage.

EVERYONE BELIEVES HE KILLED THEM.

In the furious hive of the foyer, amid the butterflies scattered across the parlor walls, by the hedge maze outside—wherever Nicky floats, gathering stories, Sebastian Trapp's guests pronounce the same verdict.

Three starchy gentlemen recall his misadventures at the Baron's forest retreat—the night a former senator loosed an arrow into his shoulder; the weekend he nursed a sickly fawn back to health, even though "most of us wanted to eat it"—before adding, "Course, Basher's got a temper, as we know." (What do they mean? "Why, nothing at all!")

A nonagenarian librarian, balding like a dandelion: "Even if he did get rid of that busybody wife of his," she tells Nicky, "I'm sure he had his reasons. No, I don't know what his reasons *were,* I'm just sure he had them."

A classical composer: "What bothers me about Trapp, you ask?" Nicky had not asked. "It isn't the murders he committed. It's his damn quotes! Oh, he cites his sources. But I don't want to know what Sherlock Holmes thought! I want to know what *Sebastian Trapp* thinks!"

"'A quotation for everything saves original thinking,'" observes Nicky.

"Beautifully said!"

"Dorothy Sayers said it. What were you saying about the murders?"

A pet psychologist recalls how, at the New Year's Eve party in 1999, Sebastian seemed distracted. "Planning for later, maybe," she muses. "Has he, like, said anything to you? About killing anybody? Definitely let me know if he does."

A Portuguese architect scoffs. "Gossips everywhere. There is an expression: moral indignation is envy with a halo." He sips champagne. "And he is not well, I understand?"

Nicky turns to behold Sebastian the sun king, heliocentric, a universe of hangers-on swirling around him. "He isn't," she replies. "What was it you said? Moral indignation—"

"—envy with a halo, yes. Although obviously he killed them."

THE KITCHEN: plates clash, faucets gush, Madeleine shakes shards of glass into the recycling bin. The caterers ignore her.

She slumps in the window seat. Gazes through the mesh screen at the moonlit maze, its silver leaves, its sunless sundial.

Now that he's here, beneath this roof, between these walls, Madeleine feels suddenly wary of Cole, as though she has summoned a dark genie of powers unknown. He could be anywhere, this ghost of a ghost. He could be anyone.

She says Jonathan's name, tastes it, swishes it in her mouth like it's wine. Who knows how Cole might have transformed? The last time she saw him, puberty hadn't even speckled his face with pimples, fuzzed his chin or legs. Besides, why should he rely solely on time for camouflage? He could dye his hair, grow a beard . . .

". . . lady over there talkin' to herself." A member of the waitstaff is amused. Madeleine less so: she is now a woman in a window, mouthing silent questions, a lady over there talkin' to herself.

THE EVENING SPINS like a roulette wheel, Nicky slotting into one conversation after another with varying degrees of luck. At some point, she sees that Madeleine has disappeared from her post by the strings; from time to time, Diana treks across the foyer, refreshes herself at the bar. And in the center of the room,

Sebastian is a popped bottle of champagne, fizzing and sparkling and overflowing.

Just as the clock strikes ten, two fingers tap-dance on Nicky's shoulder. She turns to find Lionel Lightfoot, his backside bulging into the crowd with such prominence that other guests must curve their paths around him.

"Good eveni—yes, hello, you—good evening, Miss Hunter. Now"—Lionel swings his bulk to one side—"I'd like to *introduce* you to someone. Really *interesting* fellow. A *colleague* of sorts. Where did he . . ."

"Mr. Lightfoot!" A young man, fair and rail-thin, approaches with one arm aloft, fingers balancing a martini glass. "Mr. Lightfoot!" Edging forward.

When Simone barges past him, the glass empties onto his head, a tiny waterfall, the olive on its toothpick washed over the edge like a doomed rafter. Lionel extends his beefy hand in greeting, but she swats it away.

"*Dear* Simone," says Lionel, "your guests are not *flowers*. You needn't *water* them."

"*How dare—*"

"*Diana* invited me—me and my *friend* here, now wringing gin from his *hair*. Really *interesting* fellow—"

They argue in italics as Nicky makes her excuses, smiles sympathetically at the really interesting fellow—sharp nose, keen eyes—and powers forward, past Sebastian ("He told me, 'Name a venue, and I'll set a sensuous lovemaking scene set there—dungeon, abattoir, wherever,' and so I answered, 'Rope hammock'") and over Watson, until at last she exits the scrum, and flattens herself against a flank of the staircase, and exhales.

"Miss Trapp?"

A young man in a smart suit steps neatly in front of Madeleine as she nears the bar. "Timbo Martinez. I wanted to thank you for including me tonight."

This Martinez is Casper-pale and sunshine-blond, his face all angles, one cheek lightly pitted with acne scars. Serious eyes. For some reason, his hair and collar are damp. "You're looking for my aunt," she tells him. "Mrs. Trapp. Or maybe my stepmother. Also Mrs. Trapp."

"Oh, I thanked your stepmother. And your aunt knocked a drink onto me. But this is your home, too, isn't it?" Those serious eyes ticktock from side to side as he speaks. Madeleine feels as though she's under surveillance.

Then he looks past her. She turns. And there she is, the also-Mrs.-Trapp, burning bright in the center of the room, listening politely to the babbling rabble of old friends—Sebastian's and Hope's, not hers—and newcomers handpicked by Simone. And Madeleine realizes, with a jolt of pity, that Diana is still a stranger here: a copy who enters her own party beneath the gaze of the original, a visitor who hides within her own house. No wonder she's planning to leave it.

"I've read all your father's books." Timbo Martinez says it without heat, just information he's sharing. "In fact, I'm helping Mr. Lightfoot with *his* new book."

"Lionel is writing a new book?"

"It's a mystery."

"Why is it a mystery?" Madeleine's voice sounds frostbitten. "Is he or isn't he?"

"It's a mystery *novel*," says Timbo Martinez. "You didn't know?"

"And my stepmother invited him?"

Suddenly Watson jailbreaks from beneath the bar, playing hockey with an ice cube. Madeleine reaches past her guest, seizes a beer by the throat, and stalks into the fray.

NICKY ISN'T DRUNK, but Nicky isn't quite sober, either. Colors wheel past, aqua blues and absinthe greens, shrieks and roars popping like fairground balloons; the orchestra bows are dripping sweat, surely, and lights glitz high overhead, and in the center of the spectacle she sees Diana wavering bright and quivery as a flame.

She's lifting her glass to her lips when a hand clutches her own, her knuckles aching quietly in its grip. Nicky glances down at ten knotted fingers.

"Who dies next?" booms a voice, and she looks up to behold her hand-holder, teeth bared in a laugh. The floor tilts beneath her.

"That's what *tugs* the reader forward. That's what *reels him in*. Oh, he wants to know whodunit, of course; he's eager for the solution. And if our reader is the unimaginative sort, he can reduce the book to a . . . what's it called? Litmus test. Gladiator rules: thumbs up, thumbs down. 'Does the ending surprise me? If so, then I pronounce the preceding several hundred pages a success. If not, I've wasted time and money.'"

When he squeezes Nicky's hand, his wedding band rubs against her finger.

"But it's a novel, not a jack-in-the-box! Do these people screw solely for the orgasm?"

Now the music changes key—

—and now the floor tilts again—

—and now the mob slides across the room.

Bodies press in close, flesh and fabric, jangling Nicky's limbs. She tries to unravel her fingers from his, but then—

"Who dies next?" Sebastian booms. "As death stalks the cast—it stalks us, too, even as we lie in bed in our pajamas, reading! The roof might cave in. Carbon monoxide could be making itself at home upstairs. You never know when your heart's going to fail. Or perhaps your enemy will strike *tonight*, put a bullet in your temple, a blade in your breast!"

Nicky attempts to remain calm, lifts her champagne flute—but the mob pushes in, pushes her against him, his voice resounding in her ear. Through a chink in the crowd she spies Jonathan by the staircase.

"Who dies next? *Anybody*. It could be *anybody*. Yet once you turn that final page, the game is no longer afoot; it's over. For *them*—not for you. You no longer share a dilemma, no longer fear a common foe. *Your* mystery endures. *Your* death awaits."

Sweat trickles beneath her dress like underground rivers. Again she glimpses Jonathan; he mimes applause.

"And so once you learn *whodunit*, you're already alone again. No one to face death with you, or cheat it. You've said goodbye."

She looks up at him, the lights starry in her eyes. She squeezes them shut.

"For as Chandler reminds us, 'To say goodbye is to die a little.'"

"To dying a little!" somebody cries, and when Nicky dares to look, she beholds a pack of spectators with their glasses raised, gazing feverishly at their host. They repeat the toast like an ill-trained choir, at different tempos, before they try again, the words whirling in a loop around Nicky, an echo chamber:

To dying a little!
To dying a little!
To dying . . . !
. . . dying a little!
Dying!

MADELEINE PADDLES OUT OF THE FOYER, rides the surf of revelers through the parlor, and washes ashore in the courtyard. Diana is lingering by the hedge maze, a champagne flute dangled in one hand. Evening mist softens her edges.

"Lionel Lightfoot is here," Madeleine announces to her step-mother's bare back.

"I invited him. Bygones and all. His companion seems pleasant. Do you feel safe, Madeleine? In this house?"

Diana turns. She doesn't sound like herself, thinks Madeleine: she sounds slow, wary. She doesn't look like herself, either—it's the clothes, sure, but also the dark in her eyes, and the crease between her brows. She doesn't even *smell* like herself—no hint of that nameless perfume.

"Of course I feel safe. Should I not?"

Diana traces a fingertip along the rim of her glass.

"You two!" Simone's voice barrels into Madeleine's back. "Champagne pyramid!"

Diana nods, smiles, pauses by Madeleine's shoulder. "Some-time later I want to talk to you about your father."

She drifts away. When Madeleine turns back to the French windows, her aunt is gone, and Diana is gone, and the guests are gone, and all that remains is the fog creeping across the paving stones.

At last Nicky shakes free of Sebastian and wades through the crowd until Jonathan intercepts her by the stairs, flourishing his fingers like a magician.

"*Abraca*shit," he says as a shard of silver drops to the floor. He stoops, stands, key in one palm. "Ta-da!" Pressing it into her hand. "I rather feared I might arrive this evening to find you slumped against the front door, locked out and half starved."

"Thank you," she replies. "I'm taking it upstairs before I lose it again."

A half dozen paces up the staircase, she turns to find him two steps behind.

"Mind if I join? Nobody's watching," he adds, and taps his scalp. "Eyes in the back of my head."

"Sounds serious. You should consult a specialist."

"I'll prove it." Screwing his eyelids tight. "I see . . . white people."

"Remarkable."

He climbs another step, and Nicky proceeds. She wonders if his hand is hovering over the small of her back.

On the landing, the air is cooler, the colors softer. Four framed faces observe the fray, a bouquet of wallflowers at their own dance. Nicky glances back, sees Jonathan gazing past her, rubbing his jaw. He looks like a tourist in a gallery, inspecting a famous painting he's only ever seen on a page.

"So we've got your boss and—Madeleine, was it?"

"It was. Is."

"And there's the mother, the wife." Nicky says nothing; the landing has grown quieter with each Trapp Jonathan names, and the party dimmer. "And that"—his fingers drop from his chin, reshape themselves into a gun, barrel pointed at Cole—"is the boy who disappeared."

She nods.

Jonathan lifts his brows and smiles. "Cute kid," he says.

46

"I WOULD'VE KILLED for a bedroom like this when I was a little boy."

Jonathan is ogling the dormers, the ceiling, the museum, as Nicky sets the key on the desk. "Big fan of taxidermy, were you?"

He peels off his mask, hitches his trousers up, squats before the rank of stuffed bulldogs. "You don't mind bunking with this lot?"

"They don't bite."

"S'pose not. Watson the Fourth," he says, gently thumbing the collar of a plump coal-black cadaver. "Nineteen ninety-three to two thousand two."

Nicky approaches, hovers. When he doesn't stand, she tugs at her dress and maneuvers herself to the floor.

"He would've been the final family dog. Right?" asks Jonathan. "Wonder what he made of it. What he *witnessed*, even." He strokes the bulging skull, mutters, "I wonder if *Simone* got to him."

"What do you mean?"

He turns to her slowly, shoes scritching against the floorboards; then his face relaxes and he grins. "I'm just taking the piss." Bouncing lightly on the balls of his feet. "Watson—present-day Watson, the Watson currently in power—she tripped a waitress in pursuit of a deviled egg downstairs. Blink of an eye, Simone's on the spot. 'I will murder that animal,' she says, nostrils steaming. 'I will murder her with a smile.'"

He echoes Simone in a voice astonishingly like hers, sliding into an upper register without strain, the wholesome vowels rolling off his tongue.

"And I ask Fred if his mother might in fact be capable of homicide. And he answers, 'Dude, my mother is capable of genocide.'" California-speak now, slow and easy and so similar to his friend's speech that Nicky half wonders if Freddy has ventriloquized the words, hidden in some corner of the attic.

Jonathan grins. "I've a talent for voices. Served me well in school plays." Drawing closer.

Blood quickens beneath her skin, in the tracery of her veins. *Something exiting is hapening!!*

"Can you be me?" she asks.

His lips meet hers. His kiss is full but very gentle.

"I could be anyone," he whispers, and he kisses her again. She likes him for it. He cups her shoulder. She presses her hand to his chest, finds his heartbeat.

They kneel there in silence, before the jetsam of several centuries and countless voyages.

Their faces part, but linger close, as if in a magnetic field.

"We should go downstairs," she says, eyes closed, her lips grazing his.

Then she feels him smile. He rises, hoists her up after him. "Look at us, scandalizing all these dogs and one very ugly kid."

"That's my roommate you're talking about." Nicky feels strangely protective of *A Child*.

"I wonder if they've missed us," says Jonathan, adjusting the knot in his tie. "I fear someone will notice how you've ravished me."

"You should be so lucky."

He smiles again and follows her to the door.

47

"MEN ARE SUPPOSED TO WALK DOWNSTAIRS before women, you know," Jonathan is saying in the dark of the staircase. "Because if a woman trips on the steps, she'll just bump into a big strong bloke, but if *he* topples onto *her,* she shall surely perish."

"Are you about to topple onto me?"

"I mean, not on *purpose.*"

The light bends near the landing. When they emerge on the second floor, he snaps his fingers. "You told me about a library. On the water—remember?"

"Mm," she replies, not remembering.

"May I see it?"

Noise staggers up the stairs, lurches toward them: laughter, shrieks, lunging strings.

"Unless you're eager to rejoin the party," Jonathan adds.

Nicky takes his hand, squeezes it, and steals with him down the back corridor, gliding past the tall windows ("Is that a *pond*?" he asks. "Is that a *maze*?") until, at the library door, she glances over her shoulder and softly presses it open.

Gauzy moonlight swoons through the window; the bridge wears fog tonight. In the fireplace, long tongues lap at the throat of the chimney, gilding the desk, and the typewriter, and the figure in the chair.

Nicky stops.

"Who the hell's that?" whispers Jonathan.

Whoever the hell it is is bowed over the blotter, hands busy just below the desktop.

They approach unnoticed, hewing close to the bookshelves. Nicky's fingertips skim spine after spine. Foiled letters flicker in the darkness.

The figure lifts an object to its eye: a glass cube, a little box of flame in the firelight.

Nicky advances.

The figure stares at the cube.

Nicky draws near.

The figure lifts its head.

Nicky says, "Oh, God."

Livid white skin, bulbous nose and bulbous jaw, eye sockets sunk deep in the flesh, two horns like hooks curling from the brow. But most gruesome is the sick leer, lips thick and red. "A smile to eat you alive," Simon St. John once shuddered. "I'd give an awful lot to learn who's behind it."

It's Spring-Heeled Jack, St. John's archenemy. It's the last sight Laureline St. John ever beheld; it's the face that grins at Nicky in her nightmares, and it's looking right at her.

She'd give an awful lot to learn who's behind it.

"Wait," hisses Jonathan. But she moves ahead, slowly, heels sinking into the carpet, mouth dry, eyes on Jack. Firelight ripples across the glass desktop. The keys of the Remington shine like coins. Jack's head twists as he tracks her, his fingers kneading the glass cube.

Only now does Nicky notice the Webley in his other hand, staring at her.

She freezes.

Jack watches, unblinking, liquid eyes buried deep in the rubber.

Her skin crawls within her sleeves. "That won't fire," she says.

He cocks the pistol.

Jonathan steps forward. "Come off it, mate, that won't fire—"

Suddenly—roughly—Jack springs from the chair, shouldering Jonathan aside, stumbling on the rug. Jonathan reels against the shelves, but Nicky lunges one hand, rakes her fingers down Jack's arm as together they pitch to the floor. A firecracker-pop of stitches at the shoulder and the sleeve whips free, gun with it.

He lands on his side, grunts when she collapses onto him. She seizes his wrists and rolls him onto his back, straddling his stomach. Her shadow spills over his body and face, but the bare left arm, bent above his head, is white with firelight, and the tiny letters above the elbow are clear as typewriter text: I SHOULD HAVE WRAPPED THIS UP IN A RIBBON A LONG TIME AGO.

She plants a knee on his arm and grasps the clammy mask, wrenches it away.

Shadows pooled in the cheeks, clotted in the stubble—the face is barely his. Nicky glances over her shoulder at Jonathan.

When she turns back to Freddy, he punches her.

Or, rather, he swats the side of her face with one hand, and she hears the glass cube in his palm crack against the cheekbone. Feels it, too. His arm is thrashing like a snake as he struggles; he probably didn't mean to strike her, Nicky reasons, as she smashes her left fist into his eye. Thumb out, wrist locked, like she was taught. The crunch is so sharp that she nearly apologizes.

The cube tumbles across the carpet—and then two hands scoop her beneath the arms, haul her up and off. Jonathan's hands, and Jonathan's crotch she wallops when she whips her head back in protest. Her mask flies off.

Freddy has scrambled to his feet. For an instant he locks eyes with Nicky; in the firelight, skinned of one sleeve, collar stippled with blood drops, he looks half dead. And then, eyes wide, he spins and flees, his bare shoulder glancing off Madeleine's in the doorway.

By the time Nicky bursts into the corridor, he's vanished. She races to the landing, shucking one shoe and then the other, the chatter and clatter steadily louder in her ears until, just as she arrives at the top of the staircase, she hears violins flourish, as though announcing her.

There, at the bottom of the stairs, Freddy skids, and swerves, and—"Oh," breathes Nicky—collides with the champagne pyramid.

It bursts like a dam.

Strings squeal. A chorus of gasps from the crowd, now still as a frieze, and then stadium silence. Except for Freddy's shoes scrabbling on the marble as he bores his way toward the kitchen.

He vanishes. Some idiot applauds. A few others chime in, and the chatter simmers before boiling over. What was that? *Who* was that?

As caterers urge the party away from the rubble, as the orchestra strikes up another tune, Nicky feels a gaze spotlight her. Her eyes rove the foyer. The stage below suddenly dims.

Except where, in the center of the room, Sebastian Trapp stands straight as a lighthouse, watching her.

48

JONATHAN IS STOOPING NEAR THE DESK, hands braced against his knees, when Nicky and Madeleine return. "D'you know you head-butted me in the balls?" he wheezes.

"You grabbed me from behind. And I didn't need to be rescued."

"I was rescuing *Freddy*. You popped him bang in the bloody face."

"Is this that *gun*?" Madeleine picks up the Webley by its narrow barrel.

"We found Freddy over there," says Jonathan. "Fussing with your dad's things."

Madeleine marches to the desk, sets the gun on one corner. Nicky collects the glass cube, the severed sleeve, and—a little shiver—the rubber Jack mask.

"What am I looking for?" asks Madeleine. "Also, you're bleeding." Nicky touches her cheek; her fingertips are wet.

Jonathan wags a handkerchief. "Take this. Christ, my bollocks."

Diana arrives at the door, burning bright, and hurries to Madeleine. "Was Freddy—" She frowns at the open drawer.

Now Simone surges into the room, squawking, while Sebastian overtakes her with strides so long and swift that Nicky can almost feel him kick air into the fire, the master returned, flames leaping eager as dogs.

"Fred parked himself here, sir." Jonathan doesn't dwell on how they discovered this. "And when the young lady tackled him, he clocked her with that thingummy." Nicky resists the urge to present her wound for Sebastian's inspection; instead, she places the glass cube on the blotter. "So she caved his face in."

It's the firelight, probably, but when Sebastian turns to her, she detects the shadow of a smile on his lips. "She's a boxer. Freddy's, I presume," he adds, nodding at the sleeve in her hand. "And there's his coat, on the back of the chair. Left a damn change of clothes, did Freddy. And . . ." He trails off. Nicky has presented the Jack mask, its cruel lips sneering at him, its eye sockets vacant.

Simone squeaks. Sebastian grunts.

The five of them scatter like birds when he steps behind the desk; they regroup around him, heat at their backs, as he gazes at the black lining of the empty top drawer.

"He took it all," sobs Simone.

Sebastian sighs. "There was nothing to take. Except that cube. Room to maneuver, please." He begins pulling drawers open: envelopes, blank stationery . . . "Most of these are unlocked, so either young Frederick didn't bother or he couldn't find anything very interesting. Look, typewriter ribbon. Has he no need for typewriter ribbon?"

Now Sebastian reaches across the desk, sweeps his hand over the munitions: poison bottle, candlestick . . . dagger. "I keep one drawer shut up," he adds, slipping the tip of the blade into the bottommost. "These locks were made specially to fit this dag—here we are. Good! Untouched. End-of-life papers." He winks at his wife and daughter. "You'll just have to wait."

Nicky inches nearer, glimpses a block of typing paper. Glimpses the two words in black type on the top page.

Sebastian slides the drawer shut, stabs the lock, twists. "What *was* young Fred after?" He sets the dagger down and lifts the glass cube, kneads it as he scans the desktop.

"Anything missing?" asks Jonathan.

Sebastian blinks. "Who the hell are you?"

"I'm a friend of Fred's."

"Well, I wouldn't brag. But yes, all in order. This lump of glass was a bequest," he explains. "Belonged to my father. Sentimental value only. Bit of Tacitus etched here, you can see. Never knew how it ended up with a military man who didn't seem to speak much English, let alone Latin, but I liked the look of the thing, liked its heft. Miss Hunter now knows all about its heft, of course."

Nicky's cheek throbs.

Shadows flutter across Sebastian's face as he weighs the cube. *"Proprium humani ingenii est odisse quem laeseris."* To Jonathan: "Since you ask, stranger in my house, the most expensive item here is the typewriter, which you can't exactly smuggle down your—"

His body stiffens.

Nicky narrows her eyes. With his back to the fire, his face is just a dark mask.

"What is it?" asks Simone.

"Oh, no." Madeleine. "Oh, no."

Nicky frowns, nerves crackling, glances at Jonathan. He's staring at the typewriter.

Nestled in the silver scoop of the Remington's strikers is a sharp, bold, scarlet—

"A paper butterfly?" asks Jonathan. "Somehow sinister, is it?"

Nicky squints. "There's writing on the wings."

When Sebastian looks at her, firelight steals over one wide eye and the taut corner of his lips.

He lifts the butterfly and turns toward the fireplace; the paper flushes even redder.

It's like watching a building collapse, Nicky thinks, as he shudders from the ground up: first his knees buckle, then his hips give, and his shoulders sag and finally he crumbles into his chair, head bowed, butterfly in one hand, glass cube in the other.

Diana kneels beside him. Carefully, as though extracting a bullet, she removes the insect from his grip, stands to read aloud the words Nicky sees typed dark and clear on the paper wings:

TELL THEM WHAT   YOU DID TO HER

"I suppose that does sound sinister," mutters Jonathan.

Nobody else speaks.

Suddenly Madeleine hoists her father to his feet. "I'm putting him to bed," she announces, daring them to interfere, and starts to conduct Sebastian down the dark length of the library.

"Simone." Diana's voice is brisk. "Could you please help me clear everyone out of the house?"

"Certainly. But I don't understand"—without Sebastian present, Simone seems uncertain whom she ought to address—"why would Frederick would play such a . . . very odd prank? The oregano, and 'Tell them what you did' . . ." She gathers the coat, the sleeve, and—with a grimace—the mask, then fades away, muttering like the fire.

Diana stares at the butterfly in her hand until at last Jonathan clears his throat. "Can we do anything?"

She floats him a dazed stare. Lets it drift to Nicky. Props the origami on the Remington keys—carefully, lest she disturb it—and closes the empty drawer and walks off.

But from the far end of the room she calls, dim among the shadows, the color drained from her clothing:

"Was the butterfly there when you found Freddy?"

"Course," answers Jonathan.

Diana lingers. Then, for an instant, she flashes like a sunrise as she steps into the light of the corridor.

"Course it was here, right?" Jonathan reaches for the insect, pinches a paper wing. "I mean, Fred *made* it, didn't he? Unless somebody popped it on the very valuable typewriter when we were crowded round."

Nicky's mind is at work.

"*Does* that gun fire? Too old, right? Too unloaded?" Jonathan nods at the Webley. "This is America. Probably a cocked rifle in every room." He circles the desk; his hand hovers over the pistol. "Who's that Russian playwright chap? Had a theory about guns?"

"Chekhov. If you introduce a gun in Act One, you have to fire it by the finale."

"Right." Jonathan abandons the Webley. "What *was* Fred up to here, d'you reckon?"

Nicky can't begin to reckon. She shakes her head.

"Well. Last call downstairs, I expect. Could you use a drink?"

She takes his hand.

So they cross the rug, and exit the room, and travel down the corridor, and from the landing they watch the party funnel out of the foyer, the wreckage of the champagne pyramid still glittering below.

But all the while, Nicky thinks of the words typed on the paper in Sebastian's desk.

For Cole

49

IN THE KITCHEN, in the quiet, the elder Mrs. Trapp wearily announces her intent to spend the night, "in case Sebastian needs anything"—here Nicky glances at the younger Mrs. Trapp, slumped in the window seat—and marches off.

Half an hour to midnight, Nicky's phone tells her. "Should I sweep the foyer again?" she asks. "I don't want Watson limping around."

Her hostess's eyes are closed.

They open when Simone blows back in a moment later: "Madeleine won't answer." Sighing, hands on hips, as if about to ask *Whatever will we do about that girl?* "Oh, she's in there, all right. But when I knock—nobody home. What *will* we do about her?"

Nicky, filling the kettle, gazes at the courtyard window, sees Simone in the glass, unfastening her necklace; sees her pluck the tiny studs from her ears. "Would you return these to Young Miss when she emerges? I've had enough warfare tonight. Thank you." Simone tips the metal into Diana's hand. "I'll be upstairs. The room with all those death masks, I suppose."

At the door she turns: "When Sebastian wakes up, please let me know."

The kettle is singing. Nicky steeps a tea bag and sets the cup on the floor beside Diana, who has fallen asleep; then she hops to the countertop and sips milk, legs swinging lightly. Spots a small rip at the elbow of her sleeve. This party was a contact sport.

"*Proprium humani ingenii est odisse quem laeseris.*"

Nicky swallows, coughs.

Recumbent at the window, eyes shuttered and hair loose as she speaks a dead language, Diana looks almost oracular. Her words are slippery with booze. "I'd never seen that block of glass in Sebastian's desk. But I can translate it. 'It belongs to human nature to hate him whom you have harmed.'" She opens her eyes again, finds her teacup. "We hate those we hurt."

"A little bleak," says Nicky.

"A little. Just milk for you? I don't suppose there's a mystery novel about milk?"

Nicky's jaw fidgets. "Oh—*Before the Fact*. Hitchcock adapted it as *Suspicion*. There's a famous scene where Cary Grant heads upstairs to his wife with a spiked glass of milk. They dropped a working light-bulb in the glass for effect."

"So he's trying to . . . bump her off? His wife?"

"The studio didn't want Cary Grant playing a murderer. In the movie, it's all just a misunderstanding. But in the book, he kills her. Well, technically, she kills herself—lets him poison her."

"Would you ever try to kill yourself?"

The question wobbles across the island like a misshapen bubble, clumsy but clear. Nicky considers, smooths her sleeves. "I don't think I can imagine wanting to die," she says, slowly. "But I guess I can imagine not wanting to live."

Time has slowed, almost stilled. Nicky feels . . . not uneasy, exactly, but alert. She wonders if she ought to sit by her hostess, wonders—

"After I lost my husband and daughter, I struggled." Diana clears her throat. "Indescribably. And Sebastian struggled like that, too. He told me once that—it hurt to live."

Silence for a moment, as Nicky's heart aches.

"That butterfly," says Diana. "Are you certain it was in place when you arrived?"

"No," replies Nicky, after a pause. "Seems likely, but no, I'm not certain. Why?"

"Because anybody could have—plenty of our guests knew about the origami. Freddy, too, of course. But—"

Diana is slurring very sweetly. Nicky prompts her. "But the butter-fly at the door?"

The teacup is set as Diana slowly swings her feet to the floor. "Freddy again." She masks her face with her hands. "He brought it in."

Nicky leans forward. "What do you know about the disappear-ance?"

Diana drops her hands, eyes wet.

"What do you know about the disappearance?" Nicky repeats.

"I know that we never should have asked you to write this story." Pressing dry hand to damp nose. "This isn't your fault. Sebastian wanted it. But now it's too—maybe it was always too . . . strange."

Should she offer to vacate? Nicky wonders. No: the detective-fever is burning.

"Go sleep," Diana tells her. "I'll finish my tea. And then I intend to dose myself to next week."

Reluctantly, Nicky dismounts from the island.

Someone—Simone, presumably—has doused the lights in the foyer; it sprawls before her in monochrome, desolate and vast, shadows cringing in the corners. She can almost hear the echoes of hoots and howls, the clash of glasses . . .

. . . Sebastian's voice ringing above the fray . . .

A line of gold beams beneath Madeleine's door. Nicky begins the climb upstairs.

At the landing, before the Trapps trapped in oil, she pauses. They stare at her, and she stares back: Sebastian's suit, Madeleine's dress, floating like ghosts. Hope is invisible. Of Cole, just a shock of silver-blond hair—and in his unseen hands, a white butterfly.

For Cole.

Nicky imagines the strikers leaping to punch the paper, each letter glossy with ink, as Sebastian tapped those four keys: **Co—**

She senses motion down below, turns. The darkness hasn't subdued Diana's gown; Nicky watches her cross the floor, heels dangling from one hand.

When the grandfather clock starts to announce midnight, Nicky startles, but Diana merely stops, drops her eyes to her fingers. Appears to study them.

After the sixth toll, Nicky moves on. By the time she returns to the attic, a new day has been born in blackness.

And for the first time since she arrived in San Francisco, she locks her door.

50

> Freddy, is this you?

Madeleine perches on the edge of her bed, naked. Four hours in that gown and she never wants to dress again.

She waits for Magdala to reply.

When he doesn't:

> Freddy?

Freddy was at the typewriter. The butterfly was *on* the typewriter. Freddy knew Cole—better than Madeleine thought, maybe.

But nothing about this smells even faintly of body spray: not the stunts at the front door and in the library, not the sinister origami . . . nor, for that matter, the guess-who texts.

. . . Yet he rifled the desk. He scrabbled with Nicky (got his ass handed to him, too, which doesn't displease Madeleine). He wrecked three hundred champagne flutes and fled.

She finds her cousin's number in her phone.

> Are you texting me from
> another number?
>
> Are you making those
> butterflies?
>
> Freddy?

The screen blurs as she watches. After a moment, she hears the clock in the foyer slowly stutter midnight.

She watches and she waits.

Tuesday, June 23

IN A MOMENT THEY'LL FIND HER.

Find her where she floats, fingers splayed wide in the marbling water, hair spread like a Japanese fan. Fish glide beneath it, push through it; skate along the line of her body.

The filter hums. The pond simmers, shimmers. She trembles on the surface.

Fog prowled the ground earlier this morning—San Francisco swirl, velvet-thick and chill—but now the last of it burns off, and the courtyard basks in light: paving stones, sundial, a chorus line of daffodils. And the pond, that perfect circle sunk near the wall of the house, with its glowing fish, its lily pads like stars.

In a moment a scream will crack the air.

Until then, all is silent and all is still, except for the shiver of the water, and the slow traffic of the koi, and the ripple of her corpse.

Across the courtyard, the French window opens, sun sliding off glass. A breath. Then that scream.

They've found her.

51.

The scream wrenches Nicky from bed.

She flies to the door, down two switchback flights, hugging the corners, steps materializing beneath her feet—

—at the top of the grand staircase she pauses, wondering if she'd heard anything at all.

She walks to the kitchen, coffee-cup tranquil in the morning light.

The second scream could crack glass. Nicky jumps into the parlor, where the French window yawns at the courtyard.

The paving stones are cold beneath her bare feet. Flower beds. Box-woods. Sundial. A ghost.

She blinks.

The ghost stands at the edge of the koi pond, a hooded pure-white robe flowing from head to heels. The right arm, draped past the finger-tips in its sleeve, points at the water. Nicky hurries to the pond, and the ghost turns to her.

"What do we do?" asks Simone.

Floating in the water is a woman, facedown, hair sprayed about her head, her back and arms bare.

Nicky barges into the pond and promptly drops three feet, orange fish whirling like sparks around her. Cold clasps her legs, her waist; she swats lily pads to either side as the body rocks, hooks her hands under one raw shoulder, and rolls the woman onto her back.

Her gray eyes are lifeless, her lips tinged blue; the gash on her temple is deep. But she remains the most beautiful woman Nicky has ever seen.

"What do we *do*?"

Nicky stands still, one hand at the nape of Diana's neck, as fish waft past and the chop of the water calms. Should she close those eyes? Lift the thin strap of her dress?

When the pond erupts, blasting her backward, she stumbles against the sunken wall, submerged to her shoulders. She grunts, swipes at her eyes. Sebastian is rearing like a sea beast, his wife scooped in his arms. Her dress is dark. Her feet, crossed demurely at the ankles, are pale.

He gawks, eyes wild, at Diana, at her head cradled in the crook of an elbow. One of his fingers grazes her wound. He flinches.

Nicky watches him as the water sways around her. He lifts his face and looks at her with such sorrow that she can barely look back. Then, slowly, he bows to that clear brow and kisses his wife on the forehead.

Tiny claws scuffle atop Nicky's skull before Watson topples into the pond and instantly sinks. Nicky hauls her up to the surface, holds her to her chest. The dog begins to howl—not sharp barks of shock or fear, but the long, low wolf's bay of mourning.

"Is Watson out here?"

Nicky twists to see Madeleine at the French window, in a sweat-shirt and gym shorts, clutching her phone.

She frowns. "Why the hell is everybody swimming?"

52

"WE REALLY MUST STOP MEETING LIKE THIS!"

Detective B.B. Springer, glinting in a snakeskin blazer, surveys the assembled household from the doorway. "Lotta familiar faces here. Yours included." She beams at Nicky. "Remember me? My helmet was blue last time." Tapping her sleek cap of bubblegum-pink hair.

Nicky remembers.

The familiar faces surround the dining room table, Sebastian nearest the door, in his sodden pajamas, a towel draped over his shoulders and a snifter of brandy within reach. From the other end, Nicky watches him; he looks like a scarecrow in collapse, slumping over his knees, limbs unraveled at the joints. In the hour since Nicky summoned an ambulance, Simone has cycled through the five stages of grief five times; Madeleine has smoked a half dozen cigarettes; and Nicky, after a wrenching cry in her attic bathroom and a quick change into dry clothes, descended once more to watch the paramedics hover around the body.

Until B.B. Springer blew in. "We're just waiting on my partner," she explains cheerfully.

Madeleine pokes another cigarette between her teeth, fires up. Arrows smoke away from the dog lumped in her lap, glossy with pondwater.

"I'd like one, too, please," says Simone.

Madeleine hesitates before sliding the pack and lighter across the table. She watches her aunt puff with interest, the way a scientist might observe unexplained behavior in an animal already studied.

Simone exhales. "Lime green."

B.B. blinks. "Pardon?"

"Your hair. Twenty years ago. Lime green."

"Oh, I've lime-greened myself a dozen times since then. The brass let me get away with it 'cause I'm so terribly impor—*hola, amigo.*" This to the pale young man in sharp suit and strangling tie who steps quietly into the dining room. His hair is so fair that if he were to stray into the sunlight, it might ignite, Nicky thinks, and his suit and side-burns are both clean-cut. This is a Serious Detective.

"My partner, Timbo Martinez," announces B.B. "Our boy wonder. Smarter than me and you and the dog put together, so be honest. Or if not, be careful. Right, Tim?" She grins at the boy wonder, standing beside the entrance like a doorman, assessing the room. He regards Sebastian for a moment.

"I spend half my time trying to make him smile," says B.B. "I dream of the day."

"You don't look Hispanic," observes Simone.

"I was adopted," says Timbo Martinez politely. His voice is flat and neutral, almost automated.

"My hair, his childhood: we're all caught up." B.B. boosts her back-side onto the deep windowsill behind Madeleine. "Folks, I don't like this kind of reunion," she says, scales glimmering. "Your house has a history. *We* have a history. But let's not confuse the present with the past. Unless that should become necessary."

Sebastian, hanging off the chair, masks his face with one hand.

"I'm sorry for your loss," adds the detective. "What time did Mrs. Trapp go to bed last night?"

"Questions *now*?" Simone nearly splutters. "While we're in *shock*?"

"Relax, Mrs. Trapp, you won't feel a thing. What time—"

"Midnight."

All eyes on Nicky. Suddenly she feels exposed. "The clock was striking twelve as she left the kitchen," she explains, her voice still throaty. "I was on my way upstairs."

B.B. raps the diamond panes at her back. "My pal out there"—Nicky rises; by the pond squats a dreadlocked woman whose jacket advertises her as CORONER—"puts the time of death at around nine hours ago. Also midnight."

Nicky sits. "I read a lot of mysteries, and most of them say that time of death is difficult to pinpoint."

"Nowadays we can narrow it down to within forty-five minutes. Without forensics."

"Body in the water, though . . ." mutters Timbo.

"Was it—*suicide*?" Simone can barely whisper the word.

B.B. cracks a knuckle. "Any reason it should've been?"

"Her bedroom window is open. I noticed it from the courtyard before I saw her."

B.B. sighs, hops down from the sill. "Couple problems there. First, a three-story tumble isn't reliably fatal. Unless—problem two—the lady dived headfirst. In which case, either she'd belly-flop on the surface— maybe break her neck, maybe crawl outta there wetter but wiser—or she'd hit the stones and—I don't mean to be indelicate—her head would burst like a grapefruit. What're the odds she just clips the rim of the pond and slips neatly into the water?"

Simone draws on her cigarette. "But it's possible?"

"Could be someone wants us to think so."

Timbo nearly raises his hand. "Had Mrs. Trapp recently been depressed for any reason?"

"I'm dying." Sebastian's voice issues from between his fingers like wind through a door. "We're both depressed about it."

"And last night specifically? Did you notice anything?"

After a moment, Nicky realizes she's *you.* "She seemed a little edgy." Agatha Christie has not prepared her for this: answering actual questions posed by an actual officer of the law. "She wanted to talk about—"

Suddenly Nicky recognizes Timbo Martinez: he accompanied Lionel Lightfoot last night, sustained liquid damage in the line of duty. *Really* interesting *fellow. A* colleague *of sorts.*

"Ms. Hunter?" B.B.'s voice shakes her by the shoulders.

"Yes."

"Mrs. Trapp wanted to talk about what?"

Nicky glances at Sebastian.

"I'm asking you, Ms. Hunter, not Mr. Trapp."

"The past," replies Nicky.

B.B. turns to her partner, speaks low. He listens, nods.

"Of course it wasn't suicide," Madeleine scoffs.

"Why?" B.B. has crossed to Sebastian, lingers behind him.

"Because it was obviously an accident. Tipsy late-night stroll. Slipped by the fish."

"Was Mrs. Trapp in the habit of taking late-night strolls?" asks Timbo.

A drag, a puff. "I'm not in the habit of being questioned by the police at home, but it's happening today, isn't it?"

"Not for the first time," B.B. beams. "Timbo here had a front-row seat to last night's show. Sounds like a real—how would your people put it, Tim?"

"Fiesta," he says, paper-dry.

"*Sí.* But the house was evacuated . . . ?"

"Just—a misunderstanding." Ash topples from Simone's cigarette. "My son. The *ruckus* . . ."

Nicky closes her eyes. All these years reading stories about death, yet she's never seen—certainly never touched—a corpse. All those nights looming like a dark angel over the pages, spying on autopsies and checking pulses in blind alleys, drawing shut the painted eyelids of throttled dancers . . . Death was intrigue. Death was a challenge. Death seemed a thrill.

But now she has seen death, held it, only to find it strange, and sad.

". . . across its wings," Simone is saying. "Typed. Bold as you please."

"Cole Trapp made origami butterflies," B.B. informs her partner.

He frowns. "'Tell them what you did to her'—referring to Mrs. Trapp? The first Mrs. Trapp?"

Madeleine wipes Watson's eyes. "You'd need to ask Freddy."

"Meaning Freddy wrote it?" asks B.B.

"Of course," says Madeleine.

"Of course not," says Simone.

B.B. tilts her head. "Anybody keep the butterfly?"

Madeleine sighs. "I guess it's still up in the library. I can go—"

"Not yet. Not you. Who stuck around last night?"

The women glance at one another. "All of us at this table," answers Nicky.

"And Diana." Gravel still clots Sebastian's voice. His hand drops from his face; slowly his back straightens. For the first time since B.B. joined them, he looks up at her.

"Hello, sir," she says gently. The way one might greet a baby surfacing from a nap, Nicky thinks. Or a dangerous animal behind bars.

Sebastian and the detective watch each other. *We really must stop meeting like this.*

"Any trouble in your marriage, Mr. Trapp?" asks B.B. "This most recent marriage, I mean?"

He kills his snifter in a swallow. "You think it's murder," he says.

The words hang in the air like smoke. Nicky doesn't breathe.

"You don't think she jumped?" says Simone.

"You don't think she slipped?" says Madeleine.

"You think it's murder," says Sebastian again.

B.B. shrugs. "I think you're a tough guy to stay married to, certainly."

"So you suspect me."

"I suspect everyone here."

Nicky is watching herself from afar, a character in a film. *I'm a suspect in a maybe-murder.*

"If it's homicide," B.B. adds.

Timbo: "Anybody else have a house key?"

Simone: "Adelina. The housekeeper. She—"

"Freddy." The brandy has oiled Sebastian's voice.

"Freddy again!" B.B. sings. "Talk of the town. I desire a chat with Freddy. And I desire to see this famous paper insect. Timbo, would you bust out your butterfly net? Ms. Hunter, kindly lead the way . . ."

Nicky stands, and Madeleine and Simone gaze at her like prisoners watching a fellow inmate newly paroled.

"Watson . . ." calls Madeleine. Nicky turns to see that the dog has escaped from her mistress's lap and is following her to the door, wobbly as a water balloon. Sebastian watches, gullies around his eyes as they meet hers—and then Nicky leaves the room. Timbo gallantly allows Watson to trudge past.

"Oh!" Simone cries when they walk into the foyer. "Jonathan—my son's friend—he gave a key to Nicky last night. It *looked* like a key. Ask—" They lose her voice behind the curve of the staircase.

Nicky waits for Timbo to ask. But he simply hikes up the steps after her, humming softly under his breath.

53

THE DOG GIVES UP at the landing, flops down. Timbo quits humming. Considers the portrait.

"Huh," he grunts.

Spokes of ghost-white sunlight slant onto the hallway carpet, heating Nicky's bare feet as she passes through. Six days ago, she trod this same corridor, Diana ahead of her, hips swaying demurely in her powder-blue dress; six days earlier, she looked out these same windows, onto that very courtyard. And now . . .

"Do you really think this is a murder?" Foreign on her tongue, like a word she's read but has never spoken.

"I should ask you about that key," Timbo says, almost apologetically.

Yet now her gaze is fixed on the scene below, where the coroner kneels beside the body laid out on the paving stones. Diana's skin is pale, her clothes like dark blood.

"Jonathan somebody?"

Nicky moves along to the library door, to the skull knocker gnawing on its heavy hoop of iron, and turns to find the detective at a respectful distance, hands folded at his belt. "Jonathan Grant," she says. "I barely know him."

"Guys you barely know often give you their keys?"

"It was my key." She pushes the door, walks inside. The bay is bright today, tiny whitecaps like metal shavings, the bridge lunging into the headlands beyond; yet still the room—cavernous, ravenous—traps the light in its teeth and devours it.

"Gosh," says Timbo, gawking at the casement windows. "*Gosh,*" he repeats, turning to the layers of somber black shelves, the grilles and ladder, the books glinting with flecks of gold. When he bends to examine Edmund Crispin, his body in that perfect suit buckling into an angular S, the light falls on his face, and Nicky sees a faint stippling of scars. She imagines a teenage Detective Martinez staring at his skin in the mirror, despairing or unhappy or at least a bit sad, and she wonders whether others were kind. And although he's a detective and she's a suspect (what *will* Aunt Julia say?), she feels a little rub of sympathy for him.

He straightens up. His eyes, she notices, tend to flick left and right when he looks at her, like a tennis ball in play. As though he wants to absorb as much information as possible.

"How do you know Lionel Lightfoot?" she asks.

"He asked the commissioner for help with his new novel. Commissioner suggested me. It's a detective story." Timbo's fingers mountain-climb the ribbed spine of a leather-bound book: Israel Zangwill, *The Big Bow Mystery.*

"Typewriter down there? Yeah: I'm just advising Mr. Lightfoot on current police procedure. Interview tactics. Weapons." Behind the desk yawns the fireplace, mouth ablaze. "Who laid the fire?"

"Gas. It's always burning. Like the Olympic torch."

"Anyway, Mr. Lightfoot invited me along last night. I wanted to meet Mr. Trapp. I like his books."

"Did you meet him?"

"Not until this morning." The detective circles the desk, eyes roving the blotter and its exhibits—the dagger, the noose, the poison bottle. The gun.

And Nicky witnesses what B.B. Springer has only dreamed of: a smile, small but sincere.

It vanishes when he looks at her. "That's Simon St. John's revolver," he explains.

"Yes. Do you think it's murder?"

Timbo leans over the typewriter, left hand wriggling into a latex glove only slightly whiter than his skin. The butterfly has slipped down the steppes of the keyboard. He pinches one wing and lifts it to his face. Nicky wonders if he's nearsighted.

"I just got here six months ago," he says, snapping an evidence bag, carefully tucking the butterfly within, "and B.B. was on the job barely two years when she visited this house. For the first time, I mean." When he peels off the glove, the bag drops to the floor. He crouches to retrieve it. "Kind of a sad rite of—"

He reaches around the corner of the desk. Nicky watches his back stiffen, wonders inanely if somehow there's another butterfly.

Timbo stands. One hand holds the evidence bag, the other holds a—

"Mask," he says, unnecessarily.

The velvet Lone Ranger. Nicky nods. "Mine. I lost it in the—brawl."

His eyes switch side to side. "Sounds gladiatorial."

"You should see the other guy."

"I'm hoping to. Man—that's *the* Webley." Shaking his head. "I don't like most guns," he adds.

"You're a cop."

"Not because I like guns."

He adjusts his collar, loose around his narrow neck, and strides briskly to the door, the butterfly floating in its plastic bag.

Nicky hugs herself. *They really think Diana was murdered.*

And there's only one person in this house with a history of ill-fated wives.

54

"The mural I don't remember," marvels B.B., sidewinding slowly between the jigsaw tables. She lingers by the trick puzzle, the cat and canary, then drops into a chair. "Curious things, rooms. Tell you quite a lot about the people who live in them. Hey—that prostitute looks like you."

Madeleine sits next to *Madame X*. Wishes her dog were puttering underfoot.

"I met your stepmother just once, in an interview room. Quiet type. I liked her."

"I liked her, too." Strange, referring to Diana in the past tense.

"Somebody didn't." B.B. stirs the jigsaw pieces with a fingertip. "My partner liked Diana—for the Trapp case. Believed they were dead, believed she and your dad made 'em that way." B.B. glances at Madeleine. "They did end up together."

"Fifteen years later."

"Me, my money was on Isaac. You remember my husband?"

"Vaguely."

"That's why I noticed him. That and the beard." B.B. catches Madeleine blushing, grins. "Well. Didn't solve it then, won't solve it today." She snaps a spray of whiskers into the cat's cheek.

But that's just what she hopes to do, Madeleine realizes. She very much hopes to solve it.

"Besides—now we've got ourselves a *new* mystery! A *sequel*, even. How *did* your stepmother wind up in that goldfish pond?"

"Koi," says Madeleine automatically. "Why ask me?"

"Maybe you know something I don't?"

"I know less than you could possibly imagine."

B.B. sits back. "Strange goings-on in Trapp Towers, no? Something in the water, you might say. Your stepmother was 'edgy' last night, according to Ms. Hunter. Any idea why?"

"I expect hosting a party for three hundred strangers would put you on edge. Especially when it's your husband's last. Try it, let me know."

"And your cousin. Good son. Good boy. Yet last night, he's rummaging around in the library wearing a freaky mask—we know not why—then ka-pow: fight club."

"Sounds about right."

"And that origami butterfly? 'Tell them what you did,' was it?"

"'To her.'"

"To *her*. Do you think your dad knows what happened to your mom?"

"No. Do *you* think my dad knows what happened to my mom?"

B.B. holds up her hands. "Just saying: somebody threatens Mr. Trapp that way, sounds like they know *something*. Freddy, you suppose?"

"Freddy barely knows what day of the week it is." Ice in Madeleine's voice, sweat in the seams of her palms. He might have kissed the deceased, he might have killed the party—but Freddy's not a *murderer*.

"So now I'm confused." The detective frowns at the cat, taps a claw into place. "In the dining room, you said yep, he wrote those notes. Now you're saying nope, he's too—pardon the word—dumb."

Madeleine stares. She won't implicate her cousin. But she's pretty sure Diana's death wasn't an accident. Yet surely it couldn't have been suicide. Meaning—

"Who wrote that note, Miss Trapp?"

"I don't know." Except she does, doesn't she?

A redhead in uniform enters, plastic sleeve in hand. "Bedroom floor by the desk," she mutters.

"Gimme gimme," coos B.B., squinting at the paper within. Her smile falls off like a false moustache.

After a moment, she slides the sleeve to Madeleine.

> *It's an awful cliché, but I can't go on.*
> *The guilt will drag me down and drown me.*

"Is this her handwriting?"

The handwriting is soft and shy.

"Miss Trapp, is this—"

"Yes." Her throat swells. Diana wrote this. And then Diana died.

. . . Diana, who had told her, in the courtyard, that *Sometime later I want to talk to you about your father.*

B.B. narrows her eyes, as though trying to solve a riddle.

"What exactly are you investigating, Detective?" asks Madeleine.

"A murder," says B.B., the suicide note in her hand.

55

THE PALE OFFICER—Madeleine has forgotten his name—enters quickly and blondly, Nicky following at a distance. He nods at Madeleine (she expects him to "Ma'am" her), dangles a baggie before his partner. Trapped inside is the red butterfly.

B.B. mouths the words on the wings. "Who touched this?"

Madeleine: "My father. And Diana."

Nicky: "I must've. Jonathan. Freddy, presumably."

Timbo: "Did you actually see Freddy handling it?"

A pause. "No."

"You ladies hear from Cole Trapp lately?" asks B.B.

Nicky looks as if she doesn't get the joke. "No," she says, slowly.

"No." Madeleine shakes her head. "Not in twenty years." *Don't sound desperate.* "What could my brother have to do with Diana?" Better.

But the thought loiters in the corner of her mind, like a stranger whose eye you don't want to catch. Would Cole have had a reason—

"There was another butterfly," Nicky volunteers, and Madeleine wants to behead her.

B.B. frowns. "Another butterfly?"

"In a box on the front steps. Diana told me. A red butterfly, words on the wings. *Cherchez la femme.*"

"Cher said what?"

In at most three sentences, B.B. will trace the box to Madeleine. "It means 'look for the woman,'" she says. "Cole liked the sound of it. That was on Friday. Freddy found the box, gave it to me, I gave it to Dad."

"And he told Mrs. Trapp, who told your guest here?"

"It's a very chatty household." Not that chatty, though: Freddy, not Sebastian, had told Diana, right before—right before *kissing her,* that ass; another secret to keep. "But anybody could've left that box at the door. And anybody could've left *that* butterfly on the typewriter. There were hundreds of people here last night." If the detectives want to play Clue, Madeleine's not going to make it easy for them. "Besides," she adds, "Diana spelled it out for you in print."

Her voice sounds squeezed. *I can't go on.*

She sees Nicky frown at the paper in B.B.'s hand. The detective's nostrils twitch, like a horse at the post. "Either of you met any men in their mid-thirties, blue eyes, possibly but not necessarily fair-haired, who seemed unusually interested in the Trapp family?"

Here we go. "I would recognize my brother," Madeleine lies.

"Your aunt mentioned a Jonathan?"

Timbo clears his throat. "He had a key."

"He wouldn't *need* a key," says Madeleine, sighing. "Hundreds of people were here last night. Any one of them could've stuck around, killed some time in a spare bedroom before killing—" *Word choice, Madeleine.* "Look, nobody's been killed at all! You've got yourself a *letter*—"

"How old is our friend Jonathan?" asks B.B.

Nicky shrugs. "Late thirties, I guess."

Madeleine recalls his easy chat last night, his wide shoulders, that accent. Surely not, she'd concluded.

Then she recalls the texts that rattled her phone the moment he walked away.

Don't look so nervous.

And don't look for me.

"Late thirties, you guess," says B.B. "Any interest in Sebastian Trapp?"

Nicky wiggles her jaw. "He asked questions. But more to be polite, I think. We did watch a Simon St. John movie."

"His idea?"

Another shrug. "Yes."

"We'll need his details."

Sweat simmers on Madeleine's forehead. Cole reappears in the world of the living, Diana disappears from it—what are the odds?

Maybe it's gone too far. Maybe it's not too late. She tastes the words: *My brother texted me.*

. . . But doesn't she want to know what he knows about their mother?

No: the texts, the origami, and now a corpse. Fire the flare gun. *My brother texted me. I texted back.*

"When did you stop wondering? About Isaac?"

The voice is gruff and rough and her own.

B.B. tilts her head, the faintest smile on her lips. "Who says I ever did?"

He texted me.

"He tex—"

But again the redheaded officer steps into the room, steps on her words. "Could you jump in here? We got a situation."

56

NICKY GAWKS IN THE DOORWAY. Sebastian is battering the chandelier with a champagne bottle, vicious swipes that pop its bulbs and dent its limbs. Tiny diamonds rain onto the coffee table; his hair is starry with glass. The butterflies on the wallpaper have spread their wings, ready to scatter, and Simone is tugging uselessly at his robe.

Madeleine and B.B. speed forth while Nicky lingers next to Timbo. The instant his daughter touches his arm, Sebastian calms; he drops the bottle to the rug, and with Madeleine and Simone gripping either hand, he subsides into the sofa, his back to the French windows.

Nicky looks at him in his robe, at Madeleine in her sweats, at snake-skinned B.B. She feels Timbo beside her, watches Simone hurry to the kitchen. They're in a bad play, the costumes haphazard, the set in disarray: six characters in search of an answer.

Sebastian sighs. "I wanted to destroy something."

"Well," says B.B. brightly, "that's a good day's work. I don't mean to be insensitive, Mr. Trapp—"

"Then don't be," calls Simone.

"—but do you recognize this?" Circling the coffee table.

Sebastian studies the note, the plastic sleeve trembling in his hands. His face seems to age.

B.B. eyes him the way you would a crossword you just can't crack. In her whole life, Nicky thinks, the detective has probably never gone so long without speaking.

Gently she reclaims the note, passes it to Timbo. He clears his throat. "'It's an awful cliché, but I can't go on.'"

Nicky hears a gasp, realizes it's her own. She hears a cry, realizes it's Simone, who has returned bearing a water glass and a stub of paper.

"'The guilt will drag me down and drown me,'" Timbo finishes in that monotone of his.

"It's her handwriting." B.B. sounds unhappy. Sebastian and Madeleine absently nod.

Timbo frowns. "Why the guilt?"

"I knew it. I'm sorry I knew it, but I knew it." Simone thrusts the stub at B.B. "Frederick's number. He isn't answering, though. And he *always* answers me. I've put the kettle on—"

"I need to go upstairs. If I may." Sebastian is shuddering as he stands, Nicky sees, a machine about to break down. Should she—

"I'll take you," says Madeleine, wreathing one arm around his waist as he drapes a hand over her shoulder. When he looks back at Nicky, baleful, she suddenly wants to cry.

B.B. retreats a step as they drag past, Madeleine pausing to swat crystals from her soles. "Timbo, you wanna . . . ?" He nods, offers to accompany father and daughter upstairs.

Madeleine begins to object, gives up.

Nicky flattens herself against the lifeless grandfather clock, making way, as the band of three moves fitfully into the hall. In the kitchen, the teapot begins to shriek.

57

Groggily, the elevator ascends into darkness.

As a child, Madeleine spent hours in the cage, rising and sinking and rising again, happily disoriented, seeing nothing and hearing only the clack of gears and the slither of cables and the whine of metal. Cole joined her now and then, but he insisted she open the doors in the halls, so that light would waterfall onto them, wash away the dark.

"Dark," observes Timbo, shifting beside her.

Clack. Slither. Whine.

At the third floor the Otis judders and brakes. Madeleine and her father lurch into the hallway, Timbo hovering at his other side.

The second door on their left is Diana's bedroom. Madeleine, lodged under Sebastian's arm, cuts quick eyes to the officers there, to the window hoisted high. Her father slows, gawking; she steams ahead.

As she lowers him into his four-poster, a sob spurts from his mouth, then another—skirling cries that circle the room and huddle in the corners of the ceiling. Madeleine wants badly to flee; instead she pours him onto the sheets. Timbo bends over, carefully, and grasps the knobby ankles. One bare heel blasts his shoulder; with a grunt, he catches the other foot square in his palm and twists it just sharply enough that Sebastian rolls onto his side, air balloon-hissing out of him.

Madeleine wants to know how skin-and-bones Timbo pulled that off. She assesses the trim suit, the cool blue eyes. Perhaps she's underestimated him.

For now, though, she drags the blankets over her father's chest. His voice gurgles faintly in his throat; his brow is damp.

In the dresser she finds a tube of Valium and a tub of gumdrops. "Swallow both," she commands her father. "Open wide."

He opens wide, swallows both.

Beside her, Timbo's nose twitches like a rabbit's. "That pot?"

"Dad's been loopy after treatment ever since Freddy arrived. I figured he kept a stash." Sebastian's eyelids droop and drop.

"Mr. Trapp," says Timbo softly, and that anonymous voice sounds almost human. "Sorry to—you were saying something, sir? When you got into bed just now?"

With barely a rise and fall of the chest, the patient sighs, "Not again." Madeleine pauses at the foot of the mattress. "I said not again."

And he wads his eyelids tight.

Timbo bends toward him: "Would you recognize your son if he returned?"

Sebastian's eyes snap open so fast that Madeleine steps back. Her father stares straight at the detective. When he speaks, his voice is low but clear.

"I'd know him anywhere," he says.

58

HER TEA HAS COOLED during the climb to the attic. Nicky steps over yesterday's gown. When she lies down on the bed, her hand brushes Cole's diary, forgotten in the sheets. She decides to forget it a little while longer.

First the shock of the scream, then the shock of the body, then the shock of the police—and then, the shock of the note.

It's an awful cliché, but I can't go on. The guilt will drag me down and drown me.

She heard nothing last night. Then again, she wouldn't have—wouldn't have heard Diana climbing the staircase in her red dress, a torch in the gloom; wouldn't have heard her slide the window open; wouldn't have heard . . .

Did she perch on the sill? Nicky wonders. Watch the sky? Sit there for a while and remember her husband, her child? Remember Hope and Cole?

To her astonishment, Nicky feels betrayed. Not one week ago, Diana had welcomed her to the house, plied her with tea and cookies, settled her into an attic that she herself had made ready. She'd played for Nicky the soundtrack of her youth. She'd told her of her worst moment, her worst years. When did she begin plotting her surrender?

. . . Stop that. Stop. To die like this isn't a *plot*. Even Sebastian Trapp would agree with that.

And yet twenty years later she's married to Sebastian Trapp, B.B. Springer had reminded her husband. Was Nicky right to have wondered about Diana and Sebastian? Had the past—in some shape, in some guise—caught up with her?

. . . But what about that note?

Nicky sits up. All of a sudden, she craves escape—not from this house, not from the attic, but from the here and now. She wants transport: to an alternate dimension where death isn't a tragedy but a puzzle; where lives are as disposable as yesterday's crossword; where people die for money or lust or revenge, never for reasons unknown.

She hops from bed and hastens to the low hedge of paperbacks against the wall by Cole's desk. Her fingers scurry along the top of the Christies, each touch releasing a memory, like sweeping her hand over piano keys: a cruise ship on the Nile; a crowded train compartment in the dead of night; a hand carefully pasting strips of text to a poison-pen note; seven diners at a restaurant table.

The American edition is called *Remembered Death*. She'd forgotten that. *Sparkling Cyanide* she likes better.

Back in bed, Nicky sinks into the pillows and opens the book. *She had been depressed, run-down . . . It accounted, didn't it, for her suicide? How little you might know of a person after living in the same house with them!*

Nicky can't quite recall how the story unfolds. She turns the page.

Forties London, debutante in peril, poisoned sister. *The attics of the Elvaston Square house were used as storage rooms for odds and ends of furniture, and a number of trunks and suitcases.* Nicky almost smiles.

A few paragraphs later, she spreads the book across her chest. She simply can't picture Diana diving from her bedroom window. *She had been depressed, run-down*—perhaps; but a woman who entered rooms with such composure wouldn't exit one so recklessly, would she? A fall seemed very . . . out of character.

Nicky doesn't buy it, not entirely. B.B. Springer doesn't, either; she's still hunting Cole's shadow.

But *what about* that note?

It's a knot.

And the bow on top, a clue known only to Nicky: **For Cole**. That sheet of paper in Sebastian's desk drawer, with its mysterious benediction. *What* was for Cole? One might almost assume they were . . . communicating.

So escape to 1945 again. Peer into the dead woman's trunk.

As the bereft sister at Elvaston Square unpacks a dusty gown of spotted silk, Nicky unpicks the stitches of B.B.'s idea: Someone could be a killer without being Cole, after all. Maybe Jonathan did copy her key. Freddy has one, certainly.

Of course, you don't need a key if you're already inside. *Too many rooms, too many stairs. The kind of place where, at any moment, someone very dangerous could be standing right behind you.*

Nicky returns to Elvaston Square, where the heroine has discovered a surprising letter. *It might be important, one day, to show why*

Rosemary took her own life, she decides. *She smoothed it out, took it down with her, and locked it away in her jewel case.*

The chapter concludes with an anonymous note: *You think your wife committed suicide. She didn't. She was killed.*

Nicky claps the cover shut. Inhales.

She didn't.

She was killed.

Hope and Cole, two decades back; Diana, last night. And in both timelines: Sebastian, Madeleine, Freddy, Simone.

If she wants to discover what happened to Diana—and she does; the detective-fever is upon her afresh—she must find out what happened twenty years ago.

Her phone wriggles in the sheets. Let it be Julia; or let it be her god-daughter showing off a lost tooth, or Irwin and Potato grinning; let it be a colleague or a landlord or a forgotten friend—any inhabitant of her real life. Enough of this mystery she's crept into.

"Hello?" Her voice is croaky.

"Hello yourself," says Jonathan. "How's everyone feeling this morning?"

59

> Diana died last night.
>
> I'm sorry to tell you this.
>
> The police seem to think it
> wasn't an accident.
>
> They seem interested in you.

Madeleine sits at a table in the jigsaw room, back to the door, absently wedging pieces together, waiting for his reply. At last she hears Watson trot in, claws crisp on the floor. The prodigal pet.

As Madeleine leans over to pick her up, her phone chimes. She darts her eyes to the screen.

> SHHH

She nearly drops the dog.

"You okay?"

Madeleine turns, spots Nicky in the doorway. "Shut it behind you."

Nicky obeys. Waits as Madeleine gathers Watson in her lap.

What's she like?, Cole had asked. Was it a coincidence, though, that he should appear just days after Nicky did? Did he already *know* what she was like?

. . . No, probably not. Cole had heard their father's death rattle, somehow—hardly a secret—and now he's come home. Sebastian invited Nicky here—she didn't invite herself—for that same reason, staring down that same deadline. Emergencies attract all comers.

Besides, Nicky and Sebastian have written to each other for five long years. Is it likely that she knew Cole before then? If so, why contact his father? Five years is a long time to wait for . . . well, what could *Nicky* possibly want? Did she meet Cole *after* she and Sebastian began corresponding? That'd be quite a coincidence. And again: so what?

It's a knot. Still: what does she really know about Nicky?

On the table, her phone chimes again.

Madeleine glances at Nicky, patiently awaiting further instructions, and nearly grasps her head in her hands. She can't remember what she knows, or suspects, or prefers to ignore; the doubts and fears and memories are commuters toppling onto the track, a whistle in torment screaming dead ahead and a full-moon headlight barreling down. She breathes, drags air into the depths of her lungs, nearly chokes.

"Are you okay?" asks Nicky.

"Better than some. Strange theory that detective's got."

"Which one?"

"The one who can't shut up."

"I meant which theory."

"About my long-lost brother leaving little bugs around the house. How that relates to Diana, I've no idea." Except the police think he's a person of interest. Cole! A person of interest! Madeleine loved her brother, but he was never very interesting.

Nicky sighs. "I mean, if we were in a prewar mystery novel, then I'd say sure, I believe it."

"That happens all the time, I guess?"

"*The Red House Mystery, Brat Farrar . . .*"

"Thanks, that's plenty. The detective asked me if I'd heard from Cole."

"Yes, I was there," says Nicky.

"She asked you the same."

"I was there for that, too."

She's a bit spiky this morning. Madeleine almost likes it.

"He texted me," she hears herself say. "It's him. It's Cole. It is *Cole*." There. She feels as though she's sailed off-road and into thin air.

Nicky eyes are wide. "What?"

Madeleine nods. "Do you know him?"

Wider still. "Do I—how would I know him?"

"You got here six days ago. He texted me four days ago."

A frown. "Your father invited me here. After years of back-and-forth. About detective stories."

"But Cole told me to let you stick around." Keep your enemies close etc.

"What is it you think I might be doing for him?" Nicky sounds curious, not indignant. "You just heard me tell the police about that first butterfly. So I'm not much of an accomplice."

"You're not much of *anything!*" Madeleine shoots to her feet, Watson clutched in her arms, voice bursting from her like water from a hydrant. "You're not much of a *writer*—Dad said so. You're not much of a *houseguest,* you just float around freaking everybody out, like some perky little ghost. You're—ever since you got here for this *pointless, moronic memory book,* everything's gone wrong. Everything's *wrong,* Nicky!" Her eyes boil over, her body heaves; the dog paws at her chest. "People are dying and people are un-dying and I miss my mom, I *really miss* my mom. I miss—I want—I've only got *three months* with Dad until he's gone and I'm alone—*alone*—and suddenly *Cole* comes back on unfinished business or whatever fuckery he's up to, but *I'm the one who's been here this whole time!* For *all* of it. *I never left.* And I don't know what to do. And *you're not much* of a help."

She sucks air into her lungs. Her voice seems to echo; she looks away. The paupers and dandies on the walls have turned to gawk at her. The wenches serving ale are blushing.

Nicky moves toward her, her face drawn. *She's a boxer,* her father had informed the room last night, so Madeleine flinches and holds Watson tight against her chest, shielding her crumpled face, in case Nicky—

—hugs her.

Nicky is hugging her. Madeleine glances down at her damp hair. Silence.

"I'm sorry everything's wrong," Nicky tells Madeleine's shoulder. A squeeze. "I'm sorry you never got to leave." She burps.

. . . No—Watson burped. The dog is mashed between them. Madeleine steps back, scrubs at her eyes as she sits. Nicky crouches before her, lithe in her sweats.

"I can leave. I should go," she says quietly. "You should be alone. Not *you*—the family."

"No, no." Madeleine starts to strum the dog's belly. The outburst has calmed her, or (maybe) it was the embrace. "I thought—hoped, maybe— you might know him," she says, softer now. "And he wanted you here."

"For what?"

"He's asking about my mother." Madeleine swallows. "*Our* mother. His and mine. You're here with Dad, combing through his life, so he thinks—"

"Maybe Sebastian Trapp will tell me what he did with his wife and son. Or just his wife, I guess." Nicky slumps against the wall, against Jack the Ripper, and slides to the floor, her head at his feet. Her eyes close. "Yes, I'm interested in your family history," she says quietly. "It's an interesting family history. But I am here because I was asked to come."

Madeleine examines her pale face, the too-long sleeves of her sweatshirt. "Dad didn't really say you can't write."

A tired smile. "I'm glad."

"And you're not freaking everybody out."

"I hope not." The girl looks exhausted.

It's time for an alliance. To an extent, at least. "The texts," says Madeleine. "They're . . . ominous. He seems certain Dad knows what happened to our mother."

One eye cracks open. "*Does* your dad know what happened to your mother?"

B.B. Springer asked the same question just an hour ago. Madeleine's fingers idle at the dog's throat. *Does* he? "Do I tell the detectives he's here?" she asks. "What if he hurt Diana?"

"Why would he hurt Diana?"

"*Someone* did."

"What about her note?"

"I don't—" A thought sideswipes Madeleine so suddenly that she catches her breath. "Freddy."

Nicky sits up. "Freddy?"

"He kissed her." Madeleine stares at the door. "Diana. He kissed her yesterday. Or the day before. There's too much time to keep track of." Slumping against her chair. "She pushed him away. Freddy's— not *obsessed*, but . . . for years he's just drooled over her. He's been a good friend to me, you know. Ever since Cole. He's been good to Dad, even if Dad . . . well. But lately he's so *weird*. Like he's . . . up to something. I know that sounds silly, but . . ." She gives up. "Something is happening."

"Something is happening," agrees Nicky.

Madeleine eyes the phone on the jigsaw table. SHHH.

"I want to know what Cole knows. I want to keep him out of danger." What if he *is* the danger?

"You think he made those butterflies? You think he's been here but no one's seen him?"

Madeleine glances at the wall, at Jack, a distant shadow in hat and cape, dressed to kill. "No one's *recognized* him. He could've been that violinist last night. He could be your gentleman caller. He could be anybody."

Nicky blinks.

"Or he could be nobody I've ever seen," adds Madeleine.

For the second time today, they hear a scream.

Nicky jumps to her feet. Madeleine chases her into the foyer, clasping Watson against her chest.

Across the marble, in the living room doorway, stands Simone, hands masking her nose and mouth, eyes fixed on the gurney two officers are rolling over the floor. The white body bag is bulging at one end but almost flat at the other, like badly packed luggage.

Madeleine watches the officers maneuver her stepmother out of the house. Beside her, Nicky blots her eyes with her sleeves.

The grandfather clock rouses itself for one elegiac gong as B.B. Springer walks briskly toward them, fingers smoothing her hair, arm around Simone. "We'd just wrapped up with your aunt when she opened the door and . . . well, you saw it." B.B. grips the lapels of her jacket, snaps them so the snakeskin crackles. "You need some time here. We'll be back for Mr. Trapp when he's in better shape. Coroner requests you keep out of the bedroom. And the yard."

Timbo appears, toting three evidence bags—a coat, a sleeve, that nightmare mask—and reports Frederick Trapp's current whereabouts as unknown. "Landlady says she booted him out early April. No forwarding."

"He was *evicted*?" blurts Simone.

B.B. whips three business cards from her pocket. "I'll hear from you if you hear from him. Again, we're very sorry for your loss."

"Very sorry," mumbles Timbo.

Madeleine, Nicky, and Simone watch them exit the house, Timbo first, his hair flaming for an instant in the sunlight. B.B. pauses on the threshold, then turns, gazes at the foyer with—defiance? wonders Madeleine.

She smiles. Draws the door shut behind her.

Sudden quiet. The symphony of that morning plays dimly in Madeleine's head: her aunt's screams, her father's rants; the elevator groans, the wash of pondwater.

The three of them wait for a moment before scattering. "I'll look in on Sebastian," says Simone, bustling toward the staircase.

"Excuse me." Madeleine turns from Nicky, Watson panting against her, and hurries to her suite, thumbs a message into her phone:

Please answer me

Then she deletes the Please. Sends it.

A moment later, she's slumped on her sofa, face buried in palms, the dog rolled into the crevice of the cushions.

Madeleine sits there for a year.

Sits until she hears the front door close.

She walks to her bed, peers through the window at the car in the driveway. She sees Jonathan at the wheel. She sees Nicky climb inside.

Who is he?

And why *is* he so interested in that girl?

60

"Bloody hell, that's a morning."

Jonathan whistles. He's fresh in a rugby shirt and sunglasses, and any other day, Nicky would want to pick up where they left off in the attic—her hand on his chest, her mouth on his mouth, her veins lit up in excitement—but today she turns to the window, tired of talking.

"Poor woman. Poor Fred—spoke very warmly of her. And you—you all right?"

Nicky frowns. "I didn't know her very well. But still."

"But still," he sighs. "What it must be like, to feel there's no hope. No possibility."

She folds her arms across her chest, closes her eyes. "They don't think it's suicide."

"Thought you said there was a note?"

"Yep." A mound of a park outside; two men wrangling a Labrador, laughing; a mother and child hand in hand.

"So—back up: why would anyone want to . . . what, *murder* her?" Like it's a dirty word. Nicky supposes it is. "I sound as though I'm stressing every syllable in that sentence. *Why? Anyone? Her?*"

"You stressed *murder,* too."

"Murder is inherently stressful."

Yesterday Nicky would've giggled at that. "They're interested in Cole Trapp," she says.

"What, because of that little telegram last night?" Ahead of them tourists spill from the sidewalk outside a row of townhouses in summer colors; Jonathan taps his horn, taps it again. "Talk about wanting to murder. But isn't Cole Trapp dead and gone? Or gone, at least?"

Nicky says nothing.

A pause. "Where are we going, by the way? I'm happy to just wander, if you like. Yours to command."

"Any idea where Freddy might be?" *He kissed her. Diana.*

"At his, I should think. Licking his wounds. Probably tough to lick your own eye, though. I rang him last night and this morning. No answer. Should we drive to his place?"

"I don't think he's home." She bites her lip.

"What *did* he want in the library last night, anyway?"

But Nicky's fingertips are dancing on her phone screen, tracing the route ahead. "Could you take a right here, please?"

Minutes later, beneath a frail lattice of cable-car wires, they park and cross into the gauntlet of Castro Street. Rainbow flags swell like sails from telephone poles; clothing boutiques and laser-treatment centers shoulder the upper stories of Golden Age townhomes. Light blanches their bay windows, dazzles the glass doors of delis and pet shops. The lone bank in sight, clad in drab brick, looks like the chaperone at a party.

"So weird to think that somebody died downstairs while you were sleeping," says Jonathan, and Nicky nearly cries again.

They pass the regal Castro Theatre (on the marquee: BOHEMIAN RHAPSODY SING-ALONG! and a German war drama called *Phoenix,* presumably not a sing-along) and a cannabis dispensary and a pizzeria. She looks at her phone. *That uncomfortable heat at the pit of your stomach, that nasty thumping at the top of your head* . . .

When the arrow on her screen turns west, she turns with it.

And lifts her eyes to an alley flaming with fluorescent graffiti. Next to her beckons a white rabbit, pocketwatch in paw; on either side, walls throng with citizens of Wonderland: the dormouse, dreaming; the Queen of Hearts, screaming . . . all in acid-trip shades, all leering and gaping as Nicky steps deeper and deeper into the alley. Letters overhead, floating on a tide of pipe smoke: WE'RE ALL MAD HERE.

To her left squats a monstrous Cheshire cat with a grin like a scythe and a tail like the curl of a question mark.

It *is* the curl of a question mark, Nicky sees, and the spattery purple inkblot below it is a doorknob. She twists the knob, pushes the door—"Wait," hisses Jonathan, just as he did last night in the library—and steps into darkness.

The place is a cave, most of it bare floor, invisible beneath her feet. Three bashed-up booths hug one wall, each wanly lit by a sconce desperate for retirement. Across the room, stools ring a half-moon bar, and behind it, above skylines of liquor bottles, globe lightbulbs of the dressing-room variety spell the name BETTY.

Nicky approaches. She tends to like dive bars. Dive bars tend to like her.

The bartender, hulking and beefy, eyes Nicky; she wears a tank top, a tutu, and a week's stubble. "In my next life, I wanna come back as cute as you," she says, voice rich and deep. "What's your name, baby girl?"

"Nicky."

"Betty." Her handshake could crush ice. "Who's your piece?"

"Jonathan. Jesus," he adds as Betty grips his hand.

"Welcome to Betty's. Café by day, bar by night. And by day." She winks. Her eyes are frilled with sequined lashes.

Nicky hops onto a bar stool. "When do you sleep?"

"Oh, baby—I clock out at four P.M. I own the damn joint." Betty taps her phone, and unseen speakers exhale a lonesome saxophone solo, crackling with age. "Much better. What'll it be?"

"I don't drink coffee."

"So don't drink coffee."

"What do you suggest?" asks Jonathan.

Betty listens to the sax drifting across the ceiling. "A Manhattan you shake to foxtrot time, a Bronx to two-step time, and a dry martini you always shake to waltz time."

Nicky listens, too. "There doesn't seem to be a time."

"Whiskey it is." Betty spins the cap off a bottle of Hibiki, pours three shots.

Before they can toast, a cough like a volcano erupts from the depths of the room. Nicky swivels: in the far booth, a battered stork of a man in a lifeless brown suit dips his beak into a pint glass, swallows, then drags on a cigarette. Smoke churns beneath his lamp.

"Is that individual dying?" asks Jonathan.

"That's the Professor," Betty says. "He came with the place. Hasn't croaked yet."

A quick shot of light as the door swings open, swings shut. Betty waves to a woman in scrubs before turning to an espresso machine the size of a car engine.

"You waiting for someone, darlin's?"

"Looking for him," Nicky says to her broad back. "Guy about our age."

"What age is that?"

"Very-well-into-thirties," Jonathan replies.

The espresso machine begins to burble.

"Nice and tall," says Nicky.

"Gym membership," says Jonathan.

"Deep-dark hair," says Nicky.

"Easy there," says Jonathan.

The machine hisses.

"And a small tattoo on his arm—line from a book."

The machine roars, and Betty whisks a cup and a pitcher to the woman in scrubs, sucking on a Camel a few stools away. Nicky nearly smiles. The smoke roiling in the barely-there light, the hard-bitten bartender, the mournful sax . . . she's in an old noir.

"He got coffee here last week," she says. "I noticed the cup." She taps her phone, finds Freddy's staff photo from the previous year. Stares at it: he looked remarkably healthier then.

Betty nods, her smile thinning. "Cute. 'Fraid I can't help you. You drive here?"

Jonathan blinks. "Yes."

"Where'd you park?"

Jonathan names the street.

"Can't park there afternoons. You'll get towed."

"Shit," he says, clambering from the bar stool and vowing to return. As soon as the door swings shut, Betty leans forward, beckons Nicky to do the same.

"Car's fine. I wanted him gone. Now, I can't help you with Fred, but I'm not sure I like the look of your boyfriend, either."

Nicky frowns. "He's not my—what do you mean?"

"I haven't seen him before," says Betty, stroking her whiskery chin, "but I've seen his type."

"What type is that?"

"The type that's hiding something." And she downs her Hibiki.

Nicky slowly rubs her own between her palms. She likes Jonathan—likes his chat, likes his lips. Even likes the Southwest-England connection between him and Hope Trapp.

. . . Although he *had* lived in London at the same time as Diana.

And he *did* keep her key for twenty-four hours.

And he *does* know Freddy—an unlikely murderer himself, but most definitely up to something, as his cousin said.

And someone could be a killer without being Cole. Without being Sebastian, either.

Nicky knocks back her shot, grimaces, knocks back Jonathan's shot, grimaces—Betty looks on with approval—and wipes her mouth. "Thank you for the drink." She slaps three bills on the bar— "For yours and ours"—and steps backward toward the door. "See you again, maybe."

"I'll be waiting for you, baby girl," Betty calls.

It's only when she's back in the alley, blinking in the sunlight, that Nicky realizes Betty knew Freddy's name without her ever saying it.

61.

MAYBE IT'S THE DETECTIVE-FEVER, maybe it's the whiskey—but Nicky feels ready to follow the white rabbit through Wonderland to where the alley tacks beneath a blue butterfly, the caterpillar reborn. She turns left.

A moment later, a door slams behind her. She glances back to see the stork from the bar, plumage greasy, chewing on his cigarette. He looks either way, begins stalking toward her.

She quickens her pace, past letters streaming along the brick: OH, WHAT A CURIOUS DREAM I'VE HAD!

When she rounds the corner, she's exited Wonderland, though not the alley. Here it tightens, dingy walls narrowing to a distant splinter of sidewalk and sun.

"Hey." His voice staggers into the dead end, stumbles after her. "Girlie!"

She darts a look backward—nobody but the butterfly—then ducks into a shallow doorway. Taped to the glass pane of the door is a sheet of paper, marked in red ink: BEWARE OF MOTHAFUCKIN DOG.

"Girlie! I wanna talk to you." The Professor is nearing her, feet slapping the ground. Nicky can't decide whether to hide or to jump him.

He strides past, fragrant with booze and smoke, lank hair brushing his shoulders—

—and at her back a frenzy of snarls, as the door shudders and she springs into the alley, into the stranger, driving him hard against the brick wall. When he grunts, his cigarette tumbles from his mouth.

Nicky has hiked her knee into his crotch (by accident) and seized his shoulders (also by accident), so he can't double over. She clings to his oily coat, twists her head. Behind the door, some mongrel is shouting at them, jowls sudsy, paws scrabbling at the glass.

"Shit, lady," croaks the Professor. "I juss wanted to—jeez, knock it off, mutt!" The mothafuckin dog lathers the window, snaps its jaws.

Nicky releases the man, steps back—then whirls around and snarls so ferociously that the dog abruptly sinks from sight, saliva like spume upon the glass.

She turns to the Professor. "You wanted what?"

He winces. "Fred. Works in sports, like. Big guy, muscly." When he eyes the fallen cigarette, Nicky stoops to the pavement and retrieves it. "Thanks," he says, plugging the stub between his lips.

"You know him?"

He shakes his head. "I seen him in there"—jerking his thumb toward Betty's—"lotsa times. Brings takeout. Oriental-type squiggles on the bag." A cloud of smoke. "Restaurant's called Tigress. I 'member that 'cause my wife and me, we had a cat called Tigress. Woke up one morning, she'd flown the coop overnight. The cat, not my wife. Never saw her again. Then a year later I woke up and my wife'd flown the coop overnight. Never saw her again, either." He sighs. "I really miss that cat."

Nicky looks at the Professor, his sallow skin cured in sun and smoke, his yellowed fingertips, the sad eyes; she pictures him healthy, or at least hopeful, with a job and a lunch date and—why not—a cat. "Why are you telling me this?"

He smooths a shirtfront pocked with burn holes, as though some zealous assassin had sprayed him with gunfire. "Guy's off. Couple months ago, starts showin' up drug through hell backward. An' ever since, more often'n not, he walks in with his Chinese, kinda twitchy, an' a little later, a young fella shows up an' sits down, an'—"

"Who?"

"Dunno. But they talk for a minute, an' then the fellow leaves. An' so does your man, after he eats his dumplins. Maybe once a week."

"When? What day, I mean?"

"Girlie, I don' even know what day it is today." He sucks on his cigarette, flicks it to the ground.

Nicky pats her pockets, fishes out her wallet. "Thank you, sir," she says, offering a twenty. He quickly palms it.

"Watch yourself, miss." Sloping backward up the alley, back to Wonderland. "He could be a tough customer."

"So am I," she tells him.

62

NOBODY HAS TEXTED: not Cole, not Freddy, even though she's threatened him repeatedly. And who else would contact her? *You're the last one left.*

Madeleine shuffles from her room, climbs the stairs; as she steps onto the landing, the front door opens behind her and Nicky walks through, smiles hopefully.

That hug was hours ago. Madeleine keeps moving.

In the doorway of her father's bedroom she hesitates, watching him snore evenly beneath the covers, beneath the red roof of his bed, eyes shut and hands folded across his chest. *I suppose this is a preview,* she thinks.

"Any word from Frederick?"

Madeleine didn't even notice Simone at her father's bedside. Still in her bathrobe. Madeleine hasn't changed, either. Perhaps they ought to get dressed.

"Frederick?" pleads her aunt.

Madeleine shakes her head. Leaves.

How *is* Freddy mixed up in this? The butterflies, the texts—it could all be a one-man campaign. But not if that man is Freddy, surely. (Surely?) Cole's only friend: his locker-room bodyguard, his fellow Scout, his sleepover bunkmate. Had they reunited?

A limp ribbon of tape spans the doorway of what she still thinks of as her mother's bedroom: CRIME SCENE CRIME SCENE, it chants, very sure of itself. DO NOT CROSS.

She ducks beneath it.

The air seems thinner here; the violet walls have faded. The bed is made, a dark dress on top like a chalk outline, and on the floor, a garment bag.

Maybe this is what a room feels like, looks like, when someone has died in it.

Although Diana hadn't died here.

Diana had hoped to die in Samarra. Diana had hoped to travel. Diana planned a future.

Madeleine frowns at the desk. Why, then, had Diana written that note?

The police have closed the fatal window. Madeleine approaches, careful not to touch the sill, and gazes down into the courtyard, into the pond. A few lily pads shaped like hearts. Fish swirling slowly in the clear black water.

Was she suicidal?

Was she drunk?

Was she pushed?

Madeleine turns away, crosses to the vanity, bare but for a lamp and a black perfume bottle and a white jewelry box, doubled in the mirror. When she lifts the lid of the box and slowly winds a small key on the side, fragile metallic notes drift like balloons into the afternoon light. A French song: Madeleine remembers the tune from seventh-grade language class.

After a moment, she inspects the perfume bottle. Here it is at last, the name of Diana's mystery scent, clean and cool and soft: Mystery. This strikes Madeleine as unimaginative.

She mists her bare wrist. Twists the cap back on, sets the bottle on the dresser, brings her arm to her nose.

The music starts to drowse; the tinny, tiny notes dither and die. Madeleine shuts the jewelry box lid, strokes it once, then exits the bedroom. The police tape peels from the doorway; she watches it flutter to the floor, stoops to collect it, presses it firmly against the jamb.

As she walks down the corridor to her father's room and the last echo of the melody fades from her mind, she recalls its title. "J'ai descendu dans mon jardin."

I went down to my garden.

63.

Simone welcomes Nicky into the kitchen stiffly, seems surprised to learn she'd left the house—and with Jonathan ("Not sure what that Betty chap was on about," he said. "The car was fine").

"The detectives spoke to me about him." Simone is hunched over the island in her robe, mug of coffee before her. "They even asked if he *reminded* me of anybody! Meaning *Cole*. As if I wouldn't recognize my own *nephew*."

Nicky balks alongside her. Who would confuse Jonathan Grant with Cole Trapp? . . . The police, apparently.

She retrieves a milk carton from the fridge, waits for Simone to observe how she's made herself right at home; instead, she's invited to browse last night's photos.

"I thought I should take some pictures, in case you wanted any for your—memory book," explains the only living Mrs. Trapp as Nicky huddles beside her. She swipes two fingers across the screen, back and forth, regular as windshield wipers. "There's the champagne pyramid. Oh, I can't bear to look at it." Swipe. "Why was I photographing shrimp scampi?" Swipewipeswipeswipe. "Lionel Lightfoot. I'll never know what Diana was thinking."

For a moment she goes quiet.

Next up is Freddy. Simone sighs. "He's so *erratic* lately. That *scene* last night. I wish . . . I wish he'd call."

Now she conjures up Diana: bright dress and loose hair, empty glass in one hand, speaking to Freddy but glancing beyond him. "Oh," says Simone.

He kissed her.

In the next photo, Freddy holds the camera overhead, arm's-length, while he and his mother flank Diana. "He insisted on a selfie," Simone explains to Nicky. "What an angle." She frowns. She's frowning in the picture, too, and a touch disheveled—her silver hair snagged in her silver chain, her eyelashes sooty with mascara.

Diana's edges are blurred. She looks almost spectral.

"Could you send this to me?" Nicky asks, surprising herself. "I'd like to—I'd like it."

"Frederick asked for it, too." Simone hands her the phone and Nicky forwards the photo. It's a comfort, knowing that Diana has an afterlife in her hardware, a ghost in the machine.

"And here's Sebastian. Or much of Sebastian. You see how difficult it can be to squeeze him into frame when he's talking to a very short person, such as this woman in a wheelchair." Then Sebastian laughing, Sebastian bowing, Sebastian tippling beer.

"Have you always been in love with him?"

Nicky knows instantly that nobody has ever asked her this. Simone turns her head, almost in wonder, like a lonely spirit whom suddenly someone can see.

When she speaks, her voice is very, very soft. "Since my wedding day." The corners of her lips lift. "I hadn't met him before then. Our first date—Dominic's and mine, I mean—was right after he and Hope and Madeleine went off on a long book tour. I don't remember which book. Hardly matters. Then I became pregnant, and my mother wanted the baby born in wedlock—eight weeks later, shotgun wedding. They missed the rehearsal. Sebastian and company. Canceled flight, I think. Hardly matters. But the following morning . . ."

Her eyes close. "When I saw him in his best-man suit, standing next to Dominic at the altar, I thought, *Oh, no—it's* you *I want, it's* you *I love, I do, I do.*" She beams at the ceiling, the length of her throat exposed, and for a moment Nicky glimpses the woman she was, before nerves carved lines in her face and age zebra-striped her hair. "*Why you?*" she asks helplessly. "*Why now? As I'm walking down the aisle?*"

Nicky listens.

Simone descends to earth, opens her eyes. "I said I do to Dominic, of course. Said it and meant it. He was the forerunner. And I did love him, and I loved Frederick, then and now and forever. I was a dutiful sister to Sebastian and Hope, and after—after New Year's Eve, for all those years, I cared for Sebastian. We all did. Then, when my husband died, I thought—I *hoped*—that . . ."

Nicky feels her blood begin to rove. *Wouldn't it haunt you?* Simone had asked. *Taking a life . . . Never coming clean. Who could do it?*

Cui bono, Nicky had answered. Who *did* benefit by Dominic's death? For that matter, who might've benefited from Diana's?

Simone sighs. "But I couldn't work out how Sebastian would ever regard me as anyone besides the sister-in-law. Never shuts up, babies her boy, bossy busybody. Hardly matters."

Her phone screen fades to black. Automatically she taps it, and Sebastian's face surfaces again. Simone gazes at him.

"Then he brought Diana home. Didn't see that one coming."

And now Diana's dead. Diana, who probably didn't see that one coming.

Simone begins twirling the spoon in her teacup. "I don't care for mystery novels. I think they're ridiculous. Even the Simon stories. I've read all of them, of course. I read Sherlock Holmes, too. I wanted to see what *he* saw in them. I remember only the man who fell in love with a woman on an ocean voyage years earlier, the man who said to Sherlock, 'When we parted she was a free woman, but I was not a free man.'" Another faint smile. "You're a good listener. I get why people talk to you."

"Mm," answers Nicky, swallowing.

"Ever loved somebody who didn't love you back?"

I wonder if Simone *got to him,* Jonathan had said of some long-dead Watson. *I ask Fred if his mother might in fact be capable of homicide. And he answers, "Dude, my mother is capable of genocide."*

"Yup," says Nicky, her voice in a chokehold.

"It can be almost pleasurable, I find." Simone's fingertip skates atop the screen. For a moment they sit in silence. "But mostly it's unbearable. Oh—past five. The cats are probably cannibalizing one another. I need to leave. It'll be me making the funeral arrangements, of course. Sebastian can't. Madeleine probably can't." She climbs from the stool. "I think you should leave, too."

She doesn't mean for the evening. "I understand."

"There's been a death in the family. Sebastian isn't well, Madeleine is . . . Madeleine. Frederick's wrecking property and assaulting people—I'm sorry, by the way."

Nicky clears her throat. "Not the first time I've been smacked."

"I'm sure you and Sebastian can discuss your project in a little while. But for now . . ."

"I understand. Really."

Simone pockets her phone. In the doorway, she pauses, examines her robe. "I guess I'll wear this home," she says. "It's his."

When she leaves, Nicky downs the rest of her milk, exhales. *The fever will lay hold of you.*

She doesn't play chess, but still she can picture the board: Simone sacrifices a knight in order to take her place beside the king. Queen appears out of nowhere. Eventually Simone claims her, too.

Nicky picks at her thumbnail. Why would Simone strike just months before Sebastian's death? Perhaps, if you've killed two people for a single reason, you feel obliged to finish what you've—

She bows her head, grips her glass.

Why not three people?

And now a roaring in her ears as the fever lays hold: what about the first queen?

Where was Simone that night? At home, she said, with her husband and son.

And Cole.

64

UPSTAIRS, SEATED ON THE BEDSIDE CHAIR in the pale lamplight, Madeleine stares at her father's hands. Pianist's hands, her mother used to say, fine-boned, long fingers. Madeleine examines her own fingers in her lap. Chunky, she knows, or at least clunky.

He's now lost two wives. And a child.

"She had a sad life."

Madeleine jolts. His eyes are closed, the lids bruised, dark as sockets in a skull.

A moment passes, until she suspects that she imagined his voice. Beyond the window, the last of the evening light burns away.

"A sad life," he repeats, eyes open. Madeleine wonders if he's still floating on weed.

"She had five years with you," she says. "You traveled. You . . ." They were companionable. They laughed, often enough. ". . . loved each other," she finishes.

But he rolls his head against the pillow, back and forth. "Her real life was over before me."

Madeleine remembers.

"So she withdrew. Into the past, where the sets were familiar. I believe that's why she returned here: not to live her life but to wait it out." Now he turns his face to his daughter. "We weren't each other's first choices. But that's why we fit: we were both resigned to it. Neither one of us really wanted lives beyond those we had already led. We were each other's afterlives." His eyes are damp.

Then, with a sad smile: "Please come in."

Madeleine glances behind her. Nicky hovers in the doorway like an angel of death unsure whether she's arrived late or early. "Sorry to intrude," she says. "I ought to take off. You'll want the house to yourselves."

Madeleine nods, satisfied. She and her father have waged this war before, two against the world, two against this house: peering together down its dark halls, shouldering side by side the weight of that attic, shying from the windows—

"Miss Hunter, I would feel bereft were you to leave. Maddy"—he offers his hand to her—"please tell our guest that we insist."

She squeezes his fingers, irritated. "No one's going anywhere tonight, certainly."

"Stay a moment, Miss Hunter. You know, girls, what I most wished for Diana was motherhood. She had that essential, that *elemental*, quality of a good mother."

Madeleine nearly raises her hand. "Kindness?"

"No. She *was* kind, but no." He looks at Nicky.

Who, after a pause, says, "Diana was ferocious."

"Very good. She needed to be, to survive such loss. Not many would sense that in her, but you did."

Madeleine glares at her father, willing him to address her, not this stranger—and now he does. "'A mother's love for her child is like nothing else in the world,'" he says. "'It knows no law, no pity, it dares all things and crushes down remorselessly all that stands in its path.'" His hands shift in hers. "So sayeth Agatha Christie. And a woman as ferocious as that would make a wonderful mother." Sebastian is sinking deeper into bed, his voice dwindling. "But she didn't want to try again, to risk again. Didn't want to lose again."

A moment later, he's snoring, and Madeleine dims the lamp. When she turns to the door, Nicky is gone.

In the lightless hallway—it was Diana who always switched on the sconces, of course—Madeleine stumbles over the goddamn dog. The two of them descend to the courtyard. As Watson nitrogenates a boxwood, Madeleine glances into the dark corner where earlier today (was it really today?) she discovered her father, roaring, his wife in his arms; where now the fish drift indifferently through the water.

She shivers.

In the nighttime parlor, its chandelier pitiful as a dead Christmas tree, Madeleine paws at the bookshelf until the wall glides toward her. The hangover room is lit low.

She sits on the chaise inside. Her eyes tour the walls, the gallery of maps and prints—had Diana visited all these places? Madeleine never asked.

The lights die.

Now she listens to a low rustle of pondwater near the floor, seeping through the grate. Diana's body steeped in that pond. Her blood flowed into it. What Madeleine hears, that sound of water, is the sound of blood.

And as it washes into her head, she finds her phone, taps a message to her brother.

> Magdala.
>
> I'm starting to get scared.

A moment later:

> Magdala.
>
> I don't think you're scared
> enough.

65.

"Evening," says Jonathan.

"Evening," says Nicky, phone wedged between shoulder and ear.

"Too late for a chat?"

It's barely nine thirty, but she could sleep for a year. *Go sleep*, Diana said, just last night (was it really just last night?). *I intend to dose myself to next week.*

Jonathan proceeds. "So I was wondering. After I dropped you off. I thought that butterfly on the typewriter or whatever—thought it was only a laugh."

Nicky aims one leg into her shorts, misses, stumbles across the floorboards, grunting.

"Sounds like a rugby match."

"Feels like one." She stabs the speaker, tosses the phone onto the bed.

"But they—the police, I mean—they believe it's a threat?" he continues. "They think this origami artist, Cole Trapp or not, knows what happened to the wife, the mother? And he's trying to force Sebastian to come clean? And is not Fred?"

Nicky rucks the shorts up to her hips. "That's one theory."

"And he's trying to spook Sebastian?"

She perches on the edge of the bed, flops backward. "Or entrap. Or blackmail. Or torture. But he seems very certain that Sebastian is responsible."

One hand stirs the sheets, brushes against the diary.

"I don't think I could even make origami. Can you fold little paper animals?"

"I can barely fold a napkin."

His laugh is pinched. "They want to speak with me. The coppers. Feeling a little uneasy here."

"I wouldn't be afraid. The truth is the best defense." Nicky folds herself into bed, props the diary on her stomach.

". . . he was a little kid," Jonathan is saying. "And the wee lad grew up to be a strapping brute like me, is that the idea?"

As he chatters somewhere by her hip, Nicky locates the last entry she read (only yesterday—was it really only yesterday?). *Something exiting is hapening!!*

She flips the page, then the next few—all blank. Cole's voice goes silent there, in June of 1999.

Her eyes are caving in. She shuts them, splays the book across her chest. When Jonathan pauses, she murmurs, "Yes," and like a pull-string doll, he continues speaking.

Only in that final instant before sleep does she hear him clearly once more, his voice low and soft:

"What makes you so sure there's nothing to be afraid of?"

Wednesday, June 24

66

—A BUZZ.

Madeleine opens one eye. Her phone shivers on the pillow. "Hello?" she slurs.

"Ms. Trapp, I'm calling from the *Chronicle*. We'd love to talk to you about your father's wife—"

"*I would rather explode,*" screams Madeleine.

Thirty-three missed calls stacked onscreen, all unknown numbers. Thirteen voicemails. "Madeleine," coos a stranger, "sorry for your loss. I'm with the newsroom at—" Delete. "Good morning. We're hoping you can verify some details—" Delete.

She murders each message, sweat in her blood, acid in her gut— *Leave me alone, leave us alone*—but when the phone shakes again, as if in self-defense, she answers. "Wrong number."

"This is the *Oakland Star*. Please come have a quick word."

"Like hell I'm going to Oakland," Madeleine spits.

"No need. Just come outside."

Madeleine dives to the curtains, yanks them back.

A dozen strangers have congregated at the foot of the drive, like vampires waiting to be invited in. Two shoulder cameras; the rest peck at their phones, except for a woman mouthing the words in Madeleine's ear.

"If we could borrow you—"

Madeleine whirls from the bed, startling Watson, and charges into the foyer in her pajamas. Tongue dry, throat tight, not enough skin: it's New Year's Day again, and the rest of that month, and the rest of that winter. She'll open the front door and scream into the past.

The front door is already open. A blade of light cuts across the marble. Madeleine freezes.

". . . the family asks for privacy at this—this time. Mr. Trapp hopes to make a statement soon, but for now, please just . . . give him space to grieve."

Madeleine hovers beside the door. On the steps, Nicky is addressing the cockroaches like a little town crier, bag slung across her chest.

"Please." She waves her phone. "Nobody wants to see themselves online, harassing a widower."

The crowd begins to melt away as she comes back inside, closes the door. "What was that?" hisses Madeleine.

"Whoa." Nicky hops in surprise. "Sorry. I saw the mob from the attic, and I asked myself, *What would Simone do? Simone would probably clear them out before you or your father—*"

A low woof. Watson has appeared at the bedroom door. "Here, come in," says Madeleine, before stepping into the bathroom to catch her breath, splash her face.

She emerges to find the dog snoring where she woofed and Nicky across the room, standing before the optical-illusion print. "The police reporter published a very brief item late last night," Nicky explains. "Just 'Diana died, no foul play suspected at this time.'"

Could've fooled me, thinks Madeleine.

"Hashtag-MurderSequel was trending when I woke up."

"Oh, nice. That's nice." Madeleine crosses to the bed, glares out the window. The last of the roaches are scuttling away. "Off you fuck," she mutters.

"Sorry?"

"I was just swearing." Turning to Nicky. "Thank you. For—doing what Simone would've done. Are you headed out?" Eyeing the bag.

"Change of scene. Gotta write." Nicky clears her throat. "Also: I know your dad asked me to stick around, but—I think I ought to go. I do. Like I said out there, you're grieving, and . . ." Her voice cracks in her throat like a pane of ice.

Madeleine watches in horror. Her arms rebel, floating up for a hug, before she folds them firmly across her chest.

"Sorry," mutters Nicky, smearing her fingers beneath her eyes. "She was—a very decent person."

Madeleine pats her on the head, as though she's a good dog. Hears herself saying, "You'll find it's not so easy to leave this house. Besides, Dad's used to having women around. Me. Diana. Watson." The dog kicks in her sleep. "And maybe the past is a better place for him. Even if it's gone."

"Or it's waiting."

Madeleine frowns.

"He said that," says Nicky. "'The past isn't gone. It's just waiting.'"

Madeleine thinks of her brother, also waiting. But for what?

Suppose Cole were . . . *involved*, say, in Diana's death. Maybe he thought she knew something about their mother. Or maybe he wanted Sebastian to pay attention. Never mind why, really—just assume he's graduated from paper butterflies. Should she alert the police after all? Would they guard the house, guard her father?

I don't think you're scared enough.

The shadow he casts in her head gets darker by the hour. She needs an ally.

"Please stay," Madeleine says.

Nicky's phone chirps. "My ride. I'll be back," she adds, stepping carefully over the dog.

Madeleine jumps onto the bed, stares out the window. No spectators, just a banana-yellow taxi that slides up the driveway and whisks Nicky away.

Watson fixes her with one rolling eye as Madeleine approaches. In the foyer, she can almost hear herself breathe. The party caterers had scarcely swept up the ruins of the champagne pyramid before Simone ordered everybody out, and napkin wads still litter the corners like tumbleweeds, tiny toothpick swords splinter beneath her feet. The place seems poised to crumble: *The Fall of the House of Trapp*, she thinks. She's never much liked Poe, but she remembers that story, that house, with its decaying Gothic hall and the doomed woman who dwelled there. Madeleine.

67

In the cab, Nicky catches up with Irwin (who has read about Diana's death) and Julia (who has not). She assures them she'll be leaving soon—but she survived the night, didn't she?

No smile from Irwin, not even with Potato heavy-breathing in his lap. "Bad people love innocence, Nicky." His voice is low. "And you're the most innocent person I know, with the biggest heart. And there's only one of you." A squeeze on her big heart.

"You're the most stubborn person I know," says Julia. "This is exactly what I feared—didn't I say it?" No gurgle of a straw; just her voice closing up. Nicky tries to distract her with recent words of the day, but she can't remember any of them, and Julia isn't in the mood.

Texts crowd her screen, even a few old-school voicemails: friends and colleagues are concerned. Nicky vows to circle back this afternoon, once she's cleared up this nasty thumping at the top of her head.

She disembarks at the Dragon Gate in Chinatown. The car coasts away, heading off a funeral procession as it crawls east down Bush Street.

She pauses in the shadow of the three pagodas, scaly with green tile. Twin sea serpents salute each other atop the roof, and a sign painted like an exotic rug sways from the rafters, gold characters piped across it. Beside the east and west gates, a stone lion apiece, both wearing raspberry lipstick.

And beyond the Dragon Gate, up the steep pitch of Grant Avenue, the rumble of voices.

Nicky begins to hike—past antiques dealers, a few small restaurants, storefronts all introducing themselves bilingually. Just ahead, a gaggle of blond women in designer sweats rail against income inequality. The blondest thrusts a flyer at Nicky. "Educate yourself!"

Grant levels off at the intersection, just as Pine Street suddenly lifts to the west, as though the city were folding itself upon Nicky. She approaches the ragged edge of a swarming crowd.

The block heaves beneath plump Chinese lanterns, jewel-red and dripping tassels, strung across the street from fire escapes to balconies, from windows to rooftops. Crowds throng the stalls—stir-fry cooks assaulting woks, children hawking silk scarves and San Francisco tees. Exotic fauna here, too: dragons slither through the mob, a flight of them, colors shocking bright, giddy shrieks beneath the skin. Nicky peeks at the belly of a molten-red monster—a half dozen school-children, wielding stilts and commanding bystanders to "MOVE! MOVE!"

The sidewalks are jammed, people papered against storefront windows. Nicky checks her phone. Can she elbow her way two hundred feet forward?

The dragon circles back into the crowd. Nicky grasps a fistful of blue tailfeathers and hitches a ride.

Halfway down the block, she spies an opening, darts to the door of the Tigress restaurant. Cases the joint: white tablecloths, golden Buddhas laughing. Five diners, none of them Freddy.

When the hostess approaches, Nicky shows her Simone's selfie, points to Freddy. The woman smiles and says, in gentle English, "To see."

"I'd like to see him, yes."

"To see."

Nicky frowns.

"To see, to see!" the woman insists, and ushers Nicky out the door, steering her a few steps along the sidewalk, amid tourists brandishing selfie sticks like rapiers, and into a doorway.

Nicky tips her head back. A vertical marquee clings to the façade, tapering to an arrow-point aimed at the sidewalk. THE BEARDED DRAGON HOTEL, the sign reads, silver letters on dying green paint.

She turns. The hostess is gone.

From her shelter, Nicky watches the surge of passersby, catches her breath. Idly examines the intercom, stickers peeling: 1A. 1D. 2B. 2C.

To see indeed. *Eureka,* she doesn't murmur, although she's tempted.

She presses 2C. Presses again, for as long as she can endure the whine of the buzzer. Then she punches button after button until the intercom rasps at her.

"Delivery," she blurts, and waits, wincing.

The door drones. She enters.

Dank lobby, its only twinkle of color a pink Post-it pasted to the elevator doors: OUT OF ORDER FOREVER. Below the corkboard on one wall, sheets of paper have flaked away like shed skin.

Nicky heads for the stairs.

She climbs four zigzag flights—the first two bleached with fluorescents, the next deeply dark—until she turns into a short hallway, each of five doors marked with a strip of masking tape. No apartment 2C on the second floor.

Another glaring-white staircase, another hallway, street noise roaring beyond a distant window. She finds 2C on the left.

The temperature has risen with her; she blots her temple with one sleeve. Raps on the flimsy plywood.

Nothing. She raps again.

Nothing.

Softly she twists the knob, twists until it won't budge. She sighs.

Then she rocks back on one heel, angles her shoulder, and rushes 2C.

The wood grunts but holds. She retreats, lunges, hurls herself against the door. It springs open.

68

THE APARTMENT IS TINY—how does Freddy fit in here?—and the daylight straining through a grimy single window shies from the room as if suspicious. A microwave on the floor, a steel sink in the corner, a flatscreen poised atop three flipped supermarket baskets. Duffel bags disemboweled at Nicky's feet: clothes, sneakers, a can of body spray.

All four walls bare.

She pushes the door shut and walks toward the low coffee table, where pill canisters stand in a row, short and stout and slim and tall. Nicky crouches, squints at a label:

OXYCODONE 40 MG

She examines the prescription. The name is NANCY HOUGHTON. The address is in Oakland.

The next bottle, PERCOCET 10 MG, belongs to ROBERT ANDERSSON in Sausalito, and the one after that—OXYCONTIN 15 MG—was filled for A. H. CHATHAM of San Francisco. Nicky shakes each canister; just a few pills rattle.

The door beside the television sighs when she opens it, as though tired of this ritual. She steps inside. Her eyes go wide.

Sebastian smiles at her.

Madeleine pauses midspeech.

And Diana looks to her left, lips parted.

They're candids, but clear and fairly well-composed, some in vivid color, others gray or sepia. Dozens of them cover two devil-red walls in a corner of the room, where a torchère lamp sprouts from the floor and spouts a white beam upon the photographs and headlines and news clippings, all movie-lights dramatic, electric whites and liquid blacks:

**WIFE, SON OF BESTSELLING AUTHOR DISAPPEAR
THE LADY VANISHES!
POLICE CHIEF: "LITTLE PROGRESS" IN TRAPP CASE**

10 YEARS LATER, WHERE ARE THE TRAPPS?
IS SEBASTIAN TRAPP'S NEW NOVEL THE KEY
TO HIS FAMILY MYSTERY?

—fitted together like puzzle pieces. Behold the living and the dead: Lionel and Cassandra Lightfoot; Dominic Trapp and his pregnant bride; B.B. Springer and a ruddy older cop; Isaac Murray and, in the former life before her former life, Diana Gibson.

Across the room stands a folding chair and a card table on frail legs. A laptop, folded shut; a sleek color printer; several candles, flames shimmying on overgrown wicks.

Nicky's heart stalls. He must be close.

She moves past the mattress on the floor, past the miniature fridge squatting in a puddle, until she stands before his desk.

In the chair is a severed head.

Nicky swallows a gasp.

No—just a face: that rubbery skin, that death-rictus. Spring-Heeled Jack, leering from the seat. Evidently Freddy keeps a spare. Nicky shudders, glances back at the mosaic on the wall.

Strange he should turn his back on his shrine.

Beside the computer, a folded sheet of paper and an envelope. She smooths the letter flat, reads by candlelight. Green ink, shaky hand:

Meet the newest member of the cast

And, laser-printed at the bottom:

BUYER AGREES NOT TO DIGITIZE ENCLOSED CONTENTS.

The other side of the page is blank.

The envelope, then. She lifts it: an address in the Mission.

Out tips a photograph, facedown. On the back, the same cursive: *Hard at work.* Nicky turns it over.

There she is at the vegan joint, giving peas a chance, gazing sternly at her computer screen, phone on the table, Corona bottle choked with lime. A lone woman in a lonely diner, like a Hopper painting. He caught her through the restaurant window, in black and white, so that even with her gadgets, the scene appears ageless.

Goosebumps prickle on Nicky's arms. And when she turns, when she approaches the gallery again, she picks out two more photos of herself. Scaling the grand staircase with Jonathan on the night of the party. Isaac Murray warning her at his front door.

Your ride just took a picture of you. Of us.

She frowns at the print in her hand. Why would anyone sell a picture of her? Who would *buy*—

—glass crunches.

She freezes.

Silence.

The doorway is to her left. But she can't look through it from here—she needs either to edge backward into the center of the room or to travel sideways along the wall. The wall, she decides: if he enters, she can surprise him. She begins to move.

A slow crunch now, a careful tread on the shards. Nicky goes still.

Silence again. She breathes quietly, clutches the envelope and photo.

"Who's here?" He sounds uneasy. Perhaps she should reveal herself, Nicky thinks, stepping toward the—

"I have a gun."

Her nails dig into her palm.

She waits—for the click of a pistol, maybe, or for her own voice. That's the best play, right? To call to him, calmly, and identify herself. Right?

As she fills her lungs, the photograph falls from her fingers, slices into the doorway. Drops soundlessly upon the floor, face up.

Nicky stares down at the diner, wishes she could jump into the booth alongside herself. Her heart thrashes against her ribs.

Finally, warily, she peers around the edge of the frame.

Freddy, in stained tee and sweatpants, gawks at her, one hand grasping the knob, the other throttling a takeout bag. HAVE A NICE DAY, the bag encourages her, above a smiley face.

She can hear the din of the street fair, hear her heart pumping.

She steps toward him.

He runs.

69

SHE RUNS.

He has already plunged down the first flight of steps when she bursts into the hall. The stairwell lights dazzle her eyes; she grimaces, clatters after him, hits the landing and spins.

Another flight. Below her, his footsteps slap the cement. The stairwell is hot and narrow as a throat.

Bam on the landing. She seizes the rail, glances over it, glimpses his shoulder one dim floor below, whirls onto the next flight, where the lights die too fast for her vision to adjust, and thunders blind—

She hears him cry, rushes forward, smacks the wall, whips around the landing, deeper into the dark—

—the collision is rough, a clash of bones, and now that yelp again, loud in her ear. She's pasted him against the wall: a young Chinese man.

She grunts an I'm-sorry and charges down invisible steps. Lunges one leg, hopes to stick the landing.

Stumbles, bashes the wall with her shoulder. Keeps moving.

Over the rail, she sees him barrel down the bottommost steps and out of sight. Fluorescents light her arrival at the next turn. She narrows her eyes.

At the final landing, her foot skids hard on a mound of linguine like a bloody mop. She crashes onto one haunch, slides down the steps, head between her elbows, and drives her foot forward to brake.

Her heel mashes into the floor, pinning a plastic bag to the linoleum— HAVE A NICE DAY—and she hauls herself up, vision strobing—

—lobby, front door—

—into the street market, colors brighter, traffic rougher, roar louder. Nicky chops one arm into the stream of pedestrians, cuts across the sidewalk. Wriggling to the curb, she notices the twist of papers in her hand.

Please meet the newest member of the cast.

A stir-fry cook backs into her, shouts. *Go,* Nicky orders herself, stuffing the envelope and letter into her bag—

—and then she freezes, because eyes are on her and she knows they're his. She lifts her head.

Panic has drained years from his face; he looks like a frightened little boy. Between them, thirty teeming feet of gridlocked sidewalk. She cuts her eyes to the street, where pathways shift like cross-currents.

He moves.

She moves.

Between the stir-fry stand and a table heaped with knockoff handbags, squaring her shoulders, holding her breath as though she's plunged underwater. Crushed fruit beneath, lanterns swinging overhead—and everywhere, dragons writhing. She glances behind her: a jade-green beast approaches, nostrils flared, pedestrians scuttling to either side.

Back to Freddy: the curb boosts him half a foot, so she can track his head while he pushes forward—and then she feels a blast of chilly air as the herd around her screams and scatters.

She snaps her head back to the dragon, stares down the mist billowing into her face. Deep within the beast's jaws, lodged in its throat, a Chinese teenager grips a blow-dryer.

"Fog juice!" she explains, her glasses misty. "Water and glycerin!"

"Do it again," says Nicky, and turns around.

At her back, the dragon exhales vapor, cold and curling, and bystanders flee. "Dead ahead," she calls over her shoulder. "You're flying." The dragon hiccups in excitement, gushes fog.

Nicky strides down the street in a cloud of dragon breath, wearing it like a cape, the crowd unzipping before her, the lanterns shivering on their strings above. To her left, beyond the fruit stalls and florist's booths, she watches Freddy. She's gaining on him.

A low steel barricade spans the northern intersection. "Fly faster!" Nicky shouts at the beast, and the command chatters down its spine.

There, twenty feet in front of her: he's ditched the sidewalk and now thrashes his way forward in the street, arms flailing. Lobs a bloodshot look behind him.

She springs ahead, wisps of fog clinging to her, burning off her body.

"Move! Move!" she yells, squeezing between shoulders, karate-chopping her left hand to cleave a path. She's quick and fluid, slipping through the mob like oil, her own voice in her ears: "Go! Go!"

Ten feet away. He twists his head, makes her, moves faster.

She dives into his wake before the crowd can stitch itself together again. Casualties litter the pavement: gutted dumplings, a bouquet of rainbow chopsticks. A spray of baby-pink plum blossoms lashes her in the face. She runs, petals flurrying from her hair.

Nobody between them now. Close enough to watch his shoulder blades surface and subside with each lunge. Close enough to see California Street sloping to the east. The soles of his sneakers flash at her, the barricade suddenly looms, she flings one arm at him, her fingertips skim his shirt—

—smooth vault, lands on his feet with a clap like quick applause, and he hurtles into the path of a black sedan, a memorial wreath fixed to its grille.

Tires shriek. So do the people behind Nicky. When Freddy rolls across the hood, it's a drum solo.

Nicky seizes the barricade. He's dropped out of sight. The wreath rests on the pavement, a halo of lilies circling the portrait of a happy Chinese gentleman. It's the hearse Nicky saw outside the Dragon Gate.

Car horns blare. The driver lurches from the sedan. Clutches the door.

And then Freddy jack-in-the-boxes up by the far headlight, eyes Nicky, swivels, and sprints across the intersection, skipping nimbly between two Teslas.

At her back, the crowd relaxes. Some idiot applauds.

Already the hearse driver is stepping inside the car—no time for Nicky to cross the road—and already Freddy is half a block away.

The sedan clears its throat, resumes its journey, crushing the lily wreath beneath its tires, jolly Chinese gentleman and all.

70

"Got a minute?"

Detective B.B. Springer has swapped snakeskin for—is that jacket dripping with indigo peacock feathers?—though her hair still glows lava-lamp pink. She smiles.

Madeleine does not smile. She merely steps back and draws the front door open.

In the parlor, B.B. suggests they chat outside. Madeleine leads the way, resisting the urge to glance at the koi pond.

"Nice labyrinth you got there," says the detective. "Don't hear myself saying *that* too often! You mind if I head in solo?"

It will be a distinct pleasure, thinks Madeleine, to watch B.B. Springer stumble and wander.

B.B. heads in solo. Where the path splits in two, she licks her fingertip and points at the sky, then swivels and strides with assurance down the lane.

Madeleine begins to follow at a distance. The detective never hesitates more than a moment, just looks both ways, as though crossing a street, and then onward. Right, left, left, right again . . .

At the sundial, she raises her arms, triumphant, like a gymnast who just nailed the dismount.

"You know your way around," Madeleine concedes.

B.B. moves to the wrought-iron table, plops into a chair. "Couldn't have done it without you. Left there, my friend," as the lady of the house, flustered, wavers at an intersection.

"But you did do it without me." Madeleine's cheeks are flaming.

"Well, I spied on you a *little*. Corner of my eye. If I turned in the wrong direction, I could see you pull up short. People spot trouble, they tend to apply the brakes. Tend to give themselves away."

Madeleine emerges from the maze, seats herself by the sundial. B.B. has claimed the chair facing away from the pond; beyond that pink bob, Madeleine can see the loose constellation of lily pads, the dark water. The window three stories up.

"Hey, where's your pooch?"

"Oh—she'll track us out here at some point. Then she'll get lost in the maze like it's the end of *The Shining*."

B.B. whoops. "Isaac always said you were funny."

"Did he?" asks Madeleine, mildly.

"Yeah. He also said that if your brother were back, he'd contact you."

Madeleine feels as though a hostess has just invited her inside only to jam a pistol between her ribs. "Cole disappeared twenty years ago," she growls.

"And yet this infestation of butterflies! Think your cousin made 'em?"

"No." It's a relief to speak the simple truth. She wonders if her voice sounds different.

"Think your brother did?"

Back to lying. "No."

"You said you two weren't all that close back then. Maybe you are now?"

"We're nothing now."

B.B. nods for a moment. "I do like that jigsaw room of yours. That's how I'm approaching Diana Trapp's death. It's a puzzle."

When Madeleine doesn't react: "Let me show you what I'm hoping to piece together. One: She died by suicide. Unhappy lately, jittery all night. Odd strategy, jumping from that height into a body of water— you just might survive—but it did the trick. The grit in the head wound matches the rim of the pond. No water in the lungs, which means she died before she could drown. In case that's some comfort."

Madeleine swallows. Imagines Diana's pale face in some chilly morgue, imagines the flash of the scalpel.

"You've got her note," she reminds the detective, reminds herself.

"Boy, do we. 'It's an awful cliché, but I can't go on. The guilt will drag me down . . .'"

"And drown me," says Madeleine after a moment. "Fairly unambiguous."

"That's our first option."

"What's the other?"

"Who says we've only got two? Two is an accident. Of some description. Tough to square that with the note, though."

"And three?"

"Diana did not die by suicide. Diana was murdered."

"You seem quite interested in that idea."

"I suppose I am. Four, or really three-A: Diana was murdered."

"You're repeating yourself, Detective."

"By Cole."

B.B. looks like a child who has just pushed a button and wants to see what happens. Madeleine shifts in her seat. "Why would he murder Diana?"

"Beats me. Motive is where the mystery lies." Sitting back. "Maybe she knew a secret. Maybe payback."

"Payback?" Madeleine tries to scoff. "You don't know Cole."

"No, he disappeared before I had the pleasure. And don't you mean I *didn't* know him?"

Madeleine wants to slap her.

"Or maybe," says B.B., "Cole decided to punish his father and Diana was the casualty."

"Punish him for what?"

Shrug. "I'm guessing he thinks your dad was responsible for whatever happened New Year's Eve. Maybe he *knows* your dad was responsible."

"Dad wasn't—nobody was responsible. Nobody in this house."

"See, the note, the jitters, even the pond—all that I can just about swallow. Except for the Cole of it all." B.B. leans in close. "The origami. 'Tell them what you did to her—'"

"Anybody could've done it," says Madeleine, mercury rising to her brain. "Anybody at *all* could've brought that box to the door. Maybe this person is trying to knock some information out of Dad. Thwacking a piñata. You know about the Trapper Keepers, right?"

"Wouldn't wanna meet one in the wild."

"One of them might have crashed the party. But not Cole. Anybody *but* Cole. There is no *Cole!*" Her voice breaks.

B.B. watches her for a long moment. Then, lifting slender fingers one by one: "Suicide. Accident—why not. Murder by person unknown. Murder by person once known." The fingers curl into a fist. "So what we do, me and Detective Martinez, is we *stare* at our theories, our if-this-then-thats. Stare real close, through magnifying glasses and monocles and such, until all the information, all the noise, all the details . . . You can *sense* it sharpening. Like a kaleidoscope."

"Sounds very satisfying," murmurs Madeleine, wishing Watson would thunder through the boxwoods.

"Madeleine." The railroad switch in B.B.'s tone shocks her. She looks at the detective, at the smile blown from her lips. "I need the truth here, cold and hard: are you in contact with your brother? He might not be so sweet anymore."

No, he isn't. "Not in twenty years."

B.B. stares her down. "Please call me," she says at last, "when your dad's got some pep in his step." Then she stands, stretches her feathered arms. "I can show myself out."

Madeleine watches her navigate the tangle of hedges, pausing not once, a woman out for her usual stroll. As she nears the exit—or the entrance—she turns, peacock feathers shivering, and calls, "I'll say hi to Isaac for you!"

Then the bitch disappears into the parlor. Madeleine sags with relief.

She can make out, at the edge of the courtyard, the kitchen window where she sat twenty years ago, on the worst day of her life, while a gruff cop with beer on his breath asked for her movements between midnight and nine o'clock that morning.

B.B. Springer's interrogation just now felt rather more sinister.

Her eyes scale the backstage of the house, story by story, then wander along the six attic windows, and at last descend again to the pond. She waits for the fish to scatter and the lily pads to tremble and the body to erupt from the black water.

Then she swipes her phone screen and sends a text.

The police think you murdered Diana.

71

"I'D LIKE TO DISCUSS a private matter, please." The beady eye of a video camera glares at her.

"You'll need to make an appointment." The woman's voice is so calm and clear, Nicky expects to hear that calls may be recorded for quality assurance.

"It's urgent."

"Please make an appointment or dial nine-one-one if the emergency is medical."

"This concerns Cole Trapp."

The woman kills the call.

Wait and hope, as Sebastian had told Nicky. As Dumas had told Sebastian.

She inspects first her coat—somewhere in Chinatown she tore it; red fabric glimmers within the gash like blood in a wound—and then the townhouse façade, a waterfall of glass and granite, glinting coldly. Up the hill, she sees the tail of Lombard Street—famed as the crookedest street in the world, although not actually the crookedest street in the world—slithering down the slope, pushing like a garter snake through the greenery.

She glances at Freddy's empty envelope, at the initials printed above the address. This address.

She has never met a Trapper Keeper. She feels like a detective going undercover.

A moment later, the slate door retreats, and a woman appraises Nicky sternly through rimless specs. She's dressed as she speaks: crisp, neutral, cardigan gray and fluffy as ash. Early fifties. Thoroughly respectable.

"Afternoon," says Nicky.

Instantly the woman transforms, like a business-casual werewolf: her eyes glitter, her teeth gleam, her hands rattle as she claps them beneath her chin. "It's *you!*" she squeaks. "Come *in*, come *in*—" She grasps her visitor by the arm, drags her inside. *I will die here,* Nicky thinks.

A shallow staircase rises to the second floor, where they cross a tract of granite slabs the color of pale smoke. The house is see-through at both ends; the air is chilled. An ice-cube home. Nicky slips into her coat again.

"People tend to be more truthful in a cooler climate," the woman explains. "It also discourages aggression. Come!" she says, aggressively.

Nicky glances back at the stairs. She could still run for it.

"Longtime Trapper here," the woman admits, girlish, beaming over her shoulder. "Since day one. Not too many of us left." Leading Nicky to the back of the house, where a wall of windows float above a small yard, gray-green grass and frost-blue shrubs. Two chairs, a low table, a shag rug, all the same aloof shade of white.

"Welcome to my office." The woman drops into a chair. "Clients find the view comforting. Sit," she commands, sharp enough to chip glass.

Nicky obeys. "What do you do?"

"No, tell me about *you*. You're *living* there! *Writing* there! Sebastian's *life story*!" That leer again. "Don't deny it. Jack told me."

"I'm not denying it. Jack who?"

"I don't know his *name*," laughs the woman. "He wouldn't give me yours, either. But at least I got your picture. Never imagined you'd deliver it yourself!"

"How does this—work?" Nicky taps the envelope. "With Jack."

"You must know?"

"Pretend I don't."

"Why, he's an auctioneer! And a former employee, apparently, who knows someone inside the house. So he's able to offer—well, he's able to *sell*—a selection of personal effects, he calls them. Nothing too *valuable*, obviously. A monogrammed napkin, a set of cufflinks. A family photo. Cole merch is especially rare."

She smiles. Sharp teeth.

"You can face-to-face online before bidding. He's so theatrical"—said fondly—"candles and music and photos tacked behind him like a murder board. And he wears that *very* sinister mask." She shrugs off her cardigan. "It was Jack who told us about your project.

Which is *truly* exciting. We can finally get to the bottom of the business."

"Bottom of what business?"

"Hope and Cole, of course." Eyes sparkling. She lifts a pitcher and glass from the table. "Water?"

Nicky suspects that anything she touches will someday be entered into evidence. She shakes her head.

"Sebastian Trapp is playing a game with you. Daring you to catch him. I know a thing or two about the human mind." The woman pours. "Ask yourself: Why am I here, in this house, writing this story? Can't he write his *own* story? Ask yourself. Out loud."

"Why am I here writing this story?" says Nicky obediently.

"Asking ourselves questions out loud forces us to think more deliberately. Any insights?"

"I'm writing this story because I was invited to. There's an insight for you."

"Why were you invited?"

"Because—"

"Ask yourself."

Nicky sighs. "Why was I invited. I was invited because I've read the Simon St. John novels, and also—"

"You were invited *because Sebastian Trapp killed his wife and son.*" Flat as a horizon. The woman is no longer smiling. "His brother, too, I'm certain. And he is *dying* to tell somebody. Dying in the other sense, also—everyone knows that—but first he wants the world to know that *he got away with it.* He *must* have given you clues."

"You know this?"

"As I said, I know the human mind. Can I *prove* it? I could if I were in that house, with that man. He's playing a game with you, whether you know it or not."

"What happens if I win?"

"Then we all do. But now ask yourself: what happens if I *lose?*"

Nicky does not ask herself that question, not out loud. Through the skylight, the early-afternoon sun slides toward them like a guillotine blade.

"What do you love in this world?"

Nicky frowns. *My friends*, she thinks. *My goddaughter. My dog. My aunt. My cousins. Some of my students. Mystery novels. Night swimming. Traveling by—*

"For the sake of whatever or whomever you're thinking of," says the woman, thin smile, "be very, very careful around Sebastian Trapp." She extends her hand. "My photograph, please."

Nicky grips the envelope—her hostess will be displeased to find it's empty. "Sure, but—do you have other photos of me?" She hopes she sounds flattered.

The woman rises, beckons. Nicky follows her to a door in a dim corner, tucking the envelope into her bag.

The closet houses four filing cabinets, waist-high. The woman crouches, hauls open a bottom drawer. When she looks up, her face is glowing. "My collection," she beams.

Nicky watches her pluck clippings and headlines from folders ("All originals") and lay them gently on the floor. She shows her guest a copy of *Simon Says* ("Signed first edition"). Then she finds an envelope, tilts a print into Nicky's hand. ("Don't smudge it.")

Nicky stares at Diana, in her red dress, flanked by her in-laws. It's the selfie Simone shared.

"Probably the last picture ever taken of Diana Trapp," says the woman happily. "She doesn't look suicidal, do you think?" She pulls a second photo from the envelope, stands. "And *this*," she says, pressing it into Nicky's hand, "is you."

A green car pulling away from a sidewalk. Sebastian's Jaguar, Sebastian himself, Nicky at the wheel. Freddy tailed them to the Baron Club. Freddy witnessed her driving lesson.

"No! *No! No!*"

The scream is like a smoke alarm. The photograph bends and buckles into Nicky's palm ("*No! No!*," the woman scrabbling at her with talons) as she strides from the room.

"*Stop!*"

But Nicky is retracing her steps across the granite floor.

"Wait!" At the top of the stairs, the woman scrambles ahead of her. She pushes her hair from her eyes, sits her glasses on her nose. Exhales.

"Could I get your autograph?" she asks.

Outside, in the warm air, the chill burning off her skin, Nicky twists her neck to check that her hostess hasn't followed. She notices, fixed by the door, a placard she missed earlier:

DR. ELIZABETH ROME, PSYD
BEHAVIORAL PSYCHOLOGIST

Fucking hell, as Sebastian liked to say.

72

"'To what do I owe the pleasure?" asks Jonathan.

"I need a bathroom," Madeleine tells him.

She only needs the mirror, really, so that she can eyeball herself, remember the blueprints of her face before she examines his. Is the man outside the door possibly her brother? Well, he's taken such an unaccountable shine to a member of the household. There's the Dorset of it all, too.

Besides, someone's got to be.

She flushes the toilet for effect, rinses her hands for effect, emerges into the living room. A double-height window, holy-red brickwork, a pair of stunted pews—Madeleine has infiltrated a onetime church, it seems, resurrected for new life as a bachelor pad. The bookshelves floating on the walls are bare; a potted snake plant lurks in one corner, leaves like forked tongues. Low glass coffee table rustling with papers and receipts. Cardboard boxes everywhere.

"I was happy to receive your text," says Jonathan, thumbing his phone. He's crammed his curls beneath a cap. His T-shirt—blue, some Latin motto across the chest—lights his eyes like gas jets. His nose, unhelpfully, appears to have been busted at some point. "I could use more friends here. Spotted your houseguest lately?"

"No," Madeleine lies, because she's not here to talk about Nicky.

"I see. Oldies all right by you?"

Motown booms from invisible speakers. He dials it down, smiles at her. "Apologies for the mess," he says. "Boxes and more boxes."

Madeleine nods. "So are you in San Francisco for—a while?"

"Making myself comfortable, anyway. You should do the same." She sits on the sofa. He opts for the far end. "I'm terribly sorry about your stepmother. I had a colleague die by suicide, and—"

"Who said it was suicide?"

"Your—" Frowning. "Wasn't it?"

"I'd like to know."

The frown deepens. "An inspector called this morning. Hernandez, I think, or Fernandez. Unexpectedly blond. Unexpectedly requested my birth certificate. I told him that even if it weren't in England, I wouldn't supply it."

When Jonathan taps her hand, she flinches. Looks at his fingers; examines the skin where he touched her. Is that her brother's temperature she feels?

"Mine is a fine lavatory," he says pleasantly, "but perhaps not worth traveling across town for?"

Deep breath. "I thought we should talk in person."

He waits. Madeleine gazes at him, tries to blow twenty years of time off his face.

"Right," he announces, standing, screwing his cap on tighter. "Splash of white? Red?"

Thank Christ. "Any lager on the menu?"

"Girl after my own heart. Sit tight. I was just about to arrange some charcuterie very prettily, all by my lonesome," he says as he vanishes into a hallway.

Beyond the windows, evening is sifting onto the park, clotting in the trees, dimming the grass. Next to her, atop a martini table, two picture frames lie facedown. She lifts each. Both blank. Was she expecting a family photo? Her family?

Now the Four Seasons strut through the speakers, and Jonathan warbles from the kitchen: "'*Walk like a man, talk like a man, walk like a man, my son . . .*'"

Uncanny. His falsetto could be Frankie Valli's.

Mounted on the brick wall behind Madeleine is a poster, stark black letters against a Union Jack: QUI AUDIT ADIPISCITUR, they proclaim, and under this, in smaller text, [WHO DARES WINS].

"Do you speak Latin?" she calls. "Or know it?"

His laugh rolls down the hallway. "I'm *wearing* it. Audi cap. University motto on the shirt. I am a living dead language."

Madeleine twists in her seat so that she's facing the poster. "Where did you grow up again?"

He appears in the hall, grinning, a long butcher's knife in his hand. "As I said the other night." He thrusts the blade at the flag on the wall. "Dorset. Same as your mum."

"When?"

"When did I spend my childhood there? Around the time I was a child. Approximately."

"Is that near Wiltshire?" She knows it isn't far.

He cocks his head. "Where Diana Trapp was from?"

Madeleine waits.

"About ninety minutes away, depending. Why?" Still beaming. "You reckon the two ladies knew each other in their previous lives? Before either one got married to Sebastian Trapp?"

"My mother moved to America when she was twenty-four."

"So much for that." He traces one fingertip along the edge of the blade. Then he returns to the kitchen as girl-group shoo-be-doos stream from the speakers like tinsel from a fan. "*One fine day . . .*"

"*. . . you're gonna want me for your girl,*" mumbles Madeleine.

She glances down, spots two squat moving boxes stacked against the back of the sofa. The lid of the top box is blank; Madeleine bends forward to inspect the side. MAGAZINES, in black marker, and on the carton below, XBOX. Cole never really cared for video games. Not twenty years ago, anyway.

She lifts the MAGAZINES lid. The *Economist* and *GQ*, glossy piles of them, plus a yachting journal and a British video game quarterly. She decides to go for a sail (the cover promises *breathtaking Caribbean vistas!*, which sounds calming) and resettles herself on the sofa, *Ahoy!* in hand. Catches herself in the television screen. Alone.

Did Jonathan really ship all this over from England? She checks the address at the bottom of the cover: a street in London. She reads his name.

GRANT JONES

That's not his name.

"Have you got an alias?" Her mouth has outrun her brain.

He stops singing. "What's that?"

Just before she replies, the Chiffons fade away. "Who's Grant Jones?" she asks.

Silence.

Madeleine wonders if he heard her at all, if he's just preoccupied with hospitality. She should check another magazine.

But now she sees, in the television screen, a shadow sliding along the hallway wall, and finally Jonathan steps into the living room.

He halts—a faceless shape behind her. His hand still grips the knife. "What did you say?"

He could be anyone.

"I was just browsing this copy of *Ahoy!*," she tells him, pretending to study its pages, voice casual, "and I saw the name Grant Jones on the label."

"Ah." Voice casual. Madeleine turns, feigns surprise at the sight of him. *Could* he be? In the right light? "Grant. Mate of mine back home. Always gave me his magazines once he'd finished with them. Not the racy stuff, though." Once more he retreats. "Almost ready," he calls. "This blade wants sharpening."

Madeleine stares at the name, then slaps *Ahoy!* on the coffee table. A few loose papers sigh. She leans forward: assorted property-rental materials, all addressed to Grant Jones. Receipts, too, in his name. How many identities does a person need? Two?

More?

"So this isn't just a social call," she announces.

Through the glass tabletop, on the rug, she spies a single white sheet, rumpled, almost imperceptible beneath the flock of pages on the table.

She recovers it. The sheet is blank on both sides but densely creased, like panes of diamonds folded and flattened again. Madeleine presses its edges, pushes into its corners. The pleats and wrinkles buckle.

The paper metamorphoses into a butterfly.

"It's piss-poor, I know."

Her eyes snap to him towering over her.

He places the charcuterie platter on the table, sets down two sweaty bottles. "Recent events have inspired me a bit." He sits beside her, grabs a beer. "There's a swan round here, too. S'posed to be a swan, anyway. The video made it look so easy."

He grins stiffly. Doesn't drink. Neither does Madeleine. That accent, clipped sharp. Cole always did like games.

"Look," he sighs. "It's scrunched-up paper. Nothing sinister. Let me assure you like I assured that Ramirez chap, I'm not your brother back from the dead."

"Who says he's dead?" She swallows. "And did you, under any name, happen to meet my stepmother when you both lived in London for many, many years?"

Jonathan stands his bottle on the floor. "Are you seriously implying that I might've been . . . *involved* in her death? A woman I hardly knew?"

"Were you?" she asks, gripping the butterfly like it's a weapon. "You relocate from London to San Francisco and promptly befriend the nephew of a woman who also relocated from London to San Francisco. And who soon winds up dead. You could've camped out in her house that night. You could've copied a key, too. And you've got Grant Jones's mail in your apartment." Again she searches his face, the hair, the unruly teeth. Should she touch him again? She tries to lift her hand to his cheek—

He glares, eyes dark. "So who am I, exactly? A *lover*? Past or present? Or a confidant—'This is what actually happened to the Trapp family many moons ago'? Presuming she knew, of course. Is that who I am?" He snaps his fingers as though he's had an idea. "Did I track her down, blackmail on my mind? Or possibly I'm some stalker she can't recognize, torturing her with arts and crafts? Tell me, Madeleine, please: *who do you think I am?*"

Her breath is faint.

"You could be anyone," she says.

His hand strikes like a snake, snatching the butterfly from her fingers, and instantly she rises, scoops her bag from the floor, marches to the door, as the Righteous Brothers complain that she's lost that lovin' feelin'.

Outside, in the blue evening, she crosses the street but detours at the median. Leans against a palm tree, bark rough against her back. Breathes deep. Taps at her phone with two shaky thumbs.

The Internet teems with Grant Joneses. Especially in the United Kingdom. And this Grant Jones never did name an employer, did he? At the party, he shared colorful trading-floor stories, spoke of friends with names like Hugo and Rafe, but he never told her whom he worked for. She tries "grant jones" "lyme regis." The Internet merely shrugs.

73

WHO DO YOU THINK I AM?

Madeleine brakes hard by the curb, strides up the driveway. Inside the house, the typewriter trills like a metal songbird.

At the bottom of the staircase, she hesitates, looks up at the portrait, at her father's grave face.

What *is* he writing?

And what *does* he know?

She feels her nerve fail like a bulb sputtering out. Retreats to the kitchen, fixes a sandwich—shame about that charcuterie—and for an hour she rehearses the lines that for twenty years she's been too afraid to say aloud:

Dad, we should've had this conversation a long time ago.

Dad, there's something important we need to discuss.

Dad, about that night . . .

The songbird goes silent upstairs. He's headed to his bedroom. She eyes her sandwich, uneaten. Her stomach is too full of dread.

By the time Madeleine arrives at his door, beef and Swiss on a plate, the room is dim, his suit and shirt and tie left for dead on the rug. She scans the line of his body beneath the blanket.

"What is it, Maddy?"

She startles. "I didn't mean to wake you."

"You didn't. Your aunt was here earlier today, making arrangements for Diana. I'm tired and miserable, but very much awake. Come in, darling, come in."

As he switches on the lamp, Madeleine seats herself in the armchair, sets the plate beside him—"I made a sandwich just for you"—and points to the clothes on the floor. "You dressed up today?"

"That's not me dressing up, Madeleine, that's merely me dressing." In the lamplight, beneath the shelter of the canopy, he appears half-destroyed, thin lips chapped, whiskers flourishing upon his chin and cheeks; the skin on his bare shoulders is plaster.

"I heard your typewriter," she says. "What are you writing?"

"What are *you* writing, my girl?" He smiles as she frowns. "I've looked in on you from time to time these past few weeks, you know. Well, you *didn't* know. Silent as a shadow, was I. Found you bowed over your computer machine."

"Oh. I—actually, I've wanted to ask." Might as well. She clears her throat. "So—I mean, I already—but—maybe another Simon film?" Before he can object: "I'd like to adapt the books. The first one. For the screen. Again."

It trickles from her mouth like baby formula. She feels childish.

For an instant he stares. Then a grin spooks the surprise from his lips, chases it into his eyes. "I think that's quite an idea, Maddy."

"Oh." Her heart begins to swell. "Well, good. I'm sure you'd hate it. You won't need to see it, though."

"I won't, no. But that's not really your question, is it?"

She drops her gaze to her lap. Wishes Watson were here. Looks at her father. "Daddy, I think we should talk."

"Darling," he says, "I think so, too."

74

THE DOOR HAS SCARCELY CLOSED behind Nicky in the dark foyer, her fingers barely dug behind Watson's ear, when—

"Miss Hunter, I wish you'd join me upstairs, please."

She finds him sitting up in bed, pillows banked behind his back, Madeleine in the chair beside him. The lamp sheds mellow light on their faces: his drawn yet alert, hers satiny with tears. Madeleine stares at the lampshade as though it's a campfire. Watson waddles over, parks on her feet.

Sebastian clears his throat. "Would you breakfast with me in the morning, please? I'll drive. I've only got so many more rides in that car. I hope to die in it, but not tomorrow."

Nicky nods.

"Speaking of which, you should know that I've decided to end my treatment, as I've just informed my daughter here."

Madeleine continues to gaze at the lamp. Nicky feels as though somebody has kicked her in the stomach but she hasn't yet registered the pain.

"Thank you for your restraint," Sebastian continues. "I dislike dramatic scenes."

Madeleine lifts raw eyes to Nicky. "Would you mind if I kept Watson tonight?"

Nicky can only shake her head. Madeleine hoists the dog onto her lap. "That's a good girl," Sebastian murmurs. It's not clear to whom he's referring.

In the attic, Nicky showers—her arms and legs are leopard-spotted with bruises; that was quite a street fair—and drags herself into bed. Switches off the lamp. Looks at the constellations above. Closes her eyes.

Opens them.

Switches on the lamp. Yanks her bag from the floor and studies the two photographs: driving-student Nicky Hunter, white-knuckling the wheel of Sebastian's Jag outside the Baron Club; and Simone and Diana and Freddy, mid-selfie.

She wiggles her jaw.

. . . No, nothing here.

Lights out again. Eyes shut again. Nicky drops into sleep as if through a rotting floor.

75

THE THING BURNS IN MADELEINE'S FIST all the way downstairs. Was his hand smoking as he gave it to her? When she reaches her darkened suite and drops it onto her desk, she expects the wood to smolder and ignite, expects to see her palm seared.

She steps back, trembling. Retreats another step, and another, before turning away.

In the dim mirror, she beholds a frightened woman, clothes weary, hair sloppy. She wonders how that woman got here.

They approach each other. As Mirror Madeleine nears, they both gaze down at the reliquary on the dresser: Cracked snow globe. Sicilian cigarettes. Dog collar. Jewelry box. Small rosy conch. Exhibits of her little life.

You're the last one left. Diana said so, in this very room. *If you'd like to escape for a while, you're welcome to come with me.* But Diana has gone where Madeleine can't follow. The invitation is rescinded. She is alone, inescapably.

She locks damp eyes with the woman in the mirror.

And suddenly Madeleine sweeps one arm across the top of the dresser, erasing that little life of hers in a hail of glass and shell, the snow globe bursting and the conch shattering and the jewelry box snapping at the hinges, its glittery trove strewn across the floor.

Across the room, on the desk, her phone cries in protest.

Slowly Madeleine turns her head. Only one person texts her these days.

The room appears to stretch and narrow, the floor to extend itself, like a trick effect in a film, so that the walk feels like weeks (past the sofa, past the shelves, the walls squeezing in on either side), and every minute the phone chimes again, until at last she reaches over her chair, over the desk, over the combustible substance her father tipped into her hand, and taps the screen.

Magdala.

My diary.

You know where to find it.

Be careful.

Madeleine waits for more.

What should I do with it?

He's typing.

Do what you always did.

Read it.

Thursday, June 25

76

BENEATH THE SOMBER STARE OF AN OWL, Sebastian thanks a succession of mourners ("Most kind of you, Reynold"; "No, Walker, the second time certainly isn't any easier") while Nicky discreetly eyes her phone:

> Fancy a hike through Muir Woods on this cloudy afternoon?
>
> Otherworldly in the mist one hears.

Three emoji tacked on: the foggy Golden Gate Bridge, a tree, a boss-eyed ghost. *The type that's hiding something,* Betty had warned her.

Now the last well-wishers flake away from their table—the same table as before, in the same low-lit corner, only this morning it's Nicky in the velvet wingback and her host sunk in leather, dressed in a grave-gray suit and blood-red necktie. He has aged greatly and badly since their previous visit.

"Eggs'll be cold now, beer'll be warm." Sebastian pokes his yolks, nods, sips his lager, nods. "But I'm pleased by your most recent pages," he tells her. "Better than I deserve. The family will—" His lips audition a few syllables. "What's left of the family will enjoy it immensely."

"I'd like to finish it."

"We've time enough," he says, sitting back. "Am I being recorded?"

"Would you like to be?"

"No."

"I'll switch it off." Nicky swipes her screen, taps record—her hands are shaking—and sets the phone facedown beside the candle. Whatever he's going to say, she wants it on tape.

"You see," he continues, and then hesitates for a moment. "You see, following that unforeseen plot twist, I'm no longer certain how our story ends."

"Your story."

"*Our* story. A person isn't a slipknot—you can't just tug a string and untangle him. His story is inextricably bound up with the stories of others." Sebastian sips his beer, hands trembling. "Madeleine's story, Diana's story, Hope's story. Yours, too; you're not exempt for showing up late. And I cannot predict how *this* story ends now."

"What about Cole?" **For Cole.**

"My son's story ended long ago," he replies. "The butterflies are a spooky sequel, of sorts, but I won't say they're Cole's."

"Did you hate him?" asks Nicky, surprising herself.

For a long moment he doesn't blink, just gazes at his guest. His eyes are trapdoors. "What a question," he says at last.

"You don't talk about him with much . . . affection."

Nicky looks into those trapdoor eyes, and as he speaks, she slowly lowers herself into them.

"You'll remember," says Sebastian, "I'd grown up tough on the base. And rowdy. And ambitious, and pretty clever, although I didn't much care for classrooms. I liked girls, liked books, liked swimming, liked sweating. Liked taking a punch, because that was license to punch back. I can't recall ever feeling anxious, except on my fifteenth birthday, when a chubby prostitute named Greta took me to bed. Local ritual." His face softens for a moment.

"And then: manhood. And the wolves descended upon me. Day after day, year upon year, I survived, if only just. So I wanted a son . . ."

Nicky drops deeper into the dark behind his eyes.

He proceeds carefully, the way you descend steps at night: "I *expected* a son who—not *deserved*, but *validated* my survival, and would himself survive. And *live*. As I had not."

"You haven't lived?"

"Not as I would have liked. Not as *anyone* would have liked. It hurts to live, Nicky."

Her name sounds unfamiliar dressed in his voice, and she realizes that this is the first time he's spoken it in her company. Slowly, his finger traces the rim of his glass. She watches him, listens to him story-tell.

"The night after we rescued Watson the First, I stayed up past midnight, past dawn, watching her lift and sink on my chest as though she were floating on water. Watched in awe. With joy. But already I feared for her—she was so vulnerable, in a world so wild with danger, where she could so easily perish."

Shadows huddle around. The votive flame wriggles.

"Madeleine put me at ease from the womb. Kicked like a black belt. Bossy baby, bossy little girl, bossy wherever she is right now. As for Cole . . ." He sighs, closes his eyes. "Emergency cesarean eleven weeks early. Four pounds and change. Straight to intensive care." Now he looks at Nicky. "Even before I met him, he had crumpled like a leaf.

"He was slow to walk, slow to talk. Slow to grow teeth! Pale as a ghost, as though he were only partly there. Couldn't read, couldn't write. Night after night I would trudge through a book with him: picture books, chapter books . . . He—tried, I know that, but . . ." Raising the beer to his lips. "He liked the illustrations, anyway."

Not bitter, just weary. From behind his eyes, Nicky listens carefully.

"I tried to show him how to compete. Signed him up for soccer, Little League. Sailing. Other boys mocked him. Other fathers, too. That hurt my pride. It's a petty feeling, but it hurt my pride. Cole, I assumed, either didn't notice or didn't care, so I tried to ignore it, too. Because surely he would change, wouldn't he? Surely he would evolve to survive? Duck his head out of the clouds, ditch the origami, make some friends?"

He drinks, swallows. "Well, he didn't change. Didn't grow, either. I asked his doctor about hormones, but my wife threatened murder. So Cole remained small, and strange, and too sensitive, like a person who's lost his skin, all exposed nerves and visible heartbeat.

"Someday, if you do have children—and thank you again for taking me into your confidence; I sincerely hope you'll find a way, if you decide you want to—you'll learn that the rumors are true: you're only as happy as your least happy child. I couldn't survive our unhappy child; he would doom me. I *needed* for him to change. For his sake, certainly, but for mine as well. Otherwise, the wolves would drag me into the woods and strip me to the bone. And what if they then began hunting Cole? How could I defend him while my carcass rotted on the forest floor?"

Nicky feels the mossy ground beneath her feet. Her descent ends here, in a dim clearing—with, yes, a body on the ground and, sound-lessly circling it, beasts in view.

"In Cole I saw the weakness I had for so long struggled against in myself. Now it was in front of me, looking me in the eye."

He looks her in the eye. Still she watches him, and she watches the body in the woods as she approaches it, leaves scratching at her ankles.

"I didn't hate Cole. I feared him. I feared *for* him. For myself, too. So I tried desperately to sculpt him into a sturdier shape—tried to make him stronger. Even when I lost patience, lost my temper, I thought I was helping." He grasps his glass with one jittery hand, the lager frothing within it, a tempest in a pint.

"I wish I could have done it another way instead," he says. "I wish I'd figured that out in time."

Wolves growl behind her. She nears the body.

Sebastian exhales, drains his glass. "Have I answered your questions?"

"Not all of them." Nicky reaches to clear away the leaves clouding the face. "What *do* you know about your wife and son?"

Sharply he sets the glass on the table. A tug between her shoulder blades and she's whipped backward through the clearing and into the Baron Club. The trapdoors in Sebastian's eyes snap shut as one.

"I assume you mean their disappearance," he says calmly.

"You said that maybe you and I could solve a mystery or two. Your wife and son—that's one mystery. And perhaps there's a link between whatever happened back then and Diana. That's another."

He steeples his fingers. For a moment he is very still.

Finally: "Ye olde ghosts-of-long-ago. An instance in the present echoes an instance in the past. You certainly can't write a traditional mystery without it. But, my dear child," he says, his voice warm yet ominous, like winds whispering about a storm, "you're not in a tradi-tional mystery. You're in a psychological thriller."

It's a silly line, thinks Nicky as her blood freezes.

"This is a story without heroes. Perhaps without villains, as well." His teeth glint when he bares them. "A story where identities are slip-pery." His tie drips scarlet from his neck, as though his throat were slit, and pools on the table. "Where the mystery and the violence are mostly within you, and where the clues almost ineluctably lead you someplace you don't want to go." Glitter in his eyes like knifepoints.

Then he smiles, gently. "We're all in that story. Life is a thriller. The ending is fatal and the conclusion is final."

For a long moment Sebastian studies her face, until at last he sits back again. "You don't accept the suicide," he sighs, inspecting his pocketwatch. "Hell, maybe you shouldn't. But what is it you think *I* know? What story would you like me to tell you?"

"A true story," says Nicky.

"Good morning."

She turns. Lionel Lightfoot has silently materialized beside the table like a rogue planet.

"Basher, I wanted to tell you—how very sorry I am."

Sebastian's eyes are flat. "About anything in particular?"

"*Diana* in particular. Ah. She was a—*rare bird.*"

Nicky checks her phone. The text arrived three minutes ago: a map, pin dropped just off Castro Street.

"Am I to look forward to another fiction about my family?" asks Sebastian.

"No, no—I . . ."

Nicky glances up, braced for bloodshed—but Sebastian is wearing a faint smile.

"You couldn't write it quickly enough in any case. I'm kicking the oxygen habit early."

"Ah." Lionel nods. "Tumbling solo over the Reichenbach Falls."

"Unless you'd care to join me."

"Soon enough, soon enough."

"You hurt Maddy."

Lionel flinches, skin bulging around his eyes; when he speaks again, his words stand upright. "I regret it. Cassandra never forgave me. She said it was the *worst* . . . Ah—young lady, might I have a moment with our friend here?"

Already Nicky is on her feet. "Please. We'll pick up soon. Thank you for breakfast."

Sebastian inclines his head. One minute later, a car arrives to whisk her into the otherworldly mist.

77

THE ATTIC DOOR CREAKS as Madeleine opens it. This isn't Nicky's room, she reasons; it's Cole's. Cole, who wants her here.

And she knows indeed where to find it.

She had read her brother's diary as he recorded it, or at least the first few weeks' worth; such was her right as a sister. The material failed to engage: *Today me + Freddy rode our bikes to Frot Point and played spies.* Or *[indecipherable] stuck gum in my hair, I cut it out with sizers, now I have a bald patch. I told mama its a joke.* Et cetera.

He knew all along, it seems. Should she have paid closer attention?

Her phone buzzes. An alert: another online death notice. The coverage has been muted, though, mostly just-the-facts write-ups, only moderately ominous. Her father isn't as interesting as he was. Or else uxoricide isn't as interesting as it was.

On the desk sits a Magic 8 Ball, coated in a fine pelt of dust, except for ten small fingerprints like markings. Madeleine grasps it, and with a shake, the blue triangle tumbles into view.

CANNOT PREDICT NOW.

She forgot to ask a question. A pause, then she hears her own voice, and she shakes the ball again.

BETTER NOT TELL YOU NOW.

Madeleine frowns, sets it on the desk. Stupid toy.

She crosses to the madding crowd of horseshoe crabs and silver-tipped arrows—what *will* she do with all this when the time comes?—and then, by the Watsons of yesteryear, she treads carefully, waiting for the give beneath her foot.

Strange, though: Madeleine is sure—almost sure, anyway—that many, many moons ago, sometime after Cole disappeared, she searched for his diary, only to find it . . . well, not to find it at all. The police must have taken it. *Somebody* must have, anyway. And yet Cole claims it's beating beneath the floorboards, a telltale heart.

The floor sags. Madeleine crouches eye-to-eye with that powerfully ugly urchin (*A Child*, reads the plate at the bottom of the frame, unhelpfully), then she lifts the plank.

A red butterfly pasted to the cover spreads its wings before her. Madeleine had forgotten that. She regards it warily as she brings it to the bed.

She sits, feet flat on the floor, and opens to *December 31 1997. Please dont' read my dairy!*

How his voice has changed.

    Do what you always did.

    Read it.

In the morning light, she begins to read.

78

"Been waiting for you, baby girl."

Lights tint the liquor shelves a bright blue; the popcorn bulbs blaring her name aurify her wig, too, a cluster of Marilyn Monroe curls. "Come wet your whistle," Betty calls, whisking a bottle over a pair of shot glasses.

Nicky approaches the bar. "What are we drinking today?"

"You're drinking bourbon. So's the gentleman."

Nicky turns to find him in the corner booth, rolling an empty tumbler along the tabletop.

She slides in opposite, pushes a shot across the vinyl. He peers at her from within the cave of his hood. Stubble dusts his cheeks and jaw; the skin below one bloodshot eye has warmed to a sallow green.

"You broke into my place," says Freddy.

"Guilty. You're a Trapper Keeper?"

He glares, scratches his hands. "Hell, no. Vultures. I just take their money. Believe me, I hear myself."

"Oh, good. And how long have you been using?"

He blinks. "How long have you known?"

How long *has* she known? Nicky looks away.

"Nine months." Freddy speaks into his shot glass, voice hollow. "Ever since I busted my shoulder. Doctor prescribed OC, couple weeks. Man, I liked it. But street drugs cost a fortune in San Francisco. Everything does." He scratches his hands. "February I started swiping Oxy at work—we keep it in the sports infirmary, for emergencies. Nobody noticed. Until somebody noticed." Another sigh. "In April. Athletics director is a buddy—was, I guess—so he told the headmistress he was bouncing me for erratic behavior.

"Two days later, I'm evicted. Rough week. I couldn't go home to Simone; I'm amazed she hasn't worked it out yet. Besides, I can't stand those goddamn cats. So I moved into—you saw it. Then Sebastian got his walking papers, and Diana asked for help. School year was ending, so she assumed I had time. I mean, she wasn't wrong." He's scratched his knuckles raw. "I already knew about those groupies desperate for

Trapp swag. Figured nobody'd complain if a photo went missing, or a fountain pen, or a book, even. But now . . ." He sighs. "Now I need money. Big-game money. That's why I raided the desk: I figured he kept the serious hardware there. If that failed, and it did, I could just grab something handy."

"Like that glass cube."

"Yeah, sorry about that."

"Me, too." She watches him gingerly touch his eye. "Why the mask?"

"Sometimes the TKs wanna chat online, inspect the merchandise. Can't show my face. That night in the library, I was gonna make a quick video. You know—Jack at Sebastian Trapp's typewriter, Jack by Sebastian Trapp's fire."

"And your apartment? The walls, the candles?"

"It's all theater. Same with the tattoo." He tugs his sleeve up. The letters are flaking away. "These Trapper Keepers—such a dumb name—to them this is just some spectacle, just some entertainment. I offer an *experience*."

"Trading on your family's tragedy."

Freddy crushes his eyes shut, nods—and begins to weep. "Yeah," he agrees, shoulders hopping.

After a minute, Nicky starts to move her hand toward his, until—

"That's the good stuff, kids." They both look up at Betty, knock back their shots together.

"Burns, though," she adds, pouring water as Freddy wipes his nose.

Light flops into the room. Freddy swivels, eyes snapped wide. In the doorway hover a pair of seniors, old enough to golf and wearing his-and-hers polos.

"These two are lost," declares Betty. She goes to greet them.

Freddy has receded into his hood. "Used to swing by this place for coffee," he mumbles. "Lately I swing by for you-name-it. Guy I know's a home aide for seniors. Lots of 'em got prescriptions they don't use much. His office is nearby. My bones itch." He hugs himself. Nicky wants to hug him, too.

Not so fast: she's here for Diana. Whom Freddy kissed. Freddy, who is capable of violence.

"Oh," he says, "listen: some detective left a voicemail for me. He'd like a word about—"

"Diana."

Shaking his head. "I felt, like . . . *disembodied*. When I read about her. In a chat room, even."

Nicky says nothing about Cole, doesn't care about Cole right now. She cares about Diana. "I want to know what happened to her."

"You *don't* know?" Freddy tilts his head. "The obituary said she died suddenly. Which sounded like"—he nearly whispers—"like she did it herself."

"Did she?"

"What's the alternative? Murder?"

"The police think so. And you knew Diana. You know the house."

"So does my uncle. Whose wives keep checking out early."

"But you kissed her." Nicky pauses.

If he's surprised, he doesn't show it. "I was high."

"Probably not much comfort to her."

"I loved her, you know."

Nicky pauses. She did not know. A *crush*, maybe, but—

"I knew it when I was a kid, knew I'd love her forever. Then she came back, and . . . I mean, there was Sebastian, of course. But that always seemed temporary. And now I'll never be with anyone." His voice is full and soft and achingly sad. "I won't love another woman, no matter how much I want to. Not like I love Diana. And that's— that's unfair to a person. Living in someone's shadow like that." He wipes his eyes. "The way Diana did."

The way your mother does, thinks Nicky as his arm twitches, knocks the tumbler to the floor. How much glassware has Freddy destroyed this week?

She climbs out of the booth, bends down to collect the rubble, piles it on the table. Considers him in his hoodie, twitchy and teary and little-boy frightened, and suddenly she finds herself sitting beside him.

"So do I have a conversation with this detective?" he asks.

Nicky shrugs. "Conversations are only dangerous if you have something to hide."

Another nod. "Sorry I've been a douche to you."

"You haven't been a douche to me." She gathers his hands in hers, studies them. Did they strike Diana down?

His wrists rattle—"Got the shakes"—and when she squeezes his fingers, he bows his head to the tabletop, cheek against the vinyl, eyes on the bar. "Betty's checking me into a clinic this afternoon. She sees everything."

"I do!" their hostess calls.

"Hears everything, too."

"Can you afford it?" asks Nicky.

He smiles. "It's on San Francisco."

She dips her hand into her bag, cleans out her wallet, piles twenties beside his nose. "Who uses cash?" he mumbles.

"Do you want it or not?"

He sits up. "Why?"

"You've taken good care of me. I'm taking care of you a little."

Her phone chirps: Jonathan. Whom she hasn't seen since their visit here. She stands. "Freddy, do you ever wonder about your dad?"

"Like, whether he's in heaven?"

"No, like—who . . ."

"Ah—who killed him. My mom asks me the same question sometimes. Nah. I mean, I would *like* to know, but, like, that knowledge plus two seventy-five gets me on the bus, right?" He scratches his wrist. "Some stories, they just end without you finding out what happened. You know?"

"I know," says Nicky. "I don't like those stories."

79

HER BROTHER CUT HIS WRISTS in February 1999. Madeleine never knew.

> Today mama and me saw a lady who is a spycologist who asked
> why I wanted to die. I said I don't but it hurts to live.

She gazes at the window. Hears a little whine in her throat.
Her back aches. Still she keeps reading, diary on her thighs, feet on the floor.

> Poeple at school tell me to kill mysefl. Why are you even alive freak?
> Kill yourself there is to much bullying at shcool.
>   They make up story's about me call me loser lyer, weirdo. They
> hurt me. Last week I say I was a restling champion at summer camp
> to scare them and 3 restlers jumped on me in the bathroom said PIN
> US FAGGOT and I bite my tounge so hard it bleed.
>   I know how to spell faggot becase I see it alot on my locker.

Her blood bubbles. Next page.

> Also I told the spcyologist dad always is frustrated by me. I
> dissapoint him.
>   I am a burdin. I said that to the spcoglog lady and also said I felt
> hopless. I am here to be humileated. I do not belong.
>   THERE IS SOMETHING WORNG WITH ME

Madeleine cringes at the mob of capital letters. Squeezes her eyes shut. Opens them.

> Magdala said before Chritsmas that I need to be different. She told
> me to pay attentoin to what poeple say about me.

She can't remember this. Did she say this?

I am an embarassment, to my father and my sister

Next page.

Magdala said.

Did she *say* this?!

Today the lady asked why isnt dad here, mama said he is out of town. Not true, this morning I heard him tell mama that, if I had left a sucide note no one would be able to read it.

Madeleine's afternoon wears on, and with it Cole's next few months. He borrows forlorn words from *The Count of Monte Cristo*—which, of course, he was reading in order to please their father. (*I will finish it.*) His cursive slopes and his doodles wither. He writes less and less; he writes more than enough.

She turns the page into June.

Just four words: *Something exiting is hapening!!*

The next page is blank. And the next: nothing hapening there, either, exiting or otherwise. Six months before his disappearance, Cole simply stopped writing.

She frees her phone from her pocket.

I read it.

I hadn't realized how bad it
was for you.

Downstairs, the jittery tattoo of the typewriter.

I hadn't known how hard Dad
was on

She deletes these last words. She'd known enough.

Even if I'm saying that too late.

She waits. No signs of life.
Even the Remington goes quiet.
After a minute:

This is why I need you.

Not because of what he did
to me.

But because of what it did to
him and Mama

It was destroying them

Yes.

He was killing their marriage.
He couldn't help himself.

But he couldn't let her go
either.

You think he killed more than
the marriage.

Yes again.

How?

I need you to rattle him.

Ask him about what he knows
about New Year's Eve.

You still haven't told me what
YOU know!

I know you don't believe me.
Or at least you have doubts.

Because if you believed me,
you'd be scared.

Please believe me, Magdala.

Please be scared.

Tatter-tatter-rat-tat-Trapp!

She drops her eyes to the diary beside her. *Something exiting is happening!!*

When she lifts it to her lap, the pages flop to the left. On the back of the final sheet, Cole has made one last entry.

December 31, 1999.

New Year's Eve, he clarifies.

His penmanship has shape-shifted with time, the letters taller, the curves whetted sharp. This time, the hand is sure and the spelling perfect:

> *"Die? Oh, no," he exclaimed—"Not die now, after having lived and suffered so long and so much!"*
>
>   The Count of Monte Cristo
>   (I finished it)

Madeleine gazes at the red board of the back cover. Drums her fingertips against it.

Feels a ridge beneath the endpaper.

Her eyes narrow. She looks closer.

The ridge runs parallel to the length of the cover—and also, Madeleine sees, along the top and bottom. Tiny waves frill the edges of the endpaper, as though someone had carefully slit them before resealing with paste.

Her fingernail chivvies at the paper until she can peel it away like a flap. Fitted within is a postcard: a flurry of bright clownfish, orange and white. Madeleine slides it from the diary, turns it over.

June 3 1999 (jagged hand, barely legible)

Dear Cole,
    Thanks for the wonderful model trolley! We sure don't have these in Seattle. Good things are ahead!

Signed, in that same lie-detector scrawl, *Your friend, Sam Turner.*
The name is unknown to Madeleine.

Why had this man sent a postcard to her thirteen-year-old brother? Why would Cole hide it in a secret sleeve of his journal? Her pulse quickens.

She could ask.

But she doesn't.

She chews her thumbnail. Slumps against the pillow.

Seattle.

Cole has recorded half a dozen mother-son road trips in his diary—Los Angeles, Tahoe, even Vegas—but never Seattle, and nothing after the suicide attempt. Did they just stay put throughout 1999? . . . Well, how would Madeleine know? She was at Berkeley in the spring and autumn, after all, and she'd spent all summer at tennis boot camp in Florida.

Still: if they *did* travel, why not mention it?

Beyond the half-open door, the scrabble and wheeze of an asthmatic animal charging up a staircase. Watson peeks into the attic with a Glasgow smile, and Madeleine softens. "Hello, goblin," she says, clapping the diary shut. "Let's scram."

She smooths the bed, fits the floorboard into place, carries the dog and the diary down the stairs. In her room, she punches sam samuel turner seattle into a Washington State directory. Thirty-one individual records in the Seattle area, twenty-two listed phone numbers.

One hit for samantha turner seattle.

Past ten o'clock—too late to call, and too soon for her to work up the nerve. Instead Madeleine taps out a text to her cousin:

Do you know (of) a Sam
Turner in Seattle?

Also, for the last time: pls
come home. No one is mad
at you.

"I'm so mad at him," she informs Watson.

In bed, Madeleine studies the postcard, the spiky writing. She won't say anything to Cole.

Because she's not sure he's remembered the postcard. And that means she might know something he doesn't.

Friday, June 26

80

NICKY EMERGES FROM THE JUNGLE-STEAMING SHOWER to see her phone shudder on the sink and slide into the basin. She fishes it out, swipes the screen. Bashes one toe into the clawed foot of the tub.

"Miss Hunter?"

A man, though Nicky barely notices; she's biting her lip and sucking air. "Yes?" she hisses.

"Detective Timbo Martinez. I couldn't reach Ms. Trapp just now. Her cousin visited the station last night. Said somebody recommended he contact me. Didn't say who."

Nicky has one-footed herself to the toilet, where she wads paper against her wounded digit.

"Frederick acknowledges stealing personal effects from his uncle's home. He has no alibi post–cocktail party, after he fled the premises."

A pause.

"He insists he's had no communication with Cole Trapp. He found the butterfly box at the front door, he claims, but nobody can vouch for that. Possibly he made those butterflies himself, although—you know, Miss Hunter, I'm telling you this because I'm hoping you might contribute."

"Where's Freddy now?"

A sigh. "His mother collected him from the station. That was very dramatic. I believe his next stop is rehab. Please have Madeleine Trapp return my call. It's important."

He's hung up.

Hurriedly Nicky dresses. That shower failed to calm her. She has a sense of foreboding, as her calendar predicted. A sense of an ending, even.

Life is a thriller, Sebastian told her yesterday. *The ending is fatal.*

And then: *What story would you like me to tell you?*

A true story, she'd answered.

Nicky wants that true story. And she wants it today. She'll find him down—

—again the phone cries for attention. Nicky checks the screen: Jonathan.

She ignores him. He'll live. Unlike some.

Beneath the attic door is a folded note. Nicky picks it up—blue stationery, black type.

Pistols at dawn. Library.

And then the curve and cross of his initials.

It's well past dawn, of course. Nicky had planned to spend time with Sebastian today in any case. She hasn't told Julia she's still lodging in the attic, hasn't told Irwin—hasn't told anyone, in fact. She belongs to this world now more than theirs, she realizes, and the thought frightens her.

As she descends the staircase, his typewriter strikes up a sudden drumroll, as though she's presenting an award, or standing on the gallows. The sound hurries with each step along the sunlit hallway, until—just when she lifts the metal loop of the skull knocker—it ceases. Winner announced. Prisoner hanged.

"Enter, please!"

Morning has clarified the room. Through the windows, the Golden Gate gleams as though freshly rinsed, a few pennants of fog flowing from its towers.

At his desk, dressed in jacket (ivory) and tie (navy blue), Sebastian sucks on his pipe, looking remarkably soigné for a man so recently widowed. Of course, he's had practice.

"How did you know I was at the door?" asks Nicky.

"I didn't know at all." Smoke billows from his mouth. "Every so often I've rested my fingers and shouted in case you were loitering outside."

She takes the chair opposite him, just as she did on the evening she arrived. But now, up close—how *tired* he appears, like a creased sheet of paper that's been smoothed out again. His white skin has grayed, his gray hair has whitened; his lips are dry, his brows unruly. She notes the wrinkles in his clothing, small cracks in an oil portrait; the misshapen knot of the tie, the limp handkerchief . . . even the pocketwatch in his palm looks dull. Perhaps time isn't the best killer. Perhaps grief is.

"I don't wear grief well," says Sebastian, and Nicky flinches, startled to find him in her head even as he sits across from her. At his back, flames slow-dance in the fireplace as though exhausted.

"Grief feels like fear. I learned to live with fear a long time ago. I ought to be more comfortable with grief. Are you?"

Nicky blinks. "Comfortable with grief?"

He nods.

"I—" For a moment she doesn't know what to say. Then, slowly: "I suppose that if I'm grieving, then I must have loved whatever I lost, however I lost it. I suppose—it's like a scar reminding me of some adventure I had. Or like the end credits of a wonderful film. So . . . no, I'm not comfortable with it, but I'm grateful for it." She considers. "Grief might feel like fear, but it also feels like memory, and with memory, there's no—a story doesn't end."

She wonders if that sounds silly. She looks at him, at his lank hair and his drawn lips; his eyes alone are alive, dark and keen as they rove her face.

"All stories end," he says. Then he leans forward, rests his hand atop a short stack of pages. When he speaks again, his voice has picked itself up off the floor.

"Your work is excellent," he says, tapping the stack. "Transporting, really. The waterfalls in Peru: I can hear the roar. Writing those early novels: I can hear the typewriter. A day at the beach: I can hear the children whining, ever so gently."

Nicky smiles. "That means a lot."

"I've bled on it a bit—in red ink, I mean—so take a gander at my edits." He slides the papers across the desk; hieroglyphs and indecipherable notes crowd the margins. Sebastian has bled more than a bit—on certain pages, Nicky sees, he has opened a vein—but she's pleased. *Your work is excellent.*

He yawns, masking his face with one hand. "Excuse me. It's been an eventful spell for me. I daresay it's been an eventful spell for *you.* Christ," he winces, "'daresay.' Write historical novels long enough and I daresay you, too, will croak speaking like that."

"It *has* been eventful," agrees Nicky.

"That's what I said. You've had yourself a summer party en masque, complete with attempted burglary. Then a *brawl*! Then hundreds of champagne glasses mass-murdered. You've had a driving lesson. You've had threatening letters—well, I've had them, technically. You've had two breakfasts at a gentlemen's club without even disguising yourself. Goes without saying you've had the wisdom and encouragement of Watson the Seventh. You've seen the maze where my son's life began and the pond where my wife's life ended. You've suffered a tragedy with us." He puffs. "Oh, young Hunter—what've you gotten yourself into here?"

Does she regret his invitation? Nicky asks herself. Will she die of detective-fever?

"Have you figured out yet what's going on?" asks Sebastian. "Have you seen through the plot?"

"No."

"But you must know by now, my dear girl. We're practically at the end of the book." Sebastian lifts a magnifying glass from the blotter, the one that Nicky gave him just a week earlier, and twirls it slowly. For a brilliant instant, the arsenal between them flashes like heat lightning: the dagger, the poison bottle, the pistol, the candlestick, flaring one after the other.

Her stomach complains. "Sorry. I ought to eat."

"If Adelina is downstairs—"

"I'll fix some tea and toast." Quickly she stands. "Would you like either?"

He gazes up at her. "I'd like both."

At her back, she hears the snap and pop of his typewriter.

When she returns, he invites her to sit by the fire. So here she kneels, like a child, as she watches the flames and waits.

"A matter we've overlooked." He dips his toast. "Do you know why I ditched Simon St. John after that last book? Of course you don't," he says, before she can shake her head. "Well, it wasn't that I'd tired of him. I simply couldn't spend more time in the company of someone who unfailingly found answers to each and every problem he faced. Because I couldn't solve *my* mystery. And I couldn't watch Simon slip into a new disguise and solve *his*." Peering into his teacup. "I tried, of course. With *The Crooked Man*. But then Dominic . . ." A sigh. "Another crime with no hope of solution. So I retired Simon St. John. And I retired myself."

As she bites into her toast, Nicky observes his toes rippling within his socks, close enough to the flames that they'd smoke if damp. Behind her, an out-of-nowhere shower drums its fingers against the windows.

"Diana steered me back to the Remington some months ago, after the doctors gave me the thumbs-down. The metal dream machine, she called it."

"About Diana—"

"I'd occasionally dusted it off for assorted correspondence and such—yours and mine, for instance—but my gracious wife urged me to write a new story. Placed my fingers on the keys and refused to leave until I'd pressed one. So I pressed '1.' Right there, in black and white, I had announced my first chapter. I had announced Simon's return."

"You're working on a new novel?" Nicky is astonished. A will, instructions for his funeral, letters—even, perhaps, a deathbed confession: One or more of these, she'd felt sure, had set keystrokes tap-dancing down the halls and through the floors these past weeks. This, however, has never occurred to her: a final mystery. Even though he told her he wanted to wrap it up in ribbon—all of it.

"Can I read it?"

Sebastian pours tea. "Easy there, lass. Not much to read. Just some ideas firing in my expiring brain. A few flames gasping their last after you switch off the gas ring. Besides, I still need to sort out the ending." Lifting the cup to his lips. "That goes for mine, too. The end of my story." He drinks it off. "Fortunately, I work best against a deadline. You and Tacitus had a tête-a-tête once, no?" Tilting his head back toward the desk.

Nicky looks over her shoulder at the glass cube. Firelight crawls up and down its planes. "'It's human nature . . . ,'" she recites slowly.

"'. . . to hate him whom you have hurt.'"

They sit in silence.

"But now," he announces, "I must shuffle off for a nap. I wonder when the lease expires on that kidney machine. I'd like to bequeath it to Freddy. He's fascinated. I expect he'll try to use it on his penis."

"Why?"

Sebastian shrugs. "He's a man."

Thunder burrs as he rises. The teacup unhooks itself from his fingers and dives to its death on the black slate of the hearth. "Piss," says Sebastian, tipping back into his chair.

Nicky collects the remains. "Can I help you upstairs?"

"Please," he replies, unexpectedly. "Suddenly I feel very fatigued."

81

TOGETHER THEY LEAVE THE ROOM, Sebastian's hand grasping Nicky's shoulder. In silence they walk down the corridor, the windows glossy with rainfall, and turn into the hall; each pace seems to drain him more and more, as though he's leaking some vital fluid on the carpet.

"Should we take the elevator?" frets Nicky.

She summons the Otis. It descends, stubborn and complaining; when it arrives, she slides the grille aside, boards the car with Sebastian, slides the grille shut. Touches the third-floor button.

Clack. Slither. Whine.

He has released her, although she hears him breathe as the elevator quakes and climbs into darkness. Nicky glances down, watches as her hands disappear. Then her shins. Then her feet.

For a moment, in their blind ascent, she closes her eyes (or does she? No telling) and wonders what might happen next.

What happens next is an unholy thundercrack, as if the bowl of the sky has shattered. Clack-slither-*screech* scream the elevator gears, and then the car brakes so hard that Nicky loses balance, arms thrashing until her wrist slots snug into the dry vise of Sebastian's grip.

"Power outage." His voice sounds scraped from his throat.

In the deep-space dark, Nicky feels weightless, his hand all that tethers her to Earth.

"Generator should kick in any day now."

She doesn't speak. The thunder returns—softer this time, as though making a point it forgot to mention earlier, but still angry.

Slowly his fingers slip down, clutching tight, until at last they alight in her palm and step cautiously into the gaps between her own. Together they fold and bow, knuckles locking.

How long do they float there in that night-box? Sebastian's hand begins to quake in hers; his breath rasps in his chest.

"Do you hear that?" Nicky asks suddenly.

No reply.

"Footsteps? In the hallway?" She hears the hesitation in her voice. His fingers stir.

Just as her lips open, so, too, does the sky, one more violent split in her ears, fabric ripped hard and fast. Fingers crush her hand, wring it . . .

. . . and then, with a judder, the elevator resumes its vertical crawl, creeping upward until a slow waterfall of light drops gray and gloomy onto them.

The car stops. Through the diamond panes of the grille, Nicky peers down the long hall of the third floor.

"For a minute there, I felt quite unsafe," says Sebastian. Their fingers unfasten and she looks at him. He's older than the man who boarded the Otis, as though they've traveled through a tunnel in time.

He smiles faintly at her. "Were you trying to frighten me, young Hunter?"

She draws back the gate, clasps his elbow, ready to guide him to his bedroom.

But the instant they step out of the elevator, Sebastian gasps, and then his legs fail, and he topples against Nicky, crumpling to the floor and dragging her down until she's buried under the flap of his coat, head pressed against his side.

"I can't tell you!" he screams as she listens to his body. His voice seems to resound within him.

Nicky shakes off his coat and examines him: silver hair tumbled over his forehead, silver eyes wild. She looks down the sleeve of his outstretched arm, beyond the finger thrust straight ahead.

Poised on the narrow hallway rug, its wings spread in greeting, is a bright-red paper butterfly.

Even in the dimness, she can see small text typewritten on the wings.

Nicky gathers herself on her knees, bending toward it—demon's horns atop the head, serrated thorax, more weapon than toy—then lifting it to her eyes.

She looks over her shoulder at Sebastian. "'LAST CHANCE,'" she recites.

His arm drops to his lap. "I can't."

Far down the hallway, somewhere in the house, footsteps pound on the stairs.

82

MADELEINE SCURRIES ACROSS THE LIBRARY PARKING LOT beneath the rain, phone wedged against ear. Detective Timbo Martinez wishes for her to return his call at her earliest convenience. Right now's not particularly convenient, and he sounds calm enough, but Timbo Martinez is probably the sort of guy who meditates as his plane nosedives, so Madeleine buckles up and dials.

He briefs her as thunder rolls across the roof of her car: Freddy, precinct, confession ("Of course we won't press charges," Madeleine snaps), no reason to believe he's in league with her brother. "Nor do we have reason to believe that such a person exists."

Her hand seizes the gearshift. "Do you have reason to believe that my stepmother's death was suspicious? Real, court-of-law reason?"

"Not yet."

"Not yet or not at all?"

"I'm afraid I don't see the difference right now. Miss Trapp, I realize that Frederick is your cousin, but please exercise caution." Such a Boy Scout. Madeleine imagines him tucking himself into bed every night in full uniform.

A titanic thunderclap so startles her that she nearly runs aground at Alta Plaza Park. "Christ," she mutters. "Sorry."

Timbo has hung up. Madeleine nudges the car back into the street, windshield wipers flickering.

Nor do we have reason to believe that such a person exists. Ah, but she does. Yet the person walking through her brain right now— shapeless though not soundless, like a museum visitor whose foot-steps you hear in the next gallery, always one exhibit ahead—is Sam Turner of Seattle.

She parks against the curb, steps into the rain. Rushes up the drive and through the front door.

"I can't tell you!"

Her keys drop to the floor.

Her shoes skid on the marble, her bag flops down the staircase, her thighs burn to and from the library, her lungs gasp as she scrambles up another flight . . . but there, at the far end of the hallway—there she finds them.

She jogs ahead, panting, and Nicky rises, a red star in her hand. No: a butterfly.

Madeleine looks at its wings, looks at Nicky, then bends to her fallen birch of a father, a tangle of white branches on the ground. Nicky helps her stack him onto his legs. Together they drag Sebastian past Diana's bedroom and to his own, where they yank off his coat and timber-tip him onto the mattress.

Is this how he'll live now? Madeleine wonders. A shock every other day—a corpse among the goldfish, a butterfly in the hall; a rotating cast helping her unload him into his bed—until he dies?

"Police," she says. Nicky obediently steps into the hall, phone in hand.

Madeleine listens to her narrate the past ten minutes—fatigue, elevator, blackout, footsteps, origami—as she unknots her father's tie, unbuttons his cuffs. His shirt is cloudy with sweat.

She kneels beside him, strokes his fingers. They're trembling, like hers.

Sebastian fixes her with one eye, the white scarcely paler than his skin.

And only now, after bobbing briefly on the surface of her brain, does Nicky's word sink in:

"Footsteps?" Madeleine asks.

83

"MARTINEZ IS COMING," Nicky announces, entering the bedroom, where Madeleine crouches next to her father. Sebastian looks like a wraith.

"I gave him a pot gummy," says Madeleine. "You want one?"

Nicky's phone twitches. She checks the screen, returns to the hall. "Hi. Listen—"

"Tough to listen," Jonathan shouts. "I'm just around the corner at Harry's Bar. D'you know you can order a literal bathtub of beer here? Porcelain, twenty-four bottles of your choice."

"Now isn't—"

"I'm British, but I'm not *that*—"

"Let me call you later."

A pause. "Everything all right? Been a while."

"Busy morning."

"What's happening over there? Should I swing by?"

"No. Please."

"Are you alone?"

She hesitates. What does he hope the answer will be? "I'll text you," she lies.

The bell sings downstairs. Madeleine calls her name.

"Look," says Jonathan, "if you're not interested in—"

Nicky hangs up.

At the front door, with Madeleine's bag and keys in hand, she stands aside for Detective Martinez, all sharp angles in a smart gray suit, with Detective Springer at his back in a mohair turtleneck and black jacket and no smile. "Where's Mr. Trapp?" asks Timbo.

"In his bedroom."

"You heard footsteps? Coming from where?"

"I don't know and I don't know." Her nerves are jangling.

"So you didn't hear footsteps?" Timbo presses her.

"Doesn't matter who heard what when," says B.B. "Somebody's been inside this house. Maybe somebody's still inside."

Nicky stares.

Timbo moves quietly to the den while B.B. approaches the jigsaw room, her hand floating by her hip. "Miss Hunter"—without turning her head—"please remain by the front door, thanks so much."

She knocks on the door frame, enters the room. Returns a moment later, motions Nicky to stay put as she retreats to the back.

Nicky listens to the last shiver of rainfall on the windows. Pictures Madeleine's face a moment ago, ashen and worn, and wishes she could help. When the clock tolls four, she nearly yelps.

The detectives reappear. "Now then," says B.B., "where's this famous elevator?"

Upstairs, Timbo snaps a plastic glove around his wrist and gingerly lifts the paper butterfly from the rug. Nicky watches his head tip toward B.B.'s as they read the fine print.

"Anybody visit the house this morning? Or last night?" B.B. asks.

"No."

Timbo inspects the elevator, his phone blasting hard light into the corners of the cage. "Was the butterfly in place when you came down-stairs this morning?"

"I used the other staircase. At the far end of the hall. Always do."

Timbo bags the evidence and they proceed to Sebastian's bedroom, where Madeleine sits beside her father. Nicky goes to the window, glass stippled with raindrops.

"You again," breathes the patient, wispy, as Timbo looms into view.

"Seems you've got an insect problem, sir," says B.B. "So once more I ask: has anybody heard from the artist formerly known as Cole Trapp?"

Nicky doesn't dare glance at Madeleine.

"That's disappointing," B.B. says.

"I should've wrapped this up in a ribbon a long time ago," mutters Sebastian, closing his eyes.

Timbo edges forward. "What?" For the first time since Nicky met him, his voice has a pulse.

"It's a line from the books," Nicky explains. "Simon St. John says it."

"I've read the books. I know what Simon St. John says. I want to know why Mr. Trapp is saying it."

I still need to sort out the ending. The end of my story.

B.B. tries again. "Miss Hunter mentioned footsteps?"

The patient nods. "Yes. Running from the elevator, I think."

"Toward the other staircase. Miss Trapp, anybody going down as you came up?"

"Sure. We stopped and had a chat, a little gossip."

"Had to ask. So you, Miss Hunter, you hear footsteps, and then you see the butterfly . . ."

Sebastian says nothing. "A minute later," Nicky finishes.

"Just as I walked in." Madeleine rubs her father's hand. Nicky feels achingly sorry for her.

"Now, if the footstepper didn't exchange greetings with Miss Trapp here, and if we didn't smoke him out downstairs just now, then either he'd already fled out the back by the time the elevator doors opened or he jumped up to the attic." B.B. picks a dot of lint from her turtleneck. "Say, either of you ladies hear from Mr. Grant?"

"I just spoke to him," says Nicky. "He's at Harry's Bar."

"Just around the corner. How very convenient. How easy to get to. Been to Harry's, Tim?"

"Bathtub of beer," murmurs Timbo.

"They still doing that? Good for Harry's. I'm thinking we head over there, it being easy to get to."

"I'm thinking we head upstairs first, finish our sweep."

B.B. faces the room. "Miss Trapp, would you mind—I'd like to talk security."

Madeleine and the detectives adjourn to the hallway. Nicky gazes out the window. The rain died young.

When she glances back, he's watching her.

"Can you make it stop?" he murmurs, weak and weary.

Nicky looks at him for a moment. Slowly walks over, touches his shoulder. At last she whispers, "I don't know how." It sounds almost like an apology.

FOR HOURS, HUNCHED AT HER DESK while her father sleeps upstairs, Madeleine speaks to or leaves messages for nearly two dozen Sam Turners. "I'm looking for information about a boy named Cole," she explains, vaguely. You never know who might be a true-crime buff.

Some Sam Turners are too young to be of help; some Sam Turners are too dead.

Next she hunts him across social media—has he ever messaged, commented, liked? She tours Instagram galleries, braves the back rooms of Twitter, sifts through Facebook.

It's like looking through the windows at a party she wasn't invited to and doesn't want to attend. Madeleine shuts down each in turn.

On the final platform, some Instagram clone, Bissie and Ben Bentley beam like Mormons while their son paws at his mother's ripening belly. All three wear pink.

Madeleine stares until her vision blurs. She deletes her account.

Then—and even though the detectives swept the house—she turns in her seat. *Someone very dangerous is standing right behind you,* she'd teased Nicky that first night. It isn't a joke now.

Ten o'clock. She finds Watson in the parlor, camped out at the foot of the bookshelf. Rebecca's name shines as she touches a finger to the spine. One tilt and Madeleine could enter a portal, rest on the divan, elude time.

The dog sighs. Madeleine sighs.

In bed, she feels sleep falling on her like snow. Before it buries her, she taps a message on her phone:

Please tell me where you are.

She needed to try. LAST CHANCE.

NICKY CLUTCHES A GLASS OF MILK IN ONE HAND and watches Sebastian sleep.

Creepy (she knows)—creepy and difficult: the curtains are half drawn, the room a canvas of shades. But how rarely she's observed him at peace! He doesn't look like much beneath the duvet: just a long craggy ridge of white, a distant mountain range in winter, and his face tipped toward her. Doesn't sound like much, either; she can hear only cool air excusing itself as it pushes through the vents.

Quietly she climbs the stairs to the attic. Sits at the desk, tugs the lamp chain, drinks off her milk. Pulls her laptop from her bag. Two slips of paper drop to the floor.

Nicky picks them up, lays them on the desk. The photos she took from the Trapper Keeper: her and Sebastian in the Jaguar, Freddy and Diana and Simone at the party.

A creak behind her.

Nicky whips around, holds her breath, scans the attic.

Nothing. Just the house cracking its knuckles as it gets ready to sleep.

In the dark, *A Child* smirks, blameless but knowing.

When Nicky returns to the photos and discovers the clue—for that's precisely what it is, a genuine clue—she rises in shock. It's as obvious as handprints on a window, as phosphorus on glass. "Oh," she says.

In the drawer, she finds the toy magnifying glass, lifts it to one eye. Leans close.

Cherchez la femme indeed.

Her legs disintegrate beneath her. She slumps into the chair.

No: it doesn't prove anything. It doesn't prove what she wants to prove, certainly. So is this where all her sleuthing has led her? Is this the end of the story?

She kills the lamp, stands. As she rounds the desk, her hip brushes the Magic 8 Ball on the desk. It plunges over the edge, wallops the wood, rolls away. Lodges in a corner. A neon-blue runemark glows within its porthole.

BETTER NOT TELL YOU NOW.

Nicky settles in the window seat, tilts her head against the glass. Thinks about that silver man in his bedroom, sleeping in silence.

Only later will she remember that Sebastian Trapp snores in his sleep.

Saturday, June 27

86

WATSON SCRABBLES AT THE SHEETS, woofs low.

Madeleine sits up, half-awake. Watson rarely woofs.

She checks her phone: five minutes past four. Squints at the dog.

The man at her bedside whispers her name before she can scream.

IN THE WINDOW SEAT, Nicky dreams of keystrokes, harder than before, loud enough that the floorboards dance, nails twisting from the wood. She dreams of Sebastian Trapp, sleeping in silence—

She stirs.

. . . Sebastian Trapp snores in his sleep. Yet the dark in his bedroom was soundless.

She begins to surface.

Why would he lie there awake, eyes shut, facing the door, knowing she was outside, but say nothing? He's not the retiring sort. There isn't a room into which he hasn't invited her.

What game is afoot?

"UP AND AT 'EM."

In the darkness blazes Sebastian in a suit the color of bone— his favorite, Madeleine knows, Irish linen, blue lining. White shirt. Lavender tie. "We haven't watched a sunrise in ages. I haven't got many left. Come on, come on. Our old spot! I'll get the Jaguar purring."

"Why so early?" Her voice sounds rusty.

"I'm feeling restless. Don't dawdle. Let's go sunrising!" He fades from the room like a star.

NICKY UNSHUTTERS ONE EYE, glances out the window.

Frowns at the car across the street.

Just beyond the streetlamp, where a faint fall of light douses the pavement.

In ten days, she's never seen a car parked there before.

AT THE WARDROBE, Madeleine pulls a sweater from a drawer. Four ten A.M., her phone tells her. She inspects herself in the mirror. Four ten A.M., her face tells her.

Her hand hovers over the jewelry box. She knows what's inside, lying in wait.

She opens the lid, seizes it, thrusts it into her back pocket.

"Stay," she reminds Watson, who has done nothing but stay, as she rushes from the room.

NICKY LIFTS HER PHONE, zooms in on the car, on the driver's window.

Then she notices movement below.

COLD NIGHT AIR FALLS IN as though it had been leaning against the front door. Madeleine hurries down the steps, jeans creaking at the knees, and crams herself into the passenger seat. Beside her, Sebastian sucks on a pipe. "I've packed oranges and some once-sparkling water," he says. Madeleine swivels, makes out his battered leather messenger bag in the backseat. "Also a sleeve of stale Oreos. Breakfast of champions. Now, buck up! Buckle up, too." He jabs the key into the ignition, twists.

NICKY PRESSES HER FACE against the window as the Jaguar opens its white eyes and slips down the drive. Was that Madeleine who climbed inside?

She jams her feet into sneakers, wriggles into a hoodie, hurries to the door. Steps on the envelope.

"FIRE UP THAT PHONE, MADDY," her father tells her as he twirls the wheel and they roll into the street. "Play us some golden oldies. Let's turn back the clock."

Madeleine tugs her seat belt across her chest, throws a longing look at the house before the hedges wipe it from sight.

NICKY TURNS TOWARD THE MOONLIGHT. Her initials are scratched into the paper.

The letter is typewritten, of course.

Dear Miss Hunter,

This won't be a long goodbye. I am in my
library late at night--so far past twelve
o'clock that we're nearly at thirteen.

Not long ago, I told you (twice!) that we might
solve an old mystery (or two!).

But I concede that detective work is easier
on the page. No dead ends, no superfluous
characters, everything wrapped up in a ribbon.

So I shall do what readers hate most: I shall
spoil the mystery for you. If you really don't
want to know, stop reading now.

Have you stopped reading?

(I didn't think so.)

And so:

Impossible though it might seem, I took the
lives of my wife and child.

If you wish to continue with your account of
my own life, I give you my blessing.

ST

Nicky blinks.

Then the floor collapses beneath her. She drops one story
down, drops another, and lands in the chair opposite his desk
two weeks ago.

Sebastian smiles at her over the typewriter.

"You can find the good in me," he says. "And I hope you won't
have to dig too deep."

This isn't real, she knows—shock dragged her through those
two floors, pinned her to this chair; the Sebastian before her, the
library behind her: mere memories—but all the same she peers
up through her waking dream, through the hole in the ceiling,
and through the hole in the next, where she now stands, in the

dark of the attic, the confession of Sebastian Trapp in her grip
and not much good to be found.

She folds back the bottom of the page.

> P.S. One piece of my legacy remains
> outstanding. You'll find the clues atop
> this letter.

There's nothing on top of the letter. Unless he means the
envelope? With her name slashed across it?

No time. His confession is finally in her hands. Now all she
has to do is catch him.

87

SEBASTIAN IS NO RIGHTEOUS BROTHER. It's always surprised Madeleine that her father should sing so badly. His ought to be a rousing barroom baritone, sturdy enough to hoist pints to, not this busted-bagpipe wheeze.

Smoke spouts from his mouth, streams out his window. Madeleine turns to her own, sees herself twinned there: lashes bristly, lips dry. As the strings tremble, as the horns gush, he elbows her—"You know the words!"—and she chimes in weakly. She does know the words.

"Attagirl," he beams, setting the pipe beside him, and sings along.

The drums thunder. She feels her heart rise in her chest and levitate there as the Jaguar revs into darkness. For a giddy moment, they race ahead of the past two weeks, the past two decades; she hears the years clatter behind them like tin cans from a newlyweds' car.

"*'So don't—'*" Faster.

"*'Don't—'*" Louder.

"*'Don't—'*" She's shouting alongside her father, voices climbing the steps of the melody.

"*'Don't let it slip away,'*" they roar, and then they chant it at each other with jubilation, and only when the song is over, one minute and fifteen seconds later, will it occur to Madeleine that this isn't the way to Lands End.

NICKY CHARGES INTO THEIR ROOMS. Sebastian's bed is perfectly made; Madeleine's is a mess. Both are empty.

Nicky doesn't expect to find anybody in the library, but those keystrokes popping in her dreams—those were real, and recent. The trail begins there.

The skull-and-bones knocker cackles at her. She presses her palm against it, pushes.

Through the windows she sees the illuminated towers of the bridge. The confession flutters in her hand as she moves through the gloom to the far end of the room, the foil markings on the books glinting like jungle eyes. Behind the desk, where bright teeth once gnashed in the grate, the fireplace yawns blacker than black. The flame has died.

Her phone flashlight examines the typewriter—no paper—then scours the desktop: dagger, poison bottle, candlestick, noose. The glass cube. The butterflies sleeping beneath the surface.

Nicky shudders.

Downstairs, taped to the fridge, she finds a note scribbled on the back of a receipt:

> *At Lands End labyrinth for sunrise.*
> *Pls take Watson outside when you read this.*

Timbo Martinez answers on the second ring. "Miss Hunter." Unexpectedly alert.

"They've left the house," she tells him.

"I know."

"How do you know?"

"Because I'm right outside."

THE SONG IS STUCK IN A LOOP as the Jaguar steals into the Presidio, low beams barely flushing the winding road before them. Somewhere amid the bungalows and the barracks is the golf course where Madeleine smoked her first joint and the officers' club where she kissed her first boy. But as they coast through the deep dark woods, trees on either side of the road linking hands overhead, silver fog like netting between their trunks, sand traps and Spanish tile and graveyards seem the stuff of another place, another age.

She slides her window down, closes her eyes. The air sharpens with eucalyptus. Her hair stirs about her shoulders, her face. Her body sways with the road.

Now the bite of salt water in her nose. To the right, she knows, is Crissy Field, airfield turned wasteland turned bayside park; beyond it, Torpedo Wharf, where the family once spent a morning crabbing, she and her father and mother hauling up box traps while Cole, by the bucket, announced that the animals were attacking one another in their panic. Finally, near tears, he tipped the entire catch into the waves. Sebastian lost his temper; Hope escorted Cole back to the Oldsmobile. When Madeleine found one laggard rock crab lurking at the bottom of the pail, she . . . did she drop him into the water? Did she turn back to the traps? She can't remember.

The car slows, stops. The music dies. Her eyes open.

Directly ahead, braced against the bay, hulking underneath the Golden Gate Bridge on-ramp, is Fort Point.

OUTSIDE THE HOUSE, at the top of the steps, Nicky inspects the street. No sign of Timbo. No sign of anybody—just fog, silky and cold, and that strange car.

Its headlights flash twice.

The door opens.

Nicky steps back, and Timbo steps out, in drainpipe jeans and a trim black sweatshirt embroidered with UNIVERSITY OF WASH-INGTON across the front, hair radiating from his scalp like solar flares in the lamplight. "Mr. Trapp didn't want surveillance," he calls. "I disagreed."

"You didn't follow them?"

"My concern is who's going in, not who's coming out. Besides, I couldn't make out the driver."

Nicky closes the front door and hurries down the steps. Timbo waits. She presents Madeleine's note to him, eyes the gun bulging from his hip.

"Also," she adds, handing him the confession.

She watches him read it. This isn't his mystery, of course. But she needs a ride and she needs a cop. And she needs to hear somebody say—

"He killed them." Timbo sounds almost puzzled.

"We've got to go to Lands End."

He frowns. "You think he'd hurt his daughter? Why?"

"Ask his wife," says Nicky.

NOW MADELEINE HEARS ONLY the idling engine, the muttering waves.

Mist slinks through the low beams like gray foxes. To one side, a rough ridge of rock, a floodlight lodged within it, and to the other, the bay; ranged before them are the broad brick walls of the fort, nicked with rifle slits and feebly illuminated. From the parking lot, Madeleine can't see the lighthouse on the rooftop—dark for nearly a century now anyway—but the vault of the Golden Gate soars overhead, the bridge above trimmed with lamps and the towers waist-deep in fog.

"Wonderful atmosphere this morning," observes Sebastian, puffing on his pipe.

The screen of brick flickers. The floodlight is dying. Madeleine turns her head to the seawall and the thick, rusty chains hammocked between thick, rusty posts.

Her father points to the far end of the lot, where it juts into the water. "*Vertigo* was filmed over there, you know." He knows she knows. "The girl jumps, tries to drown herself. That Hitchcock blonde—what was her name?"

"Kim Novak."

"No, the character."

She knows he knows. "Madeleine."

In the dark of the car she can feel him smile, softly. "Madeleine. Of course."

The floodlight sputters again. The wall of the fort blinks like a camera shutter.

"I'd have liked this place as a boy," says Sebastian. "Secret passages and spiral staircases. Hide-and-seek, spy games. Cole liked this place." A cloud of smoke. "Cole liked games."

Madeleine gazes at the chains, at the black water. She wonders how her father's face looks, in the failing light of the bulbs and the rising light of the sunrise; wonders what he's thinking—which, in the case of Sebastian Trapp, might be quite different from what he's saying.

Why have they come here? She realizes that for the first time in her forty years, she feels afraid in his presence; it's a shock, unnatural, like shivering beside a merry fire.

"'The French have a phrase for it,'" says Sebastian. "'The bastards have a phrase for everything, and they're always right.'"

More borrowed words. But Madeleine would like to know what the bastards are right about this time.

"'To say goodbye is to die a little.'"

In the Jaguar, in the silence, she deducts her goodbyes from the sum of her life. Shuts her eyes.

"It's almost dawn," she says.

TRAFFIC LIGHTS HANG LIKE CHINESE LANTERNS down the length of the avenue, an evil red eye glowing in each; one by one Timbo's car spooks them green. Nicky watches the speedometer creep past forty, past forty-five, arc into the fifties.

She chews a thumbnail, gazes out the window. Strip malls, apartment complexes, all looking tired beneath a bruise-blue sky, like they know how early it is.

Her fingers stroke the confession in her lap. Two words don't belong.

She closes her eyes, watches the strikers springing to the page as he sat at his desk, those two impossible words—and now a tiny question glows in her brain, a little firefly: what had been gone from the library? *Something:* something small but definitely absent, like a missing puzzle piece.

"What did your friend Jonathan tell you about himself?" Timbo asks.

Nicky doesn't particularly care about Jonathan right now, doesn't care about anything except the Jaguar and Lands End and `Impossible though it might seem, I took the lives of my wife and child`, but she needs to talk over *the nasty thumping at the top of her head.* "Raised in Dorset. Lived in London. Worked in finance."

"One out of three. He lived in London, which is where he's from, and he's a journalist. Freelance. Jonathan Grant isn't even his real name."

As Nicky opens her eyes and turns to Timbo, he unscrews a water bottle, gulps, his lean throat working. "We got the story last night. Couple months ago, one Grant Jones hears that Mr. Trapp's on the way out, so he decides to set up shop in San Francisco, get to the bottom of the Vanishing Act—that's the title of his piece. Wants to crack the case before the deadline. So to speak. Moves into a cousin's vacant *flat*—I gather there's family money—and tries chatting up Mr. Trapp's old acquaintances. Tells people he's Jonathan Grant, burned-out banker recharging his battery. Joins a soccer league in order to befriend Frederick, who proves to be of limited use. Then he notices you. You're bleeding on the evidence."

Nicky looks at her lap, where four bright red stains speckle the paper.

Now THE CAR ACCELERATES. The road curves and straightens, curls and uncurls, a series of question marks. They speed west, through the leafy tunnels of the Presidio, until suddenly the water opens up beside them, iron-gray and restless—and then, growling, the Jaguar bursts ahead, past shaggy trees that soon mob and block the view. Madeleine watches mansions erupt from the ground in Sea Cliff; her father streaks by without hoisting a middle finger to Lionel, for a change, and at last, regaining the sea, they sweep uphill into Lands End.

She chews a thumbnail, tastes blood. Some game is afoot. She's willing the sun to hurry up, to beat them to the ocean. *Ah, well—back home we go.*

The Legion of Honor scrolls by, a stiff stone forest of columns and arches. At the end of a half-hearted lane beyond the museum, Sebastian kills the engine.

Madeleine turns. The road behind them looks as desolate as the path ahead.

Her father checks his pocketwatch, prizes himself from the Jaguar. "Come on, come on—" flinging wide the backseat door. He hitches his messenger bag onto one shoulder. Madeleine doesn't move.

"The sun is known to be punctual, daughter mine," calls Sebastian, striding into the undergrowth. She watches his white suit disappear like a ghost in flight, the bag floating at his arm, as though he's making off with his last earthly possession.

"Sorry to break it to you," says Timbo. "Seemed like you liked him."

The type that's hiding something. Nicky feels a bit bruised—was that kiss in the attic real?—but can't work up much indignation. Later, perhaps, she'll tell off Jonathan or Grant or whatever (he wasn't kidding: the man really *could* be anyone); right now, she doesn't care about anybody other than Sebastian Trapp.

The gray road ahead of them arrows into the gray distance. She's willing the sun to rise slower.

The detective swallows a hiccup. Nicky looks at him, the cheek pricked with faint scars, and again she thinks of Timbo Martinez young and self-conscious and unhappy with his face, maybe unhappy with himself.

When he glances at her, with his bedhead and those powder-blues, he looks like a little boy.

She shuts her eyes again, returns to the library. Tracks the firefly across the shelves, into the fireplace, around the desk—

And then she sees it, or sees where it wasn't, and when she turns to the detective and tells him, he cuts his eyes to the red light ahead, swaying in the breeze, and blows through it so fast that a cyclist nearly tumbles from his bike.

Her father leads her beneath eaves of black leaves down a deep flight of shallow steps, his bag jouncing from his elbow; then, in the failing dark, they turn to walk up a dirt path, eye-high with vegetation. Step after step, his form curves further around the hedge until at last he's disappeared.

Madeleine finds him at the peak of a steep slope, where a few trails gather, mingle, untangle themselves, and press on. A long green hill flows down to Mile Rock Beach and the choppy waters beyond.

"Will you look at that," marvels Sebastian, looking at that, breathing hard, his suit a slash of white against the coloring sky.

And then he's off, Madeleine in pursuit.

Four dozen dirt steps later, she doubles over beneath a spray of cypress branches, gulping air. The water grumbles at her back.

She lifts her head to the distant bridge and the bay, whitecaps glinting like teeth. Sees her father tightrope-walking a narrow ridge of rock.

Her phone says 5:11. No reception.

Now she trudges along the ridge. Slides skittishly down a trail squeezed between a vast boulder bulging from the bluff and a killing drop to the black rocks far below, water boiling around them.

The cliff is an arrowhead, the tip aimed northwest; and at its center churns a whirlpool of small rocks, each the size of a human heart, shaped into alleys and switchbacks and dead ends. The hidden labyrinth, swirling on a secret ledge thrust into the sea.

Her father flicks a tartan blanket over the ground beside the maze, weighting it with his bag. When he turns to Madeleine and beckons her, she obeys, dragging a sleeve across her damp forehead.

THE CAR COASTS THROUGH THE PARKING LOT and brakes. Nicky bursts from the passenger seat, phone to her ear. "Voicemail," she reports, for the third time. "There's no reception out there," she adds, also for the third time.

"Text her again." Timbo claps his door shut. "You sure they're at this labyrinth? Lot's empty."

Nicky's thumb skids across her screen. In her right hand, Sebastian's confession snaps against the wind. "Then they parked someplace else." *When I took my children here, we'd stash the car in a hiding spot by the Legion.*

They hustle across the promenade and down the steps, landing on the Coastal Trail, where Nicky lifts her eyes to the vision she beheld not long ago, in that slow-motion moment beside Sebastian: the shimmering waves, the storybook clouds, the headlands . . . But today the water lifts its jaws to bite, foaming at the mouth; the sky hasn't yet revealed its true colors, and—

"Just stay back when I say so. How's your half mile?"

Nicky hikes up her sweats and follows him as he trots east along that same path hugging the curves of the bluff. The same trees reeling at the edge, flailing their branches. Same stubborn boulders in the bay. The past made present.

The past is a strange place. My past, anyway. What about yours?

But the past is gone.

Oh, no. And his smile was so sad she could have cried. *The past isn't gone. It's just waiting.*

88

ALMOST SUNRISE.

For some time they've sat in silence before the labyrinth. Sebastian, barefoot, gazes calmly at the ocean; Madeleine watches the bridge, strewn with tiny rhinestone headlights.

"Two hundred shipwrecks out here, you know."

She smiles.

"SS *City of Rio de Janeiro*. Turn of the century. Last century. Foggy morning, just before dawn. Smashed into a reef, sank in minutes. Hundreds drowned." Hundred thirty, Madeleine recalls, but let him inflate the death toll; he's killed off so many over the years.

"Their bodies washed ashore for months. Mostly Chinese immigrants, very sad, but one was the captain—do you know how they identified him?" She does. Gently, she shakes her head.

"Silver pocketwatch." Pulling his own from his vest. "Chain was tangled in his ribs. So they managed to salvage his timepiece. But—"

"—they never did salvage his head," murmurs Madeleine.

"No, they didn't." A sigh. "Imagine all that went on within that head while its owner lived. More interesting than clockwork, I'll bet. Boy, look at that."

She squints at the bridge towers, twin torches, mist burning off around them.

"I thought of ending my life here once," says her father mildly.

When she turns to stare at him, he's speaking to the mountains. "One evening years ago—very chilly April—I drove to Lands End. With G. K. Chesterton on the brain. 'What we all dread most is a maze with no center.'"

She's speechless. First Cole, now her father.

"So it was for me that night. So it is for me many nights. My whole long life long." His Adam's apple quivers in his throat. "Perhaps I thought it might help to see a maze with a center. A destination, even. Because I could wander into dead ends only so many times."

Suddenly the bay booms, like a creature rousing itself at last, yawning and flexing and storming out of bed. Madeleine darts her eyes beyond the rim of the maze, over the edge of the cliff, to the knuck-les of black rock in the bay, bulging from the deep, seething with sea foam.

Sebastian shakes off his shoes. "Your mother cracked The Mysteri-ous Case of Where I'd Disappeared To very easily. Seems I'd mentioned mazes on a number of recent occasions." He smiles.

"She found me standing right there." Nodding at the tip of the arrowhead. "In the dark, in the drizzle. Watching the water. I heard her call my name." Now he points to the nearest curve of the lab-yrinth. "She stayed just outside the maze, across from me, and she simply listened. And"—his voice shrinks in his throat—"what it must have sounded like to her! Hearing those words spat out by someone she loved. Hearing them twisted and torn by the wind and water."

The sky is rinsed soft blue and pale rose. They're the loveliest colors Madeleine has ever seen.

"It seemed we remained there all spring, though I suppose it was only an hour. Either way, I exhausted myself. I don't know how deter-mined I felt when she first spoke to me—I suppose you don't, do you, until you've done it—but by the time she spoke again, called my name again, I had no desire to drop off that cliff. This cliff.

"Your mother asked me to take one step toward her for every step she took toward me. And so we crossed the labyrinth, circle by circle, until finally we met in the center and sank to our knees. She spread her coat over the ground, and there we lay for a while, and then I fell asleep. When I woke up, the skies had cleared and she was watching the stars. She hadn't moved, even with my colossal skull on her chest."

A sigh. Sebastian closes his eyes. "I felt alive. I felt *excited.*" His fingers drift up to his tie, unpick it; they drift down to his collar, unbutton it. "And six months later, your brother appeared."

He excavates a slim flask from the messenger bag. "Made in a maze." Unscrewing the cap. "Let's drink to Cole." He puts the flask to his mouth, jerks it upside down. Smacks his lips, hands it over. "Can scotch go bad?"

Madeleine sips, passes the flask back to him. "Let's say it was always bad."

"Yes, let's," he agrees, drinking.

"Cole was—conceived here? Where was I conceived?"

"I was trying to recall. I want to say in a ditch."

"That's what you *want* to say?"

"Or the back of an abandoned mail truck outside Las Vegas. Our car had died in the desert."

"Oh."

"Sorry."

Before them, light peels shadows back from the stones like rinds of fruit. The ocean rumbles.

"Are you afraid of dying, Daddy?"

He tucks the flask away, clears his throat. "All my life, since my mother died, I've lived in fear. Fear has become my companion; I notice when he's strayed from my side, and I miss him." He watches the wind chase dust across the cliff. "Not such a bad thing to be afraid, Maddy. Not such a bad thing to live with fear."

Silence.

"Would you like to have a child?"

He says it as though he's offering a canapé. Madeleine glares at him.

"What? You'd be a mother for the ages. You've got such *love* to give. Besides, I like to think of a new generation of Trapps."

"Dad, men look at me like I'm a suspicious suitcase."

"Men." He snorts. "Men are where evolution backed itself into a corner."

She nods.

Her father scoops the pocketwatch into his palm. "Five-fifty." He smiles.

The sun remains hidden behind the Berkeley hills; still Madeleine imagines light flooding westward toward the bay, rushing past Treasure Island, pouring through the barred windows of Alcatraz, and at last leaping from wave to wave beneath the bridge and across the Golden Gate strait, gilt whitecaps and dazzled water in its wake.

After a few minutes, her father turns to her. "Dearest, take the Jaguar." Dropping the keys into her palm.

"What about the sunrise?"

"The sun will rise tomorrow. It is a very persistent star. I'd like to sit here awhile."

"I can sit here with you," she offers. "Today's wide open for me."

He leans toward her, cupping her head with one hand, pressing his dry lips to her brow. She closes her eyes; she can smell the Floris on his neck.

He pulls back. "Drive safely. I love you and I love that car."

Madeleine struggles to her feet. "How will you get home?"

"Oh, I'll phone from the Legion."

She turns and walks away, around the bulk of rock rearing from the cliff, as the sea and the shore play her exit music. She glances over her shoulder. The rock hides her father; Madeleine sees only the corner of the blanket, fluttering in the wind.

She's chugging up the slope where she stumbled earlier, trying to calculate how many stairs she'll have to climb on the return journey, when her phone trembles in her pocket. Reception once more.

She digs it out, taps the screen.

Frowns.

Hurries back down to the bluff.

Rounding the rock again, she sees her father standing barefoot at the near edge of the labyrinth, the messenger bag at his hip. The blanket trembles over the ground, weighted by his shoes.

"Dad?" she calls.

He stiffens, one hand in the bag.

Madeleine tries to laugh. "Do you have a . . ."

Slowly he turns to face her. His hair flickers across his eyes.

"I'm afraid I do, darling," he answers, the Webley in his hand, dark-silver and bony, and he sounds disappointed in himself.

89

MADELEINE'S JAW DROPS LIKE AN ANCHOR.

"Why didn't you go home?" her father cries, as though she's made a terrible mistake. "Go," he pleads. "Maddy, go home."

His arm swings away from her, gun aimed offstage, and his voice goes cold. "Please lose the weapon, Detective."

Madeleine turns her head. Fifteen yards away, across the flat sweep of pebbles and dirt, Timbo Martinez walks onto the cliff top in sweat-shirt and jeans and hip holster and, in his left hand, service revolver.

"And perhaps you'll kindly see my daughter back to Pacific Heights," Sebastian says.

"Why don't we all head home together, sir?" calls Timbo. "Lots to catch up on."

Their triangle changes shape as he advances. "Dad," calls Madeleine, speaking into the wind as calmly as she can. "I need to talk to you about Cole. This is about Cole."

"It's *always* been about Cole!" Sebastian's voice cracks and a laugh pours out, bright and bitter, as he steps backward into the outermost ring of the maze. "Stop where you are, Detective. Now toss your weapon on the blanket. Just like that. Thank you."

Timbo lifts his hands, palms out. "That's a real nice piece, Mr. Trapp," he says. "I noticed it on your desk. A Webley-Fosbery automatic."

And then, in unison with Sebastian, "Four fifty-five six-shot."

"I've read all your books." The detective moves forward. "Revolver that old, though—not gonna fire, sir."

The shot is so violent that the echo sounds like falling debris. Madeleine stifles a scream; Sebastian chops his gun arm back to Timbo and steps backward, into the next ring. The sixth.

Madeleine exhales. She counted seven circles earlier—seven concentric ripples, a sixty-foot radius. The whirlpool is sucking at his heels.

She detaches herself from the rock and reaches toward him. The Webley glances in her direction—just a quick look; already it's trained again on the detective—but the shock knocks her back a step.

Sebastian Trapp—famed, fabled, mighty Trapp—is nervous.

His voice, though, is steady enough. "I had it restored in 'ninety-two for a publicity event. Turned out I was quite a good shot."

"Maybe you'd like to talk to somebody?" Timbo suggests. "I can call whoever you want."

"Whomever," says Sebastian automatically, but his eyes glitter beneath his brows. Thinking, Madeleine knows. Devising a solution. As wind streaks across the cliff, she wonders if her father might, for the first time in her memory, stand down—stow the Webley, buckle his bag, escape the labyrinth, take her hand in his . . .

Yet it's too late, she knows; somehow she knows it's too late.

And now he smiles—an inscrutable smile, as of one grimly satisfied—and speaks: "Everybody's already here."

Madeleine slides a glance at Timbo, sees him glance at her.

Instantly the wind relaxes. Her hair settles around her face. The blanket settles upon the ground. Dust settles upon the stones.

Behind the detective appears a child escaped from bed. Pajamas slouching from hips, arms sheathed to the fingertips in long sleeves. A sheet of blue paper in one hand.

Timbo swivels. "I told you to stay away," he barks, jerking his head toward the trail, and Madeleine nearly steps back, so rough is his voice.

But Nicky continues to walk along the far rim of the maze, cool yet alert, like a hunter.

90

As if it has been waiting for her entrance, the wind stirs, and Nicky feels her hair stray from her face.

Even against the vast sweep of water and air, he looms huge; against the sloping shoulders of the headlands and the sagging suspension cables of the bridge, his angles break even harder, split even sharper. The Webley eyes her as she walks.

"Good morning, Miss Hunter," he greets her.

"'One of my names,'" she says, "'is Nemesis.'"

His smile sharpens like a knife—the man knows his Christie. "'And what does that mean?'"

"'I think you know. Nemesis is long delayed sometimes, but she comes in the end.'"

He inclines his head.

"Leave," growls Timbo. "Now."

"Miss Hunter is very tenacious, Detective." Sebastian's eyes are locked on hers. "Now she's come for me."

Nicky breathes deep. This is how she feels approaching the last chapters of a mystery—the curtain, the final problem, the end of the story: her blood hums, her eyes gleam; the heat in her stomach, the thumping in her head . . . the detective-fever is peaking.

The paper rattles in her hands. Those inky sleuths presenting their solutions to vast casts of suspects in train cars and hotel suites, fanning out their clues like playing cards—were their nerves in flames, too?

Sebastian watches her. *You're in a psychological thriller . . . Where the clues almost ineluctably lead you someplace you don't want to go.*

No. She wants to go there. Solve the final problem, bring down the curtain. End the story.

Nicky pushes the paper toward him. It snaps in the cold air. "Your note."

Sebastian nods.

"Written on your typewriter."

He nods again.

"Signed in your hand."

The bag slithers down Sebastian's arm, flops to the ground. At the far curve of the maze, seven orbits away, Madeleine watches with a strange light in her eye.

"You confess to murdering your wife," calls Nicky. Doesn't he remember?

Now Madeleine gasps like it was knocked from her, just as Timbo orders Sebastian to set down his weapon, nice and slow. A gust rips across the bluff and Nicky opens her mouth—

Then the Webley fires.

91

IN THE INSTANT BEFORE THE SHOT, Madeleine sees the blanket lift and levitate, a magic carpet—and then, when the bullet punches through, it twists in the air, drops to the ground beside the upturned shoes. The service revolver lands a few feet closer to Timbo.

She looks at her father, a cuff of smoke at his wrist; then she regards the blanket as she would a living thing—a once-living thing—as though she has just seen Sebastian kill.

"Mr. Trapp, you seem pretty edgy, sir," says the detective. He tips his head toward Nicky. "You've typed out a confession. Did you write those other notes? The butterflies?"

Sebastian shakes his head. "Cole did."

"You know this?"

"I'm sure of it."

"That's not the same thing, sir."

"As the eldest and best-dressed person here, I say otherwise."

"Has Cole contacted you?"

The words gush from Madeleine's throat like she's retching poison. "He contacted me." She swallows, looks bashfully at her father. "He wanted to find out what happened to Mom." Her gaze slips beyond him, where all those orbits away, Nicky's fingers fret at the confession. "He told me to try and . . . stir up the past," Madeleine calls. It sounds dramatic, but so does the wind circling like wolves around them.

"And I've *met* him," she shouts in somebody else's voice, raw and half-wild, as her eyes boil over. "I don't know when or where or *who*—but I know I've met him." The truth is leaking out; she feels unloosed, dizzy, a diver in rapid ascent.

When the wind relents, she turns to Timbo, sees the pale fire flickering from his skin, feels the familiar warmth. "I thought he might be you," she says, shyly.

He blinks at her.

"Are you?" she asks. "Are you . . . ?"

He remains still.

"Please," says Madeleine.

In the salt air, under a paling sky, she can see Timbo clearly: the open face, the blue irises, the rowdy blond hair. His throat flexes and softens. And now she knows he's Cole, knows it so surely that she could embrace him here, by the maze where he was made, as the breeze awakens and the air shifts at their feet. Her father sees it, too: he's shaking his head in wonder.

"Tell me you forgive me," she says, tearful, tilting her head, then a shrug, then a smile. "Or tell me you don't."

"I forgive you."

Her nerves spark like nicked wires. But it isn't Timbo speaking.

Wind elbows Madeleine from behind, whips past white-rabbit fast, running late and in a hurry. She watches as it tousles first the slain blanket and next Sebastian's trousers, then frightens some dust from the ground; she watches as it rushes—

—the wind rushes over Nicky, setting the pleats of her pajamas flapping, drawing her hair from her face.

Yet in her hands, the butterfly doesn't even shiver. It simply floats above her palm as she folds one blue wing one last time.

92

"I WAS FOURTEEN YEARS OLD when I told Mama I lived in the wrong body."

I whet my voice against the wind and square myself to look at him. I've rehearsed; I want myself heard.

"Valentine's Day nineteen ninety-nine. That morning, I'd slit my wrist with your straight razor in the attic bathroom. I was ruining the family—Maddy told me so. But I cut the wrong way. Later you said, 'He can't even kill himself properly.'"

I pull back my right sleeve, unsheathe my forearm. The little rungs of scars are faint; still, I've worn sleeves these past two weeks. Be prepared: the Scouts came in handy after all.

"Mama took me to a child psychologist. Back then, 'that kind of therapy'—he meant treatment for gender-dysphoric children—that kind of therapy wasn't commonly available. But he referred us to a doctor in Seattle. I didn't like flying, you might recall, and neither did Mama, so we traveled by train, even though it's twenty-three hours one-way. One of our long weekends, we told you. At night I lay in my bunk and imagined that somebody, or a dozen somebodies, might creep in and murder me, like in *Orient Express*. BOY, 14, FOUND DEAD IN SLEEPER CAR, STABBED 12 TIMES. 12 WITNESSES SAW NOTHING."

He watches me evenly, tie flagging in the wind, revolver in hand. "Being called 'boy' felt more unnatural to me than being dead," I add, wiggling my jaw. *You'll dislocate that thing,* he used to warn me. He's not warning me now.

"The Seattle doctor specialized in adolescent psychiatry. He didn't gawk at me; he didn't glare at me. He listened as I described myself to him. Freak. Weird. Creepy." My eyes bore into him. "Embarrassment."

Not a blink. Still the words drip from my lips:

"Faggot.

"Homo.

"Little girl."

I swallow. "That one hurt, because I *was* a girl, even if nobody really *believed* it. Except for Sam Turner. Before we said goodbye, he asked me my real name, and I answered, 'Nicole.'" I pause. "Nicholas to Nicole. Guess I lacked imagination."

I glance at Timbo. Even two decades on, I brace myself for judgment; but he just watches me, thoughtfully. Beyond him, Madeleine's hair bursts from her head in the wind. She looks as astonished as I feel.

"Sam Turner saw me for who I was and who I had always been. He heard me, too, like someone fluent in a language nobody besides us understood." These are my lines, but I'm nervous; I pause, breathe. "He introduced me to a medical doctor. I was thirteen—puberty wouldn't wait forever. We could tell Dad later.

"The process wasn't very efficient in the late nineties, but it still required extensive preliminary psychotherapy. Mama opened a separate line of credit. Once I had my green light, we visited Seattle every eight weeks for treatment. Coast Starlight at Jack London Square, King Street Station almost a full day later. Totally inconvenient, even I knew that, but at least we got ourselves out of San Francisco, away from anybody who might notice Sebastian Trapp's wife and son visiting a hospital. And we spared ourselves a flight record.

"We met his wife. Millie. Sixties, like Sam, no children. We stayed in their guesthouse. We had meals together, watched movies, played games. It felt like home. Just not my home.

"I'd been assigned a pen pal at school for a conservation project, but she never replied. So Sam suggested I write letters to my future self instead. Ask her questions, remind her of what mattered to me, of what I was looking forward to. I began sending postcards to myself in Seattle, once a month. Nicky didn't write back, of course, but every time I visited Sam and Millie, there were a couple of messages cheering me on. I liked Cole, I found. He was sweet and sincere and goofy and he deserved to be happy. I kept those postcards. The sloth. The scorpion. The butterfly.

"Then: Christmas Day. I was seven months in, although nobody appeared to notice. Santa had brought me packets of origami paper. I still don't know what upset you: I said the wrong thing, or I laughed the wrong way, or—and only later did I realize this—maybe the problem was you, not me. But that afternoon, you marched up to the attic with my paper, and by the time I got there, you were in the bathroom, and the sink was in flames. You'd torched every sheet. The blue satin, the red yuzen—burning in the basin." I can see it now, the rainbow bonfire, kindling crackling beneath my hands.

"After you walked away, I just stared at the ruins. The next morning, Mama boxed up some clothes and shipped them to Seattle. I made butterflies because I wanted to be like *you*, you know. Until I didn't."

He looks past me, at the ocean.

"On New Year's Eve, before her birthday dinner, I visited Mama in her bedroom. She gave me a round red box. Inside was a wig, long and blond and simple. And underneath that, an argyle sweater and a plain skirt. She wouldn't let me try them on, not in the house, not even for a minute, so instead I stashed it all in my overnight bag—wig, sweater, skirt, candy, books, four hundred eleven dollars I'd saved, a change of clothes for Mama—and we reviewed our escape plan: at three A.M. we would meet at Fort Point, my favorite place in San Francisco. A good place to begin an adventure, and just a bike ride away from Freddy's house. It was a half-hour walk for Mama in the wrong direction, and another half hour by taxi to the train station, but we could be sure nobody had followed us—and Cole could say goodbye to the fort and the bridge.

"'It's gonna be a long night, sweet girl,' she told me. Then we went down to the dining room."

I hesitate. *You're weak, son. You're not what I hoped for.*

The wind is biting my fingertips. "Afterward, Diana drove me and Freddy to his house. I called top bunk, in case anyone checked on us after I'd left. Fred conked out; I couldn't even shut my eyes. Dom and Simone came home and peeked in, which was my cue to sneak out, but they stayed up for more than an hour while I sweated in the sheets. The moment I heard their door close, I crept outside, wheeled Freddy's too-small old bike from the garage. I'd already chosen it weeks earlier; I knew he wouldn't notice.

"It was cold but bright that night, and I coasted through the Presidio to the fort. No sign of anybody, including Mama, so I dipped into my bag and changed my clothes, put on my hair. I felt natural. Powerful, even." For an instant I see Nicole, in skirt and sweater, blond hair pouring down her back; she smiles beneath the full moon.

"I waited for her. And waited. Two hours later—five A.M.—I found a taxi on Lake Street. Stowed the bike in the trunk, left it there when I paid the cabbie at the station."

I glance at Timbo, his hands in the air, and at my sister, arms slack, one fist clenched.

"I hoped I'd find Mama. I didn't. Maybe she'd gone home, but I couldn't. The Turners would know what to do. I remember the ticket clerk addressing me as 'young lady.' I remember realizing I'd forgotten to pack my diary. I remember the Sacramento stop, where Mama had planned to call you, before you noticed us missing.

"Sam and Millie collected me at King Street the next day. Morning after that, third page: police had declared us missing. The article said I was small and blond and a boy. Nobody reviewing security footage from that night—airports, train stations—would see Cole Trapp; they'd see a long-haired girl in a skirt.

"Sam wanted to call you. But Millie talked him out of it: what if you'd hurt Mama? So we proceeded with treatment as we waited for her, waited for news. Then you went into hiding. And we stopped waiting.

"The Turners raised me. I was the child they'd wanted. Or if I wasn't, I never suspected. Millie and her sister Julia homeschooled me through the end of the year. Julia was an English teacher, and it turned out I had dyslexia. Not uncommon. Very treatable. Vintage mysteries were my training wheels—short books, fun stories, easy language. And in September, freshman transfer student Nicole Hunter enrolled in high school. Graduated four years later, with honors and even with a few friends. Finished college a week before Millie died. Kept inhaling detective stories, because they comforted me, and because they engaged my busy brain. And because"—I shrug—"it's in my blood."

Now that blood rushes to my head. "And I also kissed boys and drove cross-country with two friends and hang-glided and hiked South America and took cooking classes for a year and bartended in Amsterdam for a summer and read so many books and broke the thumb of a guy who didn't like *no* and toured Eastern Europe and tried to play violin and flunked my driving test three times and got my heart broken and never spent a single Thanksgiving alone and made more friends, really *good* friends, to-this-very-day friends, who are *proud* of me just for *being* me, who became my family just like I became theirs. I've got a god-daughter. I've got a mortgage. I've got my own bulldog. And I still make origami. Origami and detective stories—they survived Cole.

"I lived," I say. "Even if this cliff *disintegrates,* even if you *shoot* me, I lived. I lived as myself." The butterfly jitters in my grasp; I pinch it, gently, so as not to crush it. "But only after I left your house."

Once more I cast a glance at Maddy, draw it over to Timbo. I watch them searching my face for some trace of who I was.

"I wondered about Mama, of course. Ceaselessly, at first, then a little less as my life changed, as I changed. My friends don't know who I used to be. They know I was born in the wrong body, but they don't know whose. Why should they? Only I couldn't accept that unfinished ending. Even as I sat aboard the train to Seattle, hoping she would breeze through the car but pretty sure she wouldn't, I suspected that you—who'd argued with her so bitterly for so long, who might have discovered our plan, and who had plotted so many deaths and crafted so many alibis—I suspected that you had gotten away with murder."

In the wind, in the cold, on a cliff, by the sea, I'm struggling to remember my lines. Those last words surprise me; only a fictional detective would say that.

Except I'm not a fictional detective. This isn't a setting but a location. These people aren't characters. My pumping heart is real. My sister's tears are real. My father's gun is real.

93.

"FIVE YEARS AGO, after Sam's funeral, I spent the night in the guest-house. On the bookshelf I found Simon St. John. The Turners weren't big fans, as you might imagine—must've belonged to a visitor. I read it on the eastbound flight. *Little Boy Blue*," I add. "Dedicated to me. I'd loved your books, always—at first because you were my father, and then, later, despite that. I'd loved Simon. That wasn't an act. And now I loved him all over again.

"I don't believe in signs, but this felt pretty damn close. So back in New York, I wrote a letter to you. My first father."

Timbo clears his throat. "Why?"

My first father hasn't spoken a word, so fine: questions from the audience. "I'd noticed an error. That was my excuse. But—grief, prob-ably. I'd lost my family; I guess I wanted to look through the windows at the life I'd lived before."

Back to him. "For postage I chose a stamp from a roll you had bought me at a museum decades ago. That afternoon was a good one; I suppose I'd wanted to keep a piece of you.

"Then a surprise: you wrote back. And so it began. I wondered how far I could push my luck—wondered what you might tell me about, say, your vanished wife. Because I *knew*"—for an instant I feel half-strangled with anger, hard enough that it might leave bruises on my throat—"I *knew* you could."

Waves shatter on the rocks below. Wind tugs at the butterfly in my hands.

"Every so often I asked a leading question about Mama—and Cole, too. You barely nibbled at the bait. I collected your letters like they were love notes, reread them like they were code. But mostly I waited for the chance to confront you. If only I could arrange it.

"And then you arranged it for me. 'These are the words of a dead man,' you wrote. 'Come to San Francisco.' Soon I found myself in my childhood bedroom, upstairs from my sister, sipping tea with my mother's old assistant, visiting my aunt and my cousin. And none of you—*none of you* knew me!" Even now it astounds me, exhilarates me.

"I was the Count of Monte Cristo, back from the dead and armed with a plan, my eyes a little clearer and my heart a little colder."

I'm talking like him. I don't mind.

"'Maybe we'll solve an old mystery or two,' you said when we met. Daring me. So I listened—to anyone who spoke to me, but especially to you. I listened for clues. This was a mystery, after all: what had you done to her?

"And I—my heart . . ." My throat closes for a moment, and so do my eyes; when I open them, I'm gazing at the sky, soft blue and pale rose. They're the loveliest colors I've ever seen.

So much for my cold heart.

"My heart burst," I shout. "My heart burst to see them—to see them at *all,* but to see them like *that.*

"I even found my old diary in its hiding place—I was shocked the police never discovered it. Didn't tell me much, but it cleared my head. I'd almost begun to forget who you really were, how I felt unwelcome in my own—"

Wind like a slap. I narrow my eyes, focus. "You told me that I'd make a good confessor. I'd tried nudging you; now I nudged harder. On the way back from Simone's, I swung by a stationery store. You can guess what I bought. Right before stepping inside the house, right before you greeted me, I folded the butterfly and placed it in a box on the front step.

"If you wobbled, though, I didn't see it. So I recruited an ally." Deep breath, back straight. "I downloaded an anonymous-number app and texted Maddy. Magdala to Magdala." Magdala, who now glares at the ground.

I should apologize—I *will* apologize—but first: "I needed *proof,*" I call to her. "You could confront him where I couldn't. That's why I pointed you to the diary. I needed you to see *why* I . . ."

She doesn't lift her head. I try again. "While you chased Cole, while *everybody* chased Cole, I could focus on—"

Guilt, acid in my throat. I push it down, swallow it, hot and foul. I turn to him.

"'Do you think they're still alive?' I asked you—right here, in this maze. 'Wait and hope,' you said. Precisely what I *couldn't* do. So enough nudging. I decided to shake the house like a snow globe: I didn't know what it would look like afterward, but I knew it would look different. And Diana was a question mark: maybe she knew nothing, maybe she knew everything."

He watches me, hair rioting atop his head.

"I'd typed a message on the Remington after we returned from the beach. I kept it on me during the party, so that I could set it on the keys for you to discover the following day—but then Jonathan asked to visit the library." Which was opportune for Grant Jones, of course. "Which was opportune for me, of course. Because I put the butterfly in place before you reached the desk. Everybody saw you collapse. And with Freddy on the loose, now you had a suspect. A red herring."

Freddy: another apology. I shake my head to clear it.

"Then a twist even I didn't see coming: Diana in the pond." Blunt, yes. This is a reckoning, not a eulogy. "Obviously Dad had done it— force of habit—but what about the note? What about the *motive*? Why bother killing another wife? Especially so soon before your own end?" The faintest of flinches. "A drop like that didn't look foolproof to me, but then I couldn't even kill myself properly. So maybe guilt pulled Diana out the window. She said as much in her note. Why should she feel guilty?

"Enter the detectives. They knew about the second butterfly, so I told them about the first—they would've found out soon enough, and anyway, *I* hadn't harmed Diana. They took that lead more seriously than I expected. Even that first morning, Detective Springer's nose was twitching. Maddy warned me. I told her to keep quiet." SHHH.

"She was scared, she said, but not scared enough, I said. Diana was dead. Nobody knew how or why. Jonathan Grant or whoever he is had appeared out of nowhere. And Freddy had kissed her, even though Freddy's a good boy. Always has been."

My father arches one eyebrow.

"The media showed up. I chased them away—this was my investigation, not theirs. And . . ." Another deep breath; I squeeze myself. "All the while, I'd been writing your life story, sifting through it for hints, for clues. And I liked your life. I liked your stories. I liked how you *looked* at me—you'd never looked at me before, not without sighing or wincing.

"Seems I'm not a very good detective, though. Suddenly you wanted to die sooner. Time for a third butterfly. I placed it in the upstairs hall before joining you in the library. In the kitchen, I dissolved a sedative in your tea—prescription-strength, can't fly without it—and when you got tired, I steered you into the elevator. I pretended to hear footsteps, just to throw you off. And when the doors opened—"

"'I can't tell you,'" he says, voice hollow, eyes sad. "I said, 'I can't tell you.'"

"But now you've told me." The butterfly shudders in my hands, points pricking the skin, wings tattooed with his words. "'I took the lives of my wife and child,' you wrote."

Behind him, wind chases tears across Maddy's cheeks. "Although you didn't," I admit. "Not *my* life." He watches me evenly. "Those words don't belong. So what kind of game is this? It *is* a game, isn't it? Or a trick, or something?"

"Or something," replies my father.

"I knew you were back." Madeleine's voice hobbles across the maze. "I felt it. I just didn't know you were you."

Guilt, sour on my tongue. "I had to know the story. Didn't you?"

Her shoulders slump.

And now I turn to him one final time. "The past isn't gone, you said; it's just waiting." Again I lift the butterfly. "So let's see what's waiting for us there."

Waves explode like fireworks behind him. I wait until they fade.

"When you strip and skin someone until they feel like nothing—what you told them all along they already were: *nothing*—you shouldn't be surprised to find that at last you've whittled them down to a fine point. You've made a *weapon* of them. You've made them *dangerous*. And once you rip everything away, they need nothing except air to breathe and your heart to run through. So well done: you've sculpted your very own nemesis, you've armed her, you've instilled her with one purpose and one alone. And here I am."

The wind and sea fall silent as I speak. I control the elements.

I look into his eyes.

At last he blinks. "Here you are," he agrees, a polite tip of the head. "As I've known all along."

94

THE CLIFF TILTS A FRACTION, dipping toward the sea behind me.

"I might be eccentric, Miss Hunter, but who invites a perfect stranger to bunk upstairs and poke around in his past? Especially when your past is as pokeable as mine?"

His voice clots in my ears, thick and fuzzy. I shake my head, very slightly, until the words sharpen, until at last my mind is tuned to the correct frequency.

"'Bring me the child,' I called when you arrived." Grin, sheepish. "Course, I wasn't yet *certain*. Not until we met."

Is this a bluff? *How?*

"*Limenitis archippus.*"

I blink.

"At the Natural History Museum," he says, "when you were twelve years old. We two found ourselves quite alone by the butterfly exhibit. 'Here's the monarch,' you announced. 'Poisonous. Be careful.' Which I thought rather sweet."

The dark hall, the bright display case, butterflies arranged beneath glass like gems. I do remember.

"But the monarch was larger, I explained, its blacks bolder. You had singled out a harmless viceroy, which had evolved to *mimic* the monarch. And so we whiled away an hour. 'What's this one?' you asked. I told you it was the *Diaethria anna,* the 'eighty-eight,' with markings like numbers on its wings. And as you kept pointing at butterflies and I kept telling you stories about them, it felt to me like a game of catch." His hair spills over his forehead; he pushes it away, eyes on me. "Later, in the gift shop, you asked for a roll of viceroy stamps."

Because I hoped to write letters to friends one day, like you did, once I was a better speller, and once I had friends.

"Five years ago, when I received your greeting, I recognized the stamp before I'd even read my name. *Limenitis archippus.* The game was afoot."

The cliff tilts a fraction more. Soon stones will roll toward me.

"I borrowed Diana's laptop, chased you down a few blind alleys— most Nicky Hunters seemed to be women. I backed up, tried Nicholas,

Nick, Nicky again. Till at last I found your faculty profile, and I saw your face—yours, not Cole's," he adds. "But made of the same material."

"How could you remember a stamp?" My voice sounds distant.

He squints, as though the answer should be obvious. "I had spent a happy afternoon with my child," he says. "How could I forget?"

The butterfly shivers in my hands. Waves charge the cliff. He waits until they've broken.

"What to do? Should I confront you? Write your name on the envelope—the name I used to know?" I imagine the shock of it: NICHOLAS TRAPP scrawled across the paper like a threat.

"No. Here was a *mystery* to solve! An *anthology* of mysteries! Why were you writing, and why now? How had *you* evolved? So I replied." (*Mr. or Ms. Nicky Hunter.* I inspected the flap, the San Francisco address. Smiled, softly.) "And so it began, as you said. I sensed us wrapping our fingers around the rope, felt a twitch upon the thread. You were searching for something—you had stepped out of the past in order to find it—"

"The truth." The butterfly flaps its wings.

"Sir"—I'd nearly forgotten Timbo was present—"why *would* you invite Miss Hunter here to poke around?"

He knits his brows. "Because she is my child," he says. "And because I thought that Miss Hunter might know something of interest to *me*."

"What might that be, sir?"

"My motive? Motive, I always say—I do always say it," assuring my sister and the cop, "motive is where the mystery lies."

They blur in my vision as he turns to me. I see only the man who murdered my mother.

"I would like to tell you—I *am* telling you—that I enjoyed our correspondence. I mean that. You've a wonderful voice."

I look away, watch the flaps of the waves. The riddles, the solutions, the glimpses of life off the page: I enjoyed it, too, I suppose. I want to ask what my voice sounds like. But not as much as I want to hear him confess.

So I simply wait. I'm good at waiting.

"Soon enough, I also heard the ticktock of my mortal clock. For a month or two I wondered what to do with you—should I say nothing?

Let the obituary surprise you? Seemed a bit brusque. So I flexed my knuckles, gripped the rope, and pulled you across the country to join me in my final hours. I wanted to meet you. More: I wanted to *know* you. And for you to know me. It's why I brought you here that morning." Sweeping one arm around the cliff. "To tell you your origin story."

When I look at him, I feel my mouth shape the word, although I don't hear it.

"*Why?* I already told you."

I swallow.

"It was clear to me, during our meet-and-greet in the library, that you believed I'd no idea who you were. Even as you wiggled your jaw at me. The advantage was mine. I'd already prepared the photo album, already planted your diary."

I cannot believe this.

"Of course the police found it," he continues, off my stare. "You'd hidden it beneath a loose floorboard, after all. After they returned it to me, I studied it for answers; but as you said, you were careful. The day before you arrived, I restored it to its crypt. Sprinkled some scene-setting dust on the cover. Even dragged that portrait over to keep vigil. A child somewhere between the sexes—probably in bad taste.

"Just a couple of little bee-stings to agitate you, then. I hadn't foreseen that you would sting back, and sting deeper.

"That first butterfly, in the box—very bold. Also inscrutable. What did I just say about motive? Couldn't imagine yours. Still: I liked the challenge; I liked my chances. I took you here, where we stand, all but dared you to reveal yourself. You declined.

"Next up: *Tell them what you did to her.* Plumb knocked me back. (As you saw.) For days, for *years,* I'd wondered *why* you'd written to me, what you were after—"

"What else could I be after but—"

"*Then* you mickeyed the tea. I suspected only too late; didn't think you had it in you. The storm was a happy coincidence, but those phantom footsteps—nice touch. You nearly shattered me. 'I can't tell you,' I told you. 'Make it stop,' I asked you."

I don't know how, I'd answered.

"And I played along," he adds. "Didn't want the cops closing in on you any more than you did."

Enough. Enough. Now Maddy and Timbo come back into focus; he appears to have edged closer to his gun in the dust. "You've *confessed* to it!" I shout, the bloodied paper thrashing in my hands. "You said you *murdered*—"

Suddenly he roars. "I said I *took*—"

"Tell me *how*." My throat feels like an electric current. "Did Simone help you?"

"Simone?" His tie flails, the hems of his trousers snap. The gun trembles in his hand. The whirlpool at his feet has pulled him into its fifth ring.

"I found a clue," I say, and I sound like a Junior Detective but I don't care. "In a photograph. I found the *necklace*." So loud that Maddy steps back. "I gave Mama a necklace the night she disappeared. A silver disc, inscribed, on a silver chain. How did it wind up in a photo, on your sister-in-law's neck, at a cocktail party twenty years later?"

Yet he doesn't answer; he simply looks . . . sad.

Instead, it's Maddy who speaks—Maddy who steps forward, clutching a strand of metal in one hand.

"Because I took it from her after I killed her," she says.

95

ONE HOUR AND THIRTY-ONE MINUTES into the new millennium, Hope Trapp stepped from the curb outside her home into the backseat of her brother-in-law's Saturn. Her jumpsuit flashed like a flame; then the door closed behind her and the car rolled away.

Down the block, at the wheel of a beat-up Jeep, Madeleine frowned. She had arrived home early from Berkeley so that she could surprise her parents when they woke up or when she woke up, whichever came second; instead she found the hostess fleeing her own party.

Madeleine was slightly stoned. But very curious.

Six minutes later, at a Marina District liquor store, her mother hopped from the car, wriggling into a dark coat. An arm thrust from the passenger window, chunky bracelets at the wrist, white peonies in the fist. "Oh, why don't you keep them?" pleaded Hope, her voice bouncing like a ball up the street, but Simone simply rattled the nosegay. At last Hope relented, waved the car away. "Go home!" she laughed. "I'll call a cab. Or walk, if I feel like it. Kiss Cole, kiss Cole!"

As the Saturn disappeared into the new year, Madeleine watched her mother stroll toward Better Liquor Fast, from which Madeleine had been banned years earlier after several misunderstandings involving her fake ID. Now she'd caught her mother on a beer run. She killed the engine, wondered if she ought to stage a little reunion in aisle three . . . but then, by a lonely pay phone, Hope slowed, and glanced over her shoulder, and stopped.

And headed for the street.

Madeleine climbed out of the car. Sucked air into her lungs, ready to catapult her mother's name down the block.

. . . What *was* Hope Trapp up to, though?

She locked the car door, smoothed down her sweatshirt (HOME-COMING 1999, the stitching still shiny), and beneath a full moon began tailing her mother down the tree-lined sidewalk. She'd rein her in before she got to the corner.

Hope got to the corner. Hope got past it, too, and crossed a desolate boulevard, Madeleine hanging back. She cut through a yacht-club marina, sailboats asleep in their slips, and a concrete terrace, its steps descending to the silver beach and the black bay.

Two hundred yards behind her, Madeleine asked herself, out loud, "What is happening?" She was slightly stoned, yes, but more than slightly confused.

By the beach her mother shook off her coat—the air was cool, not cold—and folded it over one arm. Madeleine watched the velvet shimmer in the moonlight. She looked up: New Year's fireworks had pounded the sky so hard that the night looked bruised.

At last Hope turned onto a broad, sandy trail trimming the coastline of the bay, between a ghost-town parking lot and a nursery of baby dunes. But soon the dunelets yielded to the beach, and the parking lot surrendered to grass—and now Madeleine was tracking her mother across a plank bridge through a tidal marsh, wetlands brimming on either side.

At some point Hope shed her heels, hooked them on her fingers, the nosegay swinging from her other hand.

Madeleine waited for her to turn, for Hope to see her.

But she didn't turn. Didn't see her.

Madeleine tipped her head to the stars, saw herself bird's-eye—her mother, too—as they trekked west: to their left, wrinkled marshwater reflecting the moon; to their right, small plots of dune flora—scrubs and wildflowers, wrapped in low chicken-wire fences—and beyond these, the dark beach and the dark bay. She saw the path bend past long-vacant Spanish barracks, a colony of disused airplane hangars . . . and as the beach narrowed to a rocky fringe, she saw the Golden Gate, flowing overhead like a river in the sky.

Now Hope was floating past the wharf where the family used to fish and crab. Madeleine glanced warily down the length of the pier, as though she might catch herself there, catch her brother and their parents, too.

The trail veered north, merged with a two-lane drive between a steep ridge and the water. Thick, rusty chains hammocked between thick, rusty posts. Madeleine heard waves lapping against the seawall. By now she knew where her mother was leading her.

There, at the peninsula tip, bathed in moonlight: the abandoned fortress. Fort Point.

Crouched beneath the bridge, brick walls, rifle slits. No lights, within or without, but as Hope approached the paved lot, Madeleine found cover behind a small utility shed; she heard her heart beating, even though the waves urged *shush, shush*.

She watched Hope slow, stop. Glance at her wrist. Madeleine did the same. Two nineteen A.M.

She'd spent almost half the new millennium stalking her mother. This would probably be one of those stories everybody laughs about later.

Hope revolved in place, as though looking for something she knew she wouldn't find. Then she strolled, leisurely, with her shoes and her coat and her flowers, to the far end of the lot, where the walls of the fort met and jutted almost to the edge of the water.

Then she was gone.

Madeleine sprang from behind the shed. Raced across the parking lot to the corner of brick where her mother had vanished.

She stared down a narrow strip of asphalt, four feet wide and forty long, all that separated the fort from the water—strung with those same low posts, those same slumped chains. Black rocks were banked against the seawall; the bay was bursting upon them.

No sign of Hope.

One hand braced against the brick, Madeleine walked the path until it curved ahead. She curved with it. Where it opened onto an alcove behind the fort, a broad court of pavement, she spotted a jagged heap: her mother's heels and coat. Hope had dropped her clothes and now slowly patrolled the seawall, plucking petals from her flowers, casting them into the bay.

"Mom?"

"*Bloody*—" screeched Hope, whirling about, hand against her heart. Surprise on her face. "Darling! What are you doing here?"

"What are *you* doing here?" Madeleine asked.

"You're not home until Monday, I thought."

"I came back early. Then your ride pulled out of the driveway, so I followed you." A pause. "To a liquor store."

Hope's smile faded.

"What are you doing, Mom?"

After a moment, her mother looked away, at the water. "That shop keeps bootleg mezcal in the back. Plump little worm and all. I said I'd grab a few bottles and be back soon."

"But you didn't," Madeleine observed. "And you aren't."

"No," agreed Hope, rubbing one foot.

Waves slapped the wall. Dread curled up in Madeleine's gut, began to hiss.

Hope remembered her flowers. "Your aunt brought these tonight. Left them in the car, insisted I take them. I can never tell with Simone." Slowly she twisted the head off a peony, tossed it at the bay. Sighed again.

Then she turned to Madeleine. "I'm taking your brother away."

Madeleine simply stared.

"You should have seen your father tonight. No—you *shouldn't* have done. He humiliated his child because of a *butterfly*. Told him he was *weak*."

"Cole *is* weak," said Madeleine.

"Then it's his father's duty to be strong for him." Hope tore off a petal, dropped it into the waves. "Although you're wrong," she said after a moment. "Cole is the strongest of us."

"So where is he?" Madeleine gestured at the bay, at the bridge above. "Is he going to row by and pick you up? All aboard for—where, exactly?"

"Enough, enough. I'll call tomorrow morning. Or this morning, really."

"You think Dad won't notice you've left?"

"Not tonight, no." She'd thought about this. It annoyed Madeleine. "The party's still at a medium boil. He'll stagger up to his bedroom thinking that I've staggered up to mine. Or that I'm sleeping it off at Dominic's. I'll ring later today. But I *don't* want *you* caught *up* in it." Calm enough, except her knuckles were as white as the peonies.

"Darling," said Hope, voice softer. "Go back to campus. Come home in the afternoon—Dad and I will have had our chat by then."

"Why don't you chat with him now?" asked Madeleine, and she heard the hurt in her voice. The anger, too.

Her mother smiled sadly. "This is more complicated than you know, my love."

Lines pulled at the corners of her lips; the breeze dragged strands of hair across her face. She looked *old*. But her eyes glinted in the moonlight, and so, at her throat, did her necklace. Madeleine glared.

"He showed that to me at Christmas. *Cherchez la femme.* Isn't that all he does? Just look for his mama?"

Hope flinched. The dread in Madeleine's gut coiled tighter, hissed louder.

"You're always *babying* him. He trots after you like he's Watson. Those little mother-son vacations. It's so . . . *weird.*"

"Stop it. I hear enough of that talk from your father."

"So why don't you ever listen?" shouted Madeleine. "Why don't you *ever* take *Dad's* side? He just wants Cole to grow up! He's trying to *help* him!"

"No," Hope said, roughly, "he's trying to make him somebody he—"

"Somebody he *isn't*? That's the point! You want him to be who he *is*?! This weird, weak—"

"*Stop it,* Mad—"

"He hops from one school to the next, yet somehow never learns to read, never makes a friend . . ."

"*Madeleine.*" So forceful that even Hope looked startled. She stepped in close. "Leave. Now. Wherever you've parked, drive back to school, and don't you dare say—"

"How can you choose *Cole* over *us*?" Madeleine cried. "He's a *freak!*"

The crack of her mother's palm against her cheek sounded like a gunshot. Felt like one, too. Even before the skin could sting, she was staring at Hope in shock.

The blow seemed to knock her out of her body. She could watch the scene like some impossible witness: her mother reaching out, speaking three words—"Mad, I'm so sorry"—and Madeleine driving her hands forward, a quick collision of palms and shoulders.

Another crack—but this time, Hope's head glancing off one of the squat posts on the seawall. She clattered to the ground; a shower of white petals drifted through the darkness.

Madeleine saw herself from a distance, down the dark strip of asphalt clinging to the fort, as she gazed at her mother, a bundle of orange and black shadows, like a dying fire.

Saw herself from still further away, trying to shake her mother awake. Shaking harder.

Pressing her mouth to her mother's, breathing.

Kneeling beside her, hugging her, the two of them rocking back and forth. Madeleine sobbing soundlessly.

And then she was running across the parking lot. Past the wharf, breath ragged, and across the tidal marsh, where she retched over the bridge. She ran through the marina, toward the dark liquor store. To the pay phone.

She barged in, lifted the receiver, hand quaking. Rummaged in her pockets—"Daddy, Daddy, Daddy . . ."—forced a quarter into the machine. Began jabbing in her home number.

Then she looked at the dial pad, the buttons painted dark red. Looked at her fingers.

She dropped the phone. Watched it thrash on the end of its cord like a fish. Grabbed it, replaced it on the hook. Scrubbed the dial pad with her sleeve. Stepped back from the phone in terror.

And glanced over her shoulder at her Jeep, parked at the curb half a block away.

Fifteen minutes later she was standing above her mother. Hope's eyes were half-lidded, her hair fanned about her head. Petals littered the ground around her—she looked like a snow angel. Except for the wound on her temple, red against her pale skin.

Tears flowed down Madeleine's cheeks. She dragged her sleeves across her face and hooked her arms beneath her mother's, began pulling her toward the parking lot, where the Jeep waited for them, its rear door open.

She braked a few houses down from her driveway, where six or seven cars still leaned against the curb.

She checked the clock: 3:24 A.M.

A tap on the window. "What did you do to her?" asked her father in horror.

Madeleine squeezed her eyes shut. When she opened them, he wasn't there. (Of course he wasn't there.) She chewed her thumbnail.

"Tell me what you did to her!" he shouted.

She spun to the passenger seat. Empty. (Of course empty.) She chewed on a strand of hair.

"Madeleine—"

She knew he wasn't behind her, but all the same she turned. The flattened backseat was bare.

Except for her mother's body, laid carefully across the carpet, her head resting on Madeleine's sweatshirt. Madeleine couldn't bear to bloody her beautiful coat.

Now, shuddering in just a long-sleeved shirt, she checked the clock again. 3:27 A.M.

The Jeep stole away.

Later, she wouldn't remember how she was feeling, what she was thinking, as she drove; she simply imagined herself from on high once more, as though a silent helicopter crew in the battered night sky of a new century were tracking her flight.

She saw her car head west, past the Russian Orthodox cathedrals and Chinese grocery stores.

She watched it speed south along the Pacific Coast Highway, famous and fatal. Houses receded and thinned out to the east as wide beaches and swells of gray grass unfurled beside the sea.

She lost sight of the Jeep when it plunged into a sudden spectral forest, headlights X-raying the trees. The road began to wiggle and twitch.

Then the car reappeared just as a steep shock of rock rose to the left, raked high over her in a frozen wave. And to the right, beyond a hopeless guardrail and one hundred fifty feet below: the ocean.

And finally she took in the jagged seaboard, a series of cliffs bristling like thorns from the coast, bases lathered in foam. The Devil's Slide.

Her high beams were two bright pinpricks.

She jerked the car to the side of the road, where the guardrail quit. Snuffed the lights and climbed out of the driver's seat. The seashell roar of the water filled her ears.

She opened the rear door.

When she stepped away, her mother was cradled in her arms like a child, her coat across her chest, her head still wrapped in the homecoming sweatshirt. Hope was taller, but Madeleine was broader, stronger, a college athlete. She was also electric with alarm. She could manage a hundred yards or so.

She walked from the hard-packed dirt across the short grass stubbling the cliff. Further down the coast, the moon watched.

Madeleine glanced at her mother's head tipped against her shoulder. Inspected her unblemished temple. Hope looked as though she were asleep.

With halting steps she proceeded down the ledge. The bluffs behind her, the scrub beneath her, the cliff face before her, and the sea below: all stone-gray, iron-black, all silver and pearl—except for her mother's velvet, still smoldering a low, smoky orange.

The ledge pitched sharply toward the sea. Madeleine descended carefully, sneakers braced against the incline. She heard the waves detonating far below.

For a moment, she paused.

Then she continued, clutching her mother tighter, until they approached the edge of the cliff. Again Madeleine sank to her knees, Hope gathered between her arms and thighs. Just a step and a fall away, black water and white foam swirled in a cove gouged from the rock.

Quietly Madeleine slipped out of her body. Saw herself as a cinematographer would, as though this were just a scene from a nightmare film.

Floating somewhere beyond the cliff's edge, she watched herself bow her forehead to Hope's, watched her kiss the tip of her mother's nose, very lightly. When she lifted her head, Hope's cheeks were damp.

The marine rumble faded as the camera drew closer, pushing past the grass, past her knees, and past the woman she held. Madeleine began to fill the frame. Her cheeks shone. Her eyes shone.

She was looking straight ahead—not at an audience, not at an imaginary lens; she was looking at the dark mutinous Pacific waves. The same waves she could no longer hear.

Silence.

Just her shoulders now, and just her face. Strands of hair wandered across her brow. She closed her eyes.

Stillness.

But finally, gently, one hand pulled the hair. And the camera slowly retreated, and again the sound of water washed in. Her other hand rubbed at her nose, her cheek.

The sea grew louder as the camera pulled back, making room for her empty lap.

Then Madeleine opened her eyes, regained her body. Saw the ocean, brushed with rough waves, and the cold moon.

Her wristwatch read 4:35 A.M.

Beside her, a glint in the blunt grass.

She tugged it free: a strand of metal. Madeleine stared at it. Held her breath. It fit the seams in her palm.

She glanced back at the ocean. But soon her hand clenched, and the chain dripped from her fist like water.

96

THE CHAIN DRIPS FROM HER FIST LIKE WATER.

"I kept it." Madeleine's voice has survived the story, bruised but usable. "That's what you're not supposed to do, I know. But I did. And twenty years later I've brought it here to—to bury it at sea."

A quarter-curve away, Timbo's face softens—just a shade, but it transforms him.

Across from her, Nicky—Cole—gawks in horror.

Their father gazes at the edge of the labyrinth, where the gut-shot blanket has settled, its tassels fluttering like the fingers of a dying man. She heard him scream, Madeleine thinks, when she spoke those words—*I took it from her after I killed her*—but his voice was muffled in the wind, the roar in the curl of a conch.

"Why didn't you leave your mother in the bay?" asks Timbo.

This is an easy one. "I once researched tidal patterns for a story Dad wrote. I knew that a body in the bay might wash up, but a body in the water further south . . ."

She shudders. "So I drove back to school. Just like I'd been told. My roommate was supposed to be at her boyfriend's frat house."

Madeleine remembers dropping her coat and shoes by the front door. Remembers standing there in socks. Remembers approaching the bathroom just as a naked man emerged from it.

"But she'd taken him to our place."

They had both scuttled back, her hand balling the necklace into her palm, his hand diving to his crotch.

Didn't realize you were still here.

Her fist throbbed, she was squeezing it so hard.

I've been sleeping. Probably some winter flu.

Well, go back to bed, champ. He clamped his other hand atop the first and shuffled past her. *It's, like, three in the morning.*

(It was actually, like, almost five in the morning. But when lime-greened Detective B.B. Springer asked her roommate to confirm Madeleine's whereabouts on New Year's Eve, the boyfriend distinctly recalled their exchange outside the bathroom: three A.M. An hour after Hope Trapp's in-laws bid her good night.)

And Happy New Year. The words had slipped past the door as it closed, seemed to echo off the tiled walls. She flicked the light switch. In the mirror, a frightened woman greeted her, clothes weary, hair sloppy.

The woman's fist unfolded. The necklace was twisted in her palm.

Madeleine clears her throat. "Later I drove home. Again. By the time I got there, Dom had already raised the alarm." Her father continues to watch the ground.

"I kept it," she repeats. "Every so often I would lock my door and open my jewelry box and look at—at the necklace. A few times I even tried it on. But mostly it just . . . hibernated. For twenty years." She feels the disc carve into the skin of her palm, presses harder. Then, to her father, she says, "I suppose it helped me learn to live with fear."

Waves clamor just beyond the drop, but Madeleine scarcely hears them. He watches her balefully. She could've remained silent, she knows; but, oh, she felt so very tired of silence.

"I doubt I'd set eyes on it within the last five years." She sets eyes on it now. "My aunt did, though. Before the party. She wanted to borrow some jewelry. Only I wasn't in my room." Just five days ago! She nearly whoops in amazement. The world has tilted off its axis since then, rolled like an eight ball into some parallel universe. Lives have ended. Diana's. Her own, too.

"So she helped herself. I barely noticed her all evening. Tried to avoid her, really. And after the party ended . . ."

Her father lifts his eyes to hers, and in that instant she understands: he will write the final chapter. Sebastian Trapp has always been acclaimed for his endings.

"After she shooed everyone out, Simone tried my door. I should've answered." Madeleine swallows. "Because when I didn't, she gave the necklace to Diana."

Timbo appears to lift one hand higher, as though signaling a teacher. "How do you know this?"

And Sebastian, hoisting his stockinged foot, says, "Allow me to explain," with the last-gasp vigor of a very tired man, as he takes a step back.

97

THIS IS THE WRONG ENDING.

Mama is dead and Magdala killed her?

I assumed Mama was dead. I assumed *he* had killed her.

"After that scene in the library," he's saying, "and it was a scene, set and staged—afterward, Maddy brought me upstairs. For an hour I lay in bed, puzzling over the not-so-mysterious Mystery of Cole. On my chest sat the lump of glass that failed to topple Miss Hunter when the idiot Frederick smacked her with it.

"Miss Hunter herself had toppled *me* with a scrap of paper. She assumed I knew what had happened to my wife. She was hardly the first. *I* assumed that *she* knew, having disappeared at the same time—that she could clear up an old mystery or two. But when I read those wings by the fire, *Tell them what you did to her,* I realized that we were both in the dark. Only now one of us knew it." A hard-luck smile at me. I want to scream.

All this time I've blamed him, *hated* him. Yet for my sister, hunched there with her knuckles bound in silver, I feel only sorrow. I remember her then and I look at her now, across the labyrinth, across twenty years. *Wouldn't it haunt you? Taking a life,* Simone had asked me.

It's haunted Madeleine.

"Then, just after midnight, Diana paid me a visit, a necklace swinging from her fingers. 'I've seen this twice today,' she said. 'I watched Cole give it to Hope on New Year's Eve. Twenty years ago. Twenty *minutes* ago, Simone gave it to *me.* She'd borrowed it from Madeleine.'

"I took the necklace, squinted at the inscription on the pendant: *Cherchez la*—well, we all know it by now, don't we? I write precisely this sort of story, I could make the proper deductions. The solution composed itself.

"Diana seemed—*entranced.* As though she'd spied a new face in a familiar portrait. That's how I felt, certainly, although I protested. 'Let's ask her how she got this,' I said, even though we both knew *how,* or at least from *whom,* which gave us a pretty good idea *why* Madeleine had kept it without ever letting on.

"But Diana continued. 'It's Madeleine,' she whispered. 'Madeleine knows what happened to . . .'

"'You're unnerved,' I said—I was desperate to trap her in the present, where I knew Maddy to be blameless. 'It's this Cole business. Butterflies being strewn about, and . . .'"

The wind rises, and the butterfly jitters in my hands. My fingers clench the paper, push dents into it; the edges slice against my palms.

"But it was too late, I knew; somehow I knew it was too late. 'I don't care about *Cole*,' she hissed. 'I care what happened *then*. I care why she has *that necklace*.'" That's when I spotted a man in the crack'd dresser mirror, wearing blue pajamas and a white face, with a little string of metal in one hand and the little lump of glass in the other. Saw him draw near, Diana behind him, just this quivering orange flame, her voice blurred." He closes his eyes. "I saw the valet box below the mirror, crammed with—oh, my cufflinks, some tie clips. And tucked into the stitching of the lid was—is—a passport photo: my daughter, age four. She could barely keep a straight face that day." He opens his eyes; they're shining. "Every morning for more than thirty-five years, when I decide how to decorate my wrists and person, there's Madeleine, trying not to laugh at me."

Madeleine is trying not to cry.

"And then the police were mentioned. I couldn't *think*. Should I claim it was a replica? Or bundle Maddy into the Jag, race to the airport? My head, my *heart* . . . But as I watched her in the glass, Diana told me, 'I am going to contact the police.' Steel in her voice. I just gazed at that photograph, at my little girl, who couldn't hear the trouble she was in."

His tie whips in the cold air, streaming toward Madeleine; the gun shivers in his hand.

"'Now please'—she did say *please*—'give me back the necklace.' I shut my eyes. Surely nobody else had noticed—not even Simone recognized it. If Diana could just . . ."

"Then she asked again. No *please* this time. I glanced up, saw her at my back, reaching. My heart punched a hole through my chest, and I whirled around and swung my hand."

A pause. "Not the hand holding the necklace," he adds. "The hand holding the lump of glass."

This is the wrong ending.

"I saw a bird die in flight once. On safari. A kingfisher. Pure blue feathers, bright orange breast. I was tracking it through my binoculars when it just dropped from the Congo clouds. As though some electric current had failed. Stopped my heart to behold it." He bumps his heel against a stone and absently steps backward, into the third circle. "That's how Diana fell. Before she even hit the floor, I knew I had killed her.

"She landed on her side, on my suit jacket. That suit is long gone, Detective." Timbo nods.

He cuts his eyes to me so fast that I step back. "I knelt by the bed. Diana's lovely face was angled toward me, her lovely eyes staring. I thought about all the lives I'd snuffed out in my books. I thought about all the murderers. I had now joined that fraternity; I had become the killer half the world swore I already was. And how absurd it suddenly seemed—not that a person could end somebody else, but that he might ever believe that that death wouldn't end him, as well. What silly characters I'd invented."

Somewhere a gull cries in mourning. Soon the sea will catch fire.

"Still, I proceeded as one of my murderers might. Placed a towel beneath her head. Checked her pockets—two tiny ear studs, Madeleine's. Stashed the necklace in my valet case. And then? I'd dissolved corpses in quicklime; I'd spiked sherry with untraceable hemlock. Never in seventeen novels had I imagined a plausible way to disguise the murder of a woman with a head wound.

"A fall down the stairs? But those marble steps are rounded, and what if somebody in the small hours were to stray into the kitchen? I needed to put distance between time of death and discovery of the—of her. The more dots there are, the tougher to connect them.

"The alternative to accident was suicide." A hitch in his voice. He pauses. "I didn't like that, but then I didn't like any of it. I opened my door—God, how I feared that dark!—and very, very quietly walked to Diana's bedroom. Like Miss Hunter, I'm not one for signs—but, auspiciously, the window was already open.

"Not surefire means of death, self-inflicted or accidental or otherwise, for the very reasons that irksome detective set out. It wouldn't quite convince. Then I recalled a storyline I'd once abandoned, and

I recalled, too, Diana's journal, long since retired, in which after the accident she'd recorded her grief and her despair and the shame she felt after losing her child and her husband. Her family."

It's an awful cliché, but I can't go on. The guilt will drag me down and drown me.

"She'd allowed me to read it before we got married—she was making herself vulnerable, and I loved her for it. So I knew where she kept the journal: in her desk, within arm's reach. Also auspicious. I didn't spend much time browsing—the guilt would've dragged me down—and the drowning business was purely serendipitous. She'd written more on that same page, but what you read was all I needed; I tore it out, set it on the chair. Would this settle the matter? Not for the irksome detective. It's difficult, however, to argue with a note authentic in letter if not in spirit. It's difficult to clock time of death with a body in water.

"I rather hoped Diana would have recovered by the time I returned to my bedroom. She had not. I collected her in my arms—her body still soft, still horribly warm—and carried her into the hallway and down the stairs. Our wedding day wound backward. We passed beneath the family portrait, the portrait I keep there to remind me of what I'd lost. I laid her on the parlor sofa, opened the French windows. When I turned back, the dog was licking her fingertips. I nearly wept.

"I brought her outside. I—I stepped into the water, knelt to the surface. For some reason, I wondered what the fish would make of it. Then I rolled her—I very gently rolled Diana over and pressed her head against the edge of the pond, so that grit would lodge in the wound.

"And there I said goodbye. To say goodbye is—well." He pulls one sleeve across his brow. "Back in my room, I inspected the rug—unsoiled—before once more creeping downstairs, this time to my library, where I threw the suit and towel onto the fire and placed the fatal cube on my blotter. It had featured heavily earlier that evening; its absence might be noticed.

"I sat at my desk and waited." He swallows. "I waited past sunrise. I waited until I heard a scream."

Today's sunrise, beyond the hills, has tinted the water a rough blue, colored the stones at our feet white and rust-red. Across the labyrinth, tears slick my sister's face; nearby, Timbo's eyes gleam.

My own are wide and dry in disbelief.

"When you saw me next, charging into the pond, reeling—that was authentic grief. Like watching in horror as your handprint surfaces on your child's skin. Diana had hurt nobody. Diana wasn't in the wrong place at the wrong time. She was simply on the wrong side of the human instinct to protect our young at any cost."

The wrong ending. My gaze travels far up the coast, where sunlight simmers above the hills.

"The following evening, I learned from my daughter that her mother—your mother, too, as Madeleine is now aware—had died in much the same manner: a blow to the skull, then a watery grave. By complete accident, I'd committed a copycat crime." Maddy bows her head, sobbing.

"So I placed the necklace in her hand—that vagabond necklace, from Cole to Hope to Madeleine to Simone to Diana to me and back to Madeleine—and made one request: bury your dead, I said." Slowly he nods. "And I took my own advice. I sat at my typewriter and confessed—confessed to taking the lives of my wife and child. Pick a wife. I took Diana's life, certainly, but Hope's, too, by failing her. Her fate is my doing. And Madeleine is the child whose life I took—the child who gave up her life to care for me—although anybody reading that letter would think I meant you."

He turns to me. "*Including* you, it seems. You left my house before I could take your life. I'm very glad you did. And that is why I surrendered myself, on the page you've transformed in your hands. I wished to take Madeleine's burden. I wished to protect your identity. I didn't want anyone searching for you if you didn't want to be found, and I'd said nothing at all to your sister. So I killed you off in black and white. And *that*, Miss Hunter, is your solution."

The butterfly crackles in my palms. A bird cries somewhere close.

"I brought my other child here to say goodbye." He clears his throat. "The scene became more crowded than I'd expected."

Across the labyrinth, Madeleine blots her eyes with her fist, drags her sleeve beneath her nose. Then, wincing at our father: "Why'd you bring a gun?" she asks.

He turns to her and says, "So that I can shoot it."

98

I cut my eyes to Timbo, catch his fingers flexing. "Who will you be shooting, Mr. Trapp?"

"Whom." His coat flies open in the wind, alarmed, broad strokes of sweat smearing his white shirt. "So much for our genre of choice, Miss Hunter! So much for helpful clues and tidy endings!"

I *knew* he'd done it, I *knew* it—but there's no triumph here, no grim satisfaction; there is only sadness, deep and dark. The most beautiful woman I've ever seen.

The winds are rising now, and the sea with them. The labyrinth begins to swirl. When a wave collides with the cliff, he steps into the second ring, as if to keep his balance.

He calls to me: "I should like to say that all thy vexations were but my trials of thy love, and thou hast strangely stood the test. I should like—"

"In your words!" My hair sticking to the tears. "In *your* words!"

A very gentle smile. "Oh, Miss Hunter. Oh, Nicole. You were stronger than I was."

My eyes are full. His white form trembles and dissolves.

"You became who you always were."

I wrap my arms around myself, weeping.

When I blink, he snaps into focus again, the Webley jiggering in his hand. I glance at my sister, at the cop.

"We hate those we hurt, my child," Sebastian Trapp tells me. "We hurt those we hate, and we hate them still more. It's a drain we spiral. It sucks us under. I learned that too late."

He calls to Maddy over his shoulder. "Be collected, darling," he says against the wind.

Timbo frowns. "Mr. Trapp."

"No more amazement, Madeleine. Tell your piteous heart there's no harm done."

In one fluid motion, Timbo steps and stoops and now his Beretta is in his left hand. "Mr. Trapp, I hope I'm not hearing some fond farewells."

My father returns to me. "You're an excellent detective, Nicole," he tells me, with what sounds something like pride, gun shaking in his grip.

I feel warm and very cold at once. "I am?"

"Your methods are unorthodox. Illegal, even. But yes."

"*Mr. Trapp.*"

The labyrinth is churning faster now, wind and light coursing through the lanes. "You asked whether I could really remember a particular stamp so very many years later."

"You'd spent a happy day with your child," I reply.

"Mr. Trapp, I'll count to five."

"More than enough time. Yes, a happy day indeed—so happy, in fact, that I bought two rolls of viceroys."

"One," Timbo calls.

"Dad." Madeleine steps forward.

"Mine is in the small metal box in the bottom-left drawer of my desk."

"This is two, sir."

"Not a single stamp removed. Not one butterfly flown away."

"Dad," says Madeleine.

The light on the stones is running like mercury between us.

He grins. "For twenty years, I've looked at them. Oh, and—"

"Three." Timbo's jaw is set.

"Please," I say. "Dad." I reach for him.

"And if you ever write a novel of your own—"

"*Daddy,*" pleads Madeleine, putting one foot into the vortex.

"Four!"

But my father looks only at me, smiles only at me.

"For heaven's sake, don't let it go on too long." He steps into the center of the labyrinth and snaps the gun to his temple.

And when the shot cracks the air, the butterfly escapes my grip with a shudder of sharp wings and flies away over the water, migrating west toward the open ocean, its first and final voyage.

99

FROM THE MOMENT Detective Timbo Martinez plunged into the woods to hunt for a signal, Maddy and I exchanged not a word—not when he returned to the cliff, not after he exited again in search of backup and coroner, not while he traffic-copped the SFPD onto the ledge.

The arms were flung wide, the stilt-legs as well; the blanket Timbo had draped over him covered only his trunk and head. My father and his funeral shroud, each with a single bullet wound.

At some point I turned away, toward the beach where he and I had strolled what felt like years ago. Glitter in the damp sand.

What secrets might you be hiding, young Hunter?

Then Timbo led us along the Coastal Trail, through tunnels of eucalyptus and pine. I breathed in mint and earth, listened to the sea growling unseen, felt wind strip my cheeks dry. And, frozen in my gut, the horror that I'd been wrong—*we'd* been wrong, together.

Five yards ahead of me, Madeleine trudged slowly, hood against her back, hair overflowing it. When she rounded the final bend and disappeared from view, I wondered, with a sudden thrill, if I would round it myself and find my sister vanished, fled from this place and perhaps from this world.

But no: she's waiting at the overlook, seated on the single bench.

Timbo jogs ahead, hops up the packed-dirt staircase to the parking lot. I watch Maddy; beyond her dropped head and drooped shoulders is the view our father shared with me, that slow-motion moment: sea, clouds, hills, all wild and defiant, supernaturally bright.

Now Timbo returns, squinting in the sunlight. "Half dozen civilian vehicles up there, none of 'em parked within twenty yards of me." He rolls a bottle of water along the back of his neck. "Like they know I'm police." He thrusts the bottle at me, then visors his eyes with one hand, winces at Madeleine. Stands a bottle beside her.

Deep inhale and he's hiking uphill again. I sit next to Maddy, tilt my head up to the blue sky. To think I witnessed his soul rising into it.

"Too much to hope you've got a cigarette." Her voice is raw; her face is bared to the light.

"A little too much," I reply.

She unscrews her water bottle, gulps. Wipes her mouth and turns to me. Her eyes are bloodshot. "Did you ever consider telling me?"

I didn't. "I did."

"Because I wish I'd known."

"I'd wish you'd known, too," I say, and to my surprise, it's true.

She sniffles, so deep that a cough bursts from her throat.

"I thought that you'd stayed at home all these years because you were so upset about Mama going missing."

"I was."

"But that isn't why."

She studies the sea. The sun on the water breaks like glass in my eyes, and for an instant, I watch Maddy tug a string from the mouth of a beer bottle, raising the sails of the tiny ship within. *This is the SS* Cole, she announces. I'm seven, and she is my hero.

"It seemed fair," she says. "It *was* fair. She didn't get to live her life. I shouldn't live mine. I should devote myself to Dad—I'd deprived him. I should . . ."

She offers her face to the sky, eyes shut; her hair begins whirling about her head like an unruly halo. "I loved her!" cries Madeleine gladly. "That *magnifi*—that *force of nature,* our mother. I *loved* her. That *stubborn,* amazing—that *beauty*—that . . . I can't believe I'm made of her." She hugs herself. "We both are."

I hug myself, too, and watch the waves.

Now Madeleine opens her eyes, blinking, and glances up the rude flight of steps to where Timbo, at the summit, is speaking without pause to a woman whose bob glows lambent pink in the sun.

As though we've tapped her on the shoulder, B.B. Springer notices us, raises one hand. Then she crushes her fingers together and hoists her thumb.

"This is not *Top Gun,* you high-fructose bitch," says Maddy. Another cough. "Decent of them not to arrest me yet."

"It was an accident."

"Failing to report it wasn't." She sounds grimly self-assured; she's researched this. "Disposing of her—her," she continues, "certainly wasn't." Then she looks at me hard. "I would've understood, you know. Some people, maybe not, but I would've been happy for you. I *am* happy for you, Nicky."

My throat is tight. "I'm sorry I deceived you."

"Don't be *sorry*." She smiles; such a perfect smile she's got. "Everybody *lies*. You had your reasons. So we never have to talk about that again."

"I manipulated you."

"Fucking hell, did you ever. But you had your reasons." She scrubs her eyes, and I scrub mine. *Let me take your hand,* I will her.

Instead she sighs. "The sister did it. Bet you didn't see that coming."

"No."

"I'm happy you got to spend time with him. And him with you."

We sit in silence. I stare at the water.

"I should've known," she says, her voice low. Then I feel a touch upon my ear. I hold my breath. I close my eyes.

Her fingertip, very lightly, traces the bone down to my chin. Brushes my nose, the hollows of my cheeks; smooths my eyebrows one by one. And now I look into Maddy's eyes, bright and full.

"You're beautiful," she says.

I don't answer. I can't.

We turn as one to see B.B. and Timbo stepping easily down the stairs.

Suddenly, as if summoned, the wind roars with such force that the words scatter as Magdala speaks them, her mouth against my ear, her palm hot when she presses it into mine.

"You always were," she whispers.

100

THE DOOR OPENS with a quick gasp, as if I've caught the house unawares.

I stand in the cool gray hall of the first home I ever knew.

After a moment, I look into the jigsaw room. All those half-lived puzzles, that wary canary eyeing the cat. And, painted on the wall, laughing as whores probably seldom laughed in East London one hundred fifty years ago: my sister.

But this isn't a history book; this is a mystery.

I turn away and face her door.

I didn't properly survey the room after she beckoned me inside a few mornings ago, the press dispersing out front. Now I take it in: Ragged paperbacks crowding the bookshelves, spines dented; a dead lava lamp; a collection of sports trophies. A gargoyle hunched at the edge of the unmade bed.

Watson licks her chops, cocks her head, asking when Maddy will return.

I squeeze her, set her down on the rug.

Room by room, in utter silence, we tour the ground floor. Then we climb the staircase.

At the top, I meet their eyes—one by one, left to right. My sister, gift-wrapped in her white sundress. My father, one brow surprised. My mother, that death-defying grin, broad as a horizon, and in her lap, me, dressed as a boy. A white butterfly in my hands.

I peer into spare rooms packed full of statues and orreries, fencing swords and undead animals.

One flight up, I walk by Diana's door, glance into my father's bedroom. Guess the spot where she must have fallen.

One flight down, I enter the library lightly, like I'm intruding. I move past the sunlit windows toward his desk, toward the cold hearth beyond it. The bookshelves on either wall bend forward—not so far as to disgorge their residents, just enough to watch me, curious, creaking. They mutter and murmur, the sound of turning pages.

The dog has disappeared.

A little lighthouse beam in my eye. The glass cube perches on the blotter, just as he said. I weigh it in my hand, press my thumb against one edge. Perhaps it's absorbed my blood invisibly. Perhaps glass has a memory. Why not? Everything else does.

Behind the desk, a black key juts from a dial in the wall. I twist it. In the fireplace, flames sit up and stretch after their night off.

I lower myself into his chair. The butterflies sleep beneath the Remington. If his typing never disturbed them, then I certainly won't.

I pull open the bottom-left drawer. Lift the lid of the metal box within. The roll of viceroys is furled tight and bright.

I fish in my pocket, pull the chain free. It's cooler than it was when Madeleine spoke those last words, when she pushed it into my hand.

I tilt it toward the flames. The silver links catch fire and the etching on the disc flashes sharp and clear:

CHERCHEZ LA FEMME

I looked for the woman, all right.

The metal feels soft against the nape of my neck. *Lost in the ruckus*, we told the police. *Fell into the waves and drowned.*

I tuck the disc beneath my collar. Then I close my eyes.

> PS One piece of my legacy remains outstanding.
> You'll find the clues atop this letter.

It's easy, now that I'm sitting where he sat, devising riddles for his readers. The clues atop the letter are—were—the first words he wrote in it. Atop all the others.

And I remember them, more or less:

> This won't be a long goodbye. I am in my
> library late at night--so far past twelve
> o'clock that we're nearly at thirteen.

Simple. It's in my blood.

I walk to the nearest stack of shelves. If there's a filing system here, it died with my father; I lose two hours dragging the ladder along the rail, touching spines and inspecting covers, before at last I find it, ten feet from the floor, jacket chipped but binding tight: Raymond Chandler, *The Long Goodbye.*

I flip to Chapter 13, look at the final page of Chapter 12, where the last line has been underlined in red ink.

There is no trap so deadly as the trap you set for yourself.

I push the books aside, reach into the darkness behind them.

The manuscript is wrapped in (what else?) a ribbon. I bid Chandler a brief goodbye and descend the ladder. Return to the desk. Tug the ribbon loose.

For Cole

I turn the page.

Here is a story just for you.

The title is printed on the sheet beneath:

DOWN WILL COME BABY
a Simon St. John mystery
by
Sebastian Trapp

And finally:

Dear Miss Hunter,

Mind your step down that ladder.

Now: it is my experience that everybody wants the truth until they find it. To wait and hope can be preferable.

In the letter left beneath your door, I claim responsibility for Cole Trapp's death or disappearance, depending on how one chooses to read it. This gives Cole—if he lives—the option of remaining undisturbed wherever he might be, whether it's a Peruvian jungle or a Venetian gondola or a library in San Francisco. Who knows?

In this, my final book, I have wrapped it all up

in a ribbon. Simon returns, of course, alongside
Inspector Trott; the ravishing Mr. Myers; Watson,
that unusually unintelligent dog; all manner
of criminals and aristocrats and poisoners and
fortune tellers ... as well as Jack, whom so many
have for so long sought to unmask.

It is to you, Miss Hunter, that I finally
reveal that secret, and it is for you that I have
produced what I would rank among my better
Simon St. John adventures. It might even be my
best. And for that I have you to thank.

I am glad I had the chance to know you, if
only briefly.

This novel is yours--and yours to do with as
you please. You may keep it for yourself. You may
share it with the world. You may burn it--I am
sure you would have your reasons.

Please be kind to Madeleine.

ST

He thought he'd get away with it, the way his culprits never did. He thought he could protect Madeleine, keep me safe and unsuspecting, drag our secrets with him past *The End*.

And night after night I listened as he wrote a story just for me.

I glance across the desk at the glass cube, tiny blazes in its depths, the inscription illuminated. *We hate those we hurt.*

Oh, he *did* hurt me. And this, I suppose, is his apology. I could keep it. I could burn it.

I bend the pages, speed them against my thumb. Words fly by in a flock. St. John. Secret niece. Dagger. Jack. Blackfriars Bridge. Mr. Myers. A sudden kiss.

I swivel the chair to the hearth.

I could burn it.

I could keep it.

I look at the book. I look at the flames.

I lift the page. I begin to read.

end of story.

AUTHOR'S NOTE

San Francisco son Paul Kantner once described his city as "forty-nine square miles surrounded by reality," a measurement adjusted very slightly in the first chapter of this novel. In that spirit, I have set *End of Story* in a San Francisco unmoored: certain streets slash one another at strange angles, fog is pumped onstage as and when, and three days of rainfall amount to three too many for an ordinary Bay Area June.

The hidden labyrinth at Lands End was created in 2004, nearly three decades after Sebastian proposed to Hope in its center. Over the next seventeen years, vandals repeatedly destroyed it, and its caretakers repeatedly rebuilt it, until sadly the labyrinth disappeared for good in 2021.

Other details—the hours of summer sunrises, the trails tangling above the sea off Lands End, and so on—are, to the best of my knowledge, reliably reported.

In other words, this is a story surrounded by reality, although reality keeps its distance from time to time. Any errors, accidental or otherwise, are mine alone.

ACKNOWLEDGMENTS

Jennifer Brehl, Liate Stehlik, Jennifer Hart, Kelly Rudolph, and all at Morrow. Julia Wisdom, Kate Elton, Liz Dawson, Kim Young, and all at Harper.

Sindhu Vegesena, Rosie Pierce, and Flo Sandelson.

My publishing colleagues in Australia, Canada, India, Ireland, New Zealand, and South Africa. Much gratitude to my international publishers, agents, and translators. (I know that this novel does not lend itself easily to translation!) Thank you for the privilege of seeing my book in your language, and thanks too to Jake Smith-Bosanquet.

°

RDF; my New cohort, then and now (Weston X!); my professors and employers who over the years have encouraged and advised me; John Kelly, David Bradshaw, Christopher Butler, Craig Raine; a great many people in the publishing industry—authors, editors, agents, booksellers, and more; my friends, my family, and my dog. I could ask for none better.

°

Unlike Sebastian Trapp, my father has given his son wholehearted love my whole life long, up through and beyond me coming out as gay. Thank you for making that so much easier for me.

I love you, Dad.

CITATIONS

Few authors write as quotably as authors of mystery fiction. Those referenced in *End of Story* include Raymond Chandler, G. K. Chesterton, Agatha Christie, Edmund Crispin, Arthur Conan Doyle, Alexandre Dumas, and Dorothy L. Sayers. Most of these are named in the text, but a handful of quotes go unattributed, so I'm noting them here in their original forms.

Chapter 8

"'Discretion,' said Fen with great complacency, 'is my middle name.'

"'I dare say. But very few people use their middle names.'"

—EDMUND CRISPIN, *BEWARE OF THE TRAINS* (1953)

Chapters 10, 78

"'Conversations are always dangerous if you have something to hide,' said Miss Marple."

—AGATHA CHRISTIE, *A CARIBBEAN MYSTERY* (1964)

Chapter 22

"'A woman who doesn't lie is a woman without imagination and without sympathy.'"

—AGATHA CHRISTIE, *MURDER IN MESOPOTAMIA* (1935)

Chapter 54

"'Curious things, rooms. Tell you quite a lot about the people who live in them.'"

—AGATHA CHRISTIE, *CROOKED HOUSE* (1949)

Chapter 60

"'A Manhattan you shake to foxtrot time, a Bronx to two-step time, and a dry martini you always shake to waltz time.'"

—FRANCES GOODRICH AND ALBERT HACKETT, *THE THIN MAN* (SCREENPLAY BASED ON THE NOVEL BY DASHIELL HAMMETT, BOTH 1934)

Chapter 76

"'That hurts my pride, Watson,' he said at last. 'It is a petty feeling, no doubt, but it hurts my pride.'"

−ARTHUR CONAN DOYLE, "THE FIVE ORANGE PIPS" (1891)

Chapter 80

"'But you must know by now, my dear fellow,' said the Major plaintively. 'We're practically at the end of the book.'"

−EDMUND CRISPIN, THE GLIMPSES OF THE MOON (1977)

LYRICS

I also wish to acknowledge the songwriters and performers of the songs referenced throughout the book. Your work has seasoned the story and made it better.

Disco 2000 (Candida Doyle / Jarvis Branson Cocker / Mark Andrew Webber / Nick Banks / Russell Senior / Stephen Patrick Mackey). © BMG Rights Management, Kobalt Music Publishing Ltd., Universal Music Publishing Group.

Girls & Boys (Damon Albarn / David Alexander De Horne Rowntree / Graham Leslie Coxon / Steven Alexander James). © BMG Rights Management, Sony/ATV Music Publishing LLC, Warner Chappell Music, Inc.

Hungry Like the Wolf (John Taylor / Simon Le Bon / Nick Rhodes / Andy Taylor / Roger Taylor). © Gloucester Place Music Ltd.

One Fine Day (Carole King / Gerry Goffin). © Screen Gems-EMI Music Inc., Shapiro Bernstein & Co Inc.

Tubthumping (Alice Nutter / Allan Whalley / Darren Hamer / Duncan Bruce / Judith Abbott / Louise Watts / Nigel Hunter / Paul Greco). © Sony/ATV Music Publishing LLC.

Walk Like A Man (Robert Crewe / Robert Gaudio). © Kobalt Music Publishing Ltd.

You've Lost That Lovin' Feelin' (Barry Mann / Cynthia Weil / Philip Spector). © Abkco Music Inc., Sony/ATV Music Publishing LLC.